KINGDOMS AT WAR

DRAGON GATE, BOOK 1

LINDSAY BUROKER

ACKNOWLEDGMENTS

Thank you to my editor, Shelley Holloway, for going along on the journey, and thank you to my beta readers Sarah Engelke, Cindy Wilkinson, and Rue Silver for sticking with me over the years. Thank you to my cover illustrator Jeff Brown and also to Vivienne Leheny for narrating the audiobook. Hey, Vivienne, I tried to do fewer six syllable names with random apostrophes in the middle for this one. You're welcome!

Last, but never least, thank you, good reader, for picking up a new adventure in an all-new world. I hope you enjoy the story.

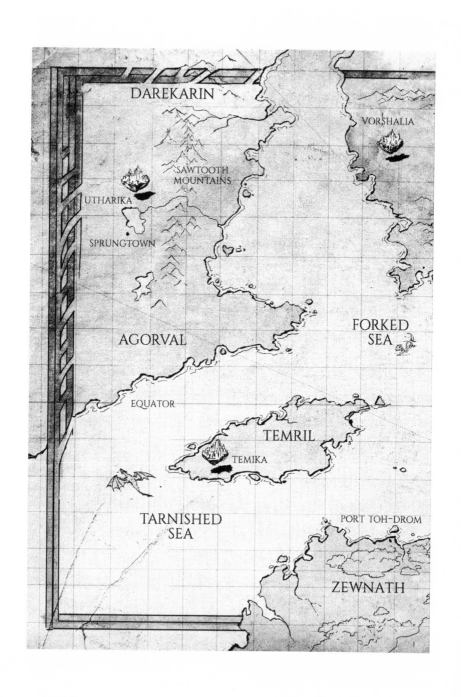

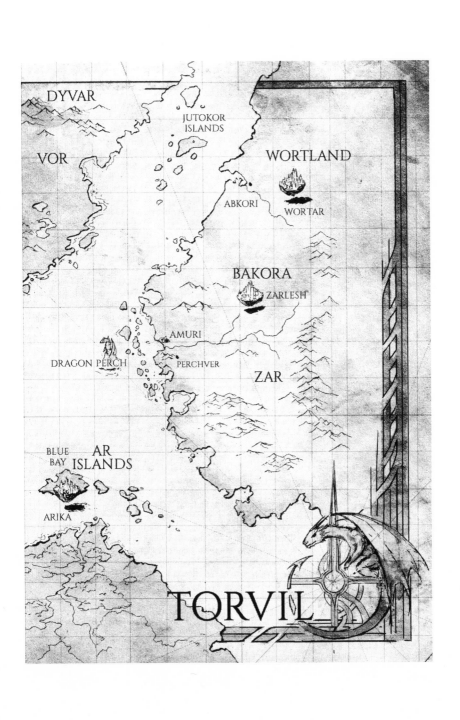

PROLOGUE

"TAKE THIS TO THE MAN SITTING OUTSIDE. AND DON'T ANNOY HIM."

The boy accepted the mug of octli, careful not to let the milky liquid slosh over the rim as he eased through the busy cantina, but he hesitated in the doorway. Scents of sulfur and ash laced the salty sea air, and the usually harsh southern sunlight had a surreal orange tint that brought to mind tales of Hell and eternal toil under a slavemaster's whip.

A single man sat outside at a table under the awning. A roamer.

The big man had brown skin, wiry black hair shot with gray, and a nose that had been broken more often than the cantina's glassware. His dark brooding eyes stared across the strait toward the volcano smoldering on the closest of the Dragon Perch Islands.

When the boy glanced back uncertainly, the bartender made a shooing motion, then rubbed his fingers together to remind him to collect the coin.

"A pox on your bunions," the boy muttered, though he dared not disobey the bartender.

He'd already been hit twice that afternoon by grumpy patrons arguing about omens and placing bets on when the volcano would erupt. His swollen eye ached at the memory of yesterday's punishment for moving too slowly.

After squaring his shoulders and taking a deep breath, the boy headed for the table.

The roamer glanced at him as he approached, but his attention returned to the volcano. A pen dangled between his fingers, and a journal lay open on the table, the pages bare except for a few lines. It was hard to imagine the big fighter as a scribe, given the sword harness strapped across his back, the worn leather-wrapped hilt of the blade poking over his shoulder, and the mage-lock pistol holstered at his hip.

No, the boy realized with a start. That wasn't a magelock but an old black-powder pistol. He remembered that roamers hated magic and hated those who used the tools and gizmos that mages sold to people. Nervously, he rubbed the band that circled his head, the source of pleasant daydreams and little zings of contentment that sometimes made him forget his lot in life.

He crept forward and placed the mug at the man's elbow. Two copper rinara rested on the table, one for the price of the drink and one... for him?

The boy peered warily at the man, afraid to be caught staring but afraid to presume. Only then did he notice the man's left hand was missing, replaced by a dark metal pickaxe head. A scar sliced through the roamer's eyebrow and halfway down his cheek. It hadn't been visible before, and it made the face seem familiar, as if the boy had seen it before, but he'd never waited on this man. He was certain of it.

A shout came from farther up the road, and he jumped. Six teenagers in ill-fitting brown and tan tunics, rope belts clinking with dangling pieces of tin and copper, were ambling this way. Several carried clubs or maces on their shoulders.

The boy glanced toward the doorway. Zone magic protected the inside of the pub from muggers and pirates, but only the enforcers imposed the laws outside, and they rarely bothered near the docks.

Had the roamer seen the approaching gang? They might assume his age and missing hand would make him an easy mark.

"Take the coins, killer," the roamer said, his gaze on the journal as he wrote a line.

Killer? The boy touched his chest.

"Both of them," the man added, his voice a baritone, not harsh and gruff as the boy had expected.

"Uhm, there's trouble coming, sir."

As the teens drew closer, they nudged each other and pointed at the table with their weapons.

"I have no doubt." The roamer looked toward the island volcano instead of the approaching gang. He squinted at a barge anchored in a bay close to the shoreline, almost hidden by ashy gray smoke wafting down from the caldera. Why would anyone sail so close to an active volcano? "You had better go inside," the man added.

"You can come in too if you want, sir."

"I like the view."

The teens had reached the seating area, and one kicked over a chair, sending it clattering across the sandstone road. Only the coarse rope strung between the pillars along the edge kept it from tumbling into the harbor.

After grabbing the two coins, the boy ran back to the doorway. He'd done his best to warn the roamer, and he'd gotten paid, so the bartender shouldn't be angry if something happened to the customer.

"Buy us a drink, Grandpa," one of the teens said as the group spread out around him, their crude weapons in hand.

"*Grand*pa?" the roamer murmured, sounding indignant, though he didn't look up from his writing.

The boy lingered in the doorway, watching even though he didn't want to see their customer beaten and mugged. He'd been generous with his coin when few were. Coin was too scarce, too hard won when half of every rinara went to the mages in their sky castles.

"Or give us your coin purse, and we'll buy our own." Another teen laughed.

The roamer penned a few more words on the page, as if the gang would go away if he ignored them. The boy shook his head. It didn't work that way.

"I *said*—" the biggest teen reached for the roamer's shoulder, "—give us your coins, Grandpa."

Somehow, the roamer managed to lay down the pen, casually flip his book shut, and still catch the hand before it gripped him. He squeezed hard as he looked in the younger man's eyes for the first time.

"You sure you want to prey on the old and infirm, kid?" the roamer asked, his voice dangerous. "When we get to a certain age, we get cranky easily."

He lifted his pickaxe arm in warning, the hazy sunlight gleaming orange on the dark steel. He didn't have the magical aura of a mage or a wizard, but he had the demeanor of someone who'd spent his life in battle and killed men. A *lot* of men.

"We don't care about your disposition." The teen winced at the pressure crushing his hand, but he managed a defiant sneer. "We just want your *money*."

He tried to yank his hand back, but the grip was like a vise, and he couldn't escape. Using his free hand, he threw a punch at the roamer's face. It never connected.

Without knocking over his chair, the roamer surged to his feet and blocked the punch. He spun, jammed the flat of his pickaxe into his attacker's gut, and hurled him over his shoulder. The teen struck one of the posts holding up the awning and crumpled to the ground.

Though startled, the rest of the gang roared and rushed at the roamer.

For a big man, he moved quickly, evading the youths' attempts to surround him, and he threw far more effective punches than they did. He never drew his sword or pistol, but he used his pickaxe as a weapon, smashing it against bone or slashing the tip into flesh. He grabbed another teen and rammed him in the solar plexus with the head, leaving him gasping on the ground. In the blink of an eye, two more youths flew over the rope and into the harbor.

The roamer faced the remaining teens, but they'd had enough. Limping and cursing, they scurried away.

During the skirmish, the mug of octli had been knocked to the ground, the viscous drink oozing into the cracks between the sandstone bricks. The roamer plucked it up with his pick and held a finger up to the boy to order another. Unscathed by the ordeal, he sat back down at the table, opened his journal, and gripped his pen again.

The boy scurried into the cantina for another drink. As the bartender had said, this was not a man he wanted to annoy.

1

THE SMOKE WAS SO DENSE AROUND THE VOLCANO THAT A NIGHT-blooming cactus flower was on full display, its purple trumpet vibrant against the rocky black slope. Jakstor Freedar—student, cartographer-in-training, and temporary lackey for the archaeology team—didn't usually pause to admire flowers, but he'd seen this one in his mother's herbalism books. She could use it for one of her headache cures, couldn't she? Or maybe it went into that vision-inducing concoction that *caused* headaches. Her alchemical repertoire was as extensive as the list of plays by Egarath the Eternal.

Since he owed her a few dozen *thank yous* for letting him come on this trip, Jak shifted the damp bandanas he carried to one arm so he could pick the flower. Snickers came from the lanky boys hacking off cactus pads nearby and tossing them onto a flat magecart that floated above the ground.

"Are you picking *flowers*?" a boy his age asked, waving a saw.

"We knew you were girlie, but we had no idea *how* girlie," another snickered.

Jak pocketed the flower and forced himself to approach the

dimwits. He knew from previous exchanges during the barge ride across the Forked Sea that a conversation with them would induce headaches far more quickly than his mother's potions, but they were part of his errand.

Crew from the barge, they'd been pressed into the cactus-cutting duty while they waited for the archaeology team to finish their dig. Supposedly, the pads were a delicacy on the mainland and worth harvesting before the volcano erupted and buried the island. Jak, having sampled one of the rubbery things the night before, would have left them to be incinerated, perhaps even kicking them into the path of lava flows to ensure they didn't show up again at the dinner table.

"You're picking cactus pads," he observed, though he should have kept his mouth shut. "Is that not girlie? Here, wrap these bandanas around your mouth and nose. My mother treated them with something to help with the smoke."

Jak tossed two of the damp cloths to them and resisted the urge to dab at his eyes—unfortunately, the bandanas couldn't keep them from tearing up.

"It's not girlie when you use a saw." The boy caught the bandanas on his serrated blade. "And sell the cactus pads for big money at the bazaar in town."

"If I sell the flower at the bazaar, will it be more masculine?"

"Nah, nothing about you is masculine." The statement prompted more snickers from the group.

"Not even my cleft chin? I've had women remark on its appeal." Not *many* women, admittedly, but Jak was positive someone he hadn't been related to had called it cute at some point.

"It looks like a butt under your lips." More snickers.

"Ah. Thanks for sharing your wit with me today."

As Jak distributed more bandanas, including to a bored man standing guard with a magelock rifle cradled in his arms, smoke made his nostrils and throat itch. He removed his hat so he could retie his own bandana before continuing up the slope to complete his errand. Once he finished, he could get to the task he truly wanted to do. He touched the sketchbook bulging in his shirt pocket.

The heckler with the saw eyed his hat, squinting at the medallion fastened to the band above the wide brim. The speculation that brightened his dull face made Jak uneasy, and he scooted away from the group. The guard was a member of the barge crew and might look the other way if one of his charges tried to steal from Jak.

The boy elbowed his buddy. "You think that hat is worth much?"

"Not covered in ash," the other worker said with a grunt.

"I think that circle thing is gold. Gold is worth a lot."

Jak hurried up the path, hoping the speculation would end as soon as he was out of their sight. Too bad he had to come back down this way after delivering the rest of the bandanas. There were few viable paths on the lumpy black mountainside, the uneven ground formed by past lava flows. Most routes ended at cliffs or fissures—or holes into ancient lava tubes where the human-hating drakur lived. There was a reason some of the crew carried rifles.

The last group from the barge came into view, their saws working on another patch of cactus, but coughs and grunts behind him made Jak stop and turn around. His hecklers had abandoned their task and were scrambling up the uneven path after him. The chatty one carried his saw, and the big one he'd been nudging had picked up an axe.

Since his mother's archaeology team was paying for passage on the barge, Jak didn't *think* any of the crew would murder him, but the way they kept glancing at his hat convinced him they had mugging in mind.

Jak hopped on a rock to lend height to his five feet nine inches, though there was nothing he could do to make his fine features and lean arms more intimidating. Still, he puffed out his chest, doing the best he could with what he had, and lifted his chin to stare unflinchingly at them.

Never turn your back on an enemy, his father had once said, *or on chest-thumping cannibals who think strangers taste amazing.*

These boneheads weren't cannibals, but Jak had no trouble filing them in the *enemy* folder. As they stomped closer, his fingers twitched toward the short sword belted on his left hip and the magelock pistol holstered on his right, but if he seriously hurt someone on the crew, the captain might leave the entire team here. And what then? The volcano could erupt this very day, and it was a five-mile swim across the strait to the mainland, the city sprawling there no longer visible through the ashy sky.

"Give us the gold medallion, *flower girl,*" the chatty one said. "Or you might fall into one of the holes while you're out here. Bet the drakur are agitated down there, what with their volcano getting uppity."

"Do you always threaten to throw passengers to their deaths? It seems bad for business, like repeat customers would be rare."

"Passengers gotta pay *taxes.*"

"Actually, we pay fares. Taxes go to the wizard rulers that we all love." Jak clamped his mouth shut, realizing he was treading on dangerous ground. Those who blasphemed the kings and queens in their floating castle cities tended to end up dead at the end of a zidarr's blade. And these were the kinds of lickspittles that would rat a man out for that.

"You think you're smart, flower girl? Then do the smart thing. Give us the hat."

"Or we'll take it," the other said. "Think he'll cry to his mommy if we take it?"

"That crazy kook? Nobody will listen to her. The captain said so."

Anger boiled up inside Jak, and for the first time, he craved the fight. He wanted to pound a fist into the boy's nose, consequences for the archaeology team be damned.

His mother was a great herbalist, who had published countless papers and won awards for her work. Just because she'd left that career to try to complete the life's work of Jak's father and prove his theories true didn't mean she deserved some grimy thugs disparaging her.

But he'd already gotten in trouble numerous times for defending her—for defending both of them—and his mother would only lecture him if he fought someone over this. He made himself unclench his fingers and respond calmly.

"This hat belonged to my father," he said. "I'm partial to it, and I'm not giving it or any part of it to you."

"Where'd he get a hat with *gold* on it? You don't come from no money." The chatty one eyed his ashy cotton trousers and shirt, the worn pockets ripped in spots. That was more because Jak jammed books and tools into them all the time than due to poor quality, but the volcano grime did make him look disheveled. "He *thieved* it, didn't he?" the boy asked.

His buddy hadn't put on his bandana, and he lowered the axe to cough and wipe at his eyes. The air was getting worse, the scent of sulfur and molten rock burning Jak's nostrils.

"I believe he bought it from a haberdasher near Sprungtown University. A mystifying place to find a hat, I'm sure. My mother could get you the address if you want to get one of your own." Never mind that the medallion hadn't come with it. Jak didn't know where it had come from but had always assumed his father found it on one of his relic hunts. "But this isn't the best time for discussing fashion. I suggest we—"

The ground rumbled, and alarmed shouts came from the

crewmen farther up the slope. Afraid they were out of time, Jak glanced toward the bay far below, at the archaeology team working just above the beach. He spotted his mother on her knees, waving over the diggers.

His breath caught. An inky blue-black patch was visible in the ground underneath her. As he watched, she swept aside pieces of ancient lava rock that she'd chiseled away to reveal more of the material.

Was that *it*? The artifact that would finally prove that his father's life's work hadn't been a waste? That the last five years since his mother had abandoned her career and taken over the quest *also* hadn't been a waste?

Jak was so enraptured by the blue-black stone—no, if the historical texts were correct, that was *dragon steel*—that he almost missed the saw blade swinging toward his face.

He ducked what would have been a smack to the side of his head and resisted the urge to scramble backward. Instead, he flung himself off the rock at his attacker and sank a punch into the boy's stomach. He must have expected Jak to try to get away, because he surged forward, making the blow even harder than Jak had intended.

Jak followed it up with a knee to the nuts, then shoved his foe backward. But the big one jumped in from the side and jammed the axe handle into Jak's ribs. Pain blasted through him, and Jak again had to resist the urge to pull one of his weapons. The big idiot *could* have used the axe blade and hadn't.

His meatpaw reached for the hat. Jak sprang away, genuine fear surging through him for the first time. Not that he would be hurt but that he might lose the only thing he had left of his father.

Alarmed shouts came from the crewmen, but Jak didn't dare look in that direction. Hoping lava flows weren't spewing out of the caldera and about to overtake them, he focused on his attacker.

The boy's swipe missed his hat, but he lunged in with his other hand and caught Jak's shirt, fingers wrapping in the cotton and ripping off a button. Using a move his father had taught him, Jak grabbed the boy's wrist, dug his thumb into the gap between bones, and twisted as hard as he could.

Yelping, the boy let go. Jak jammed a palm strike into his nose, cartilage crunching, and his attacker reeled back, dropping his axe.

Unfortunately, the chatty boy had recovered. He lunged in and snatched up the axe, murder in his eyes as he prepared to swing not the handle but the deadly blade.

Jak drew his sword. He had no choice now.

The boy lifted the axe in both arms, poised to split Jak like a piece of wood. As Jak crouched to spring aside, a massive spear whistled out of nowhere and slammed into his attacker's chest. The stone tip cracked ribs and buried itself deep in his heart.

Jak swore and dove to the side, flinging himself behind a boulder for cover.

But cover from *what*? Or *who*? The crewmen wouldn't have attacked their own people. Unless that spear had been meant for him? It couldn't have been. The crew had daggers and magelocks, not primitive *spears*.

The boy pitched backward into the dust, his eyes already dull, ash sticking to the whites. His buddy gaped at the body, utterly shocked.

"Get *down*," Jak ordered.

A rock whizzed through the air, barely missing the boy's head. It hit a boulder so hard it shattered. Finally, the boy recovered his wits enough to drop to his belly and crawl for cover.

Screams of pain tore down the slope from the crewmen. The ground rumbled again, fresh plumes of black smoke rising from the volcano. But that wasn't why the men were screaming. Jak peeked over the top of the boulder. Half of the crewmen lay dead among the rocks and cactus, spears protruding from their bodies.

Others crouched behind boulders and fired their magelock rifles. The blue charges of magical energy struck their attackers, an entire *horde* of attackers.

Jak swore as dozens of stone-skinned, rat-faced creatures with long whiskers and tiny slits for eyes poured down the slope, shouting in their growly native tongue and throwing weapons at the crewmen. They wore no clothing, and their genitalia flapped as they ran and jumped, roaring in triumph every time one of their spears sank in.

Drakur.

Jak had seen drawings in books, and even a stuffed one in a museum back home, but he'd never encountered a living drakur before. The troglodytes, some ancient mage's experiment that had mingled man with animal, didn't leave their caves. Or so he'd thought.

The charges from the magelocks took a few of them down, but there were far, far more behind them. Too many to fight. And they weren't deterred in the least by their comrades falling.

They reached the crewmen and went from throwing their spears to running up and thrusting them, knocking aside firearms, and leaving the men helpless.

Jak pulled out his own pistol. Usually, the sights on the foot-long firearm made it easy to aim. But his hand shook today as he tried to line up a shot. He'd been in fights at school, but he'd never been in a battle for his life, never stood next to someone who'd been slain in front of his eyes.

"Dummy, there's too many." The axe-wielder, who'd been his enemy seconds before, thumped him on the back and pointed toward the bay where the barge was anchored. "We've got to get back to the ship. They've got *cannons*."

Cannons would be good. So would escaping without being

noticed, but as one of the drakur raised a spear to finish off a crewman at his feet, Jak steadied his nerves enough to line up the shot and fire.

The blue charge sizzled through the air and struck the drakur in the face, leaving a charred crater in his stone skin as it hurled him backward. The tremor returned to Jak's hand. He'd never killed before, not a sentient being. Even though the drakur were trying to kill *them*, he couldn't help but feel revulsion.

The crewman scrambled to his feet and ran down the slope, shouting a thanks to whoever had helped him. Jak swallowed and told himself he could react later. There were still men alive in the cactus patch, men battling for their lives.

With his heart pounding, Jak shot three more charges, trying to make each count. His basic magelock could only fire fifteen times before it had to be recharged.

Between the chaos of the attack and the crewmen firing their own weapons, the drakur didn't seem to notice Jak. That let him get off several more shots, counting each one. Eventually, a roar came from the slope above him, only fifty yards away. A half-dozen drakur were running past the crewmen, ignoring them completely as they headed straight for Jak.

He glanced back, wondering if the axe-wielder would help him if they tried to make a stand, but the boy had taken his own advice. He was sprinting down the slope toward the bay.

Down by the beach, his mother and the archaeology team still bent over the blue-black artifact, hewing away more lava rock to reveal what lay beneath. With a jolt of fear, he realized they didn't know what was happening yet. With the roar of the sea in their ears, they hadn't heard the battle, and the axe-wielder was running for the bay and the barge, not the beach. Jak had to warn the team.

He almost bolted to his feet right away, but he stopped himself before he ran out from behind cover. The drakur were still coming.

One roared as it led the charge toward Jak, a spear hefted over its shoulder to throw. Farther back, more and more of the deadly troglodytes kept appearing out of holes and fissures in the rocks. Jak had to focus on the six that were running at him.

Forcing his hand to steady again—he only had six shots left—Jak fired at the leader. His aim was true, and the blue charge slammed into the creature's chest. It flew backward, almost tripping one of its fellows.

Amazingly, the other drakur didn't react, didn't slow down in any way. They kept coming. Two hurled spears at Jak.

He ducked below the boulder. One spear soared several feet over his head and clattered onto the lava rock behind him. The other skipped off his boulder, knocking shards of rock free that pelted him in the face.

Jak risked lifting his head. The remaining five drakur were only twenty yards away.

With nerves he hadn't known he had, he fired five times at five different chests. Four of the charges struck in the center, slamming against the stony hides hard enough to knock the drakur to the ground. From the pained groans they emitted, he knew he hadn't killed them. But he didn't care about that. He just needed them off his back so he could sprint to the beach.

But one of his charges didn't strike true enough, and the creature roared and kept coming. Against all rules of sanity, it ran toward Jak and the barrel of his pistol, not caring that its actions were suicidal.

The ground rumbled again, and with a flash of enlightenment, Jak understood the reason. The drakur weren't attacking because they hated humans—not *only* for that reason—but because they were afraid. The volcano was going to erupt, and they knew it.

They were trying to escape the island, and the crewmen happened to be in the way.

Jak gulped. Another reason he had to warn his mother.

He aimed his magelock as the drakur closed to ten yards, hating to kill these creatures if all they wanted was to escape, but it hefted a spear, the stone tip pointing at Jak's eyes. They weren't giving him a choice.

When he fired, the trigger clicked uselessly. He swore, almost ducking too late to keep the spear from removing his head. He was out of charges, the weapon useless until he could get back to camp to add more.

Worse, the drakur had pulled another spear out of a holder on its back. It didn't throw this one. It gripped it in both hands as it ran, its squinty eyes somehow allowing it to navigate—and kill—out in the ashy gray daylight.

Jak started to reach for his sword, but he worried its reach wouldn't be enough. One of the spears lay in the dust next to him, and he grabbed it. The weapon's thickness and weight surprised him. It wasn't meant for human hands, and he struggled to turn it around without rising up from the boulder protecting him. He dared not lift his head with the enemy this close. There would be no time to duck.

Shifting rocks and thudding bare feet were the only way he could time the drakur's approach. As it sprang atop his boulder, Jak lunged up and jammed the spear into it from below.

He meant to jab it in the abdomen, but he caught it in the crotch. The stone tip didn't sink deep and deliver the crippling blow he'd hoped for. It only dented that stone hide, and the weight of the contact jarred Jak's joints and almost knocked him down. He planted his feet and braced the butt of the spear against the ground.

Roaring with pain and fury, the drakur vaulted over him, its own spear flying from its hands. It hit the ground several feet away.

Jak dropped the crude spear and drew his sword, whirling to face the creature. When it leaped to its feet, it didn't even look at him. It charged off down the slope, not caring that its back was to Jak. That reinforced his belief that they wanted to escape.

But when he glanced back at the crewmen, many dead on the ground, he knew the drakur would take out anyone in their path. And more and more of them were spewing out of their volcano tunnels. The creatures raced toward the bay—and the barge and the archaeology team.

Jak sprinted down the slope, hoping he wasn't too late to warn them.

2

As Professor Jadora Freedar knelt on the hardened lava rock, carefully chiseling away pieces to reveal more and more of the blue-black object, her heart pounded as if she'd been chewing guarana seeds. The ground kept rumbling, a reminder that her team had to hurry to excavate the entire artifact before the volcano erupted, but she couldn't help but pause and rest a hand on it in wonder. The surface was as smooth as spun glass and strangely warm, especially given that it had been encased in rock for countless millennia.

"This is it," she whispered, certain that warmth indicated magic, even though her terrene blood had no affinity for sensing it. "All those years... all that research, Loran's life's work... Loran's *life.*"

Her throat tightened from more than the ash choking the air, and tears ran down her cheeks into the astringently scented bandana covering her mouth and nose. She couldn't be bothered to wipe her eyes now, not when they had finally found it, the portal to the homeland of the dragons.

"We won't know that until we get it out of here and see if it matches the descriptions in the texts," her colleague, Professor Darv Sadlik, said from a few feet away, though he was chiseling away rock as enthusiastically—as determinedly—as she.

"I know, but archaeologists have unearthed enough samples of dragon steel to recognize it when we find it. We may not know the components of the alloy, but we know it's impervious to heat and just about everything else. What else besides dragon steel could have survived being encased by molten lava? And look." Jadora waved at the side of the two-foot length of the artifact they'd revealed. "See the curve? You can already tell that it's going to form a ring. What besides the portal could it be?"

"A giant circle?" Darv asked dryly, then broke into coughs, his older lungs more frail than hers. His bandana had fallen, and he'd also been too distracted to fix it.

Jadora paused to reach over and adjust it for him, which earned her an eye roll. Old men weren't any more accepting of mothering than teenage boys.

Darv patted her shoulder. "I know how important this is to you and Jak, but let's not get ahead of ourselves. Once we have it on the barge, and we're safely on our way back to our continent, we can study it thoroughly." He glanced not toward the volcano but toward the mainland and the busy port city of Perchver five miles across the strait. "In the meantime, let's hope nobody over there is paying attention to us."

"I gained permission from the local magistrate, the Perchver University chancellor, and the archaeology department head before planning a dig here. Since they're convinced nothing could be on one of these volcanic islands—for what ancient human civilization would have been so foolish as to settle here?—they even gave me permission to take what artifacts we might find, though I did have to promise to share recipes for a few of my proprietary pharmacognostic blends in exchange."

"I notice you didn't mention King Zaruk in your list."

"I don't know what paperwork to file to request permission to dig from someone who lives in a floating castle. Can you even send mail up to those cities?"

"Funny, Jadora."

She lowered her voice. "You know why we can't ask them for permission—or let them get a whiff of what we're doing or that this truly exists. We have to hope the portal works after all this time and figure out how to activate it before they find out."

She rested her hand on the smooth metal, hoping that would take days or weeks and not years or decades.

A zing of energy ran up her arm, and she almost jerked away. But something like a dream flashed into her mind, bright and vibrant in contrast to the hazy gray world around her.

A blue sky over vast snow-covered mountains and glaciers filled her mind, the ice tinted with greens and pinks like nothing she'd ever seen. A magnificent dragon flew over the snow and ice, its shimmering scales iridescent like the inside of a mollusk shell, its body undulating through the sky almost like a snake. Jadora recognized the great creature she'd seen only in drawings based on fossils, but it was different from the artists' renditions. Who would have guessed a dragon's scales were iridescent?

Something poked Jadora, and the vision snapped, leaving her with a twinge of disappointment as her ash-choked reality returned. The surface of the artifact pulsed under her hand, shimmering slightly, reminding her of the dragon's scales.

Uncertainty and wariness crept over her. Nothing in Loran's research or in any of the hundreds of archaeology books she'd scoured had suggested the artifact could do anything except open a portal to the dragon home world. What had she seen? A dream? A preview of that other world? Proof that dragons still lived?

Darv prodded her again with his finger. "Have you figured out how to do that?" he asked slowly, as if he were repeating the question. He probably was.

What had she been saying? Oh, yes. Activation. "There's some research on that in Loran's notes." Loran's notes that had said nothing about the portal emanating visions. Jadora leaned back, removing her hand and rubbing it on her dirty trousers. "My work these past years has been focused on *locating* it. The rest, I assumed, could be figured out later. Loran had some hypotheses in his journal." Her hand strayed to the lump under her jacket, the inner pocket that held that tattered leather-bound book full of his notes and sketches.

Maybe her tone had changed—even after five years, Jadora couldn't keep the emotion out of her voice when she spoke her late husband's name—for Darv looked over, his spectacles half-coated with ash, his short gray hair damp with sweat, his dark eyes grave. "I'm sorry. You know how easily I fret. Besides, I feel obligated to give you a hard time since you've dragged me out to an active volcano in the middle of the summer heat."

"If we'd waited, the mages might have found it first." Jadora shoved aside rock, unveiling even more of the curve along the side of the artifact. Interestingly, it had a slight undulation, reminding her of the dragon's flight in her vision.

Darv's eyes sharpened. "Do you think they're still looking for it? After all these years?"

"Yes."

"How do you know? You haven't published anything, not that the university press would have allowed you to, since—ah." He cleared his throat and fell silent.

"Since I've been ostracized for abandoning my chemistry and herbalism career? I'm well aware of how most of my former colleagues feel about me, but after we get this back to the university—" Jadora started to pat the smooth metal but turned the gesture into a finger point, wary that another vision might grab her if she touched it again, "—it will have been worth it. As to the rest, yes, they've been following my research. My offices, both at home and at the university, have been ransacked and searched at least once a semester."

Darv stared at her. "Thanok and Shylezar, you didn't say anything?"

"Who would I tell when mages were responsible? Would our chancellor have rushed up to their sky cities and filed a complaint?"

"You could have told *me*. I would have avoided your office more assiduously."

"You're hilarious, old man."

He broke into another round of coughs, and Jadora regretted teasing him. He was her mentor and closest friend, one of few who hadn't turned his back on her these past years.

"Why don't you get the steam-sledge team over here?" she asked, waving to the steam-powered machinery they'd coerced off the barge that morning. That task shouldn't weary him as much as digging. "As soon as we can get the portal carved out of the rock, we'll hook it, haul it down the beach, and pull it up onto the deck."

"And pray it isn't as heavy as it looks?"

"The ancient dragon alloy is much lighter than steel."

"Right. I'm sure we'll heft it out of ground like a feather."

"Not *that* light." Jadora moved farther along the artifact's edge with her hammer and chisel, tempted to speed up the process with explosives. Normally, that would be an insane way to excavate an artifact—as the rest of the archaeology team would loudly inform her—but experiments had shown that neither black powder nor mage charges damaged dragon steel. "But it won't sink the ship."

"I trust you've done calculations."

"Of course. You know mathematics is a hobby of mine."

"And here I thought drying herbs and brewing potions took up all your spare time."

"Not these days." Maybe if this worked and they got the portal back to the university, Jadora could one day return to her original career. She would have to help a team figure out how to operate it, but then... visiting the dragon home world could be a mission for younger, sturdier people with a fondness for adventure. Adventure and grime. She eyed the black sand under her fingernails and ash in the creases of her skin, and thought longingly of her sterile laboratory back home.

"Are you sure? I can't help but notice how you still clank when you move. How many sample vials are in your pockets today?"

"Just a few. I've heard the black sand from the Dragon Perch Islands has interesting properties, so I collected some, and I picked up some irithika at our stop in Nelm. In case of relic raiders."

"Is that a poison?"

"It shares characteristics with alcohol and is an anxiolytic—it tends to relax people and make them susceptible to suggestion."

Darv waved toward the firearm-toting guards that Jadora had hired to protect their team. "Some people just shoot their enemies, you know."

"Yes, but I'm an academic and an herbalist. My preferred methods are to bore enemies to sleep by reading from my scholarly papers or to drug them."

"If my students are to be believed, the latter is more humane."

"I've heard that from your students as well."

"Ha ha. Do you—"

He frowned and peered past her shoulder toward one of the trails leading up the side of the volcano. Jadora caught a distant shout and followed his gaze. She gaped in horror, not because of the ominous plumes of black smoke—those had been wafting from the caldera all morning—but because a horde of drakur was racing down the mountainside. And—pray to Shylezar—was that Jak?

He was sprinting down the slope, flailing as he navigated

uneven ground, and shouting. With the surf roaring beyond the bay, Jadora couldn't understand his words, but she had no trouble deciphering the warning.

"Captain Nokk!" she called to the uniformed guards too busy spitting chaw, playing cards, and scratching their balls to have noticed the trouble. "Enemies!"

As Jadora lurched to her feet, pointing at the dozens and dozens of drakur racing down the mountainside, the ground rumbled again.

The guards—would the team of ten she'd hired be enough to stem the drakur tide?—jumped up, grabbing magelock rifles as they spotted the encroaching trouble. What had happened to the crewmen who'd been cutting cactus pads up there? Were they in hiding? Or dead?

"We're not going to survive that," Darv whispered.

"Yes, we are." Jadora gripped his arm, hoping to reassure him, and pointed him toward the wooden rowboats pulled up on the beach. There were enough of them to carry her team if the guards stayed behind and bought them time to escape. She would stay with the men and make sure they did exactly that. And also make sure Jak made it down to them. He was a fast runner, but the determined drakur were right behind him, waving spears as they chased him.

The wind shifted, blowing sulfuric plumes of smoke toward Jadora, and she lost sight of Jak. She fought down fear that rose up, threatening to turn into panic. He was all she had left in the world. She couldn't lose him.

"Get to the boats," she ordered her team as the guards started firing at the drakur. "Find cover, Jak!" she yelled up the slope, hoping he heard her. In the haze, the guards might accidentally shoot *him*.

"You better get to them too, Jadora," Darv called back as he ran toward the beach.

"I will," she yelled, though she wouldn't. Not until she had Jak.

Jadora rushed across the dig site toward the handful of tents erected along the edge and ducked into one to snatch a rifle. Despite her disinterest in shooting enemies, when her expeditions had started taking her into the wilds, she'd learned to use the weapon. But she also grabbed a few canisters that she'd prepared ahead of time. They would create a small explosion upon impact and spit out a lot of noxious smoke. Unfortunately, the smoke was meant to deter humans, not drakur. She didn't even know if the subterranean beings had noses.

Outside, there were fewer guards than there had been a moment before. Two men with magelocks, soft *thwomps* sounding as the weapons unleashed charges of power, were blasting the oncoming drakur as they walked backward toward the beach. The rest of the guards were jumping into the boats.

Jadora gaped at them. "Where are you *going*? Captain Nokk!"

The gray-haired leader met her eyes, shook his head, and pointed out into the bay. The barge was belching dark plumes from its steam stack as it made ready to move. No, it was *already* moving. On the deck, crewmen with telescopes were pointing at the drakur and shouting for their helmsman to navigate them out of the bay at top speed. The barge had cannons and harpoon launchers, and they were worried about the creatures?

The guards shoved Darv and several of the archaeologists out of the rowboats, so they could flee first.

Jadora swore at them and took several steps in that direction, but a cry of "Mother!" made her spin back to the slope.

Jak raced out of the smoke with two drakur right behind him. He gripped his pistol as he ran, his blue eyes wild with fear, but he must have already used all of the charges. The creatures were right behind him with their spears hefted.

Struggling for calm and a steady hand, Jadora raised her rifle. The drakur were so close behind him that she worried she would miss and hit Jak. But he saw her taking aim and ducked low as he ran.

Trusting him not to lurch up, she pulled the trigger. The stock of the magelock reverberated against the crook of her shoulder as it fired, and the blazing blue charge sped away. It slammed into the whiskered face of one of the drakur, knocking it from Jak's trail.

She shifted her aim and fired at the second one. It anticipated her attack and jumped to the side, so her charge only clipped it in the shoulder. Fortunately, that was enough to send it spinning off the trail and give Jak the time he needed to reach the camp.

Jadora fired at more drakur rushing down the same path, afraid they would attack her team. She was responsible for Darv and nine other archaeologists, none of whom had been allowed into the rowboats. The guards had shoved all of them out to make room for themselves and were rowing after the barge as fast as they could move their oars. Cowards.

Though she shook with anger, Jadora managed to stay calm enough to hand her magelock to Jak as he ran up. "Buy me a few seconds if you can. I have an idea."

"It better... be... brilliant," he panted, chest heaving after his run. Somehow, he'd managed to keep his hat.

She wanted to hug him for that—it meant almost as much to her as it did to him. "I have a couple of smoke bombs."

A clang sounded, a spear striking the steam sledge. More spears hurtled toward the archaeologists on the beach. A few of them rushed out into the water and swam after the boats.

Maybe that would be better than standing their ground. Even as Jak fired at drakur heading toward the tents, others swarmed out onto the dig site. There was no way Jadora and Jak could stop all of them, and most of the other archaeologists weren't armed with anything better than pickaxes and chisels.

Realizing her weak explosives would do nothing to scare the

drakur horde, Jadora twisted off the caps of two of the canisters. She fished in her pockets, found the vials of gray irithika powder, and dumped the contents inside.

Jak fired at two drakur who'd reached the tents and were knocking them down, jabbing ferociously with their spears.

"I don't think they like us, Mother," he said, sounding scared though he tried to hide it under bravado.

"Their world is on the verge of erupting with molten lava surging out of the volcano and burning everything in its path." Jadora sealed the canisters again. "That knowledge probably has them moody."

A *crash-clunk* came from a nearby tent, and Jak fired. "That one just destroyed the coffeepot. Moodily."

Jadora stepped up beside him and looked for a large knot of drakur to target. She kept hoping they were fleeing the volcano and would rush out into the water, that they'd only been destroying what was in their path out of fear and anger.

But they didn't head for the bay. Those not assaulting the tents and flinging camp rations all over the place arrowed toward the artifact. Dozens and dozens of them. She stared in horror as they swarmed it and jabbed at the dark metal with their spears.

Their roars coalesced into a semblance of words to her ears. She'd only studied writings that attempted to translate their language using her own Dhoran alphabet, but their vocabulary wasn't extensive, and she could pick out a few familiar terms.

"They think it's our fault that the volcano is erupting," she said.

A drakur with a spear charged at Jak, murderous rage contorting its face. "No kidding."

He fired, hitting it in the chest and knocking it to the ground.

"Because we're removing the portal. They think the gods are angry. Keep shooting." Jadora hefted one of her canisters and threw it at the mob converging on the artifact.

"That one of your smoke bombs?" Jak fired at another drakur.

"It is."

"I've only seen you use those for scaring away raccoons rooting through the garbage at your dig sites." His voice was hoarse, and he coughed at the end of the sentence.

"They've scared away thieves too."

"Yeah, thieving raccoons."

The explosion, when it came, was weak, but smoke flowed out to rival the plumes wafting from the caldera. Even from dozens of feet away, the smell stung Jadora's nostrils. She willed it to affect the drakur.

After a few seconds, a couple of them stumbled away, but the rest didn't even pause. They kept ramming their spears at the artifact. Afraid they would find some way to damage it, Jadora growled and threw the second explosive.

"I'm running low on charges," Jak said grimly, sweat plastering the side of his face, his bandana drooping around his neck.

"There's another magelock in here." She lunged into the tent, grabbed it, and handed it to him instead of keeping it for herself. Her gaze caught on a megaphone. Earlier, the guard captain had been using it to communicate with the barge crew. "That'll do." She grabbed it. "Stay here, Jak."

"Stay here? Where are *you* going?"

"To hide behind a rock and pretend I can speak their language."

Jak threw her a bewildered look.

There wasn't time to explain. She eased around the back of the tent—it was the last one standing—and toward a boulder. As she moved, the drakur spears, now chipped and splintered from striking something much harder than they were, stopped banging off the artifact as frequently. Smoke filled the air around the dig site, thick and gray and noxious. The drakur peered around, bumping into each other, disoriented.

Her formula was affecting them. But would it be enough?

Jadora darted from rock to rock, hoping they would be less likely to sniff out her ruse if her voice wasn't coming from the tent where they'd last seen her. She sank down behind a boulder where she had a view of the dig site and also the bay with the barge now well on its way, the rowboats struggling to catch up with it. Another ship was out in the strait.

Dare she hope some kind crew would come rescue them if they managed to survive this? If the rest of the day was anything to go on, that ship would sail past as quickly as it could.

From behind the boulder, Jadora lifted the megaphone and bellowed into it. *"Zarzargaresh zug resh rugt!"*

She lowered the megaphone and looked toward Jak instead of sticking her head up to gauge their reaction. Had she managed to impersonate a god and command them to flee their home? That had been the goal, but it was possible she'd spewed gobbledygook. Or told them the gods wanted that artifact utterly destroyed.

Loran, who'd spent his entire life studying languages, both dead and living, would have teased her mercilessly over her pronunciation. She wished he were still alive to do so.

The dwindling spear clacks dwindled further, then stopped completely. Jak was watching them, the stock of his rifle to his shoulder, but he didn't fire again. He glanced at her and mouthed something. Do it again?

She bellowed the same phrase, not trusting her limited grasp of the language to come up with something else. Long seconds passed, the only noise coming from the roar of the surf. The bastards on the barge hadn't bothered firing their cannons to help.

Jadora had a feeling the crew, much like the drakur, thought the volcano's eruption was imminent and there was no point in helping people who would be dead soon. She couldn't say for sure that it *wasn't*, but she'd also talked to enough volcanologists to know that volcanos could spout smoke and rumble and stew for a lot of days before they actually erupted, if they erupted at all. Admittedly, it was more hope than certainty that had driven her out here and made her willing to risk her team. If the volcano blew in a big way and buried the dig site in lava flows again, the artifact might never be recovered.

Splashes sounded, making her tense. What now?

Only when Jak lowered his weapon did she realize what she was hearing. The drakur were jumping into the water.

She peeked out, her heart soaring as they ran en masse into the bay, leaping in and swimming away. Where they thought they would go, she didn't know, but she didn't care. As long as they weren't trying to kill her team. Darv and the others were crouching behind barnacle-covered boulders in the shallows, their heads barely visible.

"It worked, Mother." Jak waved his magelock in the air after the last of the drakur were swimming away from the beach. "What did you tell them?"

"To leave the artifact alone."

"Wait, maybe that wasn't the only thing that worked." Jak's voice had taken on an odd note. He was looking toward the portal.

Jadora peered around her boulder, a sense of foreboding coming over her. Four of the drakur lay unmoving next to the artifact, their heads charred black, as if they'd been thrust in fire—or struck by lightning.

"I didn't do that." Jak glanced at her, as if she might have thought a magelock could leave such marks. "I'm pretty sure they're dead."

"They were trying to destroy the portal. Maybe it has... defense mechanisms." The memory of that vision flashed in Jadora's mind, and a chill went through her at the idea that this artifact might be sentient. At the least, it had more capabilities magically instilled in it than any of the ancient texts had mentioned. She didn't know whether to be excited or scared.

What if it objected when they tried to remove it from this resting spot?

If they still could. Without the barge, there was no way to get that artifact off the island. And she and her team were stuck here.

Another ominous rumble coursed through the ground. Jadora closed her eyes, letting her forehead thunk against the boulder.

3

WHEN JAK SAW HIS MOTHER SLUMPED AGAINST THE BOULDER, HE tried to help her back to the lone standing tent, but she brushed aside the offer. Instead, she patted him down to check for injuries, then flicked her thick brown braid over her shoulder and veered straight toward the artifact. Her jacket was torn, her trousers covered in dirt and ash, and stray strands of hair plastered the sides of her face and neck, but she wouldn't be deterred from the mission.

He shook his head and walked after her. He also wanted to see the artifact unearthed, but there was little reason to hurry to dig it out now when they had no ship to load it onto. Still, he'd spent many hours poring over the journal, notes, and books his father had left behind, and curiosity drove him toward the artifact alongside his mother. It almost made him forget the ashy smoke that had descended on the beach and that made his throat raw and hoarse.

"What did you do to scare them away, Professor Freedar?" one of her assistants asked, her clothing soggy and her boots squishing as she and the team returned to the dig site.

Mother said something vague about impersonating gods and telling the drakur they would be struck down by lightning, but she returned to chipping lava rock away from the artifact without expounding. She didn't mention that the portal itself had killed some of the drakur. Jak had seen it happen, lightning branching out from the exposed portion of the artifact and smacking its attackers in the head. It had only taken seconds for the drakur to topple to the ground, smoke wafting from their charred faces.

Maybe she didn't want to worry the rest of the team. She was, Jak noted, being careful not to bump the artifact as she chiseled.

"She also flung her raccoon-deterrent smoke bombs at them," Jak said, since the colleague was eyeing the artifact with worry. Some of the archaeologists might have also witnessed the lightning attack. "I think that was the true secret to victory," he added.

"That explains some of the stink. The non-sulfuric stink, anyway."

"Someone's coming," Darv called from the beach.

"Our stalwart guards?" Jak couldn't believe the supposedly well-trained fighters had fled, leaving a bunch of scientists and his *mother* to handle the drakur. Granted, she was in her early forties and not incapable by any means, but none of them were fighters, at least not in the traditional sense. His mother had once dealt with a strung-out homeless man who was threatening her students by mixing laboratory ingredients in a mop bucket and wheeling it down the hallway to knock him out. If she had access to herbs or chemicals, Jak would always put his money on her in a fight.

"I don't think so." Worry lurked in Darv's voice.

What now?

Jak sighed. "I'll check on it."

"Thank you, Jak," Mother said without looking up.

As he approached Darv, the older man's trousers sodden and clinging to his thin legs, the breeze shifted smoke out of the bay to reveal a large wooden rowboat heading their way. Jak's first thought was that the barge captain had stopped, regained his sanity, and sent it for them, but he didn't recognize any of the stern faces inside. Stern *women's* faces. Ten female warriors stood in the center of the boat, all wearing brown uniforms and a mix of chain-mail and hardened-leather armor, and all carrying weapons. Twelve more uniformed women manned the oars on either side of the craft. They were also armed with swords, maces, and magelocks.

"Uh," Jak said. "Are we about to get mugged by a bunch of women?"

Darv wiped his spectacles on his shirt, even though it was as ashy as everything else here. "Are female muggers inferior to male muggers?"

"I don't know, but I'd rather not admit to being mugged by them to friends back home."

"Perhaps in the retelling, we can call them pirates."

Jak didn't know if being mugged by female pirates sounded that much better.

"I will warn your mother," Darv said. "In case they are here to rob us of the artifact, she may need to produce more of her raccoon deterrents."

As Darv hustled up the beach, Jak called after him, "You're just leaving so *I'll* have to be the one to deal with them, aren't you?"

"My colleagues would not cease teasing me if I were mugged by female pirates," Darv called back.

"I *knew* it would be embarrassing," Jak muttered, keeping his voice low since the newcomers were now within earshot.

One in the front of the boat, a dark-skinned woman with short salt-and-pepper hair and a compact build, watched Jak calmly. Something about her made him want to describe her as serene rather than stern. Was she the leader? Despite the masculine haircut and uniform, there was an elegance to her strong jaw, straight nose, and pronounced cheekbones that made him suspect she'd been trailed by all the boys in the neighborhood in her younger days. She looked to be about fifty, and ten to thirty years older than the rest of the women.

Jak debated if it would be even *more* embarrassing to be beaten up by someone more than twice his age. As they drew closer, hands resting on their weapons, he worried they had come to do more than beat people up.

He was still armed, but the only other magelock in camp was out of charges. He'd checked for more, but the guards had taken all of their weapons when they'd fled. Other than a couple of swords and daggers—and pickaxes, chisels, and hammers—the group didn't have much to defend themselves with. And these women looked like they knew how to use their weapons. Several of them wore sleeveless versions of the uniforms that revealed muscles that many men would have envied.

"Welcome to the twelfth Dragon Perch Island," he called to them, hoping to put them in a good mood by being friendly. "We're camping on this delightful beach, but you're welcome to the rest of it. The natives have recently cleared out, so there are numerous caves and lava tubes. The perfect place for a camping trip. Or a military training exercise." They each wore an armband with a small metal oval that was embossed with either one, two, three, or four thorns—he assumed the symbols denoted rank. The leader was the only one with four thorns.

"Camping? I wondered what kind of idiotic tourists could possibly be out here on a volcano about to erupt." A tall, mid-thirties woman next to the leader pointed to Jak. "I guess this is a demonstration."

Her black hair was pulled back in a bun so tight it had to give her a perpetual headache. Maybe that accounted for the grumpiness. Her armband had three thorns. The second-in-command? A lieutenant?

"Who's the bigger idiot? The people on the volcano or the people rowing out to get to it?" Jak shouldn't have insulted them, given their proliferation of weapons and muscles, but he resented the implication that they were dumb tourists. If they'd truly found the ancient dragon portal, it could change the course of history.

"Can I shoot him?" the talker asked.

One of the rowers, a pretty young blonde with arms much thinner than the others, smiled at the exchange, but she was the only one. With pale skin and freckles, she was out of place in the group. The rest of the women appeared to be a mix of roamers and southerners.

"We were sent to *get* them," the leader spoke for the first time, her voice softer than Jak had expected.

"The magistrate's orders were to get the idiots off the island before they start an international incident. It didn't sound like he cared if they were alive or dead."

"True."

"We have clearance from the government to be here," Jak said as the boat came close enough for the bottom to scrape in the sand. "And it's possible the volcano won't erupt for weeks."

"Or it's possible it'll erupt in five seconds," the lieutenant said, "smothering your mouthy ass in magma."

"It's lava when it's above ground and magma when it's below ground. Do they not have any books near the gymnasium where you hurl heavy objects around?"

A hand clasped Jak's shoulder, making him jump.

"What are you doing?" his mother asked.

"Trading insults with these large, muscled women."

She gave him a stop-being-a-dolt look. Funny how similar it was to the expressions the newcomers were giving him.

"I'm Professor Jadora Freedar." Mother waded out to help the women pull their boat up on the beach, though the fit crew hardly needed assistance. "Did you say you were sent to get us?"

"That's right. I'm Captain Ferroki, commander of Thorn Company, a free-mercenary unit." The leader stepped onto the beach, waved at the ash in the air, and faced Mother. "You aren't going to resist being collected are you?"

"Ah." Mother pursed her lips and looked toward the dig site. The rest of the team was continuing the excavation, though not without numerous glances toward the boat. Without machinery—machinery that had been damaged by spears thrown into the workings—the excavation could take days. "Is your ship perhaps large enough to hold an artifact of approximately five hundred pounds of weight that measures twenty feet in diameter?"

"No," the captain said.

"You're certain?" Mother peered through the smoke toward a ferry that looked like it *could* hold the artifact, though Jak had no idea how they would get it onto the ferry with the machinery broken.

"We've been sent to retrieve archaeologists," the captain said, "not archaeology."

"It's a historic find of great importance." Mother was careful not to mention what it truly was. There weren't many artifacts that the general populace would be aware of, but *everybody* had heard the legends of the dragon portal—and the dragons who'd used it long ago to visit Torvil and soar through the skies here.

"I'm certain that you will regret losing it, but the magistrate believes the volcano will erupt soon and is paying us to remove you from his island."

"Menial task that it is," the lieutenant muttered.

"They're *all* menial tasks these days," a soldier in the back of the boat said with a sigh.

The captain looked back at her troops. It was a gaze, not an icy cold glare, but it silenced their disgruntlement.

"That was a clever trick with the drakur," the captain added to Mother. "We saw your guards swimming after their ship."

Mother's mouth twisted. "Apparently, we didn't pay them enough."

"How much would you pay us?" the lieutenant asked.

Ferroki looked at her.

"What, Captain? We've got tools, and you know we could use extra money. Pay's been sparse, and five hundred pounds isn't *that* much. Corporal Granite weighs almost that much after she porks down a bin of tallow crackers."

"Hey," a boulder of a woman in the back said. "*Everybody* eats tallow crackers when we get them."

"Not everybody eats so *many* of them."

"You say you've already been paid to give us a ride?" Mother asked.

"You, yes," the captain said. "Your artifact is extra."

The lieutenant smirked, probably pleased that her idea had been adopted. Jak caught the eye of the young blonde woman, curious how she'd ended up with this rough bunch. He smiled at her, maybe a bit of a flirtatious smile, though this wasn't the right time for that. Still, it was hard to resist. She was the first girl his age that he'd seen since leaving home.

She broke their eye contact right away without returning the smile and shrank inward a bit. He bit his lip and looked away, hoping he hadn't offended her somehow. He was certain he hadn't ogled her chest or anything his mother would have smacked him for.

"How much extra?" Mother asked.

"Ten gold oroni," the captain said.

"That's a high price. How much is the magistrate already paying you?" Mother looked at Jak.

He frowned. Was she worried they would end up being billed for this? She hadn't given him the details about the monetary situation, but he knew she'd done a big fundraiser and personally asked for donations from regular benefactors to the university to finance the trip.

"Not a large amount," the captain said. "He's only paying us to carry you off the island, possibly by slinging you over our shoulders. You're asking for more work, so the price is higher."

"I might be able to piece together a few oronis and..." Mother scanned the tattered remains of the camp.

Jak couldn't imagine what valuables they had that would appeal to mercenaries. Her gaze shifted to him, skimming over the medallion in his hat's headband, and he stiffened, but her gaze didn't linger for long before returning to the mercenaries.

"The rest of our coffee beans," Mother finished. "They're from Rabbit Roaster in Sprungtown and enhanced with culinary magic. The coffee is delicious."

Never mind that those beans were scattered all over the dig site now and coated with ash...

"*Mage* coffee," the lieutenant growled. "Isn't that the stuff that addicts you and diddles your mind so you're a more eager slave?"

"You're thinking of the magebands," one of the mercenaries said, waving at her bare head.

"They have all kinds of doodads they create," the lieutenant said, "to make us happy little minions who don't fight back when they murder our children and break our backs in their mines."

The captain held up a finger. "I've heard of that roaster. He's not loyal to the wizard kings, is he?"

"No," Mother said. "They *think* he is, but he's a supporter of terrene humans. The coffee sharpens and stimulates your mind with its magic. It's an effective counter after you've been wearing one of their headbands."

"We accept your offer." The captain waved for the rest of her people to get out of the boat. "Show us how to help."

The ground shuddered, and ripples spread across the bay.

"You'd better show us quickly," she added.

"Happy to."

Jak coughed as the smoke thickened, settling over the beach. He pulled his forgotten bandana back up, and the herbal tincture his mother had doused it with helped clean the air before it trickled down his trachea.

At a gesture from one of the other soldiers, the blonde girl stayed with the boat. Jak thought about lingering to say something friendly to her, but if she wasn't interested in chatting up hand-some-but-bruised-and-ash-covered strangers, he shouldn't pester her.

"What is *that*?" she breathed before he'd taken two steps.

She pointed toward the volcano, and he groaned, afraid lava had started to flow. But there was something hovering in the sky behind the smoking caldera, something even blacker than the smoke. His heart sank into his boots.

"A mageship."

4

THE MAGESHIP FLEW TOWARD THE BEACH, A SLEEK BLACK CRAFT similar in shape to wooden sailing ships, but with neither sail nor steam to power it and nothing but magic to keep it aloft. Jak stared glumly at it, certain nothing good could come from the arrival of mages from one of the sky cities. Most likely, they would threaten to do far more than sling the team over their shoulders and evict them from the island.

The ground shook several times in a row, and Jak feared the eruption was coming. Not days from now but today. He'd given up praying to the gods after they'd failed to save his father's life, but he thought about resuming the practice now, praying that the volcano would erupt and incinerate the mageship with lava blasted hundreds of feet into the sky.

Not that he could be certain molten lava would destroy one of those ships. They were rumored to be built not by the worker mages that crafted all of the utilitarian magical items in the world but by those talented and powerful enough to be called wizards. Building tools and trinkets was considered beneath them, but they were the only ones who could craft mageships and sky castles.

"Jak," his mother called. "Get up here."

He'd been rooted to the beach since the blonde girl pointed out the ship, but his mother, the archaeology team, and the rest of the mercenaries were frantically chiseling and digging. What was the point? There was no way they could get the portal out and onto the ferry and escape while the mages watched from above.

But as he ran up to help, he realized the team wasn't trying to dig the artifact *out*. They were trying to cover it back up.

He shook his head. The mages *had* to know about this, or why else would they have shown up at these forsaken volcanic islands? But the team had already covered up most of the blue-black metal, so he dropped down to help. Maybe there was a remote chance the mages were here for another reason—they had academics and scientists, the same as normal humans, so maybe they'd sent the ship here to study the volcano.

"Sure, Jak. That's likely."

As the mageship floated closer, the team covered up the last of the telltale blue-black metal and headed toward the lone tent. There was no doubt about the ship's destination. Had it been flying around the volcano for observation purposes, it wouldn't need to come to their dig site.

Jak joined his mother, Captain Ferroki, Darv, and several of the archaeologists by the tent, awkwardly sticking his hands in his pockets. He wasn't the only one. The words *act casual* floated through his mind, and he snorted. There was no way this would work. Even if the mages up there couldn't somehow sense the magic of the artifact, some of them might be telepaths. They could read the minds of everyone here and learn everything Jak and his mother knew, including their five years of research on the portal.

His mother closed her eyes, defeat slumping her shoulders for the first time today. The urge to comfort her or say something encouraging came over him, but he couldn't think of how or what.

"Should we start cleaning up the camp and pretend we're...

doing something besides digging for a priceless artifact?" he asked. "The captain's coffee beans are scattered in the ashes over there."

Ferroki peered over, lifted an eyebrow toward Mother, then snorted. At least she didn't appear pissed at this revelation.

"There's no point," Mother said. "I only covered it up on the off chance the dragon god blesses us with luck and the ship is carrying a team of inept teenage mages on a school field trip to observe the volcano."

Ferroki raised both eyebrows this time. "That's the *Murder Flyer*." She pointed at the front of the black hull of the craft. There was no name written on it, but a distinctive shark figurehead leered down at them, its long sharp teeth glinting silver. They were the only things on the ship that weren't black, at least from this point of view. "I don't know what it's doing in Zaruk's kingdom, but that's Malek's ship."

Jak didn't usually swear with his mother standing three feet away, but he couldn't keep an oath from blurting out. Everyone had heard of King Uthari's right-hand man, the most infamous of the zidarr. One-third warrior, one-third wizard, and one-third pure magic, they were loyal servants to the great wizard kings and trained from their earliest years to be pure killers. Malek was one of few who didn't have a name like Stone Heart or Dragon's Death. He didn't need one. Everyone knew to fear him without some stupid moniker.

Even though his mother had spoken little of the details around Father's death, Jak had heard rumors that one of the zidarr had been responsible. It had been Uthari's soldiers who came to the house after he'd been killed and questioned her and searched everything. Jak remembered two of them tramping through his own room, turning over the mattress and throwing the contents of his drawers and bookcases to the floor. They'd even torn his maps off the wall. Jak could have hated Uthari just for that.

"Isn't it named the *Star Flyer*?" Mother asked.

"They have their name for it; we have ours."

"How much would I have to pay you to fight him?"

Ferroki shook her head humorlessly. "There is no amount any mercenary company would take to face zidarr, even the Iron Fist. A rabbit does not tug at a lion's tail."

"That's what I was afraid of," Mother said bleakly.

"It may be wise for me to take my people and leave before they land. There is no logical reason they should attack us, and we did agree to remove your team from the island and take you back to the mainland, but mages were not mentioned in the contract." Ferroki scrutinized Mother, as if she might be responsible for this new development.

"They probably want the artifact," Mother said.

The mageship came to a halt floating a hundred feet above the beach. The sky was too hazy with ash for it to cast a shadow, but Jak wagered it threw an ominous one whenever the sun was out.

"Perhaps you should leave it for them," Ferroki suggested. "Unless they forbid it, we will still offer you passage back to the mainland."

Mother shot her a sharp look. Or was that an anguished look? "I can't *leave* it. Not after so many years devoted to researching it, not after so much has been given up, not after my husband—" she swallowed, and Jak patted her shoulder awkwardly.

Ferroki looked at him, as if he might be more reasonable, but Jak shook his head. He couldn't imagine getting this close and then leaving the portal to someone else. This was his mission as much as it was Mother's.

The mercenary lieutenant jogged up to Ferroki. "Captain, I trust you know who that is?" She pointed upward. "Let's get out of here. This mission isn't worth dying for."

"I know." Ferroki looked at Mother and smiled sadly at her. "If you will not come with us, then we must depart without you. It is difficult for me not to feel we are abandoning you, but if I were to incur the wrath of the zidarr or their wizard masters, it could cost me my entire unit. I have a... friend who had that happen to him earlier this year. He lost hundreds of men and did not survive unscathed himself."

"I understand," Mother said numbly.

"If you somehow manage to survive this encounter, we will owe you a favor." Ferroki truly sounded upset to leave them to the mages. Jak didn't know why she cared since they'd just met, but she saluted Mother before waving for her people to run back to the boat on the beach.

Jak couldn't keep from curling a lip, bitterness sinking into his soul. Nobody would stick around to help them today. How were terrene humans ever supposed to improve their lots in life if they didn't stand together against their magical overlords?

Several black oval disks floated over the side of the mageship, each with a person riding on it. Jak glimpsed uniformed men and someone with a black cloak that flapped in the breeze that his disk stirred. How dramatic. Was that Malek? Was there any chance that a sniper shooting him could take him down? Jak fingered the magelock he still had, positive none of the mercenaries would try it. They were as cowardly as the last group.

"Wait." Mother lifted a hand before Ferroki had taken more than two steps. "May I redeem that favor now?"

"Uh." Ferroki paused and looked up as the disks descended.

Mother stepped not toward her but toward Jak. When she reached for his hat, he was too surprised to grab it. His fingers twitched toward her to take it back, but he stopped himself. He trusted her, though he frowned mightily as she fiddled with the headband. She was removing the gold medallion.

"What?" He reached for it. "Father gave that to me."

She blocked him. "Trust me, Jak." She turned her back on him and handed it to Ferroki. "Keep this safe until I can return for it."

"I..." Ferroki held it in her palm, looking like she wanted to protest—*Jak* wanted her to protest—but she glanced at the disks. They were only twenty feet from landing now. "I will. I'll keep it safe." She buttoned the medallion into one of her pockets and strode toward the boat.

The rest of the mercenaries had pushed it into the shallows and were waiting for their captain. But before they could take off, a blast of liquid fire came from one of the discs, making Jak jump and swear. The blast struck the wooden boat, blowing it to pieces and flinging the mercenaries dozens of feet.

Ferroki, still on the beach, whirled and pointed a magelock at the disk, but a different type of magic—some invisible wave—struck her and hurled her back into the water. Her head struck wreckage from the boat, and she went limp.

Jak swallowed and stepped in front of his mother as the disks landed on the beach, the people—could mages truly be considered *people*?—now visible. There were six of them, four male and two female, all wearing gleaming black boots, black sashes at their waists with attached scimitars, and red military uniforms with silver piping. Entwined lightning bolts circled their cuffs to denote rank. Two had silver epaulets, including the man who'd destroyed the boat, the man with the black cloak, its edges trimmed in silver fur. Was this Malek? He had six circles on his cuffs, more than any of the others.

Mother gasped, as if she recognized him.

His black hair was pulled back in a ponytail, accenting an angular face with cheekbones so sharp they could have honed daggers. His dark eyes were hard, his lips thin and pressed together in irritation, and his chin had a haughty tilt as he looked down his nose at the team of archaeologists. His body buzzed with energy, as if he were made from magic instead of flesh and blood, and at any moment, he might need to unleash more of it.

Jak would have hated him on sight even if he hadn't just seen him blow up the mercenary boat. The women were swimming back toward it—clumping together as if for support—and one had grabbed their captain and was trying to rouse her. Blood ran from a gash at the blonde girl's temple, and a surge of protectiveness swept over Jak.

"Don't do anything to attract attention," Mother murmured, stepping up to his side—refusing to let him stand in front of her.

"I won't if you won't," he muttered.

"Do not fear," the cloaked officer boomed in a voice enhanced by magic. "We will question you soon. Time may be limited." He looked toward the caldera, wrinkled his nose, then lifted a hand in that direction. Wind formed somewhere, with him at the center, and spread, blowing the smoke away from the beach and somehow *keeping* it away, even when he lowered his hand and the wind died down. "Did nobody tell you that it's unwise to dig for artifacts under an active volcano?"

So much for hoping they didn't know about the portal.

"The travel brochure for the island failed to mention the active part," Jak muttered.

He didn't think he'd spoken loudly enough for this Malek to hear him, but the mage's eyes narrowed, and he lifted his hand again, fingers spread toward Jak.

Jak stepped back, but there was nowhere to go. Chilling power wrapped around him, holding him in place and applying pressure from above. It forced him to his knees.

"Stop." Mother stepped forward. "You'll want our help. We're experts on the artifact."

Malek's gaze shifted to her, and she gasped as the magic also wrapped around her and forced her to the ground.

"What I want," Malek boomed, "is you powerless animals on your knees where you belong when in the presence of wizards."

He forced the rest of the archaeology team to their knees—poor old Darv crumpled before the magic even touched him—

then sneered over at the mercenaries. Most of them had found their way to the beach, some supporting others. At least Ferroki was back on her feet, but why hadn't they swum for the ferry out in the strait? If he'd been allowed, Jak would have gotten away from this place. Maybe the mercenaries thought Malek would drown them with a tidal wave.

"Kneel!" Malek boomed. "Kneel before your superiors."

What an ass. Jak barely managed to keep from saying it out loud. But that chilling power still gripped him, and he feared for his life—and his mother's life. They *were* experts on the artifact—everyone on the team had valuable knowledge—but what if this cocky ass didn't see that or just didn't care? Maybe he had only been sent to retrieve the portal and didn't care if his master figured out how to work it.

Half of the mercenaries dropped of their own accord. Ferroki, her lieutenant, several others, and even the blonde girl glared back at him, remaining on their feet. Their resistance made no difference. With another whisper of magic, he forced them to their knees.

He pointed at the blonde girl, lust entering his hard gaze as he eyed her figure. "That one had better get used to that position. I would have sent for her myself if I'd known she existed."

Raw terror flashed in her eyes. Malek smiled and drank it in.

The fury and the desire to protect her returned to Jak, and he tried to lunge to his feet. He longed to shoot that bastard.

The rest of the officers didn't say anything or acknowledge that their boss was a toad. They were walking around the dig site, looking at the ground and pointing at it in spots—spots that were exactly where the portal lay under the rock. As Jak had feared, there'd been no point in hiding it. The mage officers could sense it.

"Any chance they'll take it and leave us here?" Jak whispered, though the idea of losing the artifact still stung him to his core.

"No," a cool voice spoke from a few feet behind them.

Jak spun as much as he could under the magical power that bound him. He almost wrenched his neck.

Another man had appeared from nowhere—Jak would have seen him if he'd ridden down on one of those disks. Unlike the others in their bright red uniforms, he wore simple clothing— tan trousers and a brown shirt and jacket—all free of adornment, save for the weapons hanging from his belt, a basket-hilted sword and a main-gauche. His short black hair was shot with gray, his hard face chiseled from granite. His whole body might have been.

Jak's first thought was to think him someone's bodyguard, but he radiated power. He was as magical as the others, maybe more so. Yes, it was even more pronounced than with Malek. This man seemed almost made of energy. That made Jak more uneasy about him than about Malek. Or, he realized with a start, was *this* Malek?

"Did you want to question them or shall I, my lord?" the cloaked officer asked, managing to ooze arrogance even as he used the honorific. His tone wasn't disrespectful, but his eyes were challenging as he met the gaze of the newcomer, as if they were equals who butted heads often rather than being higher-ranking and lower-ranking officers in Uthari's army.

"I don't know," the man Jak was increasingly convinced was Malek said. "Have you had enough yet of being flamboyant and pompous, General Tonovan?"

"Rarely," Tonovan said without missing a beat. He looked toward the blonde girl, as if he weren't done with her, but Malek gave the volcano a pointed look, and Tonovan inclined his head.

They bowed to each other, and Tonovan smiled. An edged smile that Malek did not return. The two men reminded Jak of alpha wolves circling and about to fight over leadership of the pack.

But when Malek said, "Get the portal out of the rock," Tonovan nodded in curt obedience.

Not that Tonovan did anything himself. He pointed at his men and waved at the ground. "See to it."

Jak hoped the artifact would zap them all with the same power it had used to kill the four drakur.

"Don't touch it," Malek added, pointing at the dead drakur as he looked at Jak. Reading his *mind*? Jak had been afraid the mages would have that ability. "The artifact has a lot of power pent up in it."

"Tell us something that isn't blatantly obvious," Tonovan said.

Malek's cool gaze shifted to him. "I'd make a remark about your intelligence, but I can't think of one that isn't also blatantly obvious."

"Careful, Malek. I have a lot more friends than you do."

Jak caught a couple of the officers looking at each other and rolling their eyes—it was the most human gesture any of these people had made—and Jak doubted the statement was true.

"You have allies who will be loyal as long as they believe you or Uthari will grant them political power." Malek didn't extend the rebuttal by referencing a preponderance of friends of his own.

Jak doubted anyone would be friends with a zidarr.

Tonovan snorted but turned his irritation on his men. "You heard him," he barked, though they had already started using their magic to crack and clear rock from the artifact. "Get that thing out of the ground."

Unfortunately, magic was *all* they used. They never touched the portal. There was no chance of them being zapped if contact was required. Was it? With the crowd of drakur surrounding the artifact, Jak hadn't been able to tell if they—or their spears—had been touching it when it struck.

Malek walked around the archaeologists and came to stand in front of Jak and his mother. He only flicked a glance at Jak before his gaze settled on her.

Fear for his mother coursed through Jak. And after seeing

Tonovan openly leer at the blonde girl, Jak worried about what kind of perversions this Malek might have. And if he would turn them on his mother.

Jak didn't know how attractive other men considered his mother, but about a year after his father had died, unmarried professors at the university—and some who *were* married—had started asking her for dates, so she had to be all right for her age. He hoped this freak didn't think so.

"Rise," Malek said.

And Jak found that he could. His mother pushed herself to her feet, offering a hand to Darv, who was on her other side, to help him up. The old scholar had gone pasty, and when Jak met his gaze, he read the utter fear there.

"Give me the book," Malek told Mother, not looking at anyone else.

There was no doubt about what he wanted—Father's thick journal full of notes—and Malek knew she had it. Jak was sure she did too, since she was rarely without it, but she raised her eyebrows in puzzled inquiry.

"Book? Which book? We have many." She pointed to the tents torn down by the drakur, a few books visible amid the carnage. "Are you a fan of Witiker's *Field Guide to Megalithic Artifacts of Eld*? It's a classic."

Malek's expression didn't change. Jak winced. It was the kind of flippant thing *he* would say, so he knew exactly what the probability was of it getting her in trouble. And this man—this *zidarr*—shouldn't be played around with. Surely, she had to sense all that power radiating from him.

"I have read it," Malek said. "It is not what I seek."

"You have?" Mother asked. "Is archaeology a hobby of yours?"

"Lately, Uthari has insisted it become so." His tone had turned dry, and he glanced at the now half-revealed artifact.

"Then you must have opinions on Chapter Seventeen,"

Mother said, as if she were back at the university, quizzing a student on whether he'd read the assigned material.

Jak stared at the side of her head, willing her to knock it off.

"Is that the one on the marble henge on Skyarctica that tells one of the mythological tales of how some humans came to be able to use magic?" Malek asked.

Surprise flickered in Mother's eyes. Had she thought he was *lying* about reading the book? Jak hadn't. Something about this man made Jak doubt he ever felt the need to lie.

"It is," she said. "Do you believe that version? Or the prevailing one that dragons gave some humans magical power before they left this world, thus to ensure a part of them remained?"

"The literature suggests there's not enough evidence to support either hypothesis."

"Correct, but most who study the field have opinions." Mother looked over toward the mercenaries. They'd risen from their knees and some had backed quietly into the water and were swimming toward the distant ferry. Maybe she was trying to buy time for them to escape.

So the medallion would escape with them? Jak, remembering his fear that Malek was telepathic, forced his mind away from that thought.

"Perhaps we will discuss them on the voyage back to Uthari-ka." Malek held out his hand. "Give me what's in your pocket."

He didn't modulate his voice like the general, but magic laced the words, making them impossible to disobey, and Mother's hand dipped into a pocket. Jak's fingers twitched toward his own pockets before he caught himself.

But somehow, Mother found the gumption to thwart the order, or at least interpret it creatively. She pulled three vials containing samples out of her pocket and held them out to Malek.

Instead of taking them, he pointed to the ground. "Empty *all* of your pockets."

Again, magic accompanied the words, giving them immutable power, and Mother responded. Her movements were stiff and jerky, like a clockwork soldier marching in circles, but she couldn't resist. She set more vials on the ash-dusted ground, pens, a set of fine tools for cleaning artifacts, a loupe, and canisters full of who knew what she'd collected on the journey—or just since breakfast. Even Jak, who knew her tendencies, was amazed at everything she had stashed in her pockets. She still hadn't produced the journal.

Malek's face hadn't changed much, but Jak thought he read exasperation in the man's eyes.

"Professor Freedar doesn't believe in purses," Jak said, more to distract Malek from any growing annoyance than because he expected a laugh.

"Empty your pockets too," Malek told him. "And drop the magelock."

The words were as impossible to disobey as Jak had believed, and he dropped the rifle instantly. Since he had little to hide, he didn't bother fighting the compulsion to unbutton and empty his pockets, though he hoped the men would let him take his belongings with him when they left. The idea of abandoning his fine drawing tools—the kit of pens and pencils and charcoal sticks hit the ground first, landing next to Mother's pile—filled him with anxiety. They had been a gift from his father on his thirteenth birthday.

A compass, protractor, and short ruler joined the kit, as well as the folded map of the island he'd been drawing that morning. His pile ended up almost as large as his mother's. Normally, he didn't carry *that* much around, but he'd intended to return to working on that map after running his errand with the bandanas. He was amazed he hadn't lost more of his stuff during the mad flight down the slope.

"I'm not into purses either," Jak said.

"You're a quirky family," Malek remarked.

"Yes, we are." Mother lifted her chin, as if she were proud of it.

Jak might have felt sheepish, but he was still too unnerved by these people to feel anything but uneasy. The idea of being taken prisoner and tortured for what he knew was at the top of his mind. It seemed inevitable.

Malek held out a hand, and the folded map floated up and opened, hanging in the air before him. He didn't look long—maybe he'd expected notes pertinent to the artifact rather than a student's half-finished cartography project—before folding it again. Surprisingly, he returned it to Jak before shifting his focus to Mother's pile.

Jak winced again. Father's thick leather-bound journal now lay on the top of it, the edges of the pages ragged and dirty after a lifetime of travels and having information recorded in it. More than a few pieces of paper had been folded and stuck inside, making it look even thicker.

Again, Malek floated it up into his hand. He flicked through a few pages, then closed it and put it in his jacket pocket and looked toward the artifact. With magic, the officers had dug free in minutes what had been taking the archaeology team hours.

The inky blue-black portal wasn't as uniform in hue as Jak had thought when he'd first seen a portion of it. There was an iridescent quality to it, with hints of color wavering and glinting, as if affected by the sun. But with the ash and smoke filling the sky, there was no sun.

The body of the portal also wasn't uniform. Instead of essentially being a thick ring with smooth sides, the frame was formed by four dragons, each one biting the tail of the one ahead of it so that there were no breaks. It seemed a strange message for something crafted by dragons, but he couldn't deny its elegance and beauty, and the urge to draw it filled him. Also the urge to touch it. From across the beach, he couldn't see if there were any runes or etchings on the surface, and he dearly wanted to investigate more closely.

The ground rumbled again, reminding him of their predicament. If Malek was right, they didn't have much time to get off the island.

"Shall we lower ropes with winches?" One of the younger officers pointed up at the mageship still hovering a hundred feet above the beach.

"No." Malek held out his hand toward the artifact.

The ground trembled again, and Tonovan swore and backed up, waving for his men to do the same. This time, the tremble wasn't caused by the volcano but by the portal rising out of the hard ground, quivering as lava rock sloughed away.

Jak couldn't keep from gaping as it levitated into the air, rock and ash trickling off it. How much had Mother said it weighed? Five hundred pounds? Far less than pure steel would have, but nobody should have been able to lift that with their mind.

Malek's face was tight with concentration as the portal rose higher and higher, flying straight up toward his ship. Jak glanced at the magelock he'd tossed to the ground. The officers weren't close. Maybe he could grab the weapon and shoot Malek while he was distracted. And then... and then *what*? They could never escape the other mages, and they would surely retaliate. Jak might get his mother and the whole team killed.

Malek looked over at him, not as distracted as Jak had believed.

Jak swallowed and looked away, thoughts of trying to be a hero dissipating from his mind. These people were inhuman. It would take more than a magelock to defeat them.

The artifact disappeared over the railing of the mageship. Jak hoped the crew ran up and hugged it and got zapped—unless there were normal humans up there. He wouldn't wish that on them. Only the *mages* should hug the damn thing.

With his task complete, Malek lowered his arm. "Watch your thoughts, boy," he said quietly. "There are those aboard the *Star Flyer* who would kill you for them."

Mother turned concerned eyes toward Jak. He bit his lip and shrugged helplessly. How was he supposed to control what his *mind* did?

With a flick of Malek's fingers, two of the empty disks floated over, the wafer-thin black ovals appearing far too flimsy to support someone's weight.

"Get on," he told Jak and his mother.

Apparently, the questioning that Malek had spoken of would happen later aboard their ship. Fantastic.

"Take some of the other archaeologists," Tonovan called. "To ensure *compliance*." The general smiled cruelly at Mother.

Jak didn't know whether to hope that Malek would object or not. Was it better for the rest of the team to go with the mages and get off this smoking island? Or be left here and hope the mercenaries would come back to pick them up?

Malek's gaze skimmed over the team. They all stared at the ground, their shoulders hunched, hoping not to be picked. They would all rather take their chances with the volcano.

"Professor Darv Sadlik," Malek said, though nobody had introduced him. He spread his hand toward an empty disk. "Step aboard."

Darv cringed.

"Not him," Mother blurted, raising a hand, as if she would grip Malek's arm, but she caught herself, merely holding it up in protest. "He's too old."

"There is no maximum age for riding a skyboard," Malek said, that dryness returning to his tone.

"But he—"

"Means the most to you," Malek interrupted her. "After your son."

Mother closed her eyes in defeat.

"Step aboard," Malek repeated, the magical coercion in his voice again.

Jak couldn't resist but managed to snatch up his belongings before he stepped onto a disk with his mother. She'd grabbed all of her vials and tools too, though the officers would doubtless take them from her later.

As Darv stepped onto another disk, he smiled at Mother and tried to convey that it was all right. But it wasn't.

Without any command or even a hand wave from Malek, the disks rose up. Jak gripped his mother to keep her from falling, but there was no need. The disks were as solid as ground and rose levelly, more smoothly than the steam elevators in the tall buildings of Sprungtown.

The officers shared disks, rising up with them. Jak looked for Malek, but he'd disappeared from the beach as effectively as he'd first appeared.

As they rose, Jak caught Tonovan looking down at the mercenaries swimming out of the bay and navigating the harsher waves in the strait. Many were helping those who'd been injured in his attack and were making poor progress. The ferry was heading in their direction, but what if Tonovan, whose lips were curled in that cruel sneer again, impeded their progress? Or worse.

As Jak was groping for a way to distract the jerk, the volcano finally blew. One side of its caldera crumbled inward as the other exploded outward. Huge plumes of black smoke flowed away from it, masking the entire island from view, save for brilliant orange splotches of lava already running down the rocky slopes.

"I hope the mercenaries help the rest of our team get away," Mother said quietly.

"They will," Jak said, more to comfort her than because he believed it was true. Nothing good had happened today yet.

5

THE COLD WATER DRAGGED AT TEZI TIGAN'S SODDEN CLOTHES AND armor, the short sword on her hip feeling like it weighed a hundred pounds, but she clung to the rope ladder that had been lowered from the ferry railing and helped others who were more injured than she. The swim had been horrible, waves of salty seawater smashing into her face and funneling down her throat, and she had no idea how many of their people had made it.

The memory of being in the rowboat when that huge fireball sped toward it lingered in her mind. It would be impossible to forget the white light, the raw heat, and the sheer power as it slammed into the boat, blowing it to pieces and hurling Tezi and the others overboard. Only luck had kept her from being badly hurt. Her skin was raw and pink from the close call, but others had been closer to the fireball when it struck.

With numb fingers, Tezi bent and pulled Dr. Fret closer to the ladder, making sure she gripped one of the rungs. The company couldn't afford to lose their medical expert.

A garish burn marked the side of Fret's face, part of her braid was singed off, and her uniform jacket had been torn away in the waves. The captain, lieutenant, and some of the sergeants knew basic field medicine, so hopefully, they would be able to help the doctor recover. Teeth chattering, Fret looked like she would collapse as soon as she reached the deck.

"Thanks, Rookie," Fret rasped as Tezi helped her climb past her.

"You're welcome, ma'am." Tezi was used to the title. She'd only been with the company for three months and was the youngest mercenary by several years. Maybe someday, Captain Ferroki would take on a new person, and the moniker would be transferred to her, but Tezi had a feeling she would be proving herself again and again to her colleagues for a long time. But if that was what it took, she would do it.

Pausing only to cough and spit the constant taste of ash from her mouth, Tezi helped up another mercenary and another until nobody from the company was left in the water, but back in the bay, more people were swimming this way. The archaeologists? Had the mages left them behind? She hoped so. Nobody deserved to be taken prisoner by those inhumane —no, *inhuman*—people. She had personal experience with their cruelty; that leer the general had given her hadn't been the first she'd received. People with that much power did what they wanted with no need to worry about repercussions. Usually.

"You going to turn yourself into a barnacle, Rookie?" the captain called down in her calm, even voice.

"What about them?" Tezi glanced up but pointed toward the swimmers, who were navigating out of the bay and into harsher water. "Weren't we hired to get them?"

"Yeah, we're steaming over to them now."

That was a relief. The hull vibrated with the rumble of the engines, but Tezi hadn't been able to discern the ferry's route. She was still disoriented from the swim, when the waves had kept her from seeing where she was going. It had been only by following the person in front of her that she'd reached the ferry.

"Did they all get left behind?" Tezi hadn't seen what happened after the fireball struck. All she knew was that in the time she'd been swimming, the mageship had disappeared. From out here in the strait, she didn't have a good view of the beach, but she had no trouble seeing plumes of smoke gushing from the volcano and rivers of bright orange lava flowing down its sides.

"Not all of them," the captain said grimly, looking toward the sky beyond the strait and the islands. The direction the mageship had gone? "We'll have to explain everything to the magistrate and hope we'll still get paid."

So far, Tezi had been issued her rookie salary regularly, but she always heard mutterings from the others about how few contracts were given to the all-female company, especially lately, and how low the company's coffers were. That didn't matter much to her—she'd signed on to learn how to fight and take care of herself, not to get rich—but she kept the unpopular thought to herself.

Lieutenant Sasko joined the captain at the railing and looked down. "What's our rookie doing?"

"Barnacle practice," the captain said.

"Huh."

Despite being chilled from the water, Tezi's cheeks warmed. She knew they were just teasing her—and their razzing was a lot less biting and frequent than that of the other grunts—but she wished they would see that she was being helpful. Nobody thought she belonged here, and as silly as it was, she lay awake nights, dreaming up ways she could prove herself.

The ferry closed on the swimmers, and Tezi helped them climb out of the water. She didn't see the professor they'd spoken with or the young man who might have been her son. She also didn't see the old man who'd appeared the frailest of the bunch and hoped it was because he had been captured, not because he'd drowned. Though maybe drowning would be a less painful way to go.

By the time she climbed to the deck, Tezi was exhausted and wanted to flop down, as the archaeologists and a number of the mercenaries had, but she made herself shamble over to the captain and the lieutenant to see if they needed anything from her. They were sitting on crates facing each other. It wasn't until Tezi drew close that she realized they were looking at something and that it might be a private meeting.

She faltered and stopped a few feet away, but they'd spotted her. The captain's hand closed around something.

Trying not to feel stung that they might not trust her enough to see whatever it was, Tezi straightened her back and saluted. "Rookie Tezi reporting for duty, ma'am."

She addressed the captain, but Sasko was the one to snort and say, "Don't you have a squad leader, Rookie?"

"Yes, ma'am. Sergeant Tinder." Who happened to be one of the mercenaries who razzed Tezi the most. That made Tezi disinclined to approach her unless absolutely necessary, but she made herself nod. "I'll go ask her if she needs me to do anything."

"You do that." Sasko waved her away.

"Hold on." The captain lifted a hand. "When you joined the company, didn't you say that your parents were tailors before they passed?"

"Yes, ma'am." Tezi hadn't explained much of her background, and the mercenaries hadn't asked for much. All they'd wanted to know was about her *fighting* experience, of which she'd had none, so she'd mentioned her sartorial skills in case the company might find that useful. After all, uniforms ripped and needed to be repaired, especially after being blasted by fireballs. But nobody had seemed impressed by her sewing experience, and to this day, Tezi was sure the captain had only taken her on out of pity. "Do you need something hemmed?"

She looked at everyone's torn and sodden uniforms, including the captain's and the lieutenant's.

Sasko snorted and rolled her eyes. "Everybody is going to need something hemmed after that."

"Did your family ever do hat making? Or anything with decorative ornaments?" the captain asked, ignoring Sasko.

"There was a haberdasher next door in our village, so I know a little about that business, and we'd sew shells or beads on for people if they had something special they'd found. Nobody in our community had much money for frills, but sometimes, they would find something in the woods or at the lake and think it was pretty."

"I doubt anyone found this in the woods." The captain opened her hand and revealed what she'd hidden before, handing it to Tezi.

She accepted what looked like a solid gold medallion, but it wasn't heavy enough for that. The front featured a dragon's head with star-shaped holes for eyes, while the edge was marked with unevenly spaced ridges, and the back held a pattern of raised bumps. She ran her thumb over the bumps, wondering how and why they had been embossed onto the medallion.

"Tell nobody about it," the captain warned Tezi.

"No, ma'am. I won't." She wished she had a loupe to better study it. If there was a maker's mark anywhere on it, she couldn't see it. A jeweler would have been a better person for them to consult, but Tezi doubted anyone in the company had that experience.

"But let me know if you know what it is," the captain added.

"You really think it's something?" Sasko asked. "And not some decorative trinket?"

"The kid had it in his hat *like* a decoration," the captain said, "but whatever it is, the professor didn't want the mages to get it. She took it out and handed it to me on the sly and asked me to keep it until she could come back for it."

Sasko grunted. "If the mages have a use for those archaeologists, they'll never be back. They'll get bands strapped to their heads, and they won't even remember who they are or how to scratch their own asses. You should get it appraised and sell it if it's worth anything. Is that real gold?"

She'd asked the captain, but Tezi shook her head. "It's too light. It's even lighter than if it were gold-plating over a copper or silver base metal."

"Those are the usual materials for decorative jewelry?" the captain asked.

"They're typical. They're not as expensive, obviously, and make a piece stronger and less likely to bend than pure gold." Tezi smiled, glad to have some knowledge the captain seemed to find useful.

"Does that thing bend?" the captain asked.

"Don't *bend* it if you want to sell it," Sasko said.

The captain gave her a dry look. "We're not selling it. I told the professor I owed her a favor, and keeping this for her is what she asked for."

"*Captain*. You didn't owe them anything. It's not our fault suncursed *mages* showed up."

"Mind your tone, Lieutenant," the captain said. She only broke out rank with Sasko when Sasko was getting too lippy.

Sasko sighed. "Yes, Captain."

"Malek is a zidarr," Tezi said quietly. "Not a mage. That means he's as powerful as a wizard, in addition to being a well-trained warrior." She remembered the fireball blast again and shivered. "I'm sure that general was a wizard too."

"You know about their kind?" the captain asked softly, her tone almost gentle.

Even if Tezi hadn't gone into detail, the captain must have guessed something about her past, if only because she'd admitted her parents were both dead. The gentleness—the pity—made

Tezi's emotions bubble to the surface. It hadn't been long since her world had been destroyed. It was easier to keep her feelings in check with Sasko and Sergeant Tinder, people who barked orders and didn't ask her questions about herself. Even if Tezi liked the captain more, she worried about breaking down and crying in front of her. Mercenaries didn't cry.

"Just what you learn from having a village within spitting distance of one of their sky cities," Tezi said, feigning casualness and forcing down the lump in her throat as painful memories sprang to mind. "The seekers would come by every year, looking for people to enslave and take up to their city. You can't run a good sky city without terrene human servants doing the grunt work." Tezi didn't bother to keep the bitterness out of her voice. Long before she'd lost her parents, she'd had her older brother taken by the seekers. Was he still alive up in King Darekar's city? Or a sky city from another kingdom? Tezi had no way to know. "Sometimes, they would send a zidarr along with the seekers, someone close to the king who knew his *tastes*."

The captain's and lieutenant's lips twisted. They knew what she meant. Maybe they wondered why *she* hadn't been taken during one of those visits. After losing their firstborn, her parents had gone to great lengths to hide her during the annual selection visits. And it had worked until... the day it hadn't.

"A zidarr came once when I was a girl and flicked a finger and blew up half of Main Street," Tezi said. "Killed five people, and he enjoyed it. They aren't human. None of them are. If they want this —" she held up the ornament, "—it would be best to give it to them or get rid of it before they come looking for it."

"Or *sell* it," Sasko said. "Get some money for it and make it someone else's problem."

"Gold-plated jewelry isn't worth much. If that's all it is." Not sounding like she believed that, the captain took it back and scraped at the gold plating with a thumbnail. "Besides, I agreed to keep it safe."

"That shouldn't be your job, Captain. You're a fighter, not a vault guard. Why don't you just give it to them?" Sasko tilted her head toward the exhausted archaeologists, most slumped on the deck, a couple looking back toward the blazing volcano as the ferry steamed away. "They're from the same team as that professor, right? If by some miracle she gets away, she'll go home to them, and they can give it to her."

"The mages—*wizards*—" the captain nodded toward Tezi to acknowledge the correction, "—would think to question those archaeologists if they find out the professor gave away this medallion. Maybe she didn't want her colleagues to be tortured for information." Judging by her frown as she looked at the soggy archaeologists, not a warrior among them, she didn't think they should be subjected to that.

"They'll do that anyway," Sasko muttered. "I don't know what that big metal ring was, but Malek's people crossed into another king's territory to get it, and I'm wagering they didn't have permission. That means it's valuable and they wanted it badly. And probably everything to do with it. Like *that*." Sasko pointed at the medallion. "Those archaeologists would be better off moving to a different continent, changing their names, and hoping nobody ever comes to question them."

"I don't disagree with any of that, but the professor must have given it to me because she wanted someone capable to look after it."

"She gave it to you because you were standing next to her," Sasko said.

"Capably."

"Right."

The captain drew her knife. She hadn't succeeded at scraping away any of the gold with her fingernail, but she applied her blade to one of the ridges on the edge.

Tezi shifted uneasily from foot to foot. "That could be magical, ma'am."

"Does that mean it'll zap me if I scratch it?"

"It could." Tezi didn't say more. She'd seen magic used on other people—and now had it flung at her—but she couldn't call herself an expert in that area.

"Hm." The captain put away her knife and held the edge of the medallion up for Sasko to see.

"Shit," the lieutenant said.

When the captain showed Tezi what her blade had revealed, it took her a moment to grasp the significance. She'd only seen a portion of the artifact the archaeologists had been digging up and from afar, but its blue-black sheen had been distinctive. The scratch in the gold plating showed that the base material of the medallion was the same color.

"You better get rid of that thing as soon as possible, Captain," Sasko whispered, glancing toward the sky, as if the crew of the long-gone mageship—as if *Malek*—might somehow hear her. "And hope they never find out it's missing."

"What do you think it is?" the captain mused.

"A key?" Tezi guessed, thinking of the oddly placed bumps and ridges. "To that... whatever they were digging up?"

"Maybe so." The captain also glanced toward the sky. "I made it to the ferry in time to see them lifting it up to their mageship. It was a giant ring."

"With a keyhole?" Tezi asked.

"My vision isn't that good," the captain said.

"If it *is* a key, and that thing has a keyhole, they're going to figure out real quick that this is missing." Sasko pointed at the medallion. "Captain, I know you're in charge, and what you say goes, but please promise me you'll get rid of it. There's no need to keep your promise to a dead woman, and that's what she'll be if she isn't already. You've got to think of the company. The sixty of us don't want to die because some cranky wizard comes looking for that while hurling about gouts of fire." Sasko grimaced and rubbed her arm.

Tezi touched a gash at her own temple, the memory of the fireball returning. In that instant, she'd believed she would die. Now, she found herself nodding in agreement with the lieutenant. The captain barely knew that professor. A favor for a stranger wasn't worth dying for.

The captain sighed. "You're not wrong. I know that. But I feel compelled to do right by that professor, since we were supposed to retrieve her, and we couldn't." She gazed toward Perchver, the big trade city sprawling along the shoreline on the opposite side of the strait from the volcano. "I know someone in town who has... retired from the mercenary business and now hunts down relics for those who can pay. After we see the magistrate, I want to visit him."

"And after you have a nice chat with him, you'll chuck that thing into the sea?" Sasko asked hopefully.

"We'll see." The captain carefully buttoned the medallion into her pocket and headed belowdecks.

"I have a bad feeling about this," Sasko muttered.

6

THOUGH THE HULL AND THE ENTIRE EXTERIOR OF THE MAGESHIP were black, there was red trim on the deck and even more color when their captors forced Jadora, Jak, and Darv down steps and into the surprisingly open and bright interior. Rather than narrow corridors crammed with cabins and machine rooms, spacious holds flowed from one into another with few walls or floors. Railing-free staircases linked platforms that floated in the air, allowing access to the magical infrastructure that replaced what would have been engines, pipes, and a boiler on a mundane steamship. Uniformed men and women stood on some of the platforms, accessing interfaces full of glowing domes, spheres, and panels, everything curved rather than angular.

Everything was so alien that Jadora would have believed they'd been transported to another world. The only normal things she spotted were wooden crates filled with food and supplies. They sat on the bottom of the hold, no straps visible that would have kept them from shifting around. Maybe that wasn't necessary. Jadora had yet to notice the movement of the ship, though she knew they'd flown away from the volcano.

A warm yellow light provided illumination to every corner of the holds, though there was no obvious source. As far as she could tell, it emanated from the walls. She had the urge to scratch one with a fingernail to see if some interesting biological or chemical substance had been applied. The thought of bioluminescent paint made from a natural source teased her imagination as she envisioned dozens of applications, but she highly doubted there was anything natural about this ship. Magic didn't interest her nearly as much as biology and chemistry.

Jak gaped around as they descended stairs and walked across platforms. He bumped into Jadora more than once as he took everything in, almost tipping off the side when he paused to peer down at a huge yellow orb in a strange nest on the floor. It made her think of an octopus with thick glowing tendrils stretching from it like tentacles and snaking along and disappearing into the walls. Maybe the octopus body was the mage equivalent of an engine.

"I wish I could *draw* this place," Jak breathed.

For him, that meant making a map.

Malek, who was leading their trio, with two uniformed mages walking behind them, glanced back, but he said nothing. He seemed to notice *everything*, and Jadora worried he was reading Jak's thoughts—and that those thoughts weren't properly reverent. She couldn't blame him for that, but they had to be careful. With the mages so close, she wasn't permitting herself to think about anything related to the artifact—and certainly nothing irreverent.

Jadora also tried not to mull over plans for escaping, if doing so was even possible. The mageship was flying hundreds if not thousands of feet above the ocean. Even if they could slip away from their guards, a jump from such height, even into water, would be certain death.

If they somehow *did* get the opportunity to escape, how could they leave without the artifact? Her goal—her late husband's goal

—had always been to recover it for their people, so they could use the portal to find allies who could help mundane humans free themselves from the shackles placed on them by their mage and wizard rulers. Maybe they could even find the powerful dragons who'd made the portal all those millennia ago.

Malek stopped in a wide green-walled corridor they'd entered and looked back at Jadora. She shoved her thoughts out of her mind and chastised herself for having them when he was so close.

"You'd be wise to forget those notions," Malek said softly, meeting her eyes, his face unreadable.

Jadora's heart hammered so hard she heard it in her ears.

Jak came up to her shoulder, as if he would step in front of her and protect her if Malek lashed out. She held out her arm to keep him from trying. The last thing she wanted was for a mage's annoyance with her to shift toward her son. It would be best if these people forgot about him or dismissed him as nobody to worry about. Just as she hoped they would dismiss Darv and let him go. That they'd brought him along to force her into good behavior hadn't escaped her, and she struggled not to think resentful thoughts—resentful thoughts that Malek would sense.

This close, with Malek less than two feet away from her in the corridor, she could feel his power, feel that he was not fully human, not like her.

Were the stories true? That wizards, through some occult ritual with the slavemasters in Hell, funneled magic into the children they turned into zidarr? Warping them and stealing their humanity even as they bound them to be loyal servants? Or were they simply boys with potential trained and indoctrinated from youth? Either way, the zidarr were remorseless killers, so she had to be careful.

But he wasn't only that, she reminded herself. She dared not think of Malek as only a weapon. He'd read Witiker and who knew what other authors of academic texts. He wasn't dumb. He was far more calculating and dangerous than the general who'd shown off his power.

If Malek was reading these thoughts, he didn't comment on them. He stepped back and used his power to flick a lever on the wall.

A clank came from the floor, startling Jadora. A grate she'd barely noticed before slid aside. It was one of several in this corridor, a spot tucked away in the back of the ship and not lit as brightly as the holds they'd passed through. The cell below the open grate was even darker with shadows hiding its depth.

Power wrapped around Jadora, making her gasp. The memory of the general forcing her to her knees was fresh in her mind. The power lifted her off the deck and pushed her over the open grate. What if the bottom was thirty feet down and she broke her legs falling?

"Mother," Jak blurted, grabbing her.

But the power lifted him as well, pushing him over the opening right behind her.

Fear rushed through Jadora's limbs, though she struggled to keep it off her face, not wanting to give Malek the satisfaction of seeing it. Why she bothered, she didn't know. If he could read her mind, he *knew* she was scared.

He didn't smirk or sneer the way Tonovan had at seeing pain, but that didn't mean he didn't thrive on the emotions of his enemies. Especially after reading her thoughts and knowing what she wanted.

Without so much as a twitch of his fingers, he lowered Jadora and Jak into the cell. He didn't drop them, as she'd imagined, merely using his power to levitate them to the bottom. A bottom that was twenty feet down with vertical walls creating a tall box. A box that nobody could climb out from.

As their feet thumped down, the grate slid back into place, a lock *thunking.* Darv leaned over, peering down at them, his worried and haggard face still in the light.

"What about Darv?" Jadora called up, not wanting to be separated.

"He will have his own cell, so you cannot conspire," Malek stated, his voice muted by the distance and narrowness of the cell. "And so his fate is not a certainty to you."

Darv gasped as he was hefted into the air. He floated past their grate and who knew where after that. To a cell at the end of the corridor? Or in another part of the ship?

"What does that mean?" she muttered, though a dozen guesses came to mind.

"That they can kill him tonight and we won't know it," Jak said. "But that we'll still jump to obey them, because we believe we can gain his freedom."

"You've grown cynical, my son." Jadora sighed and leaned her shoulder against the smooth featureless wall.

"This day has made me cynical."

No, five years earlier, his father's death had done that. It had taken a couple of years for him to regain his curiosity and interest in the world, to find joy in his studies and hobbies again. But he'd never lost that edge, his tendency toward sarcasm that hadn't been there before.

She couldn't blame him for that. Loran's death had made her cynical too.

"I think it's night now," was all she said, aware that the mages were still up there.

"And they didn't drop down pillows? Inconsiderate."

"I will summon you if I have questions about the journal, Professor," Malek called, his voice distant.

That probably meant he'd put Darv in a cell at the end of the same corridor, but he was far enough away that they couldn't communicate without shouting to each other. Even that might not work.

"Won't that be a fun chat?" Jak muttered.

Red-uniformed legs and polished boots came into view, standing on their grate. One of the soldiers—one who'd used magic to help unearth the portal and was a mage in his own right —peered down at them, annoyance on his face. Either for Jak's comment or because he was stuck on a pedestrian duty.

Jadora sank down with her back to the wall, some of her vials poking her through her clothes. She was surprised Malek hadn't taken them, but she didn't have anything that would assist them in escaping. Maybe he knew that. All he'd cared about was Loran's journal. Now that he had it, he could take it off to whatever lair he had on this ship and peruse it at his leisure. He would read all the notes Loran had made and know all about him through his work, and he would read the notes she'd later made in the margins and on blank pages she'd stuck in, and learn all about her as well.

If he cared. Likely not. What he wanted, she had no doubt, was to learn how to operate the portal for his master.

Jak sat beside her, his rangy form barely visible in the shadows. He pulled his knees to his chest and wrapped his arms around them, as he might have as a boy, and let his forehead thud down.

Jadora draped her arm around his shoulders, glad he didn't pull away—it had been several years since he'd allowed *comforting* from his mother, but these were extenuating circumstances. At least Malek hadn't separated them. Why hadn't he? Because he didn't think Jak was someone she might *conspire* with? That wasn't true, but it was just as well if he believed that.

"Is it safe to think now?" Jak whispered. "To speak?"

"I don't know." Jadora looked up at the boots. The soldier didn't react. "We probably won't be safe for as long as we're on this ship." Or ever again, she thought but did not want to say. Such words weren't comforting.

"They'll keep us alive, right? Because we know about the portal and they may need our knowledge?"

"Probably until they figure out how to work it, yes."

"And then?"

She squeezed his shoulders. "I don't know, but that should take some time." Time in which they could figure out a way to escape, she hoped. "Like you, I've memorized Loran's notes, but he never got a chance to study the actual artifact. And we haven't either, so it's all hypotheses at this point. I wish I'd gotten a chance to see if there were any symbols—and hints of a language—on the surface. Translating them would be a chore, and maybe not possible at all, but it would be amazing simply to find out that dragons had the equivalent of a written language. Everything we know about them comes from the fossil records and oral stories passed down over tens of thousands of years."

"I know." Jak lifted his gaze toward the grate and lowered his voice so that she could barely hear it. "Do you think he's the one who killed Father?"

Jadora glanced at their guard, then realized he meant Malek. "There were... speculations about that, among the professors and staff, since it happened on campus at his office, but nobody saw any strangers go in or out. We only know the mages were responsible because they came to our house."

"And ransacked and searched everything. I remember. But people said it was probably a zidarr because of exactly what you said, that whoever did it got in and out without being seen."

Yes, she'd heard those suggestions, and she didn't reject that it was possible, but she didn't want to fuel any notions Jak might be brewing about attacking Malek. He was hot-headed enough and of the right age to do something foolish and impulsive like giving his own life to try to avenge his father's death. The thought of losing him too made her throat tighten so much that she couldn't speak for a moment. The worst part was that she knew it would be in vain. A human boy with a pocket full of pencils wasn't going to take down a zidarr.

"It was nighttime, and few people were on campus working," Jadora said when she recovered her voice. "I don't deny that it *could* have been a zidarr, and obviously our city is in Uthari's kingdom, so it could have been Malek, but it also could have been any mage with a sword or any cutthroat hired off the streets."

"It was someone with a sword. You told me they decapitated him. That they delivered his... severed head to you in a bag." Jak swallowed and looked at her, though the shadows hid the haunted expression that had to be on his face.

And hers as well. As if it had happened yesterday, she remembered the freshly decapitated head of her beloved husband thudding to the floor like wet meat, leaving blood everywhere. It took her a moment before she could reply.

"I did." She'd been frantic to clean up the mess before Jak came out of his room, before he could see it. Strangely, in those first moments, she'd been more panicked about that than about the fact that her husband was dead. The reality of that had settled in that night—and forever after.

"It was one of Uthari's soldiers who brought you his head, right?" Jak sounded like he was trying to remember exactly what had happened that night. Since he hadn't witnessed it all—thank the dragon god Shylezar—it was more of a blur for him.

"Yes. They had swords. It could have been one of them."

"But it *could* have been Malek," he said with mulish determination.

"Yes, but please, Jak. Let's just figure out how to stay alive and get out of this situation. No suicidal heroics, all right?" She squeezed his shoulders again, though she wanted to shake him until he agreed wholeheartedly.

"You recognized that officer," he said, as if he'd just remembered. "The general. I thought *he* was Malek at first, but I saw your face. You'd seen him before."

Jadora leaned her head back against the wall. What boy—or man—paid so much attention to people to notice such details? The gods had gifted and cursed her with an artist with a keen and observant eye.

"Yes," she admitted reluctantly, not wanting Jak to have revenge fantasies about General Tonovan any more than about Malek. She sensed that Malek was the more dangerous of the two, but either of them could obliterate Jak with a thought.

"Where?"

She hesitated. She didn't make a habit of lying to Jak and didn't want to start, but maybe she could refuse to answer...

"Mages don't come to the university campus often," Jak said slowly, the gears rotating in his mind. "Was it the night of Father's death?" He stiffened. "Was he one of the ones who came to the house?"

"He was." The words trickled out of her with defeat. "Since Uthari first learned about the portal, it must have become a priority for him, so he put his top men on it." She realized that was another reason to believe Malek might have been the one to kill Loran and search his office while the other soldiers were sent to search the house. "I don't know how many of those wizard kings know about the artifact—maybe we're lucky and it's just him—but they'll all want it when they find out. Even if they don't care about getting it operational, it would be a trophy, bragging rights."

If only that was all they wanted it for. Jadora worried she'd just put a powerful weapon—or the means to *get* powerful weapons—into the hands of the enemies of humanity.

"Maybe they'll fight over it."

"Some believe," Jadora said, glad to divert his attention in another direction, not wanting him to figure out that Tonovan had been the man to open the bag and dump Loran's head on the floor, "that having the wizard kings at war would be good for the rest of us, since it could distract them for years, if not decades and generations, but they would use us as pawns, just as they do now. Throw us away as cannon fodder. A wizard war would ravage the world and make it an even harder place for us to survive."

"Then what do we do?" Jak asked in a small voice.

Find a way to dump that portal in the ocean, she thought but didn't say. Even that wouldn't be enough. After witnessing Malek wave his hand and lift the big artifact hundreds of feet in the air, she had no doubt he had the power to retrieve it from even the deepest chasm on the bottom of the sea.

"I don't know yet," she said, "but I'll let you know when I have a plan."

He snorted. "Hiding behind a boulder and ordering all of the mages to jump into the ocean probably won't work."

"You don't think so?"

After a pause, he spoke again, his voice even quieter. "Mother?"

"Yes?"

"I'm sorry I got you into this."

"You didn't lead a mageship to our dig site." If anything, she was the one who'd made a mistake. Somewhere along the line, she'd left a trail that Uthari's people could follow. She'd been careful in arranging her expedition, never talking to anyone who might be on the payroll of the king's intelligence people, but it hadn't been good enough.

"I'm the reason for all this though. If I hadn't... It's my fault. You never would have left your career if I hadn't threatened to quit school and take up Father's quest myself."

She blew out a long, slow breath, remembering that day at Loran's funeral. And remembering Jak's rage and frustration and ultimatum. She hadn't blamed him, neither then nor now. He'd been so close to Loran, always dreaming of one day accompanying him around the world, making maps that would help them bring ancient relics back to the university for study. His determination to carry on Loran's work had been understandable. But he was right that, as much as she'd loved her husband, she wouldn't have given up her career to obsessively try to complete his quest. She'd been doing important work, studying herbs and creating compounds that could cure illnesses and help people with all manner of ailments, and she'd loved it. She'd been respected, her papers praised by her peers, and now... Now she was a pariah at her own university. Her colleagues shook their heads when they saw her in the halls, wondering why she'd given up everything for this frivolous quest.

Because if she hadn't, thirteen-year-old Jak would have run away from home to take it up himself.

"It's not your fault," she said, wanting to comfort and protect him, even if there was some truth to his words. "I did it because I wanted to do it." So much for not lying.

Jak fell silent, and she had a feeling he didn't believe her. She didn't know what else she could say that wouldn't be a lie. Now more than ever, she missed her old life and questioned whether she'd made the right decision. If all they'd done was find and unearth the portal to hand it over to the wizards...

Glum, Jadora tried to shift her mind to more useful thoughts. Like planning an escape.

She ran her fingers over the floor and wall, wondering what they were made from. The surfaces had a satiny smoothness that made her positive magic had been involved in the creation. Would that make them impervious to acid? Mundane explosives? Anything she could concoct if she could somehow finagle access to chemicals and a lab? Hoping to find either on a mageship was probably pointless, but if she got a chance to search those supply crates, she would.

"How are you doing, Darv?" she called in ancient Zeruvian, Jak's silence making her uncomfortable.

Her mastery of the language wasn't much better than her mastery of the drakur tongue, but Darv taught it in his first-year linguistics and philology course, so she trusted he could work out her execrable pronunciation. If he heard her. Was he too far away? The deep cells muffled sound.

"My oubliette is without a latrine," came Darv's distant response in the same language.

She smiled, more because he'd been able to reply than because of the subject matter. "Does that mean you're doing poorly?"

"You know I have a sensitive system."

She doubted he was airsick—the flight was so smooth they might have been resting on solid ground—but there were numerous reasons to feel queasy today. "That's unfortunate. Are you otherwise uninjured?"

"I'm as hale now as I was this morning."

"That's discouraging."

"Thus I tell myself every day."

Their mage guard stomped his boot. "No conspiring in foreign tongues," he growled down.

"Can we conspire in Dhoran? Or Wizards' Common?" Jak, who probably hadn't taken Darv's first-year class, asked.

"*No.*"

"We were just discussing the lack of toilets," Jadora said, switching back to Dhoran. "Have mages evolved to such an extent that they no longer have biological needs?"

"It folds out of the wall across from you, woman."

"Delightful to know. Thank you."

A distant clank came from the corridor, or perhaps Darv's cell. "My day has improved at least three percent with this knowledge," he called in Dhoran.

The soldier issued a long-suffering sigh. Guarding terrene humans had to be tedious.

Jak dropped his forehead against his knees again, and his shoulders shook.

"Are you crying or laughing?" Jadora whispered.

"It's a laugh, sort of. I was imagining you discussing toilets with Malek or that horrible general."

"Presumably they have biological needs too."

He shook his head. Jadora patted his shoulder and went back to contemplating the composition of the walls—and that grate up there, should they come up with a way to reach it—and chemicals that one might find and put to use on a mageship.

7

"Six... seven... eight... Rookie, you're not *tired* already, *are you*?"

Tezi, arms quivering, face flushing redder by the second, made herself bark out, "No, Sergeant!" with as much energy as she could muster.

"Haven't you worked those scrawny sticks for arms up to being able to do ten push-ups *yet*?"

"Yes, Sergeant!"

After more than an hour of training on the deck of the ferry now anchored in Perchver Harbor, Tezi *was* tired, her rubbery muscles unwilling to push up her body weight over and over, but she couldn't admit it. Sergeant Tinder, crouching low to the deck, her lips close enough to funnel accusations in Tezi's ears, would only embarrass her in front of the rest of the unit if she said anything. When she'd joined the company, she'd barely been able to do one push-up, so she'd made a lot of progress, but the others were still much stronger—and they never let her forget it.

"The wind could carry that volcano stink back in this direction any minute," Tinder said, prowling among the sixty other women

—sixty other mercenaries in the company—balanced on their hands and toes, holding stiff plank positions. A stocky woman with arms larger than Tezi's thighs, Tinder probably never got tired. "We have to train while we can. Assuming you dung-sucking bags of fluff don't collapse on me. Let's go, ten more. You let your boobs hit the ground, and I'll lop 'em off."

Tinder was in rare form this morning, probably because the captain and lieutenant were out on deck, jogging the perimeter as they discussed whatever officers discussed. The mostly male crew of the government-owned ferry watched in amusement as the women trained. At least they weren't making lewd comments anymore. On the trip to the island, one crewman had joked about how women should rub *their* swords instead of pretending they knew what to do with metal ones. Lieutenant Sasko, with a temper more explosive than black powder, had flattened him and put her boot on his throat. Since then, further speculation, at least within her earshot, had been scarce.

On push-up number fourteen, Tezi's arms refused to lower her body again. She locked her elbows, hoping she could keep herself from collapsing. Sweat dribbled off her chin and splatted on the gritty metal deck. To either side, the other women kept going, arms pumping like pistons.

One day, she would be able to—

Her arms gave out, and she flopped down. Damn it.

"The rookie thinks we should take a break," Sergeant Tinder said. "The sun is barely up, but she already wants nap time. Do any of you other maggots want naps?"

"No, Sergeant," came the chorus of replies.

Tezi tried to get back into a push-up position, but her arms wouldn't take it. She knelt back and shook out her muscles, willing them to grow stronger, refusing to believe that she couldn't handle this life.

The captain glanced in her direction, and Tezi's cheeks flushed hotter. Since the captain had taken a chance on her, when Lieutenant Sasko had argued vociferously that they weren't a recruit training center, Tezi wanted to show her that she hadn't made a mistake.

If there was condemnation in the captain's gaze, Tezi couldn't tell. She only looked over for a moment before turning her eyes back toward the volcano and up toward the sky. Fortunately, there weren't any mageships in sight.

"Corporal Stacks, *you're* not getting tired, are you?" Tinder had found someone else to harass. Good.

"It's hard work actually *doing* the exercises, Sergeant," came the gruff reply.

"You think I don't train? You think I wasn't out here before dawn with the LT while you cockroaches were snoring in your racks?" Tinder dropped and knocked out twenty push-ups in about ten seconds, then hopped to her feet again. "Rest if you have to. Once we're done with our warm-up, we'll start sparring."

A few sighs and groans came from the others, but Tezi was glad. The sword-fighting and especially the unarmed combat were what she wanted to master. Then nobody would be able to take advantage of her again—or anyone she cared about.

"Why do you bother, Rookie?" Corporal Jinx, the mercenary at her side, asked.

She was the only other fair-skinned blonde woman in the unit, but their similarities ended at skin and hair color. Jinx had the build of an ox, a scar across her chin from a sword fight, and her hair was cut aggressively short and stuck out in all directions. Everything about her was aggressive.

"Being a soldier isn't for someone who can't pull her own weight," Jinx added. "Why would you even want to do this? You're *pretty*. You could work in a brothel or bar, make money a lot easier on your back."

"Such an appealing option," Tezi muttered.

"Or go flirt with some useless rich mage, and be his mistress. Get paid to walk around on his arm and thrust your boobs out."

"I want to be a soldier." At least for now. Once she learned how to take care of herself, maybe she would try something else—something less dangerous—but she didn't know what. The idea of going back to the family business when her family was *gone*... It made her throat tighten with emotions. She blinked and looked at the sky, refusing to let tears form when others were around.

"You're not cut out for it. Nobody could depend on you to have her back."

A few other women were listening while pretending not to be listening, and they nodded to themselves. The lack of faith stung Tezi, even though they'd been hazing her since the beginning, and she expected it.

"I'm getting better," she said. "Just give me time."

"Time will get you in trouble. You're going to be a target any time we're out in the field against enemies that like to take advantage of the weakest link. They'll pick out your scrawny stick body from miles away. And if you get that face all cut up, you won't have the option to do anything else." Jinx shook her head. "You don't belong here."

Tinder ordered everyone to grab their sparring gear, and Jinx pushed herself to her feet.

"I will," Tezi muttered, standing up.

"Over here, Rookie," Lieutenant Sasko called.

She and the captain had ended their jog and gathered up the archaeologists. Tezi's legs weren't as rubbery as her arms, so she managed to run over and salute.

"Grab your gear," the captain said. "We're going into town, and I want your expertise."

"Yes, ma'am." Normally, Tezi wouldn't want to miss weapons practice, but if she could prove useful, she wanted the chance to do so.

"Expertise?" One of the archaeologists raised her eyebrows and looked at Tezi, as if it might turn out that she was an academic with numerous degrees.

"On sewing," Sasko said dryly.

"Oh." The archaeologist's interest faded, and she looked to her comrades. Dr. Fret was walking among them, checking wounds that she had treated the day before. Her *own* wounds had been patched up, a bandage on her cheek smeared with a pungent burn cream. Half of the company smelled of the stuff this morning.

"Actually on gold plating," the captain said. "Go, Rookie. You've got three minutes."

Tezi ran belowdecks to change into her uniform and shove all of her belongings into her pack in case the unit left the ferry while they were out. It was a temporary spot for the largely nomadic Thorn Company, and now that they'd completed their task, they would be back on the road soon. From what Tezi had heard, the company leased a small stronghold north of Amuri, but they hadn't been there in the months she'd belonged to the unit.

As she jogged back up the steps and through the hatchway, someone stepped into her path. Corporal Jinx.

Tezi couldn't dart aside in time and collided with her shoulder. It was like bumping into a brick wall.

"Sorry, Corporal," she blurted and tried to go around.

But Jinx gripped her arm, halting her. "Sucking up to the captain won't get you anywhere, Rookie."

"I'm not sucking up."

"You're not going to get any favoritism from her. She sees right through suck-ups."

Worried the captain would leave without her, Tezi tried to jerk her arm free.

But Jinx was as strong as a bear and only tightened her grip. "Go find some other work in town. We need people we can count on here."

"Is there going to be a fight?" a soot-faced crewman carrying a shovel asked. "Because I'd pay to see that. *Girl* fight. Will you take your clothes off for it?"

"Go sit on that shovel, you perv," Jinx growled at him, letting Tezi go.

Tezi wanted to scurry off—the captain and lieutenant were at the gangplank, frowning back at her as the archaeologists walked off ahead of them—but she made herself stay and see if Jinx would need help with the man. She *was* dependable and people *could* count on her.

But the crewman focused on Tezi, not Jinx, giving her a speculative once over. "You want to help me, girl? I'll let you hold my... shovel."

"Wouldn't that be an honor for her?" Jinx asked. "Go back to the boiler room, scum."

"Nobody's talking to you, you ugly cow." He sneered at her. "Go back to pretending to be a soldier. Me and the cute one are going belowdecks."

Jinx's eyes blazed as she curled her fingers into a fist.

The crewman's eyes narrowed, and his grip tightened on his shovel. "Just try something," he whispered harshly to her. "The captain said to leave paying customers alone, but if you attack me..."

"We're not looking to fight the people giving us a ride." Tezi smiled at the man, though she was tempted to let Jinx have at him. "We have places to go, battles to fight. The captain is waiting for us." Tezi pulled Jinx away, half-surprised when Jinx allowed it and walked with her. She kept glaring over her shoulder at the man, who was eyeing them—no, eyeing Tezi—with speculation as they left. "I'm glad we're leaving soon," she muttered.

Jinx grunted. "It doesn't matter. They're always like that, the world over. They think every woman who's not some man's wife is a whore. You might as well get paid for it."

Jinx veered off as they reached the gangplank. Tezi shook her head, wondering why she couldn't get it into the other woman's mind that she didn't want to spend her life as a bed slave to strangers.

"Problem?" the captain asked when Tezi joined her.

The lieutenant had already walked down the gangplank with the archaeologists.

Tezi shook her head. "Just trying to keep the peace. I suppose that's a weird job for a mercenary, but..."

"The Parable of the Fleet-footed Rabbit reminds us that it's only worth venturing into the thicket of foxes when juicy berries await."

"So, only fight when we're getting paid?"

"Correct. Anything else is a chance to get hurt for no gain."

"Does Jinx know that?"

"She knows. Sometimes, it's hard to get the body to do what the mind knows it should."

"Like push-ups?"

The captain snorted. "Like push-ups. Come. We're going to drop off our charges at the local university, then see the magistrate about getting paid."

"Will the volcano erupting affect things?" Even though the city was across the water and miles away, Tezi couldn't imagine anyone sitting in an office today, calmly holding audiences and doling out funds, not with those ominous black plumes filling the horizon.

"Not the volcano, but the mageship showing up and taking some of the archaeologists we were sent to collect may be problematic." Jaw set and face grim, the captain strode off the ship.

As Tezi followed, she wondered what would happen if the magistrate didn't pay.

8

JAK SLEPT FITFULLY, CURLED ON HIS SIDE ON THE HARD FLOOR NEXT to his mother. He didn't think she'd slept at all. The ship was eerily quiet, no hum of an engine suggesting forward momentum, no whistle of the wind penetrating the hull. The strange metal the *Star Flyer* was made from was like nothing he'd encountered before.

It vibrated with magical energy that pulsed through his body, and an alien feeling came over him when he rested his bare skin against it. The odd mixture of longing and contentment bewildered him. Contentment was the last thing he should feel right now.

"What do you think the ship is made from?" he asked quietly when he was certain his mother was awake.

"I was wondering that earlier," she said, "and if it's susceptible to acids."

"You think there's a laboratory here they'll let you use to make something to break us out of our cell?"

She snorted softly. "No."

"Or—" he lowered his voice to a whisper, "—do you have something in one of those canisters that could corrode metal?"

Jak hadn't been shocked that Malek hadn't bothered to take his drawing materials, but he was surprised nobody had confiscated Mother's mysterious powders and herbs, or at least asked what they were. When it came to plants, she had an encyclopedic memory and knew hundreds of substances capable of poisoning or killing—not that she would ever use her knowledge that way. Her proclivities ran toward stink bombs, something that had amused him vastly as a boy, especially when she'd taught him to make something he'd ended up using on a neighbor kid who'd been picking on him.

"I'm afraid not," she whispered back. "We may be stuck waiting until we get to their sky castle to try to escape."

"I've heard that's not easy to do."

"Not if they band you, no, but they should have numerous mageships in their harbor. They transport up all manner of food and goods for their citizens—and what comes up must go back down."

"Do you know how long it will take us to get there?" It had taken more than a week's travel on the steamship that had carried them from his hometown of Sprungtown on the continent of Agorval to the Dragon Perch Islands, but he'd heard mageships could travel four or five times faster than sailing vessels.

"I'm sure we'll arrive by tomorrow. King Uthari's sky city isn't much farther than Sprungtown."

Jak's mind boggled at traveling from continent to continent so quickly. He didn't know whether to be glad they would arrive soon or not. This cell wasn't appealing, but they hadn't been tortured for what they knew yet. That fate might be waiting for them in the sky city.

Sighing, he slid his hand over the floor. A warm tingle flowed up his arm.

"It can't be metal," he said, going back to their earlier conversation. "I can feel... I guess I feel magic in it. Like that sensation you get when you hold a magelock or some other tool made by mages, but this is much stronger."

"You feel magic?" Mother asked neutrally.

"Yeah. Magical things." The question puzzled him. "Don't you?"

"Not generally. I can recognize them since they're usually familiar and distinctive, but a magelock doesn't feel different from a black-powder rifle to me. In the dark, I wouldn't be able to tell them apart."

"Really? It's always been like that for you?" Jak wondered if his mother lacked some sixth sense that most people had. He knew she didn't have his knack for navigation and finding his way back to camp after exploring in the woods.

"Yes." Her voice had that careful neutral note again. "I did feel something when I touched the artifact."

"Oh, no kidding. I could feel it buzzing with power before we even started excavating it."

"Did you? I'd wondered when you stopped right on what became our dig site."

Jak bit his lip and sat up. "Are you saying you didn't feel it until you touched it?"

"Yes."

"But the others felt it, right? The rest of the team?"

"I doubt it, Jak."

"Does that... mean something?" He tried to remember if he'd ever had a conversation like this with his mother before. It hadn't always been like this for him. When he'd been a boy, his father had given him a magical marching-soldier toy that never needed to be wound up, and Jak hadn't sensed anything special about it. Now that he thought about it, it hadn't been until these last few years—specifically, after his father's death—that he'd started being able to feel the magic in things. Strange.

"Maybe, but let's not worry about it right now. We need to—"

A clang came from above, followed by a faint rattle as the grate slid aside. Two red-uniformed soldiers came into view, their faces indifferent as they gazed down. Neither was the guard who'd been there earlier telling them about the toilet.

"The woman is to be questioned," one said, lifting a hand, fingers spread.

Mother gasped in surprise as power wrapped around her and lifted her from the ground. Jak jumped to his feet, afraid that Malek or one of the others would hurt her—*torture* her.

"Take me too," he blurted.

"The boy is not needed."

"I know lots of things, things my mother doesn't know." Never mind that they were things about drawing, cartography, and *Roktar the Roamer* novels. "They'll want to question me."

"Ssh, Jak." Mother made a cutting motion as she rose. "It'll be fine. Don't draw attention."

"Better me than you. You're a *woman*." He shoved a hand through his hair, knocking his hat to the floor.

"The general likes boys too," one of the soldiers said wryly.

The other one snorted. "Maybe we *should* take him."

"He's too old and not that pretty. You know the general's tastes."

Jak curled a lip. "What kind of *questioning* is this?"

As his mother was lifted into the light, he glimpsed fear on her usually stoic face before she disappeared from view and the grate closed again. Damn it, why hadn't he grabbed her? He should have kept them from taking her. Or at least forced them to take him with her.

With rage roaring in his ears, he pounded his fists against the wall. The metal offered no warm tingle or comfort this time.

Above, the mage guard returned to his place, indifferent to Jak's outburst.

Tezi leaned her shoulder against the whitewashed stone wall in the hallway outside of the magistrate's meeting chamber and attempted to look like a fierce, fit, and competent mercenary instead of like a little girl who was out of place in a military uniform adorned with weapons. At least she'd had the know-how to make adjustments to the hand-me-down tunic and trousers one of the women had given her, so her cuffs no longer caught under her boots.

"When we get the money, I want to stop at the blacksmith's place before the medical-supply shop," Sergeant Tinder told Dr. Fret. The three of them were waiting for the captain and lieutenant to finish their meeting with the magistrate. "You always spend everything on fancy potions and medical kits when all we need are bandages and sutures and painkillers."

"I didn't hear you complaining last night when I slathered your burns in magical healing ointment." Fret was about half Tinder's size with an impish face and perennially worried eyes. The only weapon she carried was a slender dagger, and she used it more often for cutting bandages than staving off enemies, though rumor had it she wasn't afraid to bite people who tried to drag her away from the company. "I bet they don't even hurt today."

"They don't, but I'd rather have bombs than magical healing."

"You'd rather have bombs than anything. Your nickname should have been Sergeant Boom."

"I agree. Is it too late to change it?" Tinder smirked. "Would you call me Boom in the bedroom?"

"No, I'd call you Little Minx, the same as I do now."

Tezi grimaced and wondered if anyone would notice if she

slipped through the open doors into the meeting chamber. She'd been honored to be asked along, even if it was only because the captain thought she had a smidgen of knowledge about jewelry, but she'd envisioned going with her and the lieutenant, not waiting in the hall with the company's least discreet lovers. The temptation to go out and stand in the courtyard came over her, but the wind had shifted since their morning exercise session, and the air outside stank of the volcano. Ash fell on the coastal city like snow back home. Inches of it coated the sandstone streets, the fine gray powder swirling around people's feet as they walked.

"They've been in there a long time." Fret peered through the open doors. "Do you think it's going all right? Do you think we'll get paid? Funds have been so tight. I only have a few shreds of bandages left after yesterday. We're lucky we didn't lose anyone. Mages are awful."

"Relax." Tinder thumped her on the shoulder, almost tipping her over. Little Minx indeed. "We'll get paid."

"You will *not* be paid," a man's raised voice echoed out into the hallway. "You let one of Uthari's mageships swoop down to our island and steal what I've been told is a priceless artifact from our territory."

"You didn't hire us to fight *mages*," Lieutenant Sasko's voice rang out. "You hired us to pick up the archaeology team, and we did that and dropped them off at the local university here. Go see them if you don't believe me. And then come back and pay us if it's not too terribly inconvenient for you."

The captain said something quietly, probably a warning for Sasko to be more diplomatic.

Before, Tezi hadn't been able to make out any of the muted words from the conversation inside, but now, half of the participants were yelling.

"Do not speak with such insolence to a government official appointed by King Zaruk himself, woman. And what's *inconvenient* to me is the fact that one of Zaruk's zidarr is on his way here now to discuss *my* failing." A hint of panic edged the magistrate's angry voice. "As if I knew about the artifact or that Uthari was sending people for it."

"Didn't you know a team of archaeologists was going out to hunt under the volcano?" the captain asked.

"They didn't say they were hunting for a *special* artifact. And they paid all the necessary permits and fees for foreigners to study our lands."

"You were paid?" Lieutenant Sasko asked brightly. "Then you can afford to pay us, as you agreed to."

"I must use all extra funds to protect and clean up my city. Do you see the mess that volcano is making? The old and infirm are dying from the foul air. There is nothing extra in my coffers for mercenaries who did nothing to thwart those thieves. I was a fool to hire a bunch of *women* playing at being soldiers. Get out."

Tezi bristled on behalf of the captain and the company. They were *good* fighters. She'd been on three missions now and knew it to be true, and in between missions, she'd trained every day with them. Yes, she was a rookie and had been taken in without any martial experience, but she was an exception. Every other woman in the unit had been a trained soldier or bodyguard or boxer or duelist before joining Thorn Company.

Fret bit her lip and whispered, "This is not good."

Concern also entered Tinder's eyes as she peered through the doors. "Uh oh."

At first, Tezi thought they meant the fact that the company wasn't going to get paid, but weapons clashed, and shouts sounded amid boots thundering across the marble floor. Tezi also peered inside.

Lieutenant Sasko had swept behind the magistrate, a heavyset man with the jowls of a bulldog, and held a dagger to his throat.

The captain had magelock pistols in each hand pointed at the guards who'd charged in to help their official.

"He won't be hurt," the captain said calmly, "as long as the funds we are due are delivered to us in the next ten minutes."

"You *dare* hold a blade to the magistrate's throat." One of the guards yanked out a magelock of his own.

The captain fired, the charge striking his hand.

He screamed and dropped his weapon, then cursed at her. "You won't get out of here alive, bitch."

"The money," the captain said. "Arrange it."

Tinder and Fret drew their own weapons and took a few steps into the chamber, but a clang sounded somewhere in the complex, and two guards charged around a corner in the hallway. They raced straight toward Tezi.

Though her first thought was to flee, she took a deep breath, drew her magelock pistol, and squeezed behind a support column for cover. This was what she'd been training for. She dared not flee and abandon her teammates.

Fortunately, Tinder ran back out to help her—the captain and lieutenant had the situation inside under control, at least until more guards showed up.

Both men ignored Tezi, drawing their weapons and focusing on Tinder as they ran closer. That surprised Tezi and then annoyed her. Did they not think she was a threat?

Tinder jumped back into the chamber a split second before they fired at her. Their blasts blew holes in the wall and the column framing the doorway. Tezi kicked out as the men tried to run past her. She hooked one of their legs, surprising him, but he flailed and recovered his balance.

Even though Tezi had a pistol, he gave her a dismissive glance and focused on Tinder. She'd jumped back out into the hallway, and she charged them, knocking aside one man's pistol before he could shoot again. He threw a punch at her face, but she dodged it, kicked at his groin, and danced back. The second one thrust at her with a sword, but she saw it coming and parried. Tinder wasn't intimidated by having two opponents, but she did throw a frustrated do-something-to-help glance at Tezi.

Tezi aimed her magelock but hesitated to fire. Tinder was so close to the men that she might hit her ally.

After parrying several more blows, including a blade whistling toward her head, Tinder jumped back and pulled out one of her favorite weapons. A grenade.

That gave Tezi an open shot at one of the guards. Worried they would get into a lot of trouble for killing people here, she fired at his shoulder.

The blue blast struck like a cannonball and sent him flying backward down the hallway, his sword falling from his hands.

Tinder dodged an angry blow from her remaining opponent, then darted in and feinted to his face with her short sword before stabbing him in the chest. Chainmail clanked under his tunic, but the weapon struck hard enough to make him grunt and stumble back. Tinder poked him twice more, drawing blood on either cheek, then held up the grenade.

"I don't think you need to..." Tezi started to say but broke off at the sound of boots thundering on the floor in the hallway behind her and turned to see two more guards charging in to help.

"Duck," Tinder ordered.

Seeing magelocks aimed at her, Tezi was already doing more than that. She dropped flat to her stomach. A blue charge buzzed over her head and slammed into the support column, blowing stone everywhere. Shards ricocheted off the walls and floor, barely missing her.

She knelt back up, raising her own magelock, but a dark projectile sailed over her head. Tinder's grenade.

Even as Tezi lurched to her feet to run backward, Tinder grabbed her by the shoulder and hauled her into the meeting chamber. She started to shut the doors, but the grenade blew first, brilliant yellow light flashing in the hallway.

The half-shut doors blew inward, and Tezi stumbled farther into the chamber. In the hallway, something crashed to the floor— one of the columns? Smoke hazed the air, making the inside of the building as smoky as the air outside, and the stink of black powder stung Tezi's nostrils.

Farther into the chamber, Fret was crouching behind a column with her hands over her head. Tinder had her magelock pointed at the open doors in case the guards recovered and charged in.

At the other end of the chamber, the lieutenant hadn't moved. She stood calmly with her dagger to the magistrate's throat. The captain had somehow disarmed the two guards inside and now held their weapons. She pointed her own pistols at them, though they lay in crumpled heaps on the floor now, groaning and barely moving.

Tezi longed for the day when she could fight like the captain. There wasn't even a bead of sweat on her brow.

"Now," the captain said calmly, "please arrange for our payment and do not force us to further damage your establishment or your employees. Even though we are merely women *playing* at being soldiers, we insist on being paid for our time, and we cannot allow people to take advantage of us. It's death to one's reputation, as you might imagine."

"Maybe we should kill him, Captain," the lieutenant said, a growl in her voice. "As an example to other government officials who may be tempted to screw over mercenaries."

Tezi couldn't tell if she was truly contemplating it or if it was a bluff. The magistrate couldn't either. A bead of sweat ran down the side of his face, and he licked his lips.

"Bookkeeper Crudar." He glanced toward a door in the back wall behind a podium and several massive desks. "Are you still back there?"

"Yes, sir, but I'm busy."

"Busy doing *what*?"

"Cowering under my desk."

"Get out here and bring—"

The courtyard doors banged open, and hazy daylight flooded the hallway and the meeting chamber. Tinder aimed at the opening, and Tezi mirrored her, though she couldn't yet see anyone outlined in the doorway. Strangely, she couldn't hear anyone out there either. On the way in, a handful of vendors had been hawking their wares in the courtyard, unfazed by the ash. Now, the courtyard was quiet.

"Who—" Tinder started to ask, but it turned into a curse as her magelock flew from her hands. It hit the ceiling with a clank and clattered down ten feet away.

Tezi tightened her grip on her own weapon, but it didn't matter. A burst of tremendous power tore it from her grasp, leaving her palms bleeding. Her magelock hit a wall instead of the ceiling. She ran to retrieve it, half because she knew the sergeant would yell at her if she lost her weapon and half because she didn't want to be near the door when whoever had done that walked in.

A mage. It had to be. One of the ones from the island? Coming to get the medallion?

An invisible force wrapped around her before she reached her weapon, immobilizing her. It was only luck that she'd been glancing back and was able to see the three figures that strode into the chamber.

Two men in dark-blue uniforms walked to either side of an imposing white-haired man in black clothing with a black cloak swept back from his shoulders. He had that same dangerous energy about him that Malek had, and Tezi knew without asking that this was another zidarr. And dark-blue uniforms meant these were Zaruk's people.

They looked around the chamber, faces indifferent to the injured guards on the floor and to the mercenaries responsible. Only the zidarr's face held any expression, a faint smirk as he met the magistrate's eyes.

"It appears that you are irritating many people this week, Magistrate."

"I—" Even more beads of sweat ran down the magistrate's face now. "Yes, Lord Stone Heart. It was not my intent. I didn't know about the artifact. These mercenaries were there. They did nothing to stop Uthari's people."

The lieutenant's eyes narrowed at this attempt to blame Thorn Company, and her grip tightened on her dagger. Would she kill the magistrate in cold blood?

The zidarr snorted. "What would magic-dead mercenaries have done? You should have informed King Zaruk the instant Malek's mageship entered our air. You have scouts, do you not? Watchtowers along the coast?"

"Yes, my lord, but with the volcano, we were distracted. We did not know until it was too late."

"The king does not accept excuses for incompetence," Stone Heart said softly, and a shiver went through Tezi as she remembered her previous encounters with their kind. Would this go as badly for the company as it inevitably would for the magistrate?

Stone Heart's gaze swept over the mercenaries again. It halted when it reached Tezi.

She looked down, hoping he couldn't read her thoughts, hoping that he hadn't heard about what had happened up north to a mage in Cedarworks who'd come for women to please his master. And hoping that he wasn't shopping for women to please *his* master while he was here today. Surely, with her back to him and that fresh wound on her temple, she couldn't look like some appealing bed toy to sweep up, not now.

I know what you've done, his voice sounded in her mind, a whisper.

The magical power rooting her in place didn't keep her from shivering.

Had it been one of King Zaruk's mages that you slew, I would be obligated to kill you. By the Zidarr Code, I should kill you regardless for daring to stab one of our kind. He sounded like he was contemplating it.

Tezi didn't reply, tried not even to think a response. She hated that these people could hold her powerless, keep her from even running. There was no chance against them, nothing one could do to fight back unless one of them was asleep atop a girl, drunken and sated. Then... then they were only human.

A chuckle sounded in her mind. *Yes. Sleep is the great equalizer, is it not? I will let you live because Zaruk is irked with King Darekar this month, but you had best not show your face in Darekar's lands again. Also know that his people will not let the murder of a mage go unpunished. They will be looking for you, and justice for such a crime is pursued beyond borders. Do not cross paths with mages in other kingdoms if you value your life. They will be looking for you.*

Why are you warning me? Tezi dared ask.

Because you had the courage to kill your tormentor. Courage is the third tenet.

Finally, his gaze left Tezi. Tremors shook her body. She hated herself for the relief, the weakness. One day, she would be stronger. The captain, she was certain, would not shake even if a zidarr was speaking to her.

"Leave the chamber, Thorn Company," Stone Heart said, power making the command impossible to disobey.

That he knew who they were worried Tezi, and she was relieved when the magic wrapping around her forced her to pick up her magelock and walk woodenly toward the exit. Much better to be shooed out than be punished alongside the magistrate. The captain, Tinder, and Fret were also forced toward the exit. For a long moment, Sasko remained with her dagger to the magistrate's throat, though she also did not appear to have control over her own body.

"I am tempted to have you make good on your threat," Stone Heart told her, "as some form of poetic justice, since I gather he has refused to pay you despite the completion of your services. But the king insists that those who fail be made examples of, and a throat-cutting by some mercenary would be too benign for his theatrical requirements. The public, and anyone who assumes the magistrate's position after him, must know that the zidarr came for him, per the king's orders."

Stone Heart flicked a finger, and Sasko lowered her knife. Without a word—it must have been magic keeping her usually sarcastic tongue still—she marched out after Tezi and the others.

Once they were in the courtyard—all of the vendors and people who'd been in it earlier were gone—the doors thudded closed behind them. *Most* of the way closed. The forced opening had mutilated the hinges.

"So much for getting paid," the captain said with a sigh.

"Mages are getting in the way far too much for my tastes this week," Tinder said.

After her conversation with the zidarr, Tezi agreed. She hoped the company moved on soon, especially after his warning. When she'd fled a thousand miles and across two kingdoms to get away from King Darekar's minions, she'd thought she would be safe, but clearly that wasn't true. Would she have to look over her shoulder for the rest of her life? What might be the rest of her *short* life?

"Guess we're not getting any more supplies, explosive or healing," Fret said wistfully as their group hurried toward the arched doorway leading out of the courtyard, the thick ashy air tickling Tezi's throat again.

"Not true." Once they'd slipped into the street and made sure no more blue-uniformed men were around, Lieutenant Sasko pulled out a fistful of silver rin coins. "There's not enough here to make payroll, but we can resupply before traveling to our next assignment."

"You robbed the magistrate while you held a dagger to his throat?" the captain asked blandly.

"I didn't *rob* him. I extracted as much of our fee as I was able to locate in his pockets."

The captain took it, split it between Fret and Tinder, and waved them toward the shopping district. "Get what supplies you can with that. We'll leave Perchver and look for work up north. Where ash isn't filling the air and mages, hopefully, aren't stealing artifacts from each other."

A scream pierced the heavy air, and Tezi jumped. It came from the meeting chamber through the ill-shut doors, and she had no doubt it belonged to the magistrate. More screams followed, screams of sheer pain that echoed through the streets. The few people who were out hurried inside, slamming their doors and shutters.

Was the zidarr handling the torture himself? What strange code valued courage but allowed torment? Tezi could not imagine living in their world, and she hoped she never saw another of their kind again.

But as the captain led her and the lieutenant on their next errand, Tezi doubted she would be that lucky. As they walked, she looked over her shoulder often, terrified she would see a mage stalking her, ready to exact revenge.

9

HOPING FOR INSPIRATION, JADORA PEEKED IN EVERY ALCOVE AND open door she passed as the two soldiers led her to a portion of the ship she hadn't seen on the way in. Maybe she would spot something that she could slip into a pocket, take back to her cell, and use to escape.

She regretted using all of her irithika powder and smoke-bomb canisters back at the volcano. All she had left in her pockets were vials of yargo, a substance that could be mixed with water and glycerin to make molds of objects too large to remove from the field. That wouldn't get them out of their cell.

Unfortunately, her captors didn't give her much time to snoop. The soldiers were staying close, watching her intently, and hustling her along. She reminded herself that they were not just soldiers but mages too, possibly telepathic, and she had better not spend too much time thinking about escape, now or when she was questioned. Her captors might punish her for such thoughts.

Her only relief was that they hadn't taken Jak from the cell. As much as he wanted to be with her, to try to protect her, she was terrified he would anger them and they would kill him. If only he and Darv had been left with the rest of her team, and only she were here in danger.

But she didn't know if the rest of her team was safe. That weighed on her shoulders. This had been her expedition, her passion. She'd arranged the funding and talked them into coming. If they didn't make it back home, it would be her fault.

They turned into a wide side corridor, the first to remind her of a sailing ship with doors and presumably cabins to either side. Was this where the officers' quarters were? The soldiers pointed her to wide double doors at the end. The cabin of the head officer. Would it be Malek or the general? Or the ship's captain?

When she'd seen the shark figurehead, Captain Ferroki had identified this as Malek's mageship, but that didn't necessarily mean he commanded it. He might simply be the most powerful person who rode around in it, causing people to refer to it as *his*.

As strange as it seemed, Jadora found herself hoping for Malek as her questioner rather than the general. He might be the more dangerous of the two, but she also suspected he had fewer vices. Those comments about Tonovan's tastes disturbed her. Even in her youth, she hadn't been enough of a beauty to tempt any mage to sweep her up for their master's pleasure chambers, and surely, she was past the age now where that would be a threat, but unease crept down her spine nonetheless as they approached the end of the corridor.

The doors opened before anyone knocked. A girl, naked except for a silver slaveband around her head, waited for them with a flagon of wine in her hands. She was beautiful but couldn't have been more than fourteen or fifteen, and unlike the voluntary magebands, slavebands couldn't be removed by the person wearing them. Grunts came from the side of a large cabin furnished lavishly, and the air smelled of sex and floral perfumes and incense. It created a heady mix that was possibly intoxicating.

Jadora's unease increased with the certainty that there wouldn't be anything normal about this questioning.

"Inside." One of the soldiers poked her in the back, making her realize that she'd stopped on the threshold.

"Are you sure?" Jadora asked, trying to muster some courage. "He sounds busy."

"He's *always* busy."

The wine girl stepped aside, and the soldier shoved her again. Mentally bracing herself, Jadora walked in.

She wasn't surprised, though she was strangely relieved, that it was General Tonovan naked on a plush couch next to an unmade poster bed. Three more girls were with him, no older than the first, two on his sides, kissing and stroking him, and one on her knees between his legs. Though he was *busy*, that didn't keep him from focusing on Jadora as she walked in.

Instead of looking at his little orgy, she stared at the wall straight ahead and tried to inhale shallowly as she clasped her hands behind her back. A huge painting showed a battlefield full of mages with terrene men dead on the ground all around, others being defeated by magical blasts slamming into their armored chests. It was labeled *The First Magic War*. Even though it showed her distant ancestors being slain, it was the most innocuous thing in the cabin. Elsewhere, sex toys and torture implements dominated the decor, with pornographic paintings mounted on the walls around the bed. She felt like she'd been thrust straight into Hell and could hear the slavemasters' whips cracking.

One of her guards sighed and joined her in studying the painting. The other watched the more active exhibit in the cabin with interest.

Despite looking at her, Tonovan didn't otherwise acknowledge her until he climaxed. He draped his arms across the back of the couch while the girls continued to stroke him. Strange how mages —even powerful wizards—didn't look any different naked than normal men. It seemed that monsters should have green skin and fangs dripping saliva.

"Welcome to my sanctuary in the air, Professor. Let's have a chat." Tonovan tilted his head. "Do you remember me? You didn't say."

Jadora swallowed. She had wondered if *he* remembered her.

"I remember," she said quietly.

"When I came to your house that night, I was seething with disappointment. We'd scoured your husband's office and hadn't found his journal, the journal King Uthari believed held the secret to the artifact's location. The journal that King Uthari wanted very badly. He'd given me the simple task of acquiring it, and he's never pleased when his tasks aren't completed. On the other hand, he rewards those well who complete his tasks adequately. It is a great pleasure to be rewarded by a wizard more powerful than oneself." He smiled and slid a hand down his chest.

Jadora had no idea if he was hinting at something sexual or some form of magical pleasure she couldn't guess at, and she didn't care. All she wanted was to get out of this cabin with its muddled smells—she was *positive* that incense was burning a drug that would affect her brain. It annoyed her that she couldn't identify it, but it was mixed with other substances. She picked out bergamot, cedar, and dok-naruth amid the more floral scents. Already, her thoughts seemed muzzy, and she caught herself glancing toward Tonovan when he spoke.

"And I *will* be rewarded," he continued. "When I dumped your husband's head on your kitchen floor, I saw the fury and determination on your face. You wanted to kill me, but you also wanted to find what it was he'd been killed for. I knew you would locate the journal eventually, and that if we kept track of you, you would lead us to the artifact."

Yes, Loran's journal had come in the mail later that week. That meant he'd known someone was hunting him, but he hadn't said anything to her. Maybe there hadn't been time. Maybe he'd only had minutes to wrap it and post it from campus.

"Why did you kill him?" Jadora caught herself whispering, though she didn't want to participate in this conversation in any way.

"He refused to answer our questions, and we could not read his mind. Even the zidarr could not, and it is part of their training to learn to use their powers to sift through the thoughts of enemies. Strange, that. I suspect he was one of the untrained who slipped through the cracks." Tonovan lifted his eyebrows in bored curiosity. "Was he?"

"No," she said, trying not to think of her recent conversation with Jak and how he had admitted to being able to *feel* magic in magical items. She was positive that Loran hadn't had any ability to sense or use magic in any way, so she couldn't imagine how Jak could have developed such a knack. "Knowing Loran, he probably had some magical trinket he'd found and wore for protection from mind reading."

That *had* to be it. In the years Jadora had known Loran, he hadn't done anything to suggest superhuman abilities. And neither had anyone in his family. She knew his parents well and still had dinner with them occasionally—she got along better with them than with her *own* father. As far as she knew, the ability to use magic was hereditary, so someone in Loran's family would have demonstrated such aptitude if it existed. Loran hadn't had any such abilities, and neither did Jak. It wasn't possible.

"Are you sure?" Tonovan chuckled. "I may not be the mind reader a zidarr is, but you're a poor liar. Academics are all the same; their faces are as open as the books they read. Does the boy have power?"

"No." Jadora tried to sound as truthful as she could, but Jak's words in the cell put uncertainty into her.

Jak was far past the age when children found with power were adopted and taken to the sky castles for training—training and brainwashing—never to be seen by their families again. Those older than twelve were deemed too dangerous, too indoctrinated in the terrene human way, to become truly loyal to the mages, and they were killed. She could not allow that to happen to Jak.

"What questions did you have for me?" she asked, hoping to change the subject.

Fortunately, Tonovan was fondling a breast and watching two of the girls kissing each other in his lap, acting out his fantasies for him. Jadora prayed his interests would keep him from wondering further about Jak.

"What does it do?" Tonovan murmured.

Jadora blinked. The portal? She kept herself from blurting, *You don't know?*

King Uthari had to know. He wouldn't care this much about it otherwise. He wouldn't have risked sending a ship into another kingdom's territory to retrieve it.

"It's a portal?" Tonovan asked.

Had he read that in her mind, or had she uttered it out loud? She caught herself mumbling. Dear Shylezar, was she so drugged that she couldn't keep her lips shut? She had to get out of there.

She took a step back but bumped into the chest of one of the guards. His hand wrapped around her biceps.

"I thought it might be something like that," Tonovan mused.

Heavy breathing sounded in Jadora's ear. The guard was watching the women's show. They both were now. Of course, the incense would be affecting them too.

"How do you activate it?" Tonovan seemed less addled by the drug than she. Maybe he used it all the time and had built up a tolerance. "And where does it go?"

"I don't know," Jadora mumbled, distracted by the guard being so close. She tried to move away from him, but he gripped her tightly and shifted closer, his chest against her back.

"But you've done research and have ideas. We have the journal now. We'll soon know all you know. We will set up the portal in the main courtyard of Uthari's castle, and all will know that his greatest and most powerful general was responsible for finding it. And we'll explore the place this portal leads to and perhaps find resources that can be used against our enemies. There will be no further need for all this wretched diplomacy between kings or fear of upsetting the tenuous peace, lest we be distracted by war, and the discontented beasts below take advantage." Tonovan smiled at her, making it clear that normal *humans* were the beasts in his eyes. What did that mean then that he was willing to have sex with them?

Tonovan laughed. Had she spoken aloud again? Damn it, she had to escape that incense.

"Come take your place, Professor." Tonovan pushed the women aside and spread his legs. "You were not bad-looking before, and the dakya makes everyone beautiful."

Dakya, of course. That was the drug. It was even more intoxicating than irithika, and it enhanced libido. Just what she needed.

The guard's grip tightened painfully on her biceps, and he wrapped his other arm around her, as if he meant to keep her for himself. She reacted before she could think better of it, stomping on his instep and trying to surge out of his grip. But his mind was as drugged as hers, and if he felt the pain, he didn't react to it. He only growled and held her tighter.

"Release, Rowtar," Tonovan growled and flung up an arm. Both guards flew back, one hitting the wall and one tumbling into the door. It might have been her opportunity to flee if one hadn't still blocked the way. "The professor will be mine. Just as the portal and all the glory will be mine."

"What about Malek?" Jadora glanced around desperately for a weapon. Could she grab one of the guard's swords? Tonovan's power had struck them so hard they were gasping for air.

Wait, there was a bar of soap on a shelf by a washbasin. Glycerin to go with her yargo. And perhaps unsurprisingly, there was a tin of lubricant as well.

She crept toward the washbasin, but power wrapped around her, freezing her before she could grab the items.

"Malek," Tonovan growled, "can suck my—"

The door opened, and Malek walked in without knocking. The guards stumbled out of his path, though Malek wrinkled his nose and didn't go far into the cabin.

The power freezing Jadora disappeared as Tonovan focused on him. She pretended to stumble before recovering her balance by catching herself on the washbasin. She grabbed the soap and lubricant, stuffed them in a pocket, and tried to suck in some of the untainted air that flowed in through the open door.

"I have questions for the professor." Malek's voice turned dry. "She wasn't in her cell." Other than his mild distaste for the heady air, he seemed unsurprised and indifferent to the scene.

"I also had questions for her," Tonovan said. "I have learned much."

"Oh? Do you know what the artifact does yet?"

Jadora crept toward the door. The guards weren't paying attention. Maybe Malek would end up enraptured by the drug and the show and not notice her slipping out...

"It is a portal," Tonovan said grandly, "to another world."

"Which world?"

"I was about to ask her."

"Clearly." Malek flicked a dismissive glance at Tonovan's genitals. "I'll take over the questioning."

Great, just who she wanted to talk to while her brain was addled.

Jadora eased into the corridor and made it several steps. She started to believe they might be distracted enough not to notice her departure, but a hand clamped down on her shoulder. She winced. It wasn't a hard grip, not like the guard who'd left bruises on her arm, but it was firm and unyielding.

"Next door on your left," Malek said.

Jadora sighed. At least she still had the soap. For the moment. Malek might have noticed her take it. Remembering his propensity for reading minds, she forced her thoughts away from it and walked to the indicated door. There wasn't a knob or latch—none of the doors had them—but it opened when she turned toward it.

She braced herself for whatever macabre horrors Malek's cabin would be full of.

It had none. It was half the size of Tonovan's cabin and had only a neatly made bunk, a desk, chair, and clothes wardrobe with the doors closed. Everything was tidy, save for a grimy towel hanging on a hook by the door. There was no artwork, pornographic or otherwise, and only a single sign hung on a wall. The Zidarr Code, it read at the top in unembellished print, with the five tenets listed below: integrity, duty, courage, austerity, and honor.

The air in the cabin was blessedly clean, and already, Jadora's head was clearing, thank the gods. But her feeling of gratitude was fleeting, for she spotted Loran's journal open on the desk. Several pages of freshly written notes rested beside it, along with two archaeology books. She recognized the titles as the most prominent in the small field of dragon philology.

She stared bleakly at the journal, the reminder of her husband's death. The feeling of defeat crept into her again, along with fear that she couldn't get out of this, and that even if she could, she wouldn't be able to get the portal away from these people.

"Sit." Malek pointed toward a chair.

"Which one of you is in charge?" Jadora moved toward the chair, keeping her pocket with the pilfered items turned away from him.

"Tonovan commands the Utharian mage army, more than ten thousand men."

"Does that mean he outranks you?"

"I am not a military officer."

"But he defers to you."

"Uthari likes me more."

"That shouldn't take much," she muttered, sitting gingerly.

Malek remained standing, leaning against the wall across from her, his arms folded over his chest. "It's presumed to be a portal to the world the dragons came from, the world where they originally evolved. The author of the journal didn't know why they came to Torvil or why they later left, but there are hypotheses that the climate may have shifted and grown inhospitable to their kind, or that, after creating humans, they wished to leave us to evolve without interference from their greater kind. That hypothesis, of course, requires that one's religious beliefs allow that dragons might have created mankind, instead of the more typical opinion that the farm god Thanok convinced the sun and moon gods to help create men, so that he would not be alone in this form."

Her mind had snagged on *the author of the journal*, and she barely heard his summation. Loran. Did Malek not even know his name? Or did he not care? One dead archaeologist was the same as another...

It took her a moment to realize he'd paused. Waiting for her opinion on the origins of mankind?

"Much to my priest father's consternation, I subscribe to the nonreligious theory that humans evolved naturally from other species, constructed the notions of gods to suit their needs, and that dragons came along later, perhaps through this very portal, to visit us and perhaps influence our kind." Belatedly, she wished she could retract the comment about her father. She'd barely spoken to him since her mother died, but these people could easily find him and use him as a way to manipulate her.

Malek's eyes narrowed thoughtfully, but it might have been because he shared her father's opinion of how blasphemous her beliefs were. When he spoke again, it was to continue his summary. "The journal also puts forth the hypothesis that the dragons were at war with each other or another unknown enemy and that they were driven to flee this world. It sounds like there's no proof and that there is little evidence to support any of these notions. That the portal goes to another world at all is also in question since legends of it all predate humanity's written tongues. And most examples of what were once believed to be samples of the dragon language, carved into ancient pillars and stones, were later proven to be human-made." He pointed at the philology books, then tapped the journal. "Nine-tenths of this was dedicated to *finding* the portal. It was presumed that once it was found, the secrets—directions on how to operate it—would be evident on the artifact itself. I've been studying it, and there are indeed symbols on it. A language perhaps."

Jadora kept herself from gaping at the revelation. She'd *hoped* for symbols—symbols that could be translated and would turn out to be instructions on operation and information about the builders. Under any other circumstances, she would have been delighted about this, but *she* wanted to be the one studying those symbols, not hearing about them from an enemy.

"They emanate magic—the entire portal does—but neither physically pressing them nor magically pressing them does anything."

Jadora stared at the desk, trying to tamp down annoyance that he'd already gotten to examine it and she hadn't even seen it up close. *She* was the one who'd spent the last five years searching for it. And she was the one who'd located it. These people never would have found it if not for her. But despite all her care, she'd led them right to it. Tonovan had said they'd been tracking her somehow. Watching her more closely than she'd realized. Was that truth or bluster? If they'd been watching her all these years, and she hadn't known it...

"Tonovan didn't know anything." Malek snorted softly. "One of your people at the university is on Uthari's payroll. The king has spies all over his realm and in all of his fellow kings' realms. They have the same. It's the way of things."

"Who was it?" Jadora doubted he would tell her. Did she even want to know? It wasn't as if she would ever be permitted to return home. Would she even be allowed to live after they'd scoured her mind for everything she knew? What about Jak?

He twitched a shoulder. "Professor Nugyarin. Perhaps if you confront him, he'll share the bribe money with you. And there's no reason you can't live. Cooperate with us. Uthari wants the portal and to know how to operate it. That's all."

"That's *all*?" Her voice cracked, but she didn't care. "You people killed my husband."

Maybe she should have said *you* killed my husband. Had he? Tonovan had said a zidarr did it. Was she looking in the eyes of her husband's murderer?

"He didn't cooperate," Malek said quietly.

He must have heard the rest of her thoughts, but he didn't respond to them. She glanced at the sign on the wall. Integrity, duty, courage, austerity, honor... Words that only applied to the way he interacted with his master, no doubt. No need to have integrity with mere humans.

"Do you want to see the portal?" he asked. "I've cleaned it off."

"Yourself?"

Surely, that was the kind of thing mages made their enslaved minions do.

"The *minions* got zapped when they touched it. No, not when they touched it, but when they started scrubbing it too aggressively." Malek glanced toward the grimy towel. "I can scrub something without touching it."

Jadora almost choked on the idea of *scrubbing* an ancient artifact. As impervious as dragon steel was, she would have used the
tools in her archaeology kit for delicately removing sand and grit
from bones, potsherds, and other brittle finds.

"It doesn't look that brittle. Come, I'll show it to you." His eyes
narrowed again. "There's something I want you to see."

He'd seemed almost friendly for a moment—or at least like a
normal human being—but that last sentence put her on edge. He
hadn't yet questioned her, merely shared what he'd learned from
the journal. Maybe he'd been reading her mind to verify that he'd
interpreted it correctly.

"You haven't asked me any questions yet," she said.

"I will." Malek led the way into the corridor, trusting that she
would follow him.

And she would. Even if escape should be her priority, she
dearly wanted to see these symbols. After all these years of searching, just to see the portal cleaned up and out in the open would be
a delight. And to touch it, hopefully without being zapped. It
sounded like the men trying to clean it had activated the same
defenses that had been employed on the drakur.

"Did your, uhm, minions get badly hurt when they were
zapped?" Jadora asked the back of his head as she followed him—
his hair was as tidy as his cabin, freshly trimmed along the hair-
line. A strange thing to notice.

"They said it stung, but they weren't killed. Not like those
drakur." He glanced back. "I assume the portal did that?"

"Yes."

Maybe it was pressure sensitive. Or could it somehow sense a
person's intent? A warning zap to those who knocked against it
and death to any who genuinely tried to destroy it? She shook her
head. Pressure sensitivity seemed more plausible. She wasn't
ready to assign sentience to the portal, though when she remembered that vision, she did wonder about it.

"They were stabbing it with spears," she added.

"And you worried about me scrubbing it too vigorously with my towel."

Jadora blinked. He was facing forward again, so she couldn't tell if he was amused, but it *sounded* like it. That unnerved her for some reason. Enemies were supposed to be like—well, that idiot with his orgy. Given all the dreadful stories that existed about the zidarr, she wasn't prepared to think of them as capable of having senses of humor. Especially when one of them—maybe even the one she was following—had killed her husband.

Fresh air swept over her face as they climbed up stairs leading high over the spacious hold to an open hatch. The octopus of an engine throbbed below. There were no railings, making the climb precarious, and she stepped carefully. Beyond the open hatch, the side of a uniformed soldier was in view.

Remembering the one who'd grabbed her, Jadora shifted to the far side of the hatchway as she climbed out. The pocket with the soap and tin clunked against the jamb, and she grimaced, hoping Malek hadn't heard that. But he kept walking, heading across the black deck under a black sky full of stars. That puzzled her since she'd thought the full night had passed and it would be daylight by now, but she supposed if they were traveling in a westerly direction, they had been chasing the sunset the evening before. Strange to think that the mageships moved quickly enough to either shorten or extend a day, depending on their route.

A half moon beamed silver light onto the massive portal taking up most of the space on the deck. Artificial yellow light, the source indiscernible, further brightened the area.

Her gaze caught on four lifeboats mounted near the railings on either side of the deck. They were more sophisticated than escape craft she'd seen on sailing ships, having cabins with windows up front and open seating areas in the back. In each cabin, a navigation wheel was visible, glowing a faint silver-blue. Jadora had no doubt that magic powered the lifeboats and could keep them aloft in the sky; what she didn't know was if someone without magic could pilot one. If so, maybe she, Jak, and Darv had a better shot at escaping than she'd believed.

If they could get out of their cells and launch a lifeboat without anyone noticing. Given that half a dozen uniformed mages were out on the deck, even in the middle of the night, that was questionable.

Malek walked to a particular point on the far side of the portal and waited for her. She navigated around it more slowly, trailing her fingers along the smooth surface—as the portal lay on its side, it came up higher than her waist—and gawking at its beauty. The entwined dragons were even more elegant than she'd realized, each one symmetrical and each with a symbol she'd never seen before.

To her shock, three familiar runes were engraved at what might have been the bottom. They were in Ancient Zeruvian, the first written language believed to have been developed. She stared at it, amazed even as she was puzzled. The dragons and the artifacts they'd left behind on Torvil all pre-dated any known occurrences of that language. By millennia. That meant that language had either existed longer than anyone realized, or this had been added later. Had early Zeruvians presumed to carve into the portal? Would it, with its propensity for defending itself, even have allowed that? And if so, how would humans have done this when dragon steel was impervious to everything scientists had thrown at it in their experiments?

"That's not the dragon tongue," Malek said.

"No."

"Can you read it?"

She thought about lying, but he would see the lie in her mind. Besides, she was fairly certain these words didn't hold the key to its operation or origins. "Gateway to the stars."

"Ah." A few feet away, Malek rested his hand on the surface, not on one of the symbols but on something else that was located on one of the dragon tails. A circular hole with jagged, uneven edges.

Recognition and alarm jolted Jadora. She'd thought that might be there—she should have known to expect it.

"This wasn't mentioned anywhere in the notebook," Malek said, watching her intently.

"You've read it all already?" she asked, buying time to think.

"I'm a fast reader." His tone was cool now, making her wonder if she'd imagined the earlier humor. The humanity.

"I don't know why there's a hole." She didn't know for *certain* why there was a hole. And she tried to keep any thoughts related to it out of her mind while his eyes bored into her like drills.

"But you think it's a *key* hole."

"It's possible. It may simply be decorative. Or for drainage."

"Drainage," he said, his tone flat.

She smiled, hoping vainly that it would disarm him. "Yes, drainage. In case water gets inside."

"Professor Freedar." Malek did not sound disarmed. "I've read your papers. I've scoured your notes. I know you are intelligent. Please allow that I am, at the least, not an idiot."

An unfortunate truth she'd figured out immediately. And the fact that he'd read her papers, papers that had nothing to do with archaeology or dragon artifacts, only alarmed her further. Just how long and how closely had these people been following her?

"You are, however, my enemy," she said quietly.

"The Magic Wars were two thousand years ago. The kings are your rulers, not your enemies."

"We did not *choose* them as rulers. We are enslaved by them."

"You have a house and a career that you freely chose. You are not a slave."

"I will grant that I have it better than many," or so it had been until she'd been captured, "but I do not have the right to speak freely, to choose the type of rule or ruler I wish to guide society, or to live without fear of punishment for saying or doing the wrong thing. People disappear *all* the time. My husband was blatantly killed. Those *born* into the ruling caste, in their cities in the clouds, have little idea what it is to live as we do. To live in fear and oppression, to struggle to earn enough to feed our families, while our *rulers* take half of what we earn in taxes and live in opulence. Why do you think you find it so easy to bribe our people to become spies for your kings? Because they need the money. Everybody always needs money. Woe to she who falls ill without family to take her in. Come live as we do without your powers and then see how you feel toward your rulers."

"I am well aware of how you live," he said but didn't elaborate, instead stepping forward.

Too close for comfort. If she skittered back, would he allow it? Or use his power to hold her?

Malek reached for her—no, for her *pocket.* Before she could think to block him, he pulled out the two items she'd taken from Tonovan's cabin.

He looked at the bar first. "Soap?"

"We haven't been allowed to clean."

He read the label on the tin, his eyebrows drifting upward. "And lubricant?"

"My skin is rough. Digging by hand gives you calluses."

He gazed at her—his face wasn't far from hers, his dark eyes seeing far too much as they studied hers. "I'm tempted to give these back to you to see what you do with them."

"I'm open to that."

Instead, he set the items on the portal and again rested his hand next to the conspicuous hole. "Tell me if a key goes into this and what it does? Is it what allows the portal to operate?"

"I don't know." Jadora looked toward the night sky and imagined dragons flying among the stars and what it might be like to ride on the back of such a magnificent creature, to speak with it of the ancient times, to ask why it had left Torvil so long ago. She thought of anything that she could that had nothing to do with the portal and Jak's medallion.

Malek sighed and leaned back. Had she succeeded in keeping him from extracting the information from her mind?

He studied the deck, scrutinized it intently though there was nothing down there. He looked like... A sickly feeling came over her. Like he was trying hard to remember something.

"The hat," he said, looking up. "There was something in it when I first came down to your camp."

Damn it, she'd removed the key before the disks had arrived on the beach. Malek must have come down before the soldiers. He'd been back there watching everything.

"Some kind of golden medallion with embellishments." He touched the hole. "That's the key, isn't it?"

She didn't verify it for him.

"Did you give it to one of the archaeologists? Or the mercenaries?"

She kept her mind blank. His eyes narrowed again as he contemplated her. Thinking of torturing her to get the information? Maybe he would return her to Tonovan's foul den until she blurted everything under the influence of that incense.

"I'll find it," he said. "You—"

He broke off and looked toward the sky behind the ship, suddenly as intent and alert as a wolf.

"We have company coming," he said, his voice icy cold. "Sergeant." He waved for one of the ubiquitous soldiers to come over. "Take her back to her cell."

"Yes, my lord."

"Secure the artifact," he yelled to another soldier, then took off across the deck at a sprint.

Before her guard arrived, Jadora snatched the soap and tin and stuffed them back into her pocket. The man's eyes were toward the stars, and he didn't notice. Concern tightened his face.

Whatever company was coming, it wasn't friendly.

Jadora looked back as the soldier led her below and glimpsed another dark shape blotting out the stars. Another mageship.

10

A SENTRY DISK PROPELLED BY MAGIC FLOATED THROUGH THE sandstone streets of Perchver, the silver globe mounted atop it glowing slightly. Tezi had seen them before in big metropolises and knew they were eyes for the government, watching the citizens and making sure nobody fomented rebellion. Since most land-based cities in the kingdoms were overseen by terrene humans who didn't have magical power themselves, they were given numerous tools with which to do their jobs.

In the past, Tezi hadn't worried much about sentry disks, but the zidarr's warning burned in her mind. She turned her face away from it and walked close behind Sasko and the captain.

"You sure he's still living in Perchver?" Sasko asked. "And are you sure he's still *alive*? It's been almost a year, hasn't it?"

"He's still alive," the captain said. "The last I heard, he hadn't finished his book yet."

Sasko grunted. "Is he going to kill himself after he finishes?"

"He might. Honestly, I thought he'd take his life after the massacre." The captain's voice held a note of distress, if not anguish. Who were they talking about? "He's determined to tell his story first and out everyone who betrayed him, but I don't know who he thinks will risk the wizards' wrath by printing it."

"Nobody will. It would be career suicide if not *actual* suicide."

"More than that. The wizards would probably destroy the print shop and everyone who witnessed the book being created." The captain turned at an intersection, leading them into an old merchant district that had fallen on hard times. Cracks meandered through the white plaster walls of two-story buildings with shops on the bottom and apartments on the top. The roofs were full of broken terra-cotta tiles, some having fallen off and shattered in the alleys. Laundry hung over rusty railings on narrow balconies, nobody caring that it was collecting ash while it dried.

"Everyone already knows the story anyway," Sasko said.

"Every mercenary, maybe."

Tezi didn't. She wanted to ask for details, but she didn't want to intrude or remind the captain and lieutenant that she was with them, listening to their conversation. They might decide to send her back to the company alone, and she didn't want to be alone with mages in the city. Even without that threat, Perchver wasn't the safest place, especially now that they'd traveled away from the government sector.

Beggars hunkered at corners, gaunt from starvation and their eyes glazed, magebands around their heads distracting them from reality. Children ran around without shirts or shoes. Every other alley had a fight taking place in it. Tezi's village had been poor too, but people had worked together to help make sure everyone was fed and had a roof. The citizens here seemed much worse off.

"Are you thinking of leaving the thing with him?" Sasko glanced at the pocket where the captain had tucked the gold-plated medallion. "Or *selling* it to him? You said he's an expert in acquiring stolen artifacts now, right? Maybe he knows how to get rid of them too."

"He might, but I mostly want to ask him if he knows more

about it, and see if he has any darkeye fabric to hide it so mages can't sense it."

Sasko groaned. "You wouldn't care about hiding it if you weren't planning to keep it."

"I'd also like to check in on him, as long as we're here in his city. And make sure he's... doing all right."

Sasko eyed her, and Tezi waited for her to point out that the captain hadn't responded to her statement. All she said was, "You two never got horizontal, did you?"

The captain eyed her back while Tezi gaped, having a hard time imagining her in a relationship. She seemed so indifferent to such things and so dedicated to running the company.

"You know we didn't," the captain said. "I've just known him a long time."

"As long as you trust him not to sell us out," Sasko grumbled, eyeing the pocket again. "Or try to steal that thing from you. We're no pushovers, but he was—probably still is—an elite fighter. Nobody ever got the best of him until those mages set him up."

"He won't betray us. He's honorable."

Sasko turned a skeptical expression on the captain. "People change, Captain. Especially after they lose everything."

"Some things don't change," the captain said with certainty.

They stopped in front of a curio shop with bars over the windows and a *Closed* sign on the door. Above the shop, a balcony led to an apartment with the door open, but there was no obvious way up to it.

The captain knocked and called up, "Mountains of Midnight Mourning."

Sasko raised her eyebrows. Was that a song? A play? Tezi had never heard of it.

Another sentry disk floated down the street, and she turned her back again, pretending to be interested in a dusty vase sitting in the window display.

A creak came from the balcony, and a cloaked and hooded figure peered down at them, shadows hiding the face.

"Shop's closed, Captain Ferroki," the figure said in a dry baritone. "When it's raining ash, lava, and sulfuric bits of hell, it's not good for the more delicate artifacts."

"We came to see the owner, not the wares."

"The owner's retired." The man clunked a metal tool on the balcony railing. The head of a pickaxe? At first, it looked like he was holding it, but Tezi realized he didn't have a hand on his left side. The pickaxe head was a replacement for it.

"We're not trying to hire you."

"As if we'd have the money," Sasko muttered.

"We just need information, Sorath," the captain added quietly.

Sorath? *Colonel* Sorath?

Tezi stared up at the man with more interest. Even before becoming a soldier, she'd heard that name. He'd led one of the most famous mercenary units, a battalion of exceptionally well-trained warriors under a commander who'd been renowned for his tactical brilliance. Even the wizards had reputedly been made nervous by him, aware that he'd found ways to best elite magical troops more than once.

The dry voice turned hard as the man—Sorath?—said, "Don't use that name. That man is dead."

"You didn't tell me what name that man is going by now."

"Vorzaz."

"A roamer name?"

"Yes. It means scribe and outcast in my mother's language." Some of the hardness left his tone, but his voice was bitter when he added, "Among her people, those two words were synonymous. Education wasn't valued, not like the power of a sharp blade." He stepped off the balcony and back inside, closing the door behind him.

"Uh." Sasko looked around as long seconds passed. "Are we invited in?"

"I don't know." The captain tried the door. It wasn't locked.

Sasko didn't look like she wanted to follow the captain inside, but the sentry disk floated back in their direction, and Tezi hurried to squeeze past her. That disk was showing up a lot more frequently than typical. Usually, they floated around the cities on established circuits. They only deviated from their routes if they came across something interesting and were sent by their government controllers to investigate.

Tezi hoped this errand wouldn't take long and that the company would head to a less populated part of the world, somewhere where mages and mage tools were scarce.

After Sasko closed the door, the captain led them through tidy but dusty aisles of books, globes, and trinkets from all over the world. Cobwebs lurked in the corners, and there was no light, other than what came through the barred front window. This had nothing to do with the volcano; the shop had been closed for a long time.

The captain climbed stairs along a back wall that led to a landing, then stepped through an open door.

"Go ahead up," Sasko told Tezi, drawing her sword and staying by the entrance to the shop where she could watch the street. "I'll keep an eye out while they talk."

Maybe she'd also found the disk's route suspicious.

"Do you think the captain wants me up there?" Tezi was curious about the legendary colonel and what he might say, but it was strange that she'd been invited along. Rookies didn't go to meetings with captains.

Sasko twitched a shoulder. "You're her expert on sewing and stuff."

Which had little to nothing to do with the medallion, but Tezi padded up the stairs and crept into the small apartment. Unlike the shop below, it was free of dust. It was also sparsely furnished and decorated, like a place a traveling merchant stayed in on occasion but didn't live in year-round. A desk with an open notebook, several sheets of paper, and a few pens was the only suggestion that someone was here working on some project.

"What brings you to the abode of *Vorzaz*, Captain Ferroki?" Sorath leaned against the wall behind the desk with his arms folded over his chest. He'd removed the cloak and hood, revealing bushy hair with as much gray as black. Even if Tezi hadn't known his name, the scar running through his eyebrow and down his cheek, the oft-broken nose, and the pickaxe hand replacement would have assured her he'd seen a lot of battles. His button-down shirt was half open, showing a lean, muscular chest despite his age and apparent retirement. He glanced at Tezi. "And who's the killer?"

"Killer?" Tezi mouthed. Nobody had given her such a ferocious moniker.

"He calls everybody that," the captain told her.

"Only soldiers," Sorath said. "And those who look like they could use an ego boost."

"And anyone else whose name you can't remember?"

"Really, Captain. I can't believe you came all the way here to tease me." He didn't sound too annoyed.

"That's true. This is Rookie Tezi, and you've met Lieutenant Sasko." The captain pointed toward the floor.

"Wasn't she Sergeant Sasko last time?"

"Yes. I lost Red."

"It happens." The words might have seemed aloof, but his dark eyes held compassion, and the way he softened his voice made Tezi think he was offering condolences.

"Yeah. It's a tough life." The captain swallowed, then unbuttoned her pocket. "As I said, I need information. I can pay a little for it, though work has been scarce for Thorn Company of late.

For all mercenaries, I hear. There's a lot of tension between the kings, but as usual, they haven't been attacking each other openly."

"That may change soon." Sorath looked out the window in the direction of the volcano. "But you already know to be wary of any contracts the wizard kings offer you."

"Very wary. But they have no reason to waste time and money to set us up. I'm not a military genius leading an infamous unit that makes them uneasy."

"They don't have to set you up to kill you. If they can gain something, they'll happily throw entire companies away like the wrapper around a fig bar." Sorath flicked his fingers to demonstrate the motion. "And you might be surprised who's heard of Thorn Company. You've been around a while, and you're known."

"We're known because we only take women, not because we've won tremendous battles on the field of war."

"Modesty, Captain? You come up with clever and creative ways to deal with enemies, as I well know." He smirked and bowed to her, making Tezi wonder if they'd met as enemies in battle before. "The wizards don't like anyone who's clever or creative."

"I'll keep your warning in mind. Will you examine something for me? We believe it's an artifact of some value."

"You should see an archaeologist then. Or a dealer."

"An archaeologist gave it to me before she was kidnapped by Malek and his mageship."

"You were on the island?" Sorath didn't sound surprised about the rest. Maybe everyone had heard by now that Malek had been here.

"Yes."

"Not to fight him, I reckon."

"Just to pick up the archaeologists before the volcano erupted." The captain drew the medallion out of her pocket—she'd wrapped it in a kerchief—and slowly unfolded it. "The magistrate didn't expect the mageship."

"Or that there was a priceless artifact buried out there under his nose." Sorath grunted. "You've got to wonder how it got there. The stories tell of it being placed in a beautiful jungle on the side of a lake."

"You've studied it then? That ring?" The captain watched his face.

"If it is what I think it is, it plays a starring role in the history books, a few bards' songs, and even one of Egarath's plays." Sorath held out his hand.

The captain gave him the medallion. His face didn't brighten with recognition. Instead, he frowned and squinted thoughtfully at it, then pulled out a magelight and thumbed it on for closer examination.

"We scraped off some of the gold plating on the edge." The captain glanced at Tezi, as if suggesting she'd been a part of that. "It seemed like a recent addition."

"I see."

Sorath tilted the medallion and held the light over the blue-black line, then pulled another device out of a desk drawer. It had a handle with a bulbous end and a button to activate it. When he held it up to the key, it emitted a high-pitched screech that made Tezi want to fling her hands over her ears. He moved it away and the volume lowered, but it continued screeching until he tapped the button again.

The captain grimaced. "What is that dreadful thing?"

"It detects magic. It's saying this has a *lot* of it." Sorath removed a loupe and examined the rest of the medallion, spending extra time on the scraped area.

Tezi walked to the balcony door so she could peer out into the street and see if the sentry disk was still around. From the second floor, there was a view past the flat terra-cotta rooftops to the strait and the volcano, the lava flowing in rivers down the side visible despite it being miles away.

"Thank you for helping us, Vorzaz," the captain said quietly.

"I haven't done anything yet."

"You're on the verge of sharing insightful information. I can tell."

"By the twinkle in my eyes?"

"You stick your tongue in the corner of your mouth when you're getting excited about something."

"I hadn't realized you knew me and my tongue that well."

"I know most of the mercenary captains well. It pays to study possible allies."

"And possible enemies."

"Yes. That too." The captain looked toward the window. "I admit that you did surprise me by staying in this area. When I heard you'd survived, I envisioned you hiding out in a remote cave in the wilderness, not living in a city of five hundred thousand."

"It's hard to get meal delivery in the wilderness. Besides, this is where I owned property." Sorath gestured toward the walls. "I was always careful to make sure that few people knew about it. I didn't think *you* were among them."

"We researched you extensively when we thought we might end up fighting against you at Senis Sarr."

"Including my property holdings? Were you thinking of assassinating me before I could show up to the battlefield?"

"Sasko might have contemplated it. She's a first-principles thinker."

"The best kind. Forget that pesky idea of honor among warriors. Assassinate the other side's leader before breakfast."

"Sadly, honor can get you killed."

Sorath lifted his chin, his dark gaze chilling the room as it settled on the captain. Even though he wasn't looking at Tezi, it made her squirm.

The captain realized her faux pas and lifted an apologetic hand. "I'm sorry, Sorath. I wasn't thinking of your loss."

"Vorzaz." Though his jaw remained clenched, he returned to examining the medallion.

"Was it honor that got them killed?" the captain asked quietly. "I thought betrayal."

"It was believing *they* had honor," he said savagely, his fist tightening around the handle of his tool so tightly that it snapped. He hurled it across the room, and it smashed against the wall.

Tezi jumped, dropping her hand to her sword hilt. The captain didn't react, merely gazing sadly at Sorath.

He drew a deep breath, spread his hand on the desk, and gripped the edge with his pick as he struggled for calm. "The real crime is that I survived when so few of my men did."

"Did you ever think of rebuilding the company?"

He scoffed. "No. It's too dangerous for others to stand at my side. My men died because the kings wanted *me* dead. Badly. What else could have driven so many of them to work together? The only reason I'm alive now is because they think they got me. And they almost did." He eyed the pick, then used it to pull aside his half-open shirt, revealing knotted pink scar tissue that ran down his dark skin from collarbone to abdomen. "My healer gave up his own chance to live by using the last of his potions on me. It would have been better if he'd been the one to walk off the battlefield. He had the wisdom and willingness to do good in the world."

"And you don't?" the captain asked.

"I'm just a sell-sword, Ferroki. Or I was."

"You always cared." Her voice was gentle, and even though they'd spoken of being enemies, or at least pitted against each other before, Tezi had a feeling the captain cared about him. That made her curious about their past. "Isn't that why you're writing the book?" the captain added.

"A book that nobody will read."

"Then why write it?"

"I feel compelled to leave a warning," Sorath said. "Even if nobody reads it now, maybe someone will someday, and maybe it'll make a difference."

"Maybe it will. I hope you survive long enough to finish it."

"I will. That's why I'm incognito."

The captain looked at the top of his head. "You think your fancy new hair and a new name will keep them from learning of your existence?"

"I did until *you* showed up at my door. The last I heard, most of my own men, those who survived, think I'm dead. How did you know I was alive?"

"I have acquaintances in the major cities who keep me apprised of who's seen and where."

"That must mean the *fancy* hair isn't as much of a disguise as I thought." Sorath waved to the bushy curls.

"Not with that face underneath it. I always assumed it was your shaved head that made your scar more pronounced and fearsome, but the hair doesn't change much. Can you fit that in a helmet?"

"I haven't tried for a while."

"Maybe you could keep small daggers in it."

Sorath tapped the back of his head, then pulled out a spare pen.

"A terrifying weapon," the captain said.

"A sword can propel one man into action. A pen can propel thousands."

"Only if you find a publisher."

"I will."

As Tezi watched this exchange, she wondered if it could be called flirting. Maybe she made some noise, for Sorath looked over at her.

"You're recruiting them young, these days, Captain."

"It's hard to find veterans who want to sign on for what I can pay right now. And Rookie Tezi's got grit."

Tezi stood straight, attempting to look like she deserved that praise.

"Huh." Sorath held up the medallion. "This is made from dragon steel—the alloy the dragons used for crafting tools. It's inherently magical and believed to be nearly indestructible. Valuable too. Dragon steel is about as common as fossilized dragon poop."

Tezi blinked. How rare was *that*?

"It would be even more valuable if people knew how to melt it down and reshape it, but it's said that only dragon fire is hot enough for that. It's mostly the scarcity of dragon-steel artifacts that give them their extreme value. Archaeologists and treasure hunters have been looking for them for ages, but very few have been found. A few artifacts are in museums in the sky cities, none in the museums of mundane humans. Probably not any in private collections down here either."

"Meaning this one could be sold for a lot?" She sounded wistful.

"Meaning you should get rid of it before someone tries to kill you for it." Sorath tilted his head. "You said an archaeologist *gave* it to you?"

"To keep Malek's people from getting it, yes. I think it's related to the big ring they took off the island. We think it might be a key."

"Malek is the last one you want hunting you down," Sorath said.

"I know. The professor asked me to keep it for her, but... what would you advise? Throw it in the ocean?"

"Yes."

The captain blinked. "Really?"

Sorath turned the medallion over in his hand. "If this is a key to the fabled dragon portal, it's one of the most valuable things in the world."

"I don't think he knew she had it."

"He'll find out. But throwing it in the ocean wouldn't be enough to keep him from getting it. With his power, he could pluck it off the bottom of even a deep chasm. I'm not sure we want King Uthari to have the key to visiting another world and maybe finding things—or beings—there that could make him more formidable here on Torvil. He's already one of the strongest kings with one of the largest and wealthiest kingdoms." Sorath clenched his jaw. "He's also one of those who banded together to betray me."

"I'm sorry," the captain said quietly.

"I'm half-tempted to suggest you sell it to someone who would take it to Zaruk or one of the other kings, if only to keep the key and the lock apart and ensure nobody can use the portal. Maybe they would fight over it, and it would start the wizard war that's been brewing for centuries." His lips twisted in a bitter smile, and he handed the medallion back to her. "You'll have to decide what to do with it."

"I thank you for the advice."

"Here's one last piece: remember that it's highly magical." Sorath pointed toward the broken device he'd waved over it. "That means it'll be easy for their kind to track. There are usually enough magical trinkets in cities that mages might not notice it or be able to pick it out from the crowd, but if you're out away from people and other magic, it'll stand out."

"I'll keep that in mind," the captain said. "Do you, by chance, have any darkeye fabric here?"

"I—"

Footsteps thumped on the stairs.

"Captain," Sasko called in a low voice. "Two platoons of armed men just showed up. They're not in uniform, but they look like soldiers. They're blocking this street from both intersections, and a squad is heading this way. There's a mage with them."

Tezi pressed her cheek to the window and peered down the street. It was impossible to miss the men, all clean-shaven and short-haired. They did have the mien of soldiers. Several of them were heading toward the shop, accompanied by a mage in a silver-trimmed cloak.

"Is there a back door?" the captain asked.

"You're looking at it." Sorath pointed to the balcony over-looking the street—the street the squad was marching up—and closed his book and put it in a deep pocket. The pen went back into his hair, and he grabbed his cloak and weapons, then pulled a dark canister out of a drawer. "I'll go chat with them. Use this for cover and then go via the balcony."

"Wait," the captain blurted as Sorath pressed the canister into her hand. "They'll recognize you."

"Maybe, but I'm not the one holding a priceless artifact." He jogged down the stairs as a booming knock sounded at the front door.

The captain swore, anguish twisting her usually calm face. "I didn't mean to bring trouble to his doorstep."

"They could be here for *him*, not us," Sasko pointed out.

"I doubt it."

Tezi drew her pistol, though they couldn't fight so many. Could Sorath convince them that the medallion wasn't here? Or had that mage already sensed it?

Downstairs, wood splintered, and something crashed to the floor. "Where is it?" a man bellowed. "We know they sold it to you, Vorzaz."

Black-powder weapons fired, magelocks *thwomped*, and more crashes sounded. The squad in the street flowed into the curio shop, and more soldiers advanced from the intersections.

"They're attacking *him*. We have to help." The captain charged for the stairs, and Tezi started after her.

But Sasko planted herself in the captain's path, stopping her with raised hands. "He's buying time for us. For *you,* so you can get out of here with that thing." She pointed at the medallion.

"That's not his job. It's better to let them have it than for him to be killed." The captain tried to push past her, but Sasko didn't move. "You know I can best you, Lieutenant. Get out of my way."

"No. What did he give you? A smoke bomb?"

More weapons fired downstairs. Something heavy crashed to the floor.

"Check up there!" someone yelled.

"I can't. He's—" A scream of pain cut off the man.

"Yes," the captain whispered.

She wrenched her gaze from the stairs and ran to the balcony. She pulled the tab and tossed the canister into the street as the platoons came together.

Smoke as thick and black as that wafting from the volcano spewed into the street. Within seconds, the men disappeared behind the dark cloud.

"Up," the captain whispered, the words barely audible over the cacophony of chaos coming from below.

She swept past Tezi and climbed the railing to pull herself onto the roof. Sasko waved for Tezi to go next.

Wrinkling her nose at the smoke, Tezi holstered her firearm and scrambled up to balance on the narrow railing. The captain leaped up and grabbed an overhang on the roof, pulling herself up with acrobatic ease.

With Sasko right behind her and shouts of, "Up there!" Tezi couldn't hesitate to follow. She jumped, grabbed the gutter, and tried to replicate the captain's feat. But the overhang stuck out far enough that there was no support for her legs, nothing to push off from. She hung, struggling to lift her body weight solely with her arms.

Swords clashed on the rooftop above. Tezi cursed and tried again to pull herself up. Sasko climbed onto the railing and gave her a boost. Tezi managed to hook one boot over the gutter. A magelock fired nearby, and terra-cotta tiles on the roof across the street blew away.

In a saner moment, Tezi might have climbed back down and turned herself in, but the soldiers below had figured out where they were. One of them fired toward her, and the blue blast of magic slammed into the gutter inches from her hand. Fear gave her strength, and she hauled herself up, rolling onto the rooftop but bumping into something. She yanked out her pistol.

Two soldiers lay unmoving on the flat roof as the captain faced off against two more. They'd closed to grappling range, and daggers glinted as they tried to flank her. With a clear view of the one on the left, Tezi didn't hesitate to shoot.

The magelock buzzed in her hand as it fired, the blue charge hurtling away and slamming into the soldier's side. He tumbled backward, leaving the captain to focus on the last one. With her in the way, Tezi couldn't line up another shot, but it didn't matter. The captain blocked his punches, then barreled into him, hooking an upper cut into his abdomen, then head-butting him when he pitched forward. When he stumbled back, she spun a side kick into his gut.

His weapon tumbled away, and she kicked it and three others off the roof.

"You didn't leave any for me, Captain?" Sasko had joined them, staying in a low crouch—the men in the street knew exactly where they were and kept firing, blowing away the eaves and gutters.

"Go upstairs!" someone yelled. "They're up there!"

A boom came from inside the curio shop. A *bomb*?

The captain waved for Tezi and Sasko to follow her, then ran and climbed to the roof of a three-story building abutting the curio shop. Fortunately, there weren't any more soldiers waiting up there. Their group sprinted across it to the next building and crossed three more rooftops before they had to spring across an eight-foot alley to the next set of buildings.

Tezi might have hesitated at the jump, but the soldiers who'd survived that explosion were climbing from the balcony to the rooftop of the curio shop. Only the varying heights of the buildings kept their trio from being targeted, but shouts promised the men were giving chase.

Fear and elation mingled in Tezi's chest as she made the jump. Thankfully, the building was lower, and her momentum got her across the gap. The captain and Sasko waited to make sure she made it, then sprinted off again.

After another block, their group had to descend, but the captain paused and looked back. Smoke wafted from the roof of the curio shop, more than the canister they'd thrown could have accounted for.

Regret darkened her eyes, but she didn't say anything. She jerked her head for Tezi and Sasko to follow, and they skimmed down the side of the building and ran off into the city. Hopefully, there would be time to get *out* of the city. Tezi worried that if a mage had tracked them to the curio shop, he could track them back to the docks and the rest of the company.

11

"Mother!" Jak forgot that he was too old for hugs and hugged her when she descended into the cell again. "Are you all right?"

"For now." She hugged him back. "But the ship may be about to be—"

Something jolted the vessel, tilting the deck and sending them tumbling against the wall.

"—attacked," she finished grimly.

"By who?"

"Another mageship. I only saw it in the distance. I don't know which king sent it. We *should* be back over Uthari's dominion by now. You wouldn't think anyone would dare attack his ship in his kingdom."

Jak closed his eyes and envisioned a map of the Forked Sea, with the continent of Bakura and its Dragon Perch Islands to the east and his homeland of Agorval to the west. King Uthari claimed most of Agorval for his kingdom—including Jak's home city of Sprungtown on the other side of the Sawtooth Mountains—but the boundaries extended well out over the sea. Assuming the mageships flew as fast as Jak believed they did, they should be most of the way across the water and into Uthari's territory by now.

"Well, the Dragon Perch Islands are in *Zaruk's* kingdom," Jak said. "He might have found out we located the artifact. And want it back."

Another jolt rocked the ship. Jak put out a hand, thinking to steady his mother, but she'd already sat cross-legged on the deck and pulled out a tin he didn't recognize and a bar of something. In the shadows, he couldn't tell what. He hoped it was food since the guards hadn't deigned to deliver anything but a jug of water to their cell.

"Are you making snacks? Because my stomach has been growling. Our captors are rudely inadequate when it comes to prisoner care."

"I agree, but it might be a while. We're getting out of here."

"Oh? What are you making? A bomb?"

"Nothing so exciting. And this may not be the best time to try to employ this, but..." Mother looked up at the grate, with the guard's boots still in sight, and lowered her voice. "I'm hoping this attack proves tumultuous and all hands are called upon to help defend the ship."

Jak didn't hear anything like an alarm gong, but distant clangs sounded, followed by shouted orders. He couldn't tell if Malek, Tonovan, or some underling was giving them. Thuds reverberated from above—soldiers running down the corridor. The boots above their grate disappeared from sight.

"See if you can make a lasso or some kind of loop on a string," Mother said as she mixed ingredients in the shadows.

String? Where was he supposed to find string? And what did she have in mind? For that matter, what was she making? The air smelled of soap and crushed flower petals, not exactly odors that he associated with explosives.

"How long of a string?" Jak bent over and poked his bootlaces, mentally guessing at their length.

"Several feet. We'll need to be able to hook it over that lever on the wall... while hanging from the grate."

"You're more athletic than I realized."

"I'm hoping *you're* the athletic one."

"When you said *we*, I thought we'd be magically spider-walking up the wall together."

"I'll try, but I may not be strong enough. Tighten the laces on your boots."

"Uh." He'd been about to make her lasso out of his laces, but it sounded like he would need them for climbing up the wall—somehow. "Right."

He carefully set aside his hat and the drawing tools in his pockets, then tugged his shirt over his head. Though the rocking deck made it a challenge, he tore the shirt into even strips to tie together. There weren't explosions and cannonballs, as there would have been in a sea battle among terrene humans, but *something* was striking the ship.

If this flying boat took enough damage, would it crash? Jak had no idea how high they were, but he was positive they would die if they plummeted down from their elevation, whether they hit land or water.

"You've made a lasso?" Mother asked after a few minutes.

"A rope with a loop on the end." Jak held up the strips of fabric he'd tied together to make a good ten feet of rope, maybe more. He hoped it would be strong enough for what they needed. He couldn't imagine it supporting his weight if they tried to climb up it, nor would there be any way to hook it over the grate. "A lasso would have been ambitious to make out of my shirt."

"Tie something in the middle of the loop that can act as weight."

"You act as if I have a supply cabinet in the corner over here."

"I know you've got a compass and caliper in your pockets."

"You want me to hurl my *map-making* tools against the wall?"

"To facilitate our escape from torture and death? Yes, I do."

"I'm already half-naked," he grumbled but complied, telling himself the caliper was sturdy and that he could get it back if this worked. "I hope there are at least cute girls up there who'll admire me running around shirtless."

"The cute girls are busy," Mother said, her voice without humor.

That made him wonder what had happened when she'd been questioned.

"Give me your hands and boots," his mother said before he could decide if he wanted to ask. "I've made a compound that will stick you to the wall. Also the rope and the grate. Be careful."

"You made glue?" Jak rubbed his fingers together. "You made really *strong* glue?"

"Hopefully. I've only made molds with yargo before, but I cut back on the amount of water I put in, and it feels quite sticky."

"Supporting-our-body-weight sticky?" He jammed his tools back into his trouser pockets and put his hat back on.

"The natives of Gora Gorak use yargo glue to help them climb coconut trees."

"The *pygmies* of Gora Gorak? Aren't they all four feet tall and eighty pounds?"

"Some are five feet tall and ninety pounds."

"That's a huge difference."

"It's good that we haven't eaten for a while. Hands and boots, please."

"Isn't it a bad idea to make a dangerous climb when you're famished?"

"We can do it," she said with grim determination.

Jak hoped he was athletic enough—*acrobatic* enough—to pull this off. He looped his rope around his shoulders a few times as she slathered her glue on the bottoms of his boots. After that, she smeared cold, moist, and extremely sticky and gritty stuff over his palms and fingertips.

"I'll go first to test it, since I'm lighter." As she took a step, a ripping sound came from the deck.

Jak didn't understand it until he stood up and tried to move. His boot stuck, and it took effort to pull it free. Mother started up the wall like a spider.

"It's working for me." She paused a few feet up. "How about you?"

"Uh." More soft rips came from his boots as he moved to the wall, then planted as much of the sole as he could on it and still climb effectively. The first time he pulled his hand free, he grunted in pain. It *was* strong glue. And fast-acting. "There's not going to be any skin left on my fingertips by the time we get up there."

"Use your palms more if you can."

"Are they less in need of skin?"

"You don't need them for drawing."

"Thoughtful, Mother. Thanks."

"Just try to move quickly, so it forms only a partial bond. It's a strong adhesive."

"No kidding." It still ripped the skin off his fingertips, but he found he could climb quickly with the stuff on his boots supporting his weight, and he soon passed his mother.

Near the top, the gluey substance started to wear off—he'd left a lot of it on the wall along with his skin—but he managed to lunge up and grip the grate with his left hand. Mother's advice not to do that rang in his mind, but until he managed to throw the loop and pull the lever, it wouldn't matter.

He wiped his right hand on his trousers, almost tearing the cloth, then on the metal grate, rubbing off as much of the substance as he could, then maneuvered the rope off his shoulders. The ship shook, and he would have lost his grip if not for the glue. Fortunately, their guard hadn't returned to see any of this.

Jak pulled himself up until his chin was to the grate, hooked his elbow over one of the bars, and tried to figure out how he was going to throw his loop up and hook the lever. It protruded from the wall only three feet above the deck, but this was one of the most awkward positions he'd been in in his life.

His first attempt to throw the crude rope was a failure since it stuck to his hand and barely went anywhere. "I don't suppose you made something to dissolve this stuff," he muttered, one boot still stuck to the wall and the other dangling free.

"The lubricant might help."

"Let's try it." Jak hadn't expected a response and didn't want to know why she had *that*, but he lowered his hand.

Whether it helped was debatable, but by hooking both elbows over bars, he managed to maneuver better. With his next throw, the caliper clanked against the wall near the lever.

"Hope they're too busy with their battle now to hear that," he muttered and tried again.

By the fifth throw, his arms were going numb from holding his body weight up by his elbows, but his loop hooked the lever.

"There we go," he breathed, then almost let go when a shout came from the entrance to their corridor.

He froze, envisioning punishment for being caught trying to escape. A uniformed man ran past, but he didn't glance down the corridor.

Jak licked his lips and pulled on the rope.

"Wait," his mother whispered. "The grate will slide into the deck. Come set yourself back on the wall before you pull."

"That will make it harder to pull. I've got to fully tug the lever down before the loop falls off." Jak maneuvered his arms off the bars anyway. He didn't know if the grate would whip sideways into the deck hard enough to injure him, but he needed his arms for drawing, so he wouldn't risk it.

Since he'd wiped off some of the glue, he slipped several times before managing to plant himself next to his mother on the wall. More than once, she reached out to press him against it to make sure he didn't fall, but that only made *her* slip.

He tugged on the loop carefully, and the lever inched downward. As it went from pointing upward to downward, the caliper inched toward the end, threatening to slip off. Jak gave a hard jerk. It slid off, but the lever thunked into place at the same time, triggering the grate.

Alarmingly loud clanks sounded as the metal bars slid into the deck. Jak yanked his rope through, not wanting it to get cut in half, but the caliper caught. He snatched it just before it would have hit the side and either broken or jammed the grate.

The motion dislodged one of his boots, and his foot skidded down the wall. Again, his mother grabbed him. She must have had her feet and other hand firmly affixed this time, for she didn't slide down.

"You go up first," she whispered.

Jak lunged up and caught the lip of the opening with both hands. He poked his head out, making sure no soldiers were peering down the corridor, then swung his legs up and rolled onto the solid deck. More skin ripped off as his hands pulled away, and the raw pain had him silently cursing Malek and all the mages on the ship.

Yellow and orange lights flashed beyond the corridor. Was there fighting going on inside the hold? If so, how would they slip past?

Another jolt shook the deck. A startled gasp came from his mother. Jak scrambled back to the edge, worried she'd fallen.

But she was still planted on the wall with the tenacity of a tarantula.

"Give me your hand." Jak lowered his own, blotches of blood oozing from his palms.

She clasped it, and he pulled her up. Once they crouched in the corridor, they separated their hands with the painful ripping of skin.

"I'm not going to be able to recommend your new product to my cartography club," Jak whispered, shaking his raw palms.

"I'll work on refining it in the future." His mother tried ineffectively to wipe the glue off her own hands, then flipped the lever with her knuckles, so the grate closed.

It was unlikely that would keep the mages from realizing they had escaped, but it wouldn't be obvious from a glance. Mother ran down the corridor, peering through other closed grates as she searched for Darv. Jak coiled his rope and followed her, a cool breeze licking at the bare skin of his chest.

His full pockets clanked as he moved. His mother clinked almost as much. If stealth was required at any point in this escape, they would both be in trouble.

But the shouts were farther away now, coming from outside on the mageship's main deck, so he hoped the crew was busy.

"Are there lifeboats?" he whispered.

"Yes." His mother stopped at the last grate in the corridor and peered in. "Up on the main deck."

"Up on the main deck where all the fighting is going on?"

"Likely so. Darv?" she called down.

"Jadora?" came his weak reply.

"Yes. Are you all right?" She pushed the lever, and his grate slid open, the clanks again making Jak wince at their noise. All it would take was one of those soldiers running past to hear that.

"I would be better up there than down here," Darv called up. "Or even more ideal, off this flying ship and down on solid land. Perhaps back at the university in my little house."

"We'd all like that." Mother waved for Jak to lower his rope.

"I don't know if it'll be long enough." He was positive it wouldn't reach all the way to the bottom, twenty feet below, but if Darv could reach up six or seven feet, and Jak could lower it a couple of feet, maybe...

"We'll add more ripped clothing to it if we have to." Mother glanced around, probably hoping the mages had left a coil of rope handily hanging next to the cells.

But if they could lower and lift prisoners with magic, why bother? Jak didn't see anything useful.

"Try to reach this, Professor," he called down, dropping to his stomach so he could lower it further. "There's a caliper on the end."

He said that by way of warning, so Darv wouldn't clunk his head on it, but he received a dry response. "Is that recommended mountaineering equipment these days?"

"Yeah, it's the new trend."

"I can't reach it."

Jak scooted closer to the edge, lowering his arm even farther. His mother sank down on his legs, adding her weight so he wouldn't fall in.

"How about now?" Jak almost suggested that Mother toss some of her glue down, but he doubted the old professor was strong enough to pull himself up a wall.

"It's hard to see in the shadows. Hang on." Darv patted around.

Jak lay the rope against the wall so it would be easier to find, but the ship jolted again. For the first time, a blast came from somewhere under them, striking the bottom of the hull. An ominous snap emanated through the deck under his bare chest.

"Ouch." Darv grunted. "Found it."

Darv put his weight on the rope, and Jak grimaced at the pull on his shoulder. He hoped he and his mother could lift the professor. Darv was slender and light for a man, but Jak's position made it awkward. He squirmed backward, his mother helping him by grabbing his belt and applying a counterweight. They shifted and grunted while they found their feet and got into a better position. At least the leftover tacky glue on their hands helped them keep a grip on the rope.

Grunts and protests came from Darv as they hefted him slowly up, his body thudding against the wall. Jak kept glancing back, half-expecting to find Malek standing there with his arms folded over his chest.

Another blast struck the ship from below, and a second later, something hammered it from above. Jak's stomach lurched as the deck dropped several inches under their feet, momentarily susceptible to gravity and physics.

"I think they're too busy to worry about us right now," his mother whispered. "There must be two ships out there. At least."

"You realize that if we manage to get to a lifeboat and use it," Jak said, "we'll be a target for their enemies, right?"

"Yes. We'll hide out, hope they defeat their enemies, then try to slip away while they're licking their wounds and before they think to check on us." Mother grimaced as one of the shredded pieces of shirt tore and Darv slipped back down a few inches.

A startled gasp came from his cell.

"Sorry, Darv." Jak winced, afraid he would break a few bones— or worse—if he fell back to the bottom. When he'd been building his rope, he hadn't considered pulling someone up with it. He should have. They couldn't leave Darv here while they escaped.

"This rope is feeble and of poor quality," Darv said, his voice near the top. Just a little farther, and they would have him.

"That's because it's made from my clothes."

Darv's knuckles came into view, white as they gripped the rope for dear life. "Perhaps you should purchase a higher quality wardrobe."

"You'll have to take that up with my mother. I'm still an impoverished student."

"Did I not once see you selling caricatures of the faculty in the square for coin?"

Jak nodded for his mother to help Darv up while he kept the rope taut. "Yes, but the pay was poor, and I didn't find the work satisfying."

"I saw the bulbous-nosed substantial-foreheaded version of the dean that you did. That wasn't satisfying?"

With Mother's help, Darv grabbed the lip and pulled himself up.

"Not as satisfying as mapping new territories, no. And I almost got suspended when the *dean* saw that."

"It wasn't a commissioned piece?" Arms shaking, Darv pushed himself to his feet.

"Oh, it was commissioned. But not by him." Jak coiled his rope in case he needed it again.

"Maybe we should save the career discussion for later," Mother murmured, throwing the lever to close the grate.

She waved for them to follow her to the entrance of their corridor, then paused to peer out. Between the distant shouts of the crew and the ominous creaks and snaps from the framework of the ship, Jak doubted anyone would hear them, but he fell silent as he and Darv trailed after her.

As they looked out into the cavernous hold with its floating platforms and maze of railing-free staircases, the biggest blow yet struck the ship. The force pitched them against the wall and into each other. Jak grabbed Darv to keep him from falling to the deck.

A thunderous snap came from the bottom of the hold, and a fissure opened up in the hull under the octopus-orb that powered the ship. Cold wind rushed in through the inches-wide gap, though nothing but dark sky was visible through it.

Jak envisioned it widening and the orb tumbling out through the hole, all of its glowing tentacles slithering out after it. That would leave the ship without the magic that powered it—and kept it in the air.

Two white-uniformed mages ran in from another corridor. Mother backed up, pushing Jak and Darv behind her. Thanks to the light that emanated from most of the walls, there were no shadows to hide in.

But the mages focused on the split in the hull. They descended to a platform directly over it, their gazes downward, their legs spread to brace themselves against sways and jolts from the ship. It was like being on a sea vessel sailing through a storm.

Pale violet light flashed outside the hole, and Jak glimpsed what might have been the hull of another mageship in the distance. How many enemies were out there? Would the *Star Flyer* be captured, so the enemies could board and take the artifact? Or would it be completely destroyed, the portal allowed to crash into the sea with the rest of the vessel?

"They're not looking this way," Mother whispered and pointed at the hole in the hull. Under the mages' power, it was mending itself together. She shifted her finger toward the nearest set of stairs that led upward.

Jak didn't think moving was a good idea—they would be in plain sight if the mages glanced up—but they also couldn't risk loitering in the corridor until a better moment came. A better moment might never come.

Mother crept out, leading the way across the platform and to the stairs. They'd climbed only a few steps, arms spread for balance since there were no railings, when yellow light—or lightning?—flashed outside of the shrinking hole, and raw magical power wrapped around their ship. The air buzzed against Jak's exposed skin and filled his ears like a mosquito's whine. The magical lights inside the hold went out, and the entire ship trembled.

Outside, the yellow light kept flashing, streaks of lightning visible through the hole. It was as if branches of it had wrapped around the entire ship and imprisoned them.

Jak dropped to his knees, gripping the edges of the stairs, afraid he would fall in the dark.

"Where are our shields?" one of the repair mages demanded.

"There are three other ships out there," his partner said. "If not for Malek, we wouldn't have lasted this long."

"The general's supposed to be a master at defenses."

"Just shut your mouth, be glad we're engineers, and help me fix this. Then we've got to get the lights back on and check on the prisoners."

Uh, no need to check on the prisoners. Really.

Mother reached back, groping in the dark to find Jak's shoulder. "Keep climbing," she breathed, her words barely audible.

He patted her hand to let her know he'd heard and reached back, giving the same message to Darv.

In the dark, they crawled up the stairs on their hands and knees. Twenty feet below them, the heads of the mages were visible every time the lightning flashed.

Above, the hatch they were angling for banged open, startling Jak. Where were they supposed to go if someone ran down the steps?

Lightning flashed in the starry sky beyond the hatch, but nobody appeared. Maybe the wind or an attack had knocked it open?

His mother must have thought so, for she kept climbing. The hatch banged back shut, but then the ship jerked, and it opened again. Jak hurried after his mother, and they didn't slow until they reached the hatchway.

The first thing Jak saw made him gape. The portal wasn't flat on the deck anymore. It floated several feet above, tilted as if some invisible sky giant were trying to grab it from one side and lift it off the ship.

Eight red-uniformed mages stood in a ring around the artifact, their arms lifted as they focused on it. On keeping whoever was trying to lift it away from doing so.

Another mageship floated in the air above and to the side of their vessel. Illumination on its deck highlighted numerous mages standing at the railing, mages in green uniforms. Queen Vorsha's people? She was the only one of the kingdom rulers who favored green. But why would she be involved? He'd expected Zaruk's people, assuming he'd objected to the artifact being taken from his kingdom.

More than ten of the green-uniformed mages were lined up along the railing, playing magical tug-of-war with the red-clad mages on the deck. The air crackled with energy, buzzing unpleasantly along Jak's nerves.

Smoke wafted from the enemy ship, and a blast of blue energy shot from one of the *Star Flyer*'s magical artillery weapons. It slammed into Vorsha's ship. That didn't keep more mages from appearing at the railing. They threw down ropes with mundane grappling hooks, guiding them with magic toward the portal. A few hooks missed their target, but several found purchase.

More red-uniformed mage defenders ran into view on the deck. Jak exchanged looks with his mother and Darv, wondering how they were going to sneak out without being noticed.

The defenders hurled fireballs up at the ropes, but they weren't as mundane as Jak had believed. The ropes and hooks glowed slightly as they repelled the fiery blasts.

A screech of metal and flash of white light came from the other side of the portal, up on the forecastle. Malek came into view, battling four green-uniformed mage-warriors who were trying to surround him.

His sword and main-gauche, the blades a startling blue, glowed white, leaving streaks in the night air as he spun and slashed, somehow keeping his opponents from getting behind him. He was so fast that he and the blades were a blur. Jak barely saw the kick that sent one of his attackers sailing over the railing to bounce off the shark figurehead and tumble out of sight. Faint screams floated up as the mage plummeted to his death.

The other mage-warriors launched attacks at Malek, trying to catch him before he turned his focus back to them, but whatever magic struck him barely stirred his hair. He sprang at two enemies, using both weapons offensively, knocking one foe's sword aside so he could stab him in the gut with the main-gauche. At the same time, he defended against an overhead blow from the other, swords clashing as they met. Malek slammed a side kick into his attacker's groin, sending him tumbling back, almost crashing into one of his allies. Malek whirled, bringing his long blade to bear on the man he'd stabbed, and finished him off with a powerful blow that cleaved off his head. It bounced across the deck, tumbled under the railing, and disappeared over the side. The body collapsed, leaving two intruders to face Malek.

They backed away while trading uncertain glances with each other. One yelled up to his ship, to a man aiming a magical harpoon launcher down at the forecastle. Without looking up, Malek pointed his main-gauche in that direction. The energy he hurled wasn't visible, but the harpoon launcher—and the person manning it—exploded into a thousand pieces.

Jak almost swore out loud, mesmerized by the fight. His mother gripped his shoulder, tugging and pointing at one of the lifeboats, and he forced himself to look away. Darv had already scooted out from behind him and was creeping along the wall toward the lifeboat.

Though Jak worried they would never reach it without being noticed, he hurried after Darv, with his mother right behind. The lifeboat was mounted on a wooden lift near the railing. Jak didn't see any levers or a way to launch it. What if magic was required?

Wind gusted across the deck, almost knocking his hat from his head. Jak jammed it down. He'd made it this far without losing it; he wouldn't lose it now.

As they rounded the back of one of the lifeboats, hoping to hide between it and the railing, they almost crashed into a soldier stationed there, the man firing a magelock at the enemies trying to steal the artifact. Mother halted before colliding with him, but he spotted her and spun. As he opened his mouth to yell an alarm, she threw some powder in his face. Startled, he staggered back, but only for a second before he used his power to knock Mother back.

Jak sprang at the soldier, tackling him to the deck. He grabbed his uniform and punched him in the gut, hoping to distract him from using his magic. Snot and tears flowed from the soldier's face —courtesy of Mother's powder—but he growled and thrust upward, power slamming into Jak. Somehow, he managed to keep his grip on the man, so they flew upward several feet together.

The lifeboat kept them from being visible to the mages around the artifact—who were hopefully too focused to notice the fight anyway—and Jak slammed his forehead into the soldier's face as they descended. They landed with a grunt, with Jak on top, his fingers still tangled in the soldier's uniform. The man's head clunked hard against the deck. Desperate to keep him from shouting out, Jak knocked his head back again and again. It kept the soldier from using magic, and finally, even as the roar of battle continued around them, he slumped unconscious.

"I can't believe they didn't take your powders," Jak panted, letting the soldier go.

"From my experience with mages, they could have locked us in their fully-stocked armory and would have still believed we couldn't escape or harm them." Mother rose to her feet, peering over the side of the lifeboat.

Darv stared up at the enemy mageship, gaping as Jak had earlier. Malek had finished his battle on the forecastle and was climbing up one of the ropes toward the higher vessel. The mages at the railing shouted and attacked him with weapons and their own raw power, but he had conjured an invisible bubble around himself, and everything they threw at him bounced off.

As Malek continued his inexorable ascent, one of the mages leaned over the railing with a glowing knife, intending to cut the rope he was climbing. Malek sent a baleful look at him, and before the mage could touch the blade to it, an invisible grip plucked him from the deck and hurled him into the empty sky beside the ship. He plummeted out of sight. A second and a third mage flew overboard before their teammates got some magical shielding of their own up to thwart Malek's grabs. Meanwhile, he kept climbing.

"Get them, Malek!" came a call from the aftercastle.

General Tonovan stood there among soldiers manning magical cannons. Blood flowed from a gash on his face, but his eyes gleamed with inhuman power and determination. He raised his arms, and glittering white energy flowed from his hands. It wrapped around the entire ship, creating a sparkling cocoon around them—a shield?

This was nothing like the rare glimpses of magic Jak had seen in his life, and he had no idea what their capabilities were or what they could create.

"Look." Darv pointed over the railing that they would have to figure out how to launch the lifeboat over.

Two other mageships were flying down there, but their lights had gone dark, save for fires burning on the decks and hulls. Nobody on board seemed to be attacking. Huge holes had been blasted in their sides, and if they'd been sailing vessels, they would have been sinking. As it was, one listed gradually downward. Jak spotted charred bodies on the deck.

"Maybe we can fly out that way," Darv added. "Use the destroyed ships for cover and slip away."

"First, we need to get this boat off the deck without being noticed." Jak pulled himself over the railing of the escape craft.

His mother was already inside the navigation cabin, staying low so nobody would see her through the windows. On the *Star Flyer's* deck, the portal lay flat again. The mages on the other ship were now busy dealing with Malek. He'd reached the top of the climb and vaulted over their railing, battling those who had been trying to steal the artifact. Fortunately, the *Star Flyer's* defenders were riveted to the scene up there—Malek's swords were flashing around again as he tore into the enemy troops—and weren't looking at the lifeboat. Jak began to believe they might actually escape.

He leaned over to help up Darv. As soon as they were all aboard, he joined his mother in the navigation cabin.

"This looks like it frees us from the clamp." She pointed at a lever labeled in a language Jak couldn't read. "The wheel is for steering. What lifts it up and down?"

"Uh, magic?"

"You're very helpful."

"I haven't taken the magical helmsman class at school yet. Maybe they'll offer it in the spring."

"Better get on the wait list. Maybe this one." Mother rested her hand on another lever, this one with a single symbol labeling it. "It says altitude."

"Sounds reasonable."

Some of the light outside diminished, and Jak risked peering out one of the windows. The sparkly shield around the mageship had disappeared. General Tonovan had also disappeared from the top of the aftercastle. Uh oh.

Mother threw one of the levers. A clunk reverberated through the lifeboat. She grimaced at the noise. Jak pulled his head down. If one of the mages had heard that...

"He's coming back," Darv whispered through the hatchway. He knelt on the deck outside of the navigation cabin, staring upward.

Malek stood on the railing of the enemy ship, as if it were solid ground instead of a narrow piece of wood, the entire craft in flames behind him. The wind whipped at his jacket, and his blades glowed as he surveyed the *Star Flyer* and the ships that had dared assault it. If there was anyone left to attack him, Malek clearly wasn't worried about it.

Jak had the eerie feeling of being looked down upon by a god and for the first time understood why humans in primitive societies —and some in his own city—worshipped the mages and wizards as if they *were* gods. How would mankind—mundane non-magic-wielding mankind—ever find a way out from under their power?

"I wish we'd gotten up here a minute earlier," Mother whispered, her hand on the altitude lever. "Now we'll have to wait until Malek comes back and they all—hopefully—go inside to help with repairs."

"I doubt the general or Malek do anything so piddling as filling cracks and painting char marks," Jak muttered, also wondering how they would manage to slip out now.

"Maybe they'll be tired after battle and need a nap."

That seemed vaguely plausible. Jak had read that drawing upon one's magic was draining. Maybe Malek would pass out as soon as he got back. It had been a big battle, after all. Jak imagined mages plopped down all over the ship, snoring heartily.

Malek crouched and sprang, and Jak caught himself gaping again. That other ship was fifty or sixty feet above theirs.

Malek dropped down at the speed of gravity, not slowing himself even if it was in his power to do so, and landed on the deck in a deep crouch. Jak sank lower under the window. What kind of human being could do that without breaking his legs? Maybe the stories about the zidarr were true, that they weren't fully human anymore, that magic infused their bodies, flowing through their veins where blood had once been.

A startled squawk came from Darv. Jak whirled and lifted a hand, about to hiss at him to stay quiet, but he let his hand fall.

Malek had sprung into the lifeboat and stood next to Darv, gazing down at him and then looking into navigation at Jak and his mother. She slumped, letting her hand fall from the lever. Malek had sheathed his fearsome weapons, but that didn't make him look any less dangerous.

"This is not where I left you," he stated, his tone dry. He didn't sound tired or even out of breath, and Jak judged the chances of him tipping over and falling asleep were microscopic.

Ignoring Darv, Malek strode toward them. Mother stood up, no longer worrying about hiding. In case it made a difference, Jak stood at her shoulder. They would face their fate together.

"The journal wasn't as comprehensive as I'd hoped. We'll need your assistance in getting the portal operational." Malek lifted a hand, and the flaps over Mother's pockets rose. Tins, vials, a bar of soap, and small field tools floated out, settling onto a console beside him.

Mother's fingers twitched, as if she meant to snatch them back, but Malek's cool gaze kept her from trying.

"And you haven't yet told me where the key is." Malek looked at Jak, then upward to the spot on his hat where his gold medallion had once been. "But you will," he finished softly.

General Tonovan was waiting on deck. Jak closed his eyes. All this had been for nothing.

12

As Jadora gazed stonily forward, the wind whipped at strands of hair that had slipped free from her braid. She was back where she'd been two hours ago, standing on the deck beside the portal, beside the keyhole in the portal, but now Jak and Darv were with her, and she worried she'd only made things worse. Darv slumped against the artifact, looking miserable.

Before, Malek had only been questioning her, and he'd been alone while Tonovan was in his pleasure palace being serviced. Now, they were both out here glowering at her. No, that wasn't quite right. Tonovan was glowering—he'd curled an indignant lip and snatched back his soap when Malek had brought her stash out and set it on the portal—but Malek didn't even seem annoyed that they'd tried to escape.

Tonovan, dark bags under his eyes and the side of his face coated with drying blood, appeared exhausted from his battle. Other than a couple of cuts to his jacket and a nick on the back of his hand, Malek looked little different than he had an hour ago. He gazed thoughtfully at Jadora as Tonovan demanded to know how they'd gotten out. She didn't appreciate the scrutiny from either of them.

"It must have been a malfunction with your magic," Jak replied when Jadora didn't. She was trying to think of how she could avoid babbling everything about the medallion—and who had it—as soon as they applied force. "The grates just sprang open," he added.

"The grates aren't magical," Tonovan snapped.

"Really? That's fascinating." Jak looked at Jadora and Darv. "Isn't it fascinating?"

"Fascinating," Darv murmured, though his heart wasn't in the sarcasm or defiance or whatever Jak was trying. He looked like he wanted to disappear.

Jadora wished she *could* make him disappear. Both of them. Back to the university or someplace else safe.

"How did you climb out after the grates sprang open?" Tonovan asked.

Jadora opened her mouth to answer, but Jak spoke first.

"We're very good climbers. Archaeologists get all sorts of practice climbing at dig sites. The interesting things are always hidden down latrine shafts."

Neither Tonovan nor Malek appeared to appreciate his humor.

Jadora leaned her shoulder against his. "Why don't you let me answer the questions?"

"Sure. You are the expert in latrine shafts." He forced a quick smile.

She could tell he was nervous and gripped his arm, trying to reassure him, though she doubted she had that power.

"Please put my colleagues back in their cells." Jadora addressed Malek instead of Tonovan, judging him the more reasonable of the two. "They know less than I do."

"They don't know how they climbed out of their own cells?" Malek asked.

"I assume there are other more pressing questions you have in mind." Not that she wanted to talk about the medallion, but if she implied she would be more open about it if they left Jak and Darv alone...

Malek stepped closer to her, startling her and making her step back. She bumped against the unyielding metal of the portal and was stuck. She remembered the eerie feeling of having her pocket flaps magically unfastened and her belongings floated out of them. He reached for her wrist, not her pockets, though he held her gaze with his.

"What are you doing?" Jak bristled and stepped closer but halted as if he'd run into a wall. A magical wall.

Jadora started to jerk her arm back, but there was nowhere for her to go, no way to fight these people. Malek gripped her wrist, firmly but not painfully, and turned her palm upward. He eyed her raw skin and rubbed his thumb on the remains of the crusted glue that she'd made. A tingle of fear ran through her, but he did nothing else.

"Interesting." Malek released her and stepped toward the keyhole, using his magic to force Jak to step out of the way.

"What is?" Tonovan asked.

But Malek didn't share his guess about how they'd escaped. He rested a hand on the artifact, next to the small circular hole, and looked at Tonovan. "This is. I believe it's a keyhole and that the portal won't activate without the key."

"Do they have it? You clearly didn't search them when you brought them aboard." Tonovan waved at Jadora's belongings resting in a pile on the artifact, as if it were some hallway table meant to hold knickknacks.

"I sensed nothing magical about their belongings." The way Malek said it suggested that he wasn't concerned about anything that wasn't magical. "And I had them empty their pockets back on the beach. You saw that. There wasn't a key."

"Do they know where it is?" Tonovan focused on Jadora. "Tell us where it is."

The words contained a magical coercion, and she almost blurted out the answer before she caught herself.

Malek gazed at the side of her face, no doubt trying to read her mind. She did her best to blank her thoughts. The tendons in Jak's neck stood out as he fought against the magic holding him in place. Darv eyed Malek's back, looking wistful, but he didn't have a weapon, and she prayed he wouldn't try anything even if he did.

"Where is it?" Tonovan growled, focusing harder on her.

"I... don't know." True. She had no idea where it was now.

Tonovan glared even harder, but then he backed off, exhaling a weary breath.

"Careful, General," Malek said mildly. "At your age, you might give yourself an aneurism."

"Hilarious." Tonovan turned his scowl on him. "You're only feeling perky because it's less work attacking a few people than defending against the combined might of three mageships."

"Yes, my task was a simple one."

Jadora, who'd seen him battling multiple opponents and climbing up to deal with the other ship while being fired at by half of its crew, might have snorted at the statement, but Malek was looking at her again. Not a glare but that same mild expression. She didn't *feel* him rooting around in her thoughts, but she was sure he was.

She looked toward the stars, focusing on them and wondering if she would ever find a way home. She occupied her thoughts with contemplating what she would do if she returned, the relaxing teas she would pick up from her herbalist friend in the market square. She *needed* relaxing teas now.

Malek snorted, no doubt knowing exactly what she was doing.

"You'll tell us one way or another," he said softly. "Work with us. As I said before, there's no reason for you to choose to be our enemies. Whether you like it or not, we all live under Uthari's rule, but also under his protection. It's better to work with him than against him. Where is the key?"

His tone wasn't angry or demanding but perfectly reasonable. That almost made it easy to believe he was right, that she should go along with him, but to hand over both pieces of the artifact to him and his loathsome ruler... Loran would have sacrificed himself before doing that.

"This is taking forever," Tonovan snapped. "Just threaten the boy. Or her friend. He's on the verge of collapsing anyway. Kill one of them if she doesn't cooperate."

Fear shot through Jadora, and she clenched her eyes shut. She couldn't let that happen.

"That's not necessary," Malek said. "She'll tell me."

"Uh huh. Your reason and your sex appeal are working wonders on her now." Tonovan strode forward.

Jak tensed, but Malek's magic still held him. Tonovan ignored him and focused on Darv, an eager light brightening his previously weary eyes. In that instant, Jadora knew that he would *enjoy* killing one of them.

She lunged forward, lifting her hands to intercept him, but two soldiers behind Tonovan pointed weapons at her. Someone's magic—she didn't even know whose—pinned her from all sides, leaving her as immobile as Jak. Unimpeded, Tonovan grabbed Darv, jerking him upright. Darv cried out, his body stiffening and his head jerking back as some new magic tormented him.

"No!" Jadora strained uselessly. Her mouth was all that she could move. "Stop. I'll cooperate. I already told you I would if you put them back in their cells."

"Stop, Tonovan," Malek said, his voice cold now.

Tonovan didn't, and Darv screamed, his face contorting with pain.

"The mercenaries," Jadora blurted. "They have it. I gave it to them. Stop hurting him."

He didn't until Malek stepped toward him and used his magic to break Tonovan's hold. When Tonovan released him, Darv dropped to his knees.

"Don't you *dare* use your magic on me, zidarr," Tonovan snarled at Malek.

"When I give you an order," Malek said, "you will follow it."

"You don't have any seniority over me."

"No, but I am more powerful than you, and Uthari has a dozen others he can promote into your place."

Whoever had been holding Jadora released her. She rushed over and dropped down beside Darv, wrapping an arm around his shoulders.

"I'm so sorry," she whispered to him.

Tonovan pointed a finger at Malek's chest. "I'll tell him you said that, that you *threatened* me. I've proven my worth in battle to him again and again, leading thousands of troops, not merely skulking in the night, some cowardly assassin with a knife."

"You think I'm a coward?" Malek's dark eyes were like chips of obsidian. "Then duel me. We'll settle this here and now."

Alarm flashed across Tonovan's face, and he stepped back. "Yes, let's fight in front of our prisoners. An excellent idea."

"Duel me to the death, or do not call me a coward, not when you fear to face me."

Darv barely responded to Jadora's hug. He was wheezing. Concern for him brought tears to her eyes. These people were awful. How could she get Jak and Darv out of this situation?

"Screw you, Malek," Tonovan said.

"I'm sure you would, given the chance. There's nothing you won't screw."

Fury reddened Tonovan's face, but he was done trading insults with Malek. "This is idiotic. Let's just retrieve this key and take the artifact back to Utharika. If we stay out here over the sea, we'll be attacked by someone else who thinks they can get it before we're behind the city's protected walls."

"True," Malek said. "Now that it's no longer buried, it gives off a powerful magical signature. I wouldn't be surprised if every mage within five hundred miles can sense it."

"And the word has clearly gotten out about what it is or at least that it's a potential game changer among the kings. They don't want Uthari to have it."

"We'll be home in three hundred miles if we hold our current course." Malek gripped his chin, eyeing the starry sky behind them. He seemed to have lost all of his irritation with Tonovan. The general's face was still flushed and angry, and Jadora had no doubt that he would shove Malek overboard if he ever got the opportunity. "I'll contact the artifact-hunters guild in Perchver. Some of them won't be afraid to face mercenaries, and for a fee, one will bring it to us. It'll probably be easy for one of them to get the key. I trust the mercenaries don't know the value of what they have."

Malek looked at Jadora. She glared at him, but if he wanted clarification, she would give it. She couldn't risk them hurting Darv further.

"No," Malek said, finding the answer in her mind without her help. "They only know that you asked them to keep it until you meet again."

Something that would likely never happen. Jadora stared down at the deck, weariness overtaking her. The fantasy of shopping for tea and returning home to her normal life had little hope of ever coming true.

"Go contact him," Tonovan said. "You're right that we'll keep being attacked if we go back to Zaruk's kingdom for it, but you know Uthari won't be happy until he has the complete artifact set."

"We'll get it." Malek waved two of the soldiers to come forward. "Return them to their cells with food and water." He eyed Jak. "And a shirt."

"Yes, my lord."

Malek jogged toward one of the hatches leading belowdecks. Jadora, wanting to be out from under Tonovan's unbalanced eye, didn't hesitate to rise to her feet and help Darv up beside her.

Jak gasped as he was finally released from the frigid hold that had locked him in place. He scowled at Tonovan, though Jadora didn't know if he'd been responsible.

"Don't start anything," she whispered, nodding for him to help Darv from his other side.

"I'm sorry for being a burden," Darv whispered, anguish in his eyes.

"You're not," Jadora said, though she deeply regretted that he was along with them.

"Now they'll be after those women," Darv said.

Something else that Jadora felt guilty about. She'd heard about the artifact-hunters guild. Most of them were thieves, and some even murdered to make their acquisitions. If even one member of Thorn Company was killed because of this, it would be Jadora's fault.

"We'll figure something out," she said as they walked across the deck after the soldiers. The words sounded inane to her ears— they'd lost their best chance to escape—but she hoped they comforted Darv.

"I wish they'd dueled and killed each other," Jak muttered. "Though I'm sure Malek would have killed that stupid general."

"What did you say?" Tonovan boomed after them.

"Nothing." Jadora smacked Jak on the back, half to berate him and half to hurry him along.

Jak kept his mouth shut, but he must have been thinking unsavory thoughts, for magic halted their group once again, forming a wall in front of them. Tonovan strode after them. The two soldiers frowned, turning around.

"He's sorry." Jadora lifted an apologetic hand, though she also wished the two men had dueled and that Malek *had* killed Tonovan.

"*I* could beat that bastard in a duel." Tonovan stopped in front of them, turning his glower on Jadora instead of Jak. Anger raged in his eyes.

She had to learn to keep her *own* thoughts under control around these people. What if he took his frustrations with Malek out on them?

"Yes, of course," Jadora made herself say in her most simpering tone, blanking her mind. "I apologize. I should not have thought disrespectful thoughts."

Jak shot her an incredulous look, but when she shook her head in warning, he didn't say anything.

"That you powerless peons even look me in the eyes is ludicrous." Tonovan jerked his hand up, and the same magic that had knocked them to their knees on the beach crushed them down again.

Darv remained on his feet—too weak a threat for Tonovan to worry about? Jadora hoped so. She willed him to get off the deck and out of Tonovan's sight.

"That you hesitated to answer our questions," Tonovan continued, working himself up to a lather, "that you thought to defy your superiors... you *will* be punished."

The magical pressure wrapped around Jadora grew tighter and tighter, pain assaulting her from every nerve. Tears sprang to her eyes.

Next to her, Jak dropped to his hands and knees, his body shaking. Anger on her son's behalf raged through her, but she was powerless to do anything.

"Go get Malek," one of the soldiers whispered, the words barely reaching Jadora's ears.

The other soldier jogged through the same hatch he'd gone through earlier.

Dare she hope it would be in time? Or that Malek would care enough to stop this? She could barely draw a breath. Blackness throbbed at the edge of her vision. If she fell unconscious, would Tonovan leave her alone?

"Stop it," came a cry from the side, not Malek but Darv.

"No!" Jadora tried to yell, to warn him to stay out of it, but she couldn't get the air to force the cry out.

She tipped onto her side, her shoulder banging the deck. She barely felt it. What did a bump matter when pain such as she'd never known tore through her body like fire burning inside her nerves?

Darv grabbed a dagger from the remaining soldier and ran toward Tonovan.

Again, Jadora tried to scream *no*, to dissuade him from the suicidal path, but he raised the knife, trying to kill her tormentor.

Tonovan flicked a finger. Darv flew through the air, slamming into the wall by the hatch with a thunderous snapping of bone. He crumpled to the deck, the knife falling from his lifeless fingers.

The hatch slammed open, and the power gripping Jadora, the pain coursing through her veins, disappeared. But she couldn't feel any relief as Malek charged out, only horror. Hot tears streaked sideways down her cheeks as she stared at Darv, his neck broken, his life already gone.

"What's going on?" Malek demanded. Too late.

Five seconds too late.

"Your wayward prisoners attacked me," Tonovan snarled, no remorse in his voice. The bastard had enjoyed that. She knew he had. "That's what happens when you're lenient. And who let that idiot have a knife?"

Malek looked at Darv's body, the knife, and the soldier who was missing it. The man patted his empty sheath and muttered, "Sorry."

"Take those two to their cells," Malek told the soldiers, then gripped Tonovan's shoulder and turned him toward another hatch. "You and I need to have a talk with Uthari."

"Of course," Tonovan said calmly, walking away with him.

As the soldier lifted Jadora from the deck—she couldn't have forced her rubbery legs to move even if she'd wanted to—Tonovan looked over his shoulder at her.

The price for defying your superiors is great, he spoke into her mind. *Do not forget it.*

Smoke wafted from the destroyed windows and charred and broken facade of the curio shop. The balcony had been blasted by magelocks, leaving most of it in pieces on the sooty sandstone below. During the battle, and once he was sure Thorn Company was away, Sorath had blown out the back wall to escape. He always kept weapons—and explosives—on him. Old habits died hard.

It was after midnight now. He'd waited hours to return to what had been his home for the last year—the last five years if he counted from the purchase date. But he'd only stopped by infrequently when he'd been leading Fang and Talon. Commanders of mercenary companies didn't have the leisure to take long periods of leave. But these days... he had too much leisure. Too much time to think.

He crouched in the shadows of an alley across the way. Originally, he'd planned to go in through the hole in the back, but he'd heard whispers and grunts. Did they belong to random looters searching for valuables or soldiers that had been left behind to watch the place?

Sorath didn't know whose soldiers they were, since they hadn't been courteous enough to wear uniforms, but he recognized military men when he battled them. They hadn't been the city enforcers.

He rubbed his shoulder and flexed muscles that had stiffened in the hours since the battle. That he'd suffered nothing worse than stiff muscles was a miracle, since he'd stayed and fought far longer than wise, trying to buy time for Captain Ferroki's team to escape. Strange that he'd never questioned the need to do that. In the field, they'd been enemies more often than allies, their units hired by opposing forces, but he'd always admired the scrappy company of female soldiers. They took a lot of flak from the other units, most all-male or predominantly-male, but they still found work and performed all the duties asked of them. And Ferroki had always been serene, even pleasant, to be around. An unusual quality in a mercenary leader.

It had surprised him when she'd walked in, asking for his opinion, but it shouldn't have. If anyone could locate him, her team could, and she'd never been too proud to ask for help. And a mercenary turned treasure-acquisitions expert had been the perfect person to ask about that medallion. Even before switching careers, he'd had a fondness for the ancient world and the relics and clues it had left behind.

Still, if Ferroki could find him, others could. Maybe he hadn't given up his old name and ways as thoroughly as he'd thought he had. He no longer glared warningly when soldiers didn't address him as *colonel* or *sir*, but he'd caught himself almost introducing himself as Sorath more than once. His father had given him the name when he'd been born, and even though Vorzaz sounded more like a treasure hunter and occasional scrivener, he'd struggled to make it feel right for him.

He let his hand stray to his pocket, needing the reassurance that his *scrivenings* were still with him. Half memoir, half distillation of all the military wisdom and strategies he'd learned over the years, he wanted it left behind in the world after he was gone, if only as a warning for other mercenary commanders.

The clank of something dropping filtered out of the building, and Sorath scowled, annoyed at the idea of thieves further ransacking the place. Hadn't the day's carnage been enough? True, he'd purchased the shop from the old owner with most of the knickknacks already inside, and they held no deep personal value to him, but it was the principle.

He circled to the back and approached the hole in the wall, avoiding pieces of plaster and brick on the ground. Though he'd managed to keep his weapons through the skirmish, he picked up a brick. He didn't want to kill simple thieves, probably kids trying to find valuables that they could trade for food.

Only two people were inside, clothed in dark rags as they plucked through the wreckage.

"Get out of my shop," Sorath ordered.

One sprinted for the front doorway—the door had been ripped off the hinges—but the other spun toward him with a magelock pistol in hand. Though surprised at the weapon, Sorath threw his brick and sprang back out of sight. The weapon went off, blue light flashing in the dark a second before the thief yelped, the brick striking home. His magelock clattered to the floor.

The blast from the weapon drilled a hole in the building behind the curio shop, and someone farther down the block yelled an order to *knock it off*.

Sorath charged back inside, sprinting so the thief didn't have time to grab his weapon again. But he didn't try. The kid scampered back, half-tripping over the stairway railing that had fallen to the floor, and flailed.

Sorath could have caught him but didn't bother. He let the kid regain his balance and sprint away. What remained here wasn't worth fighting for, and Sorath dared not stick around to rebuild. Too much attention had been brought to the place.

That saddened him, but he couldn't bring himself to feel angry with Ferroki for coming to him for help. He would find another hideout. He'd only returned because his favorite pen was in the desk drawer—if it hadn't been stolen. It was magical and never ran out of ink. He'd grown partial to it.

The charred floorboards on the stairs gave way when he put his weight on them, and he ended up jumping and grabbing the edge of the landing. His pick slipped, and he dangled from his hand. Part of the landing crumbled but not enough to dislodge him, and he thunked the pick down again, lodging it in a board this time. Growling, he pulled himself up, hating the reminder of how much harder everything was these days with one hand instead of two.

Inside the apartment, the desk was on its side, the drawers torn open. He sighed, certain the pen had been stolen, but it had skidded under a bookcase that had tipped over, all of the tomes fallen out—no thieves had bothered to take *those*. He found it under the book pile.

"Hah." He held it up in triumph, though in the dark, he could barely see it. "Now I can—"

The pulsing of a familiar artifact carved from dylorian crystal emanated softly from under the pile of books. He grunted, surprised the device hadn't been taken. Did he care about whatever message was coming in on the communications node? Most likely, it was an offer of work for someone in the artifact-hunters guild. Once, wizards, mages, and the handfuls of terrene humans with enough wealth to hire mercenaries had sent offers of employment to Fang and Talon over the magical device, but the unit was no more, and none of those people should know Sorath was alive.

Though after today... it was possible that had changed. He was certain those soldiers had come after Thorn Company and the medallion rather than him, but more than a few of them had survived and seen his face. They might have reported his existence and whereabouts.

"Better check it." He pushed aside books, and the glow of the magical device washed the sooty walls in orange light.

When he rested his hand atop the orb on its wooden pedestal, a conical beam of light shot upward. The face and shoulders of a man appeared in the beam, wavering and semi-transparent. Despite that, Sorath had no trouble identifying the zidarr, and that alarmed him. If King Uthari's Malek was messaging him... nothing good could come of that.

Could Uthari have learned that he and his fellow kings hadn't quite finished the job when they'd conspired to have Sorath's unit destroyed and Sorath killed?

"Members of the artifact-hunters guild," Malek said, and Sorath let out a breath he hadn't realized he'd been holding. It was generic, not addressed specifically to him. "I am offering a reward of a thousand gold oroni to whomever delivers an artifact that looks like this to me."

A mirror image of the dragon-headed medallion Ferroki had brought replaced Malek's head in the beam, and concern hollowed Sorath's stomach. With a reward like that, every artifact hunter in the kingdom—in *many* kingdoms—would be searching for it. The guild had some talented people in it, people very good at finding missing treasures. And most of them didn't mind taking down those who were holding the treasures at the time.

Sorath shook his head. Even if Ferroki had left Perchver—she better have after that attack—and she managed to avoid being found by artifact hunters, Malek himself would come for that medallion. Likely, he was busy with something else—like that portal—and that was the only reason he hadn't already.

Sorath swore as the image and the orange light faded, leaving him in darkness again.

Did he need to warn Ferroki? After today, she had to know that people were after that thing, even if she didn't know who. And Sorath didn't owe her anything. If anything, she owed him for keeping those soldiers busy. This wasn't his fight, but... he'd spent all of his adult life looking out for soldiers. The people in his own unit, for the most part, but he'd always believed in honor among warriors, even if they were under someone else's command.

He had to leave the city anyway—after this mess, it wouldn't be safe for him to stick around—so maybe he would find out which way her company had gone and head that way himself. If he passed her on the road, he could deliver the warning, and then head to a safe new place to lie low for a while.

Sorath eyed the communications node. "Why do I have a feeling I'm going to regret this?"

13

After the mageship landed, a few faint clanks and a shiver the only indicators that they'd docked somewhere, Malek was the one to come for them.

Jak, his shredded shirt replaced by a beige tunic the soldiers had brought with their food, glowered up at Malek, but inside, he was relieved it wasn't Tonovan. Seeing that bastard kill Darv while Jak had been crumpled on the deck and powerless to help had been the most infuriating and distressing experience of his life. And he was worried for his mother, who'd barely said a word since it happened.

She sat on the floor, her elbows on her knees and her head in her hands. She didn't look up when the grate clanked aside, only grunting in annoyance when Malek used his power to lift them out of their cell.

Jak was angry and anguished at losing Darv, but he couldn't imagine how much worse it had been for his mother. She'd known him for decades, longer than Jak had been alive. He wished there was a way to help her, but he couldn't imagine their fate would get better from here.

When they landed in the corridor, only Malek stood in front of them, his face impassive. What did he care that a prisoner had been killed? Especially when Tonovan had made it seem like Darv had been trying to kill him. Maybe he *had* been, but Tonovan had deserved it for torturing them half to death. And Jak wasn't convinced that Tonovan hadn't masterminded all that, maybe even magically putting the dagger into Darv's hands, so he could kill the prisoner without worrying about retaliation from Malek.

"I apologize for the death of your comrade," Malek stated.

Mother looked numbly at him and didn't respond. Jak was surprised he'd bothered apologizing, however stiffly; he had a hard time believing a zidarr cared one way or another about the deaths of *powerless peons*, as Tonovan had called them.

"Come," Malek said when neither of them responded. "King Uthari requires your presence."

"Fantastic," Jak muttered.

The king was probably even more of a megalomaniacal ass than Tonovan. Would he also force them to their knees and torture them to show off how powerful he was?

Malek opened his mouth slightly, as if he meant to say something else, but he turned around without speaking and led the way out of the corridor. Jak walked next to Mother in case she needed support. Her gait was wooden, like a clockwork soldier winding down. She looked back toward the cell Darv had once been in, her eyes haunted.

In that moment, Jak resolved that he would get them out of this situation. They would escape the sky city, get back to land, and then... then he wasn't sure. They might have to hide out for the rest of their lives, or at least long enough for the mages to forget about them, but that was possible. He'd heard of other refugees doing it.

Two soldiers waited on the platform, and they fell in behind

Jak and his mother as they followed Malek. Did he truly think either of them needed an escort or could put up a fight here?

Outside, the daylight was blinding after the darkness of their cell, and Jak stumbled over the lip of the hatch as he stepped out. Mother caught him by the elbow. It might have been instinct, but at least he knew she wasn't in complete shock. If they were going to escape, it would take both of them working together to come up with something clever.

Jak recovered but paused after only a step outside and stared around.

The mageship was anchored—if that was the right term for it —at an open air dock outside the pale yellow walls of Uthari's sky city, a place Jak had only seen pictures of in books. The wall rose forty or fifty feet high and stretched for a mile or more in each direction. Even though he'd known the sky cities had populations of hundreds of thousands, he hadn't imagined anything so vast.

The top of the wall wasn't flat; it undulated like an uneven wave, the style intriguing for its lack of symmetry. He briefly forgot his thoughts of escape as he envisioned drawing whatever buildings and structures lay within the city. Decorative statues of animals, men, and even geographic features from around the world were mounted along the wall, and from the top rose turrets and watchtowers, the windows surprisingly open to the elements. Maybe magic could keep out wind and cold.

"It's gone," Mother mumbled, drawing Jak's attention back to the mageship.

The portal no longer lay on the deck.

"They must have already offloaded it," he said.

"This way." The guards led them toward a surprisingly mundane-looking gangplank.

Malek had paused there to wait for them. How lovely that the great zidarr would personally escort them to his master.

Sighing, Jak led his mother to the gangplank, a six-foot-wide strip that extended from the mageship to a dock, one of dozens in a network of docks that provided berths for everything from mageships as large as the *Star Flyer* to personal yachts to massive barges to contraptions with closed cabins and wings that weren't even vaguely similar to sailing ships. Everything floated, kept aloft by magic. He wondered if the magic ever failed and shipowners came out to the docks in the morning to find that their craft had fallen out of their slots and crashed hundreds of feet below.

As soon as Jak stepped onto the gangplank and saw that *below* to either side, he wobbled, spreading his arms for balance as his entire body clenched with fear. They weren't *hundreds* of feet above the ground, he realized as he stared transfixed, but *thousands*.

The sky city floated above a mountain range—the Sawtooth Mountains, some detached academic part of his brain supplied— with its snow-capped peaks stark against the blue sky. Valleys, fields, and rivers to one side of the mountains were also visible, with clouds throwing shadows on the farmlands. That was the most surreal part. Looking down at shadows thrown by clouds. And the clouds themselves. He'd been vaguely aware of encyclopedia articles describing the sky cities as being above the clouds, but he never would have thought to imagine it looking like this.

Nor would he have imagined that the mages wouldn't have *railings* on any of their docks or gangplanks to keep people from falling off. That was strange given how busy the docks were. Someone could easily be jostled and pitch over the side. Could the mages all *fly* so this was not a problem? Jak had seen Malek levitate the artifact—and levitate *him* in and out of his cell—but he'd had to climb to reach that other mageship, so maybe flying wasn't possible. Even if the mages *could* fly, what about all the terrene humans that labored under their thumbs in these cities?

Even as Jak gaped around, dirty, scruffy workers in farm tunics that fell to their bare knees were unloading cabbages, potatoes, carrots, and other fall crops from a barge docked near the mage-ship. The produce went onto a train of floating carts, while a bored driver sat on a bench at the front of the queue. He alternated reading from a book and barking orders to the workers.

"Tax collection," his mother said, touching Jak's shoulder and nodding for him to keep going. Their guards were shifting weight impatiently behind them. "The mages own the land and allow the farmers to live on and work it. In exchange, half of their crops go to the sky cities."

"I know." Jak started walking again. "I took Sociology and read the textbooks."

"The textbooks have to be approved by the mage councils and tend to describe the system as more equitable than it is. Be glad you were born into a family with an academic charter."

"Are cartographers treated more charitably?" Jak spotted Malek waiting for them on the dock and headed toward him. Presumably, there was no point in fantasizing about sprinting off into the crowd and disappearing. Sentry disks, the same as they had in Sprungtown, floated about, keeping a magical eye on the docks. Jak had a feeling the enforcers, or whatever they had up here, could easily find anyone hiding in their city. "Or will I have to give half of my maps to them?"

"Just half the income you make from selling them." Normally, her tone would have been full of righteous indignation as she described the plight of mundane humans, but Mother seemed too weary—too sad—to speak in anything but a flat tone. "The rules are the same for all; academics just get less dirty following them."

"I get ink all over my fingers, and I can work up a decent stink when I'm drawing vigorously."

Malek's eyebrows rose slightly—despite the crowd, nobody bustled past close to him, so he probably had no trouble listening to their conversation—but he didn't comment. In the sea of red-uniformed soldiers and civilians in flamboyantly colored clothing,

Malek stood out for his simple brown and tan attire—and for the fact that nobody got close to him. No doubt the mages could sense his power and knew exactly what and who he was—and didn't want to risk irking him.

Tonovan was the one Jak worried more about irking. Thankfully, he wasn't in sight.

They headed toward a grassy peninsula in front of a great gate in the wall. The grass-covered earth surprised Jak, as did the perfectly ordinary cobblestone road leading across it and into the city. The lawn extended for a couple dozen yards all along the base of the long wall. It was as if the city were built on actual ground, an island in the sky.

Beside the road, floating carts waited to take riders to their destinations. Some were driven by people while others waited empty and took off on their own once their passengers boarded. Malek waved for Jak and Mother to board one without a driver, the gilded sides gleaming in the sun. A canopy offered shade for three rows of plush seats covered in jaguar fur.

Malek sat in the back, the two soldiers in the front, and Jak and Mother the middle. The seat conformed to Jak's body, gently supporting his butt and back while inviting him to lean back and relax. To his surprise, a slight warmth emanated from it, stealing any chill the air might have imparted. He'd never sat in a seat so ridiculously comfortable in his life.

"Is this the king's personal vehicle?" he guessed.

His mother, glum eyes toward the open gate in the wall, did not answer.

"One of many," Malek replied.

"Must be nice to have a fleet of cushy heated seats," Jak muttered.

Mother elbowed him. "No sarcasm while we're here. Don't even think it if you can help it."

He knew he shouldn't be lippy with the mages—especially

with *Malek*—but it was hard to keep the thoughts from bubbling up in his mind. "Being reverent didn't get Darv anywhere," he said, then immediately regretted the words.

Anguish flashed in his mother's eyes. She had to blame herself for Darv's death, for all of this.

"I'm sorry," he apologized, thinking again that none of them would have been in this mess if not for his insistence five years earlier that they continue Father's quest. "I'll keep my mouth shut."

"Good."

The cart floated through the gate—there hadn't been even a faint lurch when it started up—and into wide streets full of pedestrians, laborers, a handful of bicyclists, and more float carts and individual float seats. A few people, mage and terrene human alike, glanced at Malek, but they never stared. They jerked their gazes away, not wanting his attention.

"I'm sorry as well," Mother whispered after a couple of minutes. "I never should have brought you along on the dig. Had I truly believed we would find it this time, and that Uthari's men were watching my every move..." She shook her head. "I *should* have known that. They've searched my office on campus in the past. I just thought it had been a while, and they'd stopped paying such close attention. I was so careful to put together the expedition telling as few people as possible about our destination and goals."

"You couldn't have left me home alone for a month. You know I'm a horrible cook. I would have wasted away, and you would have returned to my alarming gauntness and felt vast guilt." Never mind that he never would have let her go without him; he'd skipped classes and stowed away before when she'd gone searching for the portal. It was his quest as much as hers. He'd wanted so badly to see his father's work completed.

"Don't you eat half your meals at the dining hall on campus?"

"Not when I'm working on my gauntness." Or when he'd spent his modest earnings from assisting professors and working in the library on pens, paper, and atlases instead of food. Or the signed limited edition *Map of the Legorian Labyrinths* by Dranith Dragor. He'd skipped lunches for months to pay for that.

The city inside the walls was as magnificent as Jak had anticipated, and he fell silent as he peered all around the cart. Aware of Malek behind him, he tried not to gape too openly, but the architecture was unique and striking. It was so different from the styles both past and present in the main cities on Agorval—or even in cities on other continents that he'd seen in travels and books— that it seemed alien. And he supposed it was, if one agreed with the factions that said mages were no longer human. He attributed it more to their ability to levitate building materials and place stones in ways that would have been impossible for those using only mundane tools. Further, the stones themselves didn't appear natural. The material used in many of the walls was more like a colored cement or other aggregate and appeared as lightweight as it was sturdy. All manner of dyes imbued in it made the buildings a riot of colors. Had he not hated the mages and all they stood for, Jak might have admired what they'd created up here.

The king's castle, a walled compound within the walled city, was comprised of blue and gray buildings and courtyards that sprawled across several blocks. No lesser buildings dared encroach toward its walls; it was surrounded by lush gardens of plants, shrubs, and shade trees. Laborers walked among the paths, pruning branches and clipping grass. On one of the lawns, a group of boys threw a disc for a dog, laughing and giving treats to the pup. The mundaneness of the scene was strange in this anything-but-mundane city, and Jak wondered if they were young mages or children of the laborers working in the gardens. Probably the former. From what he'd read, children of laborers were put to work young.

Castle guards saluted Malek, their fists thumping against their chests, as the cart floated through a gate into a courtyard, along a flower-lined drive, and up steps and through open doors large enough to accommodate them. Nobody asked Malek for his identity or demanded a password. To be zidarr was to be trusted.

In an open hall, the cart stopped, and they climbed out. Malek led the way, with the guards walking after Jak and his mother. He took note of the halls, the corridors, and stairs they traveled, mapping out the place in his mind, partially out of habit and partially in case they needed it for an escape later. After seeing all the ships at the dock, the idea of escaping didn't seem as impossible as it had before. If they could sneak onto one of those farm barges, maybe they could make it back to land and from there home.

"You would be easily found if you fled to your home," Malek said, not looking over his shoulder as he kept walking.

Mother gave Jak a startled look.

"I wasn't being irreverent," Jak protested. Anyway, it wasn't his fault that Malek was a big snoop of a mind reader. "Just contemplating escape."

"The ideal thing to think about with a telepathic zidarr two steps in front of us," she murmured.

"Sorry, I'll go back to contemplating the architecture."

"A good idea."

Malek led them up several wide sets of staircases and down an equally wide corridor with only one set of doors in it. They were gold-plated—or maybe solid gold—and featured imagery of dragons flying over castles.

"I doubt King Uthari has any need for the boy," Malek surprised Jak by saying. "Perhaps you could negotiate for his return home."

"What about *my* return home?" Mother asked.

"I do not know if that is the king's desire, but if he gets what he wants from the portal, perhaps."

"What is it he wants?" she asked.

"He will share it with you if he wishes."

The doors opened of their own accord as Malek approached. They were six inches thick. If they *were* solid gold, they would weigh tons. Jak wondered how much the entire city weighed and what power kept it all aloft. It boggled his mind that such a thing was possible, even with magic.

They entered a spacious parlor with numerous sofas and chairs as luxurious and plush as the ones in the cart—did they also heat one's butt?—though these were covered in rich brown leather rather than fur. A slender man with wispy gray hair stood off to one side, tinkering with a strange apparatus that looked like something from Mother's old lab. Glowing liquids in flasks flowed through a maze of tubes and clear pipes, the whole construct rising at least six feet. A reclining chair was nestled into a gap in the middle. What a strange piece of parlor furniture.

Mother frowned over at it, as if it were a puzzle to be solved. The reclining chair was empty, and the man—why did Jak want to call him a scientist?—only glanced over as they entered.

Someone else was waiting for them in the main seating area, and Jak slumped. General Tonovan. Oh, how Jak had hoped he wouldn't see the murdering ass again.

Tonovan lounged on a plush sofa, his legs crossed, and an arm resting over the back as he sipped from a glass of amber liquid. Ice cubes clinked when it moved. Did the mages magically freeze water or have giant slabs cut, packed in sawdust, and hauled up from the frozen lakes in the Sawtooth Mountains every day?

"Took you long enough, my lord," Tonovan drawled to Malek. "Did you take the scenic route?"

"Our guests were awed by the city."

"So you let them stop and gape? I would have put bags over their heads so they couldn't find their way out again."

"Your tour-guide services must be coveted far and wide."

Tonovan grunted. "Yes, that's what I'm known for."

"I know my treasured warriors aren't sniping at each other again," a voice came from one of several open doors off the antechamber. King Uthari?

The slender man who stepped out, clad in simpler clothing than half the people they'd passed in the city, wasn't immediately recognizable. King Uthari's face was on the currency in Sprung-town, but the portrait the coins were based on must have been painted when he was much younger. His pale face was leaner and sharper than the one on the coins, his head bald with wispy white tufts around the ears instead of full of thick hair. But his pale blue eyes were sharp in a way that wasn't conveyed on the coins, and nothing about them, or about his sure walk into the room, suggested frailness or senility.

"You know it's our favorite hobby." Tonovan rose and saluted Uthari.

Surprisingly, Malek only gave him a head nod. He stood with his hands clasped behind his back and behind Jak and Mother, where he could watch everybody in the room.

"Malek tried to lure me into a duel last night," Tonovan continued. "I believe he's been fantasizing about my death again."

"Haven't you been fantasizing about his?" Uthari asked.

"Every chance I get."

"One would think his *hobbies* would occupy his mind more than that," Malek said.

Tonovan curled a lip at him, then gave Mother an openly lascivious look that startled Jak so much that he almost sprang over two couches to plant a fist in Tonovan's face. It didn't seem to startle his mother, but she took a step closer to Malek.

"Control your hound, Professor," Tonovan told Mother,

glancing at Jak's closed fists. "It would be unfortunate if anything happened to him."

Jak forced his face to smooth, though he didn't have it in him to erase the loathing from his mind.

"He's too smart to do anything foolish," she said, though her glance toward Jak let him see the warning in her eyes. She *hoped* he was too smart to do anything foolish.

"It's so unfortunate that your other colleague wasn't." Tonovan waved casually. "I hadn't intended to kill him, you know. It was simple self-defense."

Mother clenched her jaw and didn't respond.

"When I *intend* to kill people, I draw out the moment more. To savor it." The smile Tonovan sent her was ghoulish, and he glanced at Jak—to check his response?

Jak also clenched his jaw and did not let himself respond.

"Are you done being sanguinary, General?" Uthari asked, his voice neither amused by nor condemning of his officer's antics.

The scientist poured some chemical or maybe *alchemical* substance into a tube on his contraption and didn't look over at the conversation.

"I could be, Your Majesty." Tonovan looked at Uthari, an eager gleam in his eyes. "Is there a new mission you called me here to discuss?"

"It's likely there will be. As you know from your midnight battle, our acquisition of the dragon portal has not gone unnoticed by other players on the field. King Zaruk is drawing in allies and has put out a call to numerous mercenary companies. According to our spies, he hasn't said what battle he wishes them to fight, but the timing suggests we may be his target."

"I would relish a chance to use our military might against piddling mercenaries," Tonovan said, "but I do hope he sends his elite forces against us. I want another chance to embarrass General Mox."

"I have no doubt," Uthari said. "See to the troops and ensure all is ready. They may intend to move swiftly, attempting to catch us off guard."

"They tried that last night." Tonovan sneered. "With superior forces, but that didn't keep me and my men from destroying three of their best mageships."

"So you reported." Uthari inclined his head. "As always, I appreciate your hard work and talent. You will be rewarded."

"Thank you, Your Majesty." Tonovan saluted again, fist to chest. "I live to serve."

"And I thank you for your service." Uthari spread his hand toward the golden doors.

As Tonovan strode out with his chin up, like a hound that had just been given a treat, Jak checked Malek's face, wondering if he was annoyed that Tonovan hadn't included *his* role in that description of who had defeated the other ships. But Malek was in the same military parade-rest stance, his features no more peeved than usual.

The doors automatically closed behind Tonovan, and Jak's muscles loosened an iota. To believe they were safe was foolish, but at least the sadistic pervert was gone. Maybe Uthari was one too—he certainly had no problem with employing one—but he looked too old to be interested in ogling Mother. And so far, Malek had only gotten close when he'd been removing things from her pockets.

Uthari walked over to murmur a question to the scientist—Jak couldn't hear the words—before sitting in a chair facing another chair and a sofa. A tea set, an alcohol decanter, and glasses and mugs rested on a silver tray on a low table next to a large plate of small sandwiches and fancy pastries.

"Join me, Professor Freedar." Uthari gestured to the sofa. "And Professor Freedar's son. Jakstor, is it?"

It would be surprising if he didn't know who they were—he

must have written their names down for Malek when instructing him on who to kidnap—but Jak still found it creepy. He reminded himself that this slender man was probably as powerful as Malek.

The wizard kings had all carved out their territories by raising armies, throwing wealth and power around, and magically blasting away all their enemies. Some ancestor of Uthari's, who shared his name, had taken over an existing kingdom and established this sky city a couple of centuries earlier, though there were rumors that *this* Uthari had been the one to do it, some magic keeping him alive far longer than humanly possible. Jak suspected he was simply the fifth or sixth Uthari since his ancestor had done the dirty work, but that didn't mean he wasn't powerful. The kingdoms didn't automatically pass from father to son—or, in a couple of cases, mother to daughter—since the mages respected power above all else and ousted those who weren't strong enough to keep their kingdoms.

"I see you're a mute family," Uthari said, then nodded to one of the guards.

Neither Jak nor Mother had moved at his invitation.

The guard came forward and bumped them in the backs, growling a terse, "Sit."

Jak was surprised Uthari didn't have Malek manhandle the guests. He was scarier than the uniformed guards, but maybe such acts were beneath a zidarr.

With her face a mask, Mother walked past the scientist's contraption and sat on the sofa facing Uthari. Jak perched on the edge of a chair where he could see the old man and also the door and Malek.

"The loss of your colleague no doubt has left you particularly irked with me." Uthari poured himself a cup of tea. "And you must be frustrated by the removal of the artifact you sought, but I trust you understand that it would have been illegal for you to claim for yourself a relic found on a king's property."

"That is not its original resting place, and King Zaruk has no right to it," Mother said. "But if we're strictly interpreting property law, is it not illegal for a king to claim a relic found on *another* king's property?"

"It is contentious, and it's possible we'll have a small war over that very issue." Uthari smiled and gestured toward the food and drink. "Are you thirsty? Hungry? Have refreshments if you wish. Malek, I would invite you to sit with us and snack, but I know your distaste for removing your weapons and how hard it is to sit while wearing swords."

"Especially hard on your upholstery," Malek murmured, not moving from his spot.

"Ah, yes. I haven't forgotten the split cushion incident. Not so egregious a faux pas as when General Tonovan decided to *entertain* here while I was away."

"Is that what he called swiving your servants?"

"It's what *I* call it. You know my distaste for uncouth language."

Jak looked at his mother, wondering what she thought of all this. It wasn't the torture and interrogation he'd expected—at least not yet—but it felt surreal and dangerous, like the eerie calm before a storm. Something clanked as the scientist made adjustments on the apparatus, and Jak envisioned being locked into that chair for an alchemical interrogation. Or experimentation. There were stories of mage scientists stealing human children off the streets or even away from their homes to test their magical gizmos on them. Or simply study them like lab rats.

"Have you heard any news on the key yet?" Uthari asked Malek.

"Not yet. I offered an enticing enough reward that I expect it will turn up soon, but if you wish, I'll return to Bakora to search for it myself."

"It is imperative that we find it, if indeed the portal will not operate without it." Uthari focused on Mother. "Or do you think it's possible to replicate the key? I know we're unable to work dragon steel, but could a replica be made of some lesser material?"

"I don't know for certain," Mother said, "but that seems unlikely."

Uthari sighed. "I concur."

"We'll get it, Your Majesty," Malek said.

"Of course." Uthari looked at Mother. "I've brought you here because I assume that activating the portal, even once we have this key, will not be as simple as propping it up in the courtyard and waving our hands. I require that you stay here long enough to figure out how it works. I understand there was little in the journal about that." Uthari lifted his eyebrows toward Malek.

"Little," Malek agreed. "The journal deals mostly with locating it."

"I am pleased that you were able to find it." Uthari nodded to Mother. "My time left in this world may not be infinite, even with magical intervention, and I should like to see my legacy left firmly in place. Can you guess what I seek?"

Jak blinked. What he sought besides the portal itself? What more was there? The dragons? That was what Father had hoped to find. Possible allies to change the course of the world.

"And why I was so pleased when you of all people took up the quest?" Uthari added softly.

Mother studied his face, but Jak couldn't tell if she was as puzzled by the question as he. She looked toward the scientist and his contraption for a thoughtful moment, then back to Uthari. "Jitaruvak?"

"Jitaruvak." He smiled at her. "Or, as it's referenced in most ancient texts, the immortality herb."

Jak had never heard of it.

"It's reputed to exist on the dragon home world of Ezarith," Mother said. "Our legends of those times say that dragons brought it here to extend the lives of the humans who worked with them.

Whether those humans were slaves or colleagues is fuzzy and depends on the interpretation of the texts, but the ones selected supposedly lived until they were killed, never dying of old age or disease. As long as they continued to receive the herb regularly."

"Supposedly?" Uthari arched his brows.

"There is some evidence in the fossil record to suggest these stories have truth to them."

"And there is even a fossil of the Jitaruvak herb." Uthari rose, walked to a bookcase, and picked up a chunk of rock. He brought it over and set it on the table before her. The rectangular hunk— some ancient mud or tar that had locked a branch with fern-like fronds inside of it—did indeed look like a fossil.

"Yes. I believe that used to be in the Forgotten History Museum."

"I acquired it from them."

"You acquire many things," Mother said, keeping her voice matter-of-fact.

"Only when it furthers my needs. I admit to having personal reasons for seeking immortality, but I seek this not only for myself. This could change the future of humanity. Imagine if the greatest wizards and scholars of the past centuries were still alive today. My quest, I assure you, is nobler than your husband's was, to gather allies to start a war against our kind." Uthari rested a hand on his chest. His pale eyes had gone frosty, and for the first time, some of his civility slipped as he glared at her, as if to punish Mother for the impudence of the man she had married.

Jak wished he'd sat beside her so he could more effectively glare back. It galled him that he couldn't do anything to protect his mother from these people.

"So," Mother said calmly, not noticeably worried by the frosty stare, "you need me not only because of my knowledge of the artifact but because I am an herbalist."

"A noteworthy one. I've read your papers."

"I assume I have no choice but to work for you."

"Until the portal is operational and the herb is found and synthesized into a drug," Uthari said. "I see no reason that you couldn't return to your regular life after that. Or, if your work pleases me, stay in my city with a generous stipend and employment at our university if you wish."

"I see."

"It is not a prison sentence."

"Just a loss of my freedom. And what of my son? If I agree to stay here, may he return to the university in Sprungtown? His new semester will start soon."

Jak shook his head, though she wasn't looking at him. He wouldn't leave his mother here alone with these people. He didn't trust Uthari for a second, didn't believe that he wouldn't have her killed as soon as she finished what he needed—or hand her over to that damn general to use as a toy.

"I believe he would cause trouble if he were permitted to return while you remained here. And I might then be forced to send someone to deal with him." Uthari gave Malek a pointed look, reminding Jak that he didn't know if Malek had been the one to kill his father. "Better that he stay here with you. I'm certain we can find some work for him."

Jak imagined being thrown in with the laborers who'd been unloading cabbages. Never had he thought he'd so wish he could return to his classes in the fall, but he wouldn't go without his mother.

"Will I be allowed to see him?" she asked.

"Of course. I am not a despot, despite what some terrene humans believe. I am only a practical man."

"I see. It seems that I have little choice but to work for you."

Jak had half-expected his mother to tell them to forget it, but he didn't want to see her do that, not when it would only get her hurt. Better to go along with them until an opportunity for escape presented itself. And surely it must. Uthari couldn't keep them penned up in a cell if he wanted them to study the portal. Sooner or later, they would get a chance.

"I am relieved that we understand each other," Uthari said, "and I needn't stoop to more draconian measures."

"Will your trusted general leave us alone?"

Mother didn't shiver, not exactly, but Jak eyed her, worried something had happened when she'd been taken away on the mageship for questioning.

"He spends more time in the field than in the castle," Uthari said, "but I shall instruct him not to disturb you."

"Good."

"Generally, he prefers more youthful prey, so I wouldn't think you'd excite him overmuch, but he will do as I say."

Mother didn't say *good* again. Judging by the tightening around her eyes, she wasn't happy with the response. Jak didn't like this line of discussion at all and found himself wanting to punch someone again. Tonovan ideally. He hoped the general lost his temper with Malek one day and got himself killed in that duel.

Malek's eyelids had drooped halfway as he watched Uthari and Mother. Nothing had changed about his stance, but something about him reminded Jak of a panther poised to spring. At his master? Probably not. Maybe he was fantasizing about killing Tonovan too.

"Why do you employ such a monster?" Mother asked, not bothering to hide the accusation in her tone.

Jak tensed, worried that she would anger Uthari, and he would lash out with magic.

But Uthari chuckled. "It is good to have someone powerful and rational with a deadly reputation on your side—" he extended a hand toward Malek, "—but it is also good to have someone powerful and volatile and unpredictable on your side. My enemies never know what Tonovan will do."

"Nor your prisoners," Mother murmured.

"Thus creating ease for me." Uthari rose. "It is time for my treatment. Malek, see them to suitable rooms."

Jak and Mother stood and walked toward the door, but Malek lifted a hand in front of Mother, making her stop. He flipped his palm upward, like a merchant waiting to be paid, and gazed expectantly into her eyes. She hesitated. Jak had no idea what Malek wanted.

"Give it to me, or I'll take it." Malek sounded more amused than angry.

Mother sighed and slid a hand into her pocket, withdrawing a vial of some dark-blue liquid. It must have come out of one of the racks of substances by the apparatus. The scientist blinked in surprise, glanced at his vials, then hurried over to take it. Jak had no idea what it was, but maybe Mother had been thinking of glues and climbing walls to escape again.

"You've a keen eye, Malek." Uthari also sounded amused. "Never would I have expected a professor to have kleptomaniacal tendencies—or the quick hand of a pickpocket."

"I'm told—" Malek glanced at Jak, "—that they're a quirky family."

"Meaning we should keep an eye on the boy too?"

"I would." Malek nodded for them to continue to the exit.

"Attend me after you've settled them into rooms," Uthari said. "We have a few things to discuss."

"I will."

14

MALEK RETURNED TO UTHARI'S SUITE AFTER LEAVING PROFESSOR Freedar and her son in rooms that had been prepared for them in the castle. He'd instructed the guards to watch the door around the clock and ensure they went nowhere without supervision.

Even if she had implied she would go along with Uthari's wishes, and had been careful to keep her thoughts still in their presence, Malek knew she had escape in mind. Earlier, he'd caught her thinking of ways to get out of the city and also get the portal away from Uthari. That she'd snatched some chemical that could presumably assist her with such a fantasy only heightened his certainty that she didn't intend to work mindlessly for them.

Not that this was surprising. When Uthari had instructed Malek to keep an eye on her, certain she would lead them to the portal, he'd researched her and read much of the work she'd published before leaving her career. Everything had been academic, related to the study of plants and her experiments in the field, and she didn't have a history of making trouble, but her late husband had been another story. He'd had ties to movements that wanted to oust wizards from power and break up the kingdoms.

How much she'd known about that or empathized with him was difficult to know, but Malek doubted Uthari's plan to offer her lucrative employment in exchange for obedience would work.

Her son's thoughts were easier to read, and he'd been peering down every hallway and into every room they passed, mentally mapping the castle. Malek knew less about eighteen-year-old Jak than his mother, but he would assume the boy was as intelligent as she was. He didn't blame them for plotting an escape, but he couldn't allow it. Even if a small part of him wanted to see what Freedar would have used the chemical for. He was still amused that she'd somehow put Tonovan's soap and lubricant to use.

Enter, Uthari spoke into his mind as he approached the gold doors again, and they opened for him.

Malek cleared away the notions of finding the prisoners amusing from his mind. Though he'd long ago learned how to wall off his thoughts so that no other mage could read them, he occasionally wondered if Uthari was an exception. It was possible his age and experience simply made him good at reading faces and guessing the motivations of men, but he might have some way of getting around the mental defenses of his zidarr. After all, he'd been the one to supervise Malek's training and teach him much of what he knew about magic. Numerous weapons masters had taught him combat, but his skills as a wizard he'd learned from the best in the field.

Inside the suite, Uthari now rested on the chair at his apparatus, leaning back as the doctor slid a needle into a vein in his arm. Above him, the strange medicines in his machine gurgled as they mixed and combined to form the life-extending substance that Uthari depended on.

They are comfortable and secured in their rooms? Uthari continued to speak telepathically. Though he trusted his doctor, some plans he kept only to his closest confidants.

Yes. Malek also replied silently.

They do not plan to cooperate. The boy is determined to help his mother escape. She is motivated to protect him, but she will also search for opportunities to get away and plans to work halfheartedly for me until then. I do not know where they believe they will escape to, since it would be a simple task to find them again in their home city. Do you believe a nomadic life of always watching behind your back could be more appealing than working for me earning a better wage than she previously did?

You know I do not believe so.

Yes, I trust you remember your youth and what it was like. You are still a young man.

At forty-five, and after more than thirty years of training, Malek would not consider himself young, but to Uthari, anyone under a hundred was a toddler.

I do remember. I confess it was with great satisfaction that I broke King Werok's neck to escape being killed for my talent. During the years I fled from his hunters and zidarr, I came to hate him a great deal.

He was a fool not to see that you were not too old to learn and that you needn't be killed. But a coward such as he was afraid to train a wild one with the potential to be his superior. Uthari smiled at whatever memory he had of thirteen-year-old Malek, orphan and runaway. *Just remember also that Zaruk knows how his father died and has never ceased to loathe you.*

As many do. Malek wasn't blithe or indifferent to the threats out there, to all the enemies who were constantly plotting to see him dead, and he maintained his wariness everywhere he went, but he was accustomed to it. The threat of danger kept him honed and added interest to his life.

But not the professor.

Malek arched his brows, surprised by the comment.

When Tonovan leered at her, she stepped closer to you. Have you done something to win her trust?

No. I believe you are misinterpreting a minute action. If she was afraid of Tonovan, it would make sense for her to stand behind me.

Perhaps.

Her son has guessed that I was sent to kill his father. It is likely she believes the same thing and would stab a dagger in my heart if she had the opportunity.

You have not corrected her?

Malek grew still, barely breathing as Uthari narrowed his eyes to slits to regard him.

I did not realize you knew there was a truth to be corrected, Malek said carefully.

You think I don't know that Tonovan did it? That he then lied *to me and blamed it on you because you were there and because he knew the professor's death was not what I wished? Had he been allowed to live and continue his work, we might have had that portal—and that herb —years ago. I was furious.*

I remember.

Had I known that night that Tonovan killed the man, I might have killed Tonovan myself. But he blamed you, and when you returned to the palace, you did not deny it. Why, Malek? Uthari's eyes were still slits, still locked on Malek as he ignored the concoction flowing down a tube and through the needle into his veins. *You let me punish you for that.*

It would have been his word against mine. There was no one else in that office, no other witness whose mind you could read.

You didn't think I would have believed you? Tonovan has lied many times to me. As far as I know, you never have.

That was not entirely true. There were truths Malek had kept to himself over the years. A man had to have a few secrets, even a zidarr man. *The Code speaks of honor. To me that means not tattling on a colleague.*

You hate Tonovan. And he tattled on you.

He is not zidarr.

Malek.

Malek twitched a shoulder. *He is a colleague. We must work together.*

You are too honorable for your own good at times.

Not sure if that was praise or admonition, Malek asked, *When did you find out? You didn't know that night.*

It was more than a year later. Tonovan was half-drunk and speaking of all the reasons I should send you away and replace you with Gorsith.

Malek snorted. He had nothing against Gorsith, a fellow zidarr who worked for Uthari, but the man wasn't the brightest. If Tonovan wanted him as Uthari's right-hand man, it was because he believed he could outthink and manipulate him.

The alcohol lowered his ability to block his thoughts. Uthari looked toward the table where the tea and whiskey still rested. It was always there when he brought in guests—and his own men—for exactly that reason. *As he spoke, Tonovan thought of that night, and I saw the truth in his mind. I almost had him punished, but a year after the fact, it seemed ludicrous. Besides, he is not as faithful a comrade as you. He would grow resentful at punishment and perhaps lose his allegiance to me. I must take care with him, until a better candidate to lead my troops rises through the ranks.* Uthari's eyes were slitted again.

Maybe it was Malek's imagination, but he thought the old king might be fantasizing about all the things he could do to Tonovan once that better candidate came along. Malek didn't care one way or another if Uthari got rid of him. He could work with anyone, and the challenge of a rival kept him on his toes.

You, on the other hand, never resented punishment, even when you were young. Uthari's gaze softened, grew almost father-like. *You always believed that surviving pain made you stronger.*

Because it does.

Of course. But let us not dwell on the past and instead focus on the future. I want that key so we can activate the portal, but I do not want to send you after it, unless we're not able to get it through your artifact hunters. Danger is on the horizon, and I need you here right now. The professor must be kept alive and safe. I will put this charge on you.

You wish me to be her bodyguard? That surprised Malek. *You believe that's necessary? In your own castle?*

Just as my rivals have learned of the portal and know that I have it, they will have learned of her and know that she is the secret to getting it to work. It is possible that others have as much knowledge as she, but nobody has her expertise in both areas that are of interest to me. Also, I'm not convinced that any of the archaeologists on her team or anywhere else know as much as she has learned about the portal. To lose her would be a great setback.

True.

She must be protected.

I understand.

I know that being a bodyguard is beneath you, but this is important.

All tasks assigned are worth performing to the utmost of one's ability, Malek quoted from the *Zidarr Handbook.*

There is dignity in all work. Uthari, who'd probably helped write that handbook three hundred years earlier, smiled. *Thank you, my friend. Watch the boy as well and test him when you get a chance.*

Test him?

He has latent talent. You did not sense it?

No.

I felt it roiling up in him when Tonovan was leering at his mother. I was most curious if he would find a way to dredge it up and use it, but I believe he does not know the talent is there. I sensed nothing from the professor, so presumably it was a gift from his father.

He is old not to have had glimpses and become aware of mage abilities.

Some terrene humans loathe our kind so much that it would destroy their entire sense of self if they suddenly found out they were one of us.

And of course, you know what happens to those who are not discovered at a young enough age to be brought into the fold.

I know well. Malek tilted his head. *You wish him dead then?*

He did not want to kill Professor Freedar's son. He was already annoyed with himself for stepping away and not foreseeing that Tonovan would kill her colleague. If they wished the professor to genuinely assist them, they could not kill everyone she cared about.

Not now. As you're aware, we need to convince her to study the portal in earnest. I do not believe the key alone will be all that is required to unlock its secrets. If we take everything from her, she'll have no reason to cooperate. Perhaps, if the boy's abilities are minor and he represents no threat, he need never be destroyed. If his talent develops into something that could be used as a weapon... Uthari spread his palm toward the ceiling. *Just as you have your Zidarr Handbook, we have our Wizard Handbook. No mage who could become an enemy to our people and our way of life may be allowed to live.*

I've read it.

Naturally. I do wish you to test him. Find out if he will be a threat.

I understand.

I also wish you to convince Freedar that it is in her interest to do as we wish, to try her hardest to find out how to operate the portal for our benefit.

Convince her? Through torture? At Uthari's behest, Malek had tortured people for information before, but he did not like the idea of hurting the professor. He'd never liked torturing women, and she was... he didn't know what, but he liked her creativity and determination to free herself—by using whatever mundane household products she could put to her use.

Uthari's eyes narrowed again, and Malek reinforced the walls around his mind. He would not disobey Uthari, but he also did not wish Uthari to doubt him. If he wanted the professor tortured, Malek would do it.

That may not be necessary. After all, she stepped closer to you.

Malek snorted again. *I can't believe you see any significance in that.*

See if you can win her trust. I care not whether she works for you or for me, only that I'm able to find that plant and bequeath the world a worthy legacy. Immortality for our kind. You deserve to live a long life, Malek, without need for all this. Uthari flicked his fingers to indicate the doctor's contraption.

Malek was positive that some enemy's blade would find his back—or some fireball that he wasn't strong enough to defend against would engulf him—long before he was in danger of dying of natural causes, but if Uthari had some fantasy of them working together for centuries to come, so be it. One had to humor old men—old mentors.

Winning the trust of a woman? This may be the first task you have given me that I am... uncertain I am capable of. You know I interact little with people. Especially *female* people. Since marriage was forbidden by the Zidarr Code, lest the love of another cause divided loyalties to one's monarch, Malek had avoided situations that might lead to temptation.

I admit, I'm amused at the idea of you trying to woo a woman. A smile stretched Uthari's lips.

You wish me to woo *her?* That was even more extreme a measure than Malek had envisioned. *Your Majesty, they fear me. The mother and the boy. I am zidarr. As you have made me.*

Women don't mind a fearsome reputation, so long as you're not cruel to them. But I'll not ask you to play Vereth to her Vira. That is not what you've been trained for. There was that smile again. Uthari truly seemed amused by this whole notion. *I believe if you simply stand at her side as a bodyguard, she will come to trust you.*

You're not going to arrange for people to attack her so she runs to hide behind me, are you? Malek believed the professor might be the type to hurl chemical smoke concoctions—or soap concoctions—at her enemies rather than hiding.

I am not. But as I said, I fear that may happen regardless. Double the reward for that key. The sooner we get the portal working, the easier our lives will be. I will increase security in the city and around the castle, but never forget that the other kings have zidarr, and they're trained as well as you.

I am aware.

You are dismissed, my friend. Uthari closed his eyes and leaned his head back as the last drips of his medicine entered his bloodstream. His patient doctor, who'd been politely looking out the window instead of watching them while they spoke telepathically, nodded to Malek as he left.

He was the only one to see a very unfamiliar expression on Malek's face, the expression of being daunted. The professor very likely wanted to kill him. Her son would be happy to help—and now Malek had been charged with testing him for mage talents. He could not do that without them noticing. How was he supposed to manage to win the professor's trust in the midst of that?

Lieutenant Sasko hated camels. More specifically, she hated riding them, and she cast a few longing looks at the magecarts that floated ahead of their unit in the caravan plodding northward. But the two they had reserved were for gear and supplies—and Dr. Fret, who'd snagged a ride by saying she had to mix up new burn ointment and tuck away her fresh bandages, herbs, and medications into first-aid kits. Funny how much lounging and snoring went on during that task.

"Looking most excellent, LT," a familiar young man called,

ambling past their unit on his camel. He made a lewd sign and leered at Sasko's chest.

She dredged his name up from her memory. "Suck your left teat, Rover!"

Thorn Company was traveling north with the Red Sabers, a similar-sized mercenary unit that had been renting camels at the same time as Captain Ferroki and Sasko. The handful of merchants also making the trip were delighted to have such well-armed company, given that the Cracked Flats between Perchver and Amuri were frequented by bandits. Originally, the company had planned to head north on one of the public ferries that ran along the coast—as the day heated up, Sasko cast longing looks toward the sparkling blue sea a half mile to their left—but Ferroki had changed her mind that morning. She'd said she had a bad feeling about going through with their original—and publicly recorded—plan now that someone might be after them.

"I'd rather have you suck it for me," came the return call, the twenty-something merc pulling open his vest to show off his chest for her.

His camel lurched to go around a pothole in the old road, half hidden by brown palm fronds and dust that scattered the pavement, and he almost pitched off its hump. Only a quick grab for its reins kept him from landing head-first on the ground.

"Idiot," Sasko muttered.

"You're not interested?" Ferroki asked, her dark eyes glinting with amusement. "He has nice muscles, and younger men tend to be spry."

"Your droll wit is a delight to all, Captain."

"Yes, that's in our services brochure."

"Thorn Company, available for military maneuvers, strategic consultation, and droll wit, all at one low price?"

"Precisely."

Sasko hoped there *wasn't* a brochure, but she wasn't positive.

Sergeant Words kept saying they would get higher quality and better-paying gigs if they worked on marketing their services more. She'd convinced the captain to have business cards made. Who knew what else was in the captain's lap desk? Usually, it was filled with maps and dossiers on other armies and mercenary outfits, but brochures could have found their way in.

After recovering his balance, Rover urged his camel into a trot so he could catch up with the rest of his company. He drew even with Rookie Tezi, her blonde hair gleaming in the morning sunlight, and called something that was doubtless lewd over to her and rubbed his chest—his vest was still open to show off his muscles. Sasko rolled her eyes. The idiot probably thought half of their company would be happy to jump off to the side of the road for a quickie with him. As if the proliferation of cactuses and other thorny vegetation wouldn't make that an even less appealing experience than usual.

Whatever he said prompted a startled look from Tezi. She nudged her camel's flanks and hurried to catch up with Sergeant Tinder and a couple of others, though they didn't acknowledge her. Before the move, she'd been riding alone, probably not by choice.

Sasko sighed. "You think they'll ever accept her as one of the group?"

"Probably after she saves someone's life," the captain said.

"You think *that* will ever happen? She can barely keep her sword up for two minutes without her little arm falling off."

"She's getting stronger, and she's a fair shot."

"I don't know why you took her in. You *never* take people in who don't have prior military experience. Being experienced and *capable* is the only thing that keeps us in demand. Semi demand." Sasko grimaced, stopping herself lest she insult the captain.

The company had a good reputation among those who could accept that hiring a unit of female soldiers wasn't a plan doomed to fail, and Thorn Company often got repeat work, but those willing to take a chance on them were few and far between. Usually, they ended up working for other women with means. In the years Sasko had been with the unit, they'd done three jobs for Queen Aryania, one of only two female kingdom rulers in the skies. Aryania understood what it was like to be underestimated for one's sex, but that hadn't kept her from using the company like cannon fodder. They'd been lucky to survive those assignments and not without casualties, but she paid better than most.

"Determination goes a long way," Ferroki said. "The bear tenacious enough to climb to the top of the tree for a beehive is rewarded with honey."

Sasko kept herself from rolling her eyes. She respected the captain and knew she liked her platitudes from the ancient fables, but she used that one a lot.

"Besides," Ferroki added, "she may not decide to stay once she learns enough to take care of herself."

"She may not *stay*? What are we training her for then?"

"Because we can."

"Are you putting that in the brochure too? Free food and training and pay. No need to stick around once things get tough."

As usual, Ferroki refused to rise to the bait. She only gave Sasko that indulging smile, one usually reserved for the very young and the very addled.

"I doubt she has anywhere else to go," Sasko said more seriously. "That's the story for most of us, isn't it?"

"You're only here basking in the radiance of my leadership because of a lack of more interesting job offers elsewhere?"

"A lack of family and obligations elsewhere." Since her mother had died, her colleagues had become her family. Sasko had never known her father, and had no idea if he was alive out there, but she didn't much care. Her only goal was to earn enough to buy a little home in a quiet town by the ocean and pay a handsome shirtless young man to nurse her when she grew too old to take care of herself. Mercenaries had to have goals.

"Hm." Ferroki's gaze shifted toward the side of the road.

Captain Lugurt, leader of the Red Sabers, had pulled his camel off into the pale cracked dirt to wait for them. Bald, beefy, and approaching sixty, he had a face dotted by dozens of small scars, as if an explosive had blown up in front of him, peppering him with shrapnel. More than once.

"I will issue a warning to you, Captain." Lugurt lifted his chin, gazing aloofly at them.

"Go ahead." Ferroki gestured for him to bring his camel up to the side of hers.

"If he says anything about teat-sucking, I'm clobbering him," Sasko muttered.

"Weren't you the one to bring that up?"

"Yes, but only because the kid was cute."

"I knew you thought so."

Sasko didn't bother denying it. The captain knew she wasn't opposed to sex now and then. She just had no interest in relationships. Having the husband she'd fallen for at a young age sell her into slavery to pay off gambling debts had taught her not to trust anyone that much ever again.

"This guy has more warts than a toad," Sasko said.

"Those are scars."

"Warty scars."

Lugurt must have caught a few words, for he curled a distasteful lip as he fell in beside them. "Gossip? I suppose I should expect nothing less from women."

"Gossip would be if we were discussing how poorly you fare with women or whether your wife is cheating on you," Ferroki said. "Discussing your appearance in front of you is considered razzing or perhaps taunting."

"Wise things to do to a man carrying big weapons and leading a mercenary unit larger than yours."

"You make a salient point. The lieutenant apologizes. What warning do you bring?"

Sasko had no interest in apologizing, but Ferroki was more diplomatic than she and kept the company out of trouble with rivals, for the most part, so Sasko didn't naysay her.

"We intend to put in a competitive bid for the job King Zaruk is offering," Lugurt said. "If you know what's best for you and your unit, you won't try to undercut us."

"Oh?"

Sasko had no idea what he was talking about, and she didn't think the captain did either. That morning, all they'd been focused on was getting out of Perchver before more soldiers showed up to attack them. If word had gone out about a new job up for bids, Sasko hadn't heard about it.

"Just because Zaruk has invited numerous companies to his castle doesn't mean he'll hire more than one. And *we're* the one." Lugurt thumped a fist to his chest.

"Working for the kings is dangerous," Ferroki said. "They tend to pit you against other kings—and their zidarr."

Lugurt's lip curl returned. "*We're* not afraid to battle magic users. We're crafty enough to figure out ways to avoid going head to head against them."

Sasko doubted it but didn't say so.

"I'll keep your warning in mind, Captain," Ferroki said.

"Remember, you undercut us, and there'll be a price to pay." Lugurt squinted at her, then slapped his camel on the flank, and it took off at the dromedary version of a trot.

"You think he knows we don't have plans to bid on that job and are just on the way back north to our headquarters?" Sasko asked.

"I'm sure he doesn't. Captain Lugurt has always been fond of jumping to conclusions."

"I don't suppose you'd field the idea of going up there and selling that medallion to King Zaruk?"

"You know I won't. I said I'd keep it for the professor until she returns for it, and I will."

"Even if it means being hunted down by the people looking for it?"

"I have a plan to hide it so they can't sense it. Again." Ferroki's face grew bleak. "I wish we hadn't been attacked while visiting Sorath. I never would have intentionally dragged him into trouble."

"He may have survived."

"Even if he did, his home didn't. Last night, I went back to check it and see if... if he made it out. Or didn't."

"You did? Without telling anyone?" Sasko touched her chest. She was second-in-command. The captain was supposed to tell her everything, not go skulking off in the night by herself. For that matter, if someone *did* need to skulk, she was supposed to send one of the troops.

"I had to know," Ferroki said quietly. "If he didn't make it, because of me..."

Sasko squinted at her. "I know you said you'd never been involved with him, but are you *sure* you two never discussed, uh, teats?"

Ferroki blinked. "Is that a euphemism?"

"Yeah. I think the mercenary handbook has rules about asking your CO if she has deep and meaningful feelings for a competitor."

"But teat talk is permissible?"

"It's not explicitly forbidden."

"Interesting." Ferroki fell silent.

Maybe she wouldn't answer. It was none of Sasko's business, but as long as she'd known the captain—more than fifteen years now—she'd never openly had a romantic relationship. Not even secretly, to the best of Sasko's knowledge. She'd assumed Ferroki was dedicated to her work or not that interested in intimacy. A lot of the women in the unit were like that, or had been—like Sasko —abused or hurt in some way and had no interest in taking that risk again. Some of the mercenaries had lovers or even farm husbands near their small headquarters in Rapuchi Roost, but with the company out in the field for two-thirds of the year, that put a strain on anything long-term. Of course, if Ferroki *had* ever had a relationship with Sorath—*Colonel* Sorath, leader of another mercenary outfit and, therefore, competition—there would have been even more reason for strain.

"We never discussed such things," Ferroki finally said. "You can't have a relationship with someone you might end up facing on a battlefield one day."

"It would bring a new dimension to the term lovers' quarrel." Sasko tilted her head curiously. "*Would* you have? If he'd been a merchant or caravan driver?"

"I doubt he would have been as appealing if he'd been a merchant or caravan driver," Ferroki said dryly.

"Ah, so there *is* appeal."

"Haven't you seen him with his shirt off?"

"No, but his cheek scar is sexier than Wart Face's up there."

Ferroki shook her head. "We've just gotten along well over the years when we've crossed paths. That's all."

"When your paths crossed and he was shirtless?"

"That was only one time in the public baths in Veru'uk."

"Uh huh."

"Are you razzing or perhaps taunting me, Lieutenant?"

"Maybe."

"I'm certain the mercenary handbook forbids that."

"I don't remember it being mentioned."

"It's under proper decorum and respect for your superior officer."

"Hm."

"Like I said, nothing ever came of it." Ferroki turned a wistful gaze out toward the sea. "It was just nice having someone to talk to about the business who perfectly understood the business."

"I imagine so." Sasko didn't mention that Ferroki could talk to *her* if she needed a confidante. Sometimes, Ferroki did, but other times, she kept her thoughts to herself, especially if she didn't want the company to worry.

A ferry chugged past their caravan, hugging the placid waters near the coast as it steamed north.

Sasko grunted. "I think that's the ship we booked passage on."

"Yes."

"The camel-free ship. We could be lounging in hammocks in our cabins right now instead of sitting atop grumpy furry beasts with our inner thighs chafing."

"You're squeezing too hard if there's chafing."

"Thanks for the tip. I—"

A fiery orange explosion ripped from the back of the steamer, the distant boom reverberating over the desert. Smoke clouded the air all around the craft, but that didn't keep them from seeing the entire boiler blow dozens of feet into the sky before splashing down behind the ferry.

"Thanok's hairy backside," Sasko breathed, stunned. Her camel veered off the road to nosh on a prickly pear cactus, and she barely noticed.

The smoke cleared enough to see that the entire back end of the ferry had been blown out. It was taking on water and already starting to sink. It was too far away to see if there were people floating helpless—or dead—in the water, but Sasko assumed so. At the least, the entire boiler crew had likely been killed in that explosion. And anyone with cabins in the rear of the ferry.

"Where were *our* cabins, Captain?" Sasko asked in a squeaky voice, certainty filling her with dread.

Ferroki must have had the same thought, for the question didn't surprise her. "In the back," she said grimly.

"Are you *sure* you want to keep that medallion?"

"No. My plan is to wrap it in darkeye fabric—I've got some in our stronghold—shove it in a safe box, and bury it in the mountains miles from our headquarters."

"I'll help you dig. We all will."

"Rider coming," their rear picket called.

"What new delight is upon us?" Sasko muttered, quoting Egarath the Eternal.

They turned warily on their camels, hands on weapons as a horseback rider galloped to catch up with them. Or maybe the hooded and cloaked figure was merely someone else using the King's Highway who wanted to pass the caravan as quickly as possible. Sasko doubted it.

The rider slowed his mount as he drew closer, the horse lathered and breathing heavily under the warm sun, but he didn't lower his hood. It moved as he surveyed the back half of the caravan, then looked out toward the smoking steamer. A hint of a strong stubbled chin was visible in the shadows of the hood.

"This can only be trouble." Sasko watched the rider's visible hand in case he reached for a weapon.

"Vorzaz?" Ferroki asked.

Vorzaz? That was Colonel Sorath's new name, wasn't it?

"Yes, Captain," he said, nudging his horse past the mercenaries in the back to join them. "I bring a warning."

"I hope it's less pissy than Lugurt's warning," Sasko said.

Sorath glanced at her but didn't reply, instead focusing on Ferroki. "I need a word with you in private, Captain."

Several of their people were close enough to overhear. Tezi, who hadn't yet managed to shed her admirer from the Red Sabers, peered back at them.

"Of course." Ferroki lifted a hand, as if she would reach out to him, but the distance would have made it difficult, and she let it drop. "I'm relieved you're alive. When I went back to your shop last night, you weren't there. There was little more than smoldering ruins."

"You came back to check on me? I'm touched."

"I worried you'd been touched by no fewer than a dozen daggers and magelocks."

"I'm a better fighter than that. I never let more than *six* enemy weapons touch me in a single battle."

"Hence your longevity."

"Hence."

"I appreciate you buying time for us to escape," Ferroki added softly.

Sorath inclined his head, not removing the hood. Not surprising since his face was well-known among mercenaries, and more than Thorn Company was present.

"We need to talk about more than my ruined shop," he said.

Ferroki nodded and rode off to the side of the road. Sasko, having no intention of being left out, tugged on the reins to convince her camel to leave behind the succulent succulent.

Sorath had started to speak but paused when Sasko rode up.

"She's fine," Ferroki said. "I don't keep secrets from my second-in-command."

"I gathered. I was looking at the cactus pad hanging from her camel's lips."

"Camels are like mercenaries," Sasko said. "They rest and eat when they get a chance."

"True." Sorath lowered his voice. "Malek knows about the medallion and is after it."

Sasko swore.

"I suppose I can't be shocked," Ferroki said, "but that's worse than I was hoping."

"He's not coming himself, at least not yet," Sorath said, "but he sent a message to the entire artifact-hunters guild."

"Any chance that guild is as small as it sounds?" Sasko asked.

"There are more than two hundred members just in the greater Perchver area," he said. "There's some bleed over with the thieves' guild."

"Both being full of honorable and noble people only acquiring things for their rightful owners," Sasko said.

"*I'm* in it." Sorath tapped his pick to his chest. "A lot of people are going to be after you. More specifically, what you carry."

"Including those who attacked last night?" Ferroki asked softly, regret in her dark eyes.

"Actually, that happened before Malek's message, but it's probably related. Malek may not be the only one who knows about it and is looking for it."

"I can't ditch it along the way," Ferroki said. "I'm planning to bury it once we get back home. I have darkeye cloth there."

"That might work," Sorath said, "but I have a feeling it's widely known by this point that *you* are in possession of the artifact. Even if you hide it, people may come after you to question you. With force."

"Remind me to give that archaeology professor a punt in the ass if we meet up with her again," Sasko said.

"Given that she was taken prisoner by Malek, I think she's being punished enough," Ferroki murmured.

The thuds of a camel running on hard earth interrupted them. Tezi rounded a patch of thorny shrubs and lifted a hand. "One of the other company's scouts said there might be some trouble a couple of miles ahead, Captain. Sergeant Tinder sent me back to get you."

"Oh, joy," Sasko said.

Ferroki waved an acknowledgment toward Tezi and guided her

camel back toward the road. "Are you going back to Perchver?" she asked Sorath.

"It won't be safe for me there anymore," he said, nudging his horse to follow their camels.

"I'm sorry we got you into our mess," Ferroki said.

Sasko lifted a protesting finger. "It isn't *our* mess. The archaeologists dumped *their* mess in our laps."

Sorath shrugged under his cloak, neither of them paying attention to her. "It doesn't matter. It's not safe for me anywhere. That's what happens once wizards with a vendetta go after you."

"They may not know you're alive yet."

"If they don't now, they will soon. It would be a disservice to you if I rode at your side to Amuri."

"Maybe, but I'll invite you to do it anyway, since there may be trouble up ahead." Ferroki nodded toward Tezi and the rest of the caravan.

"You have two mercenary companies and a bunch of armed caravan guards. I doubt you'll need my services."

"I was thinking we'd offer *you* some protection, but..." Ferroki looked toward the sinking ship. "We may need each other."

15

JADORA SANK DOWN ONTO THE SOFA IN THE SUITE OF ROOMS THAT she and Jak had been given. They were in the castle, only one floor down and a couple of hallways over from Uthari, a fact that did nothing to ease her mind. She tried to tell herself that it was good they were also close to the portal—from their windows, they could see it in a central courtyard below—so she could keep an eye on it. Normally, she wouldn't have worried about someone making off with a heavy twenty-feet-in-diameter artifact, but the mages had proven they had no trouble moving it around.

"This room is bigger than our whole house." Jak wandered from the parlor to one of two adjacent bedrooms. "So is this one. The bed is huge, but it *looks* tiny in that room. Is that a boulder-basher table? In case you get the urge in the middle of the night to knock balls into caves? And another seating area. There's a bucket of ice and some kind of alcoholic drink in a bottle. Is this your room or mine? Maybe mine isn't as luxurious." He wandered across the parlor to check out the other bedroom.

Jadora closed her eyes, having little interest in their accommodations. Oh, she acknowledged this was better than the cell on the

Star Flyer, but she didn't appreciate the promise dangling in the air —from the lush velvet curtains to the gilded mirrors and expensive paintings to the kitchen stocked with crystal dinnerware and exotic fruits—that cooperation would be rewarded. All they had to do was sell their souls to their wizard overlord and serve him loyally until he no longer needed them. She didn't believe for a second that Uthari would keep them around—and alive—longer than that, no matter what he said.

She'd heard of professors being selected from Sprungtown and other universities to teach at the mage academies and do research in the sky-city education systems, but none of those people ever returned, nor did they publish any new papers. It was possible they wrote articles for special mage-only journals that circulated only in the clouds, but speculation of their deaths or imprisonment ran rampant. All day, Darv's face had haunted her mind, and she knew it would continue to do so for a long time.

"The other bedroom is just as big," Jak reported. "It has a card table instead of a boulder-basher table." He poked into the kitchen. "There's all sorts of food in here. And what is this?" He opened a rectangular door within the cabinetry. "An icebox? It's cold, but I don't see any ice." He checked the cabinets all around it. "No ice. Magically cold. I guess when they sell their mage trinkets to us normal humans down below, they keep the good stuff for themselves."

"Magical iceboxes represent the good stuff?" she murmured.

"Obviously. Look, it's full of cold cuts and... what are these? Bananas? I've heard of bananas, but they don't grow anywhere on Agorval. I guess their mageships can fly them up to this latitude before they spoil. Or does their magic keep them fresh longer? Or maybe the icebox does. Mother, as long as we're here, we can have experiences we've only read about in books."

"Bananas and iceboxes. It's worth being enslaved for such riches."

Jak abandoned his explorations and sat in a chair across from her. "Don't forget about the boulder-basher table. It looks like the balls reset themselves."

Jadora was too weary and mournful to make jokes with him. She longed for sleep but dreaded the nightmares that would surely come.

"I'm just trying to take your mind off the situation," Jak said softly. "I know we're in trouble."

"Thank you." She forced a smile for him. It was her job to be strong for her son, wasn't it? "Jakstor?"

He blinked. "You're using my whole name? Am I in trouble?"

"No, but this is important, so I want you to listen."

"Go ahead. I am."

"I want you to know that none of this is your fault, all right?" She remembered him trying to put the blame on himself back in their cell, and that had been before Darv's death. Even though he often used jokes and flippancy to hide his feelings—the same way Loran had—she knew he was sensitive under the occasionally goofy facade. He might be carrying guilt over this, just as she did.

Jak leaned forward in the chair, elbows on his knees, and studied his hands instead of looking at her. Damn it, that hesitation meant he *was* blaming himself.

"*Some* of it is my fault," he said. "You never would have started this research if I hadn't been a pain in the butt and threatened to run away from home and finish Father's quest myself."

"That was five years ago. You were just a boy."

"But I meant what I said. And I think you knew it, and you gave in so I wouldn't run off and get myself killed."

"You couldn't have known it would lead us to this end."

"That's because thirteen-year-old boys have the clairvoyance of rocks." He forced a half smile. "Eighteen-year-old boys aren't so great at foreseeing consequences either."

"Forty-two-year-old women also have difficulty in that area."

"Really? That's depressing. I thought I'd be wise and sage by the time I was that advanced and decrepit of an age."

"Ha ha." She threw a couch pillow at him.

That earned another half-smile, but his eyes were haunted, and she feared she hadn't changed anything. She missed the days when he'd been younger and it had been easier to fix his problems.

"Do you think we can talk freely in here?" Jak waved at the walls. "Or do they have a way to magically monitor us? Or maybe the guards are able to read our thoughts through the door. Do you think the ones in the hall are capable of that?"

"I don't know."

He rose to his feet, went to the door, and opened it.

From Jadora's seat, the sleeve of a red uniform was visible. The guard turned toward Jak.

"Can you read our minds?" he asked, as if making casual conversation.

Jadora grimaced, hoping he didn't get himself in trouble.

"Stay in your room," the guard said. "Someone will come to prepare the evening meal for you."

"Is that a no?" Jak asked.

The guard lifted a hand, but when he pushed Jak back into the room, it was with magic, not a physical touch. The door swung shut in his face.

Jak shrugged and returned to his seat. "I don't think those two can read minds. To test one, I deliberately thought disparaging thoughts about the size of his... drawing tool."

Jadora shook her head. Sometimes, Jak's humor was so similar to Loran's that it filled her with painful nostalgia. And sometimes, it made her worry that his mouth would get him punched in the nose. That, and other consequences, had befallen Loran more times than she could count.

"Maybe he's too professional to be goaded into punishing a prisoner because of insults to his *drawing tool*," she said.

"I doubt it. Not if General Tonovan is an example of the quality of leadership in this place."

The memory of Darv's death—and Tonovan's smug face—sprang to mind, and Jadora only shook her head again. Maybe the same memory came to Jak, for he sank back into the chair, his expression growing somber again.

"How are we going to get out of here *with* the portal, Mother?" he whispered, then glanced warily at the walls.

"I don't think that's going to be possible."

"We *have* to escape."

"I know. *We* will. But I don't see how we can carry the portal out of here." She scratched her jaw. "Maybe we don't have to, at least right now. They don't have the key."

Jak removed his hat and fingered the spot where it had been, where he'd carried it all those years without knowing what it was. In truth, Jadora hadn't known for certain either, not until she'd seen the hole. Loran's notes had mentioned how important his favorite hat was to him and that it was *key* in his success as a world-traveling artifact locator, so she'd guessed early on that the medallion was tied in with the portal, but she hadn't known how critically until that moment. If she had, she would have made Jak keep that hat in a vault instead of wearing it to school every day.

"They'll get it though," Jak said. "Malek is on it. And he's... Shylezar's scales, you saw him fight, right?"

"Yes."

"Did you see his blades? When they're not glowing, they're blue. Is that an alloy?"

"Lesser dragon steel. As with the dragon steel the portal is made from, it's too hard for human magic or technology to melt and work, but dragons made weapons from the material back when they visited our world. The blades were given as gifts to human servants who loyally fought at their sides in battle. These days, the weapons are handed down from one generation to the next in wealthy families—wealthy *mage* families—though some are obtained in battle, usually by slaying the supreme weapons master who's carrying them around." Jadora hesitated. "I know nothing about Malek's heritage, but he seems like someone who may have gotten his weapons the latter way."

"Yeah." Jak grimaced. "You don't really think those mercenaries are going to risk their lives to keep him from getting the medallion, do you? We barely even spoke to them, and they were just terrenes, like us. And people who kill other people for coin. They probably sold it as soon as they got back to the mainland."

"It's possible. Or they might have chucked it in the ocean. I wonder if that would keep the mages from finding it. The artifact radiates so much power that I'm sure someone like Malek could sense it, but the medallion is much smaller."

"Mother, we don't want it lost forever so nobody can use the portal. *We* want to use it." Jak touched his chest. "*I* want to use it. To change things. To make the world better for our people. That's what this was always about. For my whole life, Father was working on this, so he could go through and find..." He glanced at the walls. "You know what he hoped to find. And what *I* hope to find."

"I thought you just wanted to ride a dragon." Jadora smiled, remembering an entire summer when he'd been eight or nine where he'd voiced that fantasy frequently, usually while galloping around the kitchen on her broomstick.

"Of *course* I want to ride a dragon—who wouldn't?—but I want them to come fix... the world."

"I know. But if the mages are the first ones to lead a party to the dragon home world and make an alliance with them..." She imagined Uthari explaining how superior mages were to the piddling humans that still crawled around on the earth and talking the dragons into helping *him*.

"No way would dragons align with them. They're pompous jerks, and we're delightful."

"Hm."

Jadora had no idea if dragons would find mages *or* mundane humans delightful. Humanity's interactions with them had been so long ago, forgotten in all but legends that had doubtless been altered over the centuries to suit the needs of each passing generation, that it was hard to know.

She knew Jak liked the tales that illustrated dragons as benevolent allies—and even she caught herself praying to Shylezar, the dragon god who supposedly protected humans—but just as many painted them as fierce predators who'd occasionally hunted humans. The truth was difficult to know, and there was the possibility that opening the portal that linked the two worlds could be a big mistake. Who knew what dragons had evolved into over the millennia? Nobody knew what they had truly been like. It was possible that humans had buried the portal on that volcanic island and hidden the records of its existence for a reason.

"Either way, we have to know," Jak said. "*We* have to go through the gate first."

"It might be easier later on, in a few years, when Uthari's focus has shifted to other things."

Or after he died. Jadora had picked up on the significance of the contraption in his parlor, though surprisingly, she'd only been familiar with a few of the medicines in the racks beside it. Others had to have been alchemical instead of mundane. She knew of no natural substances here on Torvil that could extend life.

"They want us to figure everything out," Jak said, "and I *really* want to figure it out too. Don't you? Once we get it working, maybe they'll send us through first to see if we get eaten as soon as we reach the other side."

"You sound hopeful."

"More about going through first than being eaten. Oh, if we

took the key through when we went, would that mean they couldn't follow?" His forehead crinkled. "Or does it only work and let you through if the key is in the keyhole?"

"I'm not sure. Loran's notes on the actual operation of the artifact were scant."

"If we could activate it and take the key through with us, they wouldn't be able to follow." His tone grew wistful. "We could escape mages forever."

"And never see our home or the university again?"

"That wouldn't be ideal. And it wouldn't keep the mages from pestering all of humanity that remained. Unless we could somehow open the portal for everyone who wanted to leave."

"Such thinking is a little premature when we don't know what's over there yet. Or even if the portal will work after all these centuries buried on a volcanic island."

"I know. That's why we have to go through and explore. And make maps. I could do that. They *need* to send me." Jak rose and went to the window overlooking the courtyard. "Are you going to do what they asked? Try to figure everything out?"

"Even though I long to study it as much as you do, I don't think I dare. It's not as if I can learn how to operate the portal and then withhold the information from them." Jadora joined him at the window. Darkness had fallen, but silver-blue lamps glowed in the courtyard, shedding their light on a handful of guards and the dark outline of the artifact. It lay on its side, as it had on the deck of the mageship.

"Maybe it wouldn't be the worst thing to work with them for now," Jak said. "We could figure out how to outsmart them later, after we get to go through."

His willingness to entertain the idea concerned her. What she knew—and so far, the mages did not—was that Jak had studied the portal almost as assiduously as she had these last five years. And he'd worked at Loran's side and learned from him in the years before his death. What if she refused to help Uthari, but Jak was lured into his service?

The door opened, and she pushed aside the thoughts.

Two female servants walked in, wearing the drab gray tunics and loose trousers of the palace staff and carrying trays. Interestingly, they wore removable magebands instead of slavebands, but their glazed expressions suggested they had them activated. Neither spoke. They simply extended their offerings.

One tray held Loran's journal, and Jadora rushed over to grab it. The other was full of drawing pads, new notebooks, pens, charcoal pencils, measuring tools, and a sharpener that looked like it was made from gold.

Jak picked it up. "It's like I'm being wooed by a wealthy dilettante."

"These are from Zidarr Malek," one of the women said in a monotone.

"So *not* a wealthy dilettante?" Jak picked up a couple of other tools on the tray, more familiar ones. They were the ones he'd had in his pockets when they'd been captured, and he smiled. "This is my lucky compass."

"Sure to help you out of any scrapes we land in."

"Maybe not that, but I've gotten good grades on assignments whenever I've used it."

"I'm Jadora Freedar," she told the servants, wondering if she could get through to them. If they were powerless up here, maybe they would be sympathetic to prisoners. And maybe they could be, if not allies, sources of information. "What are your names?"

One gazed blankly at her.

The other, her eyes slightly less glazed, responded. "I am Altrucia. It is not permitted for us to have conversations with you."

"Neither of us?" Jak touched his chest. "I'm quite charming."

"Zidarr Malek will come for you in the morning to supervise your studies," Altrucia said without looking at him.

Without further comment, they walked out of the room, closing the door behind them.

"He's coming to supervise us?" Jadora frowned. "Doesn't he have enemies of his kingdom to slay?"

"Maybe he thinks those enemies will be coming for the portal, so he better stick around."

"That's a depressing thought." Not only might she and Jak have to risk their souls working for King Uthari, but their lives could be in danger from his enemies.

"At least I'll be armed to defend myself."

"They didn't return our weapons." Nor the canisters and vials from her collection, though that wasn't that surprising. Jadora would have to look around for something else that would be helpful in escaping.

"I meant this." Jak held up the pencil sharpener. "Gold is heavy. And look at the nib on that fountain pen. It's practically a spear."

"I'm sure you'll be menacing to any zidarr that Uthari's enemies send."

"They had better watch out for their eyeballs."

Ahead of the caravan, a woman's scream floated out of a village to the side of the main road. Tezi, after giving up on getting the others to include her in their conversations, had been dwelling on feelings of homesickness for a home she could never go back to and a family that was gone. But the scream ululating across the parched earth startled her out of her dreary reverie.

Fainter whimpers followed the scream. Another woman? Or the same one?

Tezi tightened her grip on her reins, torn between wanting to help whoever was in pain and struggling with memories that stampeded to the forefront of her mind. Memories of her own village being visited by a zidarr and two mages selecting pretty females for their king—after testing the wares for themselves. The idea of facing a similar situation again terrified her, and she hoped this was nothing like that.

From the middle of the caravan, Tezi couldn't yet see more than the outline of the village, a handful of tan dome houses and a two-story rectangular structure made from brick a hundred yards back from the highway. A sign posted at the turnoff for the side road promised the Dilgar Gold Mines lay to the east and that this was the last place for travelers to get rest and a good meal.

The captain and lieutenant had caught up with Tezi and the rest of the caravan, the cloaked man riding behind them. Sorath, she realized, catching the glint of the sun on his pickaxe.

Surprisingly, nobody at the head of the caravan was turning off the road to check on the screams coming from the village. Why, because nobody was paying them to help? Tezi scowled. She knew she'd joined a company of mercenaries, but did that truly mean they wouldn't assist people in need? People in *pain*?

Tezi pulled out her magelock, laid it across her lap, and urged her camel to pick up its pace. If they wouldn't help, *she* would.

Up ahead, Sergeant Tinder and the grumpy captain from the other company reached the intersection and stopped their mounts. Good, maybe they *would* help.

They gazed toward the little village, Tinder pointing at people outside of the hotel. With cactus and prickly thorn bushes lining the road, Tezi hadn't been able to see people over there before, but now, she could make out men on their knees. Their faces were pressed into the dirt, their hands tied behind their backs. Or bound with magic?

Her gut churned as she spotted someone else, someone out there watching the prisoners from the shade of the hotel wall. He wore a mage robe, the vibrant blue standing out against the faded brick building and the tan earth. The lack of a uniform meant he wasn't one of the king's soldiers, but that didn't mean that others inside the hotel weren't part of Zaruk's army. There might even be zidarr in there, zidarr who would kill anyone who presumed to help. An entire company of mercenaries couldn't expect to win against one of their kind, and even if they were somehow victorious, they would lose many of their troops.

Tezi's heart sank, though she wasn't surprised when Captain Lugurt shook his head and waved for his people to continue on. Another scream tore from a woman's mouth—it sounded like she was on the second floor of the hotel—and several of the Red Saber mercenaries frowned over at the village, but they continued on, following their leader.

The women of Thorn Company looked back toward the captain, but none broke ranks to rush over to help. Tezi understood why, but it frustrated her. Nobody dared help, not against mages.

"Help us!" one of the men on the ground yelled to the caravan. "They're raping our daughters, our wives. They—"

The mage lifted a hand, and the man broke off with a scream of pain, his back arching so hard it looked like his spine would break. Tezi shifted her magelock pistol, her heart slamming against her rib cage as she debated if she could get off a shot, if the mage would be too busy tormenting the man to defend himself. Maybe he wouldn't see the blast coming until it was too late...

"Don't, Captain," came Sasko's voice, a warning whisper. "Where there's one mage, there'll be a dozen more inside. Even if we did stop them, you know what the repercussions would be. And if we killed one, we'd be hunted down ourselves, every one of us slain as a lesson to the rest of the world."

"We've killed mages before," the captain said, her usually calm voice like ice. She'd also drawn her pistol and was contemplating the same shot as Tezi.

"In *battle*, hired by other mages. You know how the rules work. If we take one of them out on our own…"

Sobs came from the hotel, a woman begging her tormenter to stop.

"Leave us alone," one of the other prisoners growled to the mage outside, rising up. "We're not animals to be—"

Magic wrapped around him, forcing him to jerk and writhe in pain, the same as his comrade. The mage snarled that he'd kill them all if they didn't shut up. They were already annoying him because they were delaying *his turn.*

His voice was young and cruel, and Tezi realized he might not be any older than she. Maybe younger. Was this a bunch of teenagers out for some *sport*?

Fury burned inside of her, threatening to erupt like the volcano. She was already a hunted woman in another kingdom; did it matter if she drew the fury of another king?

She stopped her mount behind a bush large enough to cover her moves and raised her pistol, aiming through the thorny branches. The mage was smirking, eyes glinting with pleasure as he tormented the men. He was so confident that the caravan wouldn't dare come over to stop him that he didn't even look up.

Tezi aimed for his chest, then shifted the sights slightly to the left. The shoulder. That wouldn't kill him, and maybe the rest of the company wouldn't be punished for her choice to injure a mage.

But someone else in the caravan fired first, not a magelock but a black-powder weapon that unleashed its bullet with a thunderous *crack*. It struck the mage in the eye, blowing it out in bloody chunks that Tezi saw even from a hundred yards away. She also saw the shocked expression on the dead mage's face as he pitched sideways, crumpling to the ground.

Tezi gaped over at the captain, certain she'd been the one to fire, but she didn't have a black-powder weapon. It took her a second to realize who'd been responsible because he was gone, his horse empty of its rider. Sorath.

Shutters on a second-floor window of the hotel flew open with bangs. Two bare-chested youths with tousled hair appeared, first gaping down at their dead comrade and the imprisoned men still bound as they struggled to rise from their knees, and then out at the caravan.

"Do we help him?" Sasko asked. "Or—"

"Criminals!" one mage shrieked toward the road.

An eerie magical wind whipped up, shrieking like the slave-master's demons in the bard Versifero's famous "Tempest in Hell." The camels groaned and made high-pitched bleats as they stamped their feet.

The captain sprang from her mount and ran toward the hotel, darting through the brush instead of heading up the road. Sasko cursed and stayed back, yelling for the company to continue on and get up the hill before all the mages came out.

Tezi's mount surged down the road, moving so abruptly she slid off. She landed in the dust as more camels streamed past, and rolled to the side so she wouldn't be trampled. When she sprang to her feet, branches alongside the road clawing at her uniform, she didn't try to chase her camel. If the captain was going to put herself in danger, Tezi couldn't leave her. She also couldn't turn her back on women in the same position that *she'd* been in before.

Yellow lightning bolts streaked across the blue sky over her head. They branched a dozen times and targeted several of the riders, mercenaries trying to obey their leaders' orders to get out of the area. The mages were taking their anger out on them anyway.

A lightning strike took Dr. Fret in the back, hurling her from the supply cart. And killing her?

Tezi rose up from behind a bush and fired at one of the mages in the window. But those two were ready for an attack, one having created a defensive barrier in front of them. The charge from her magelock bounced off, striking a house across the road.

The mages were looking toward the highway and didn't seem to see the cloaked figure run out of the brush behind the hotel and to the back door. As Sorath flung it open, he was almost bowled over by two naked women fleeing the building. After they passed, he charged inside.

The mage Tezi had fired at scanned the bushes, his hard gaze searching for her. She ducked low and maneuvered through the brush toward the hotel. The air crackled with power, her skin buzzing with its proximity, and the ground exploded scant feet to her side. Magic tore a dozen bushes from their roots, dirt and thorny limbs flying. The debris pelted Tezi as she scurried through the maze of cactuses and shrubs.

Another blast struck the ground, more like one of Tinder's explosives than magic. It left a crater in her path and pummeled her again with dirt, stones, and plant matter. As she hurried around the hole, blood dripping from cuts on her face, she hoped Sorath was making progress—and that he didn't run into any zidarr or mages too powerful for him to handle.

"There's one in here!" came a male cry from the hotel.

Gunshots fired, and a man screamed. Sorath? One of the mages?

Tezi came out of the brush behind the hotel and almost ran into the captain.

"You were ordered to stay with the company," the captain whispered harshly as she raced for the door.

Tezi ran right behind her. "My camel bolted."

"You were supposed to bolt *with* it." With her pistol in one hand and her sword in the other, the captain leaned through the doorway, checking inside before committing herself.

A whimper came from the first room.

"Stay down, girl," the captain said and hurried into a dark kitchen, the shadows thick after the bright daylight outside.

Tezi entered after her, her eyes slow to adjust. She almost tripped over an upturned cauldron.

Gunshots sounded on the floor right above them, and she jumped. Another whimper sounded. A girl huddled—*hiding*—in a corner with a blanket wrapped around her body. She couldn't have been more than thirteen or fourteen.

Footsteps thundered above, and something crashed to the floor. As Tezi and the captain entered a common area with tables and benches upturned everywhere, another crash sounded, and chunks of plaster from the ceiling rained down. The captain found a staircase and stepped over something to run up it. It was a young mage's body, robes dark with blood and a huge hole in his forehead as if someone had struck him with a mallet. No, the pointy side of a pickaxe.

Swallowing, and trying not to think about repercussions, Tezi hurried up the stairs. A boom rattled the entire building. Lanterns fell from wall mounts, crashing to the wooden steps.

"You're dead," someone snarled, panting with pain around the words. "All of Zarlesh will avenge our deaths."

As Tezi stepped off the stairs and into a hallway with open doors to bedrooms, she spotted the captain ahead and several bodies littering the floor. Some belonged to robed mages and some—Tezi stared in horror—belonged to young women.

A robed figure leaned out of a doorway the captain had already passed and thrust his hand toward her back. Tezi fired without thinking to aim for a nonvital target. The mage hadn't seen her and never saw what hit him. At this close range, the blast from her pistol was deadly when it slammed into the back of his head. A second shot went off at the same time, striking him in the chest. The captain. She'd seen the threat after all.

The mage dropped dead to the floor. The captain nodded at

Tezi, then turned and jogged through double doors at the end of the hall.

Only then did Tezi realize that all sounds of a fight had ended. A few gasps, sobs, and whimpers came from the bedrooms, but as she passed by and peeked inside, she saw only defenseless women. Those who had tormented them were either gone or dead on the floor.

One of the dead mages, a boy of fourteen or fifteen, had died with his glassy eyes open in shock. Had he not been half naked with his robe wide open, Tezi might have thought it a mistake, that he was a victim rather than a perpetrator.

"It's clear, Tezi," came the captain's calm voice from the last bedroom.

Stepping carefully over the bodies, Tezi joined her inside, the air stinking of spent black powder. The room was more spacious than the rest, with a bathtub, a huge bed, and what had been a kiva fireplace before some explosive had warped it, hurling logs all over the room. The mage who'd been casting lightning bolts from the window lay dead, a hole in his forehead similar to the other one. His buddy was also down, sprawled out as if he'd been running for the door when someone came in.

Sorath. He stood in the center of the room, blood dripping from his pickaxe and his hand clenched in a fist around something. His pistol was holstered.

"Gather the others," Sorath said to a woman in a torn dress hiding behind the bed. "Go outside and free your family."

She threw a wild look at him, as if not sure if he was friend or foe, then scrambled over the bed and sprinted into the hallway.

"Your hood came off," the captain told Sorath matter-of-factly, as if there weren't bodies all over the floor around them.

"I *wanted* them to see me. Besides, it doesn't matter. They're all dead. I made sure of it." Sorath's eyes narrowed. "The dead don't talk." He looked at the captain and Tezi, and Tezi had the weird sense that he'd been making sure nobody was left alive to talk for their sakes rather than his.

"You know those who come to investigate will have ways to find out what happened and who was responsible anyway," the captain said.

"Are you berating me when you and your rookie are in here with smoking guns?" He arched his eyebrows.

"They're magelocks. They don't smoke."

"That's why they're inferior weapons."

"How did you..." Tezi pointed her pistol at the mages, thinking of how she'd only managed to hit one, and that had been when his back was turned and he was distracted. "How did you charge right up to them and get through their defenses?"

"Distractions." Sorath opened his hand, revealing little spheres. "Mages have a hard time focusing when fireplaces are blowing up behind them."

"*Some* do," the captain agreed. "We were lucky these were teenagers and not yet well trained."

Tezi looked at the dead men—boys—and realized the captain was right. Every one of them had been her age or younger. "They start their torments young," she murmured.

"Why not when they're taught that terrene humans are animals and that their power means they can get away with anything?" Sorath said bitterly. "I'll check on the men outside."

He strode out, radiating anger.

"He's determined to get himself killed before he finishes that book." The captain sighed.

Tezi didn't point out that she'd been on the verge of firing when Sorath had. It might not matter. She'd helped kill one, and the authorities might figure that out. The captain had helped too. The whole company might be punished—or worse—if the parents of the mage boys figured out who had been responsible for their deaths.

16

FROM A DISTANCE, AMURI DIDN'T LOOK THAT MUCH DIFFERENT FROM Perchver, save for the whitewashed wall that protected the citizens from bandits and giant sand lizards—but not lustful teenage mages, Sorath thought bitterly.

A huge flying transport vessel rested on the ground outside the southern gate, looking more like a giant gilded box than a sailing ship or even the typical mageship. A large cargo door on the back end was down, acting like a ramp into its shadowed interior. The castle-and-lightning-bolt crest of King Zaruk gleamed on the side, its shimmering silver and blue metal catching the reds of the setting sun. Uniformed soldiers were queued up outside even before the caravan with the Red Sabers and Thorn Company arrived.

"It looks like Lugurt is going to have someone else bidding against him after all," Ferroki said quietly from the back of her camel. "That's Abokk's company, I believe."

After the mage battle, her mercenaries had reclaimed their mounts, though not without wasting an hour. The camels had been terrified, some having run over to the ocean and up the beach for more than a mile. Thorn Company, which had taken the brunt of the lightning attacks, had also needed to tend to the soldiers who had been struck. Lightning was a favorite magic of Zaruk's legions, if the crest was any indication. Her doctor had taken a hard hit that left her hair sticking up in all directions and her uniform charred, but at least she'd survived. Sorath, who never liked to see soldiers injured, especially for something idiotic, was glad it hadn't been worse.

Though it had only been a few hours since the attack, sooner or later, someone would miss the young mages and go looking for them. Sorath hadn't left any of them alive—in part because he loathed savage shits like that, and in part because there had been too many injustices in the past that he'd had to turn his back on to ensure his company wouldn't be punished for his choices. Now that he no longer led a company, and only his own life was at stake, it mattered little if he got himself into trouble. He should have died on the battlefield earlier that year. The only thing he cared about accomplishing before his death was finishing his book, but if he had to make the choice between stopping people from being tormented and writing those last six chapters, so be it.

Besides, Ferroki's rookie had been about to fire. That would have spelled out her death, whether she'd known it or not. Maybe the deaths of all of Thorn Company. Sorath had been happy to fire first and keep them from that fate, though it concerned him that Ferroki and the rookie had come to help and had shot a mage anyway. Even though he couldn't blame them for charging in, probably believing he needed the backup, he'd hoped to be swift enough to prevent that. He'd made sure none of the rapists had survived to point him out to the authorities that would inevitably investigate, but there had been survivors among the victims, and he had no doubt they would be questioned. He hoped none of the girls in the hotel had seen Ferroki shoot one of the mages.

"You know what that's about?" Sorath tilted his chin toward the squads of mercenaries, all in the loose white trousers and sleeveless wrap tops of Abokk's Desert Knights, a local outfit of a couple hundred. He'd battled them before, and his company had defeated them utterly. His gut churned at the unfairness that they were still around and his own Fang and Talon was gone.

"Apparently, King Zaruk is hiring," Ferroki said. "I have a hunch it's related to that artifact. It's a foregone conclusion that Malek didn't have Zaruk's permission to come loot it from his kingdom."

"That makes sense." Sorath had considered that himself when the word had gotten out. "I'm surprised he's taking action so quickly. Though perhaps not. The kings have been sniping at each other since they first built their castles in the sky."

"Maybe this time, it'll be all-out war. I'm never sure whether to wish that or not. Will it be better for simple humans living down here? Or worse?"

"Worse. After they use up mercenaries in their battles, they'll draft able-bodied men—and women—from down here and hurl them at the ramparts of their enemies until everyone is dead. And then they'll rebuild from the ruins, creating another world in which mages rule and we're powerless pawns."

Ferroki gazed over at him. "Maybe it's not as silly as I thought that you're writing a book. You like your words."

"You thought it was silly?"

"Well, you don't look the part of a scribe, running around with your broken nose, scars, and death-blow hand."

Sorath snorted at the name for his metal appendage. After the carnage in the hotel, maybe it wasn't a bad one. It was handy in close quarters, and he'd known the wounds would lead back to him instead of—he hoped—Ferroki. "I've got paper and pens in my pack. I can free them and take up the scrivener's role at any moment."

"I'm sure they're nestled in there nicely between your ammunition and whatever those spheres are that you were hurling at the mages."

"Pop-bangs. A chemist-turned-armorer in Perchver makes them. No magic involved, as I prefer." Sorath would never again be betrayed by a weapon made by mages—one they could easily turn against its user with a wave of a hand. He'd been skeptical early in his career when magic had first replaced the flintlock firing mechanism on firearms, and "magelocks" had been born. In the years that followed, bullets had also been replaced, leaving most modern pistols and rifles hurling magical charges. These days, Sorath had to hunt for smiths making bullets for what many said with a chuckle were noisy old-fashioned weapons.

"They're self-detonating?" Ferroki asked.

"Upon impact, yes."

"What happens if you fall off your horse and land on them?"

"I have a bad day."

Something blotted out the sun, throwing a shadow across the desert. Another gilded transport vessel.

It flew in from the sea, heading for a landing spot next to the first. Initially, Sorath thought it was a second craft from Zaruk's sky city, but a gold-and-green sun-and-tree crest gleamed on its side. Queen Vorsha's mark.

"Interesting," he murmured.

Ferroki spotted it too. "Her kingdom is almost a thousand miles to the northwest. What are her people doing here?"

"Recruiting troops, it looks like."

"Out from under Zaruk's nose? I thought those two were putative allies. At the least, they trade with each other without imposing tariffs."

"Yes, the rumors say they're even boudoir buddies."

Ferroki blinked at him. "Did you say boudoir buddies?"

"Yes. Like a true wordsmith, I'm experimenting with alliteration."

"All these years, I never realized what a strange man you are."

"I'm a *fascinating* man. It's not my fault you never plumbed my depths."

"Your depths didn't used to talk so much."

"Because you were usually trying to wheedle secrets about troop movements and my plans out of me before."

"It was that obvious?"

"I'm keenly perceptive." Sorath lifted a hand as wind from the vessel's landing caused grit and sand to skid across the parched earth. "Queen Vorsha doesn't permit mercenaries within her kingdom. Maybe that's why she sent her people over here. The desert is rife with our kind, so whoever Zaruk's people don't pick, she can have. Are you going to join in on their war?"

"I... hadn't planned on it. We have the little issue to resolve, though I do wonder how much they're paying. It's been a long drought, and if we don't get a good payday soon..." Ferroki turned a wistful eye on the transport vessels. "And as suicidal as it can be to battle against mages, everyone loves an excuse to kill them."

"I've noticed. If you need the cash, you might think about it. If your company is gathered with several others, and up fighting on mageships over sky cities, the artifact hunters will have a hard time getting to you. And even Malek wouldn't be so brazen as to stroll into another king's army looking for you."

"I'm not sure that's true, but you're right that it might be possible we'd be lost in the crowd. I'm nothing to Malek, and one mercenary is much like another to those outside of the profession."

Sorath didn't point out that her all-female unit was atypical and would stick out in people's memories whether they were in the profession or not. Ferroki already knew that. Besides, Malek hadn't mentioned anything specific about her or Thorn Company when he'd put word out about the medallion. Maybe he hadn't bothered to look them up.

"Are *you* going to get in line and go up to fight?" Ferroki asked.

Sorath shook his head. "I've no unit to lead into battle anymore. My plan is to spend the rest of my life in hiding while I finish my opus. If you want me to take your burden off your hands, I can go up to your headquarters and bury it for you." Sorath hoped she wouldn't think he wanted it for some personal gain. He felt compelled to offer to protect her, if he could, and nothing more, but after the words came out, he realized she might wonder if he would turn it over to Malek for the reward. He *hoped* she wouldn't believe that he would do that, but despite crossing paths numerous times over the years, they didn't truly know each other well.

"And make yourself a target?" was what Ferroki asked.

"I've been a target my whole life."

"I can't do that to you. You already lost your shop because people were looking for it." Ferroki touched the buttoned pocket that presumably held the medallion. "Besides, as you pointed out, they might capture and question me even if they can't sense it on me."

"I understand, but if they probed your mind with magic, they would see the truth. That you passed it off to a rogue survivor who's hard to find and harder to kill."

"How can you be hard to find? You're right here."

"I can disappear in the blink of an eye."

"In a black cloak in a pale desert?"

"My gifts are many."

Ferroki snorted, then shifted her camel over to talk to her lieutenant. They pointed at the new transport vessel, maybe considering his words.

Sorath was about to bow and say farewell, figuring it would be best if he didn't know their plans—or they his—in case he was caught and questioned later, but he paused when a black mage-cart sped out through the open city gates. Four of Zaruk's blue-uniformed mage soldiers sat in seats up front, and a man with short white hair and fitted black clothing stood in the back. His arms were crossed over his chest, his stance wide, and his chin had an aggressive tilt as he scanned his surroundings. Stone Heart. Zaruk's right-hand man.

"Off the road," Ferroki called to her people.

She needn't have said anything. The mercenaries saw the zidarr coming, his magecart speeding toward them without any indication that it would go around the caravan, and guided their camels into the dirt.

Sorath made sure his hood was up and shadowing his face. Not that the zidarr mind-readers couldn't figure out who he was as soon as they probed his thoughts. Hopefully, with so many soldiers out here, Stone Heart wouldn't notice him.

The zidarr's icy gaze skimmed the mercenaries, but the mage-cart sped past, heading down the road in the direction the caravan had come from. Sorath had a feeling they were being sent to find the missing mages.

"Let's go mingle with those mercenaries," Ferroki told her lieu-tenant and nearby sergeants. "And get away from the caravan."

Lugurt's Red Sabers were already lining up in front of Zaruk's transport vessel. A blue-uniformed soldier with a clipboard stood at the top of the ramp and was exchanging shouts with a green-uniformed man who'd just lowered the cargo-hold door on the queen's vessel.

"Best wishes, Captain," Sorath said as Ferroki turned to salute him before leaving.

"Stay safe, Vorzaz."

"That seems unlikely, but I'll endeavor to succeed."

"You've a book to finish and fancy words to use."

"True."

As the mercenaries moved off, Sorath nudged his horse back onto the road—the black magecart had disappeared over a hill. He intended to pass through the gate, turn in his mount, buy a less obvious costume, and disappear into the city until he could find a new hideout from which to write. But his horse had only taken a few steps when two more magecarts sailed out through the gate with more uniformed soldiers seated inside.

Several squinted at him, and Sorath realized how much he stood out, alone on the road, except for the merchants, who were all that remained from the caravan. They'd already reached the gate, and the carts swerved to zip around their loaded camels. Sorath moved his mount off the road, hoping the mages would continue past. One cart did, but the other slowed to a stop right in front of him.

"You there," an older mage said, an aura of power clinging to him. "Are you a caravan guard?"

"Yes, but the caravan has arrived, so it's time for a drink in your fine city there."

"Did you see any young mages on the road?"

"No."

The mage scrutinized him. Sorath emptied his mind of thoughts, save for boring imagery of his horse trodding along an empty road.

"You seem familiar," the mage said. "Remove your hood."

Knowing it would be suspicious if he made excuses, Sorath didn't hesitate to push it back. He hoped that his bushy thatch of hair would throw the man off, despite Ferroki's suggestion that it was a poor disguise. It wasn't easy for him to blend his scarred face into a crowd. Especially here, when he was so far away from the crowd.

As the mage kept squinting at him, trying to place his face, Sorath debated what he would do when the impending recognition came. Allow himself to be arrested? Or—more likely—shot? He wouldn't be surprised if the kings who'd betrayed his unit had learned by now that he'd survived and put out a reward for him. And if they found out about the mages at the hotel...

"Scribe Vorzaz," came a call from behind him. Ferroki.

Sorath winced. He kept trying to keep her out of trouble, and she kept insisting on standing with him to face it. Didn't she realize he was trying to selflessly sacrifice himself if need be?

"Don't forget to write about our tale for the locals," she called. "We're boarding now to hire on with the queen. The war will be momentous."

"You're a *scribe*?" The mage who'd been hung up on his face looked him up and down, his gaze lingering on Sorath's weapons and hand replacement.

"A skilled one. And an accountant. I was keeping the books for their unit until they couldn't afford to pay me anymore." Sorath lifted a hand, keeping the movement slow since they were all watching him tensely, and pulled out the pen tucked into his tangle of hair. "Of course, I fight when needed. Bookkeepers are frequent targets, you know."

"You're lying."

"Am I?" Sorath trusted the mage hadn't gotten what he'd hoped for in his mind and wasn't certain who he was. If he'd seen the truth, he would have reacted with more than an accusation. The men in the cart with him were fingering their weapons. And —Sorath caught motion farther along the road—damn. Stone Heart's cart had returned to the hilltop, the zidarr staring back at them.

A mage in the front of the cart touched his temple, probably being told telepathically to hurry along. Because his men were dawdling? Or because Stone Heart had sensed Sorath was trouble?

"Mark him, Defron," the mage said, "so we can find him in the city later if we want. The zidarr needs us for the search."

"Very well." The older mage lifted a hand.

Sorath gritted his teeth as a pulse of power washed over him, making his hair stand on end and filling him with the urge to scratch at skin that had grown itchy over every part of his body. He imagined that to any mage around, he now glowed like a bloom of phytoplankton at the beach.

"Go ahead." The older mage nodded to the driver, and their cart zipped off down the road.

Sorath looked through the gate and groaned to himself. A lot of people were in the wide main street that led into the city, many peering curiously out toward the transport vessels, and some of those people included uniformed mages stationed at points along the way. A huge sign warned of the potential for enemy incursions and ordered a curfew for sunset. More guards than usual stood in the towers along the walls, each occupied by a uniformed city enforcer and also a robed mage. Amuri was expecting trouble, and if Sorath walked in, glowing with a magical mark, he would be singled out at every step.

Hypothetically, he could pass around the city instead of going through, but what then? The Rogue Mountains rose up in the distance, hostile and filled with giant sand lizards, so settlements were sparse. That made it a five-day trip to the next town where he could buy supplies. He hadn't intended to travel all along the coast or *need* supplies. He'd only left Perchver to warn Ferroki.

"Stand up for mankind, bow down for the lash," he muttered the old expression.

Maybe if he waited for the magecarts to get a head start, he could return the way he'd come. He had food and water enough for the day trip, and Perchver was large enough to disappear into again. But the thought of riding past the spot where he'd left all those mage bodies, especially when an investigation would be going on, seemed ludicrous.

He forced his contemplation to end. Stone Heart's cart was still on the hilltop, the zidarr gazing in his direction. Mages weren't supposed to be able to read minds from a distance, but who truly knew the powers of the zidarr?

As casually as he could manage, Sorath nudged his horse toward the queen's transport vessel. All of the mercenaries who'd been lined up for Zaruk's had disappeared inside, the cargo door closing behind them. Most of Ferroki's people were boarding the other vessel, with her and her lieutenant lingering in the back. A few boys from the service that rented camels for use up and down the coast had come out and were collecting the creatures the mercenaries had ridden.

Aware of the zidarr's gaze on his back, Sorath headed for one of the kids, swung down, and handed over the reins to his horse, along with a coin. Stone Heart could only have suspicions, or he would have already taken action. It was hard to tell if he was watching Sorath or scrutinizing all of the mercenaries. Maybe he already suspected that some trouble had befallen the wayward mages and that the mercenaries in the caravan might have been responsible.

"On second thought," Sorath said, coming up beside Ferroki, "it's been months since I've been in a good battle. Maybe it's time I picked up a blade again."

"You've been in two battles since yesterday," she pointed out.

"Those were skirmishes. Whatever *this* is about—" Sorath waved at the open door, "—will involve battles."

"I have little doubt of that. We haven't been told any details yet, just that the queen is recruiting and the pay will be *legendary*." Ferroki's eyebrow twitched as she no doubt quoted the recruiter.

"It'll have to be if she wants people to take on Malek and the rest of Uthari's mage troops."

Ferroki was waiting for a couple of her soldiers to finish up with the camels, so Sorath headed for the ramp to the cargo hold. He wanted to slip into the shadows of the vessel and out from under the scrutiny of the zidarr. If that didn't work, and Stone Heart came after him, he would fight for his life and try to escape without getting anyone else hurt.

"No solo fighters." The recruiter in the green uniform lifted his hand to keep Sorath from boarding. He held a clipboard in his other hand. "The queen only wants cohesive units with years of experience fighting together. She's not paying for rogues." He wrinkled his nose as he scrutinized Sorath and his newly acquired mage mark.

In Sorath's experience, mage marks took weeks to wear off and no amount of scrubbing with soap and water would help. "I'm not a rogue. I'm an experienced veteran, and I can fit seamlessly into any unit."

He hoped this mage wouldn't do a telepathic check-in with the zidarr—or the mage Sorath had just told he was a scribe and bookkeeper. They *shouldn't* since they weren't from the same kingdom, but on the other hand, these two kingdoms looked to be allies now.

"That someone found you suspicious enough to mark proclaims your rogue status, if not outright criminality. You'll have to—"

"Is there a problem, Officer?" Ferroki asked, walking up with the two mercenaries she'd been waiting on.

"No problem for your unit. Just Solo here." The recruiter tilted his thumb toward the hold, indicating that her people could enter.

"Solo? He's one of my people."

"A *man* is one of your people? You're an all-female unit. You told me so yourself not ten minutes ago."

"That's true. He's more of a camp follower."

Sorath resisted giving her the scathing look that comment deserved.

The queen's recruiter blinked slowly. "He warms your bedroll at night?"

"With great vigor. We're boudoir buddies."

"I..." The recruiter reeled back.

Sorath almost did too. He didn't know whether to laugh or scoff.

"...didn't need the details," the recruiter mumbled.

"You did ask," Ferroki said politely. "He'll fight if needed, also with great vigor, but you don't have to pay him. I'll keep an eye on him."

Clearly flustered by the talk of vigor, the recruiter frowned at his clipboard but didn't seem to find what he was looking for. "There's not a box for camp follower."

"Like I said, you don't have to pay him." Ferroki patted the recruiter on the shoulder and headed into the hold without looking back. "Come, Vorzaz. My toes need warming tonight."

"Yes, ma'am," Sorath said, bemused since he hadn't called anyone ma'am since serving in his first command under the husband-and-wife team that had led the company. It had been a long time since he'd been subordinate to anyone.

All that mattered was that the recruiter let him board, scribbled something on his clipboard, and closed the door.

"Get that gear stowed, you slovenly maggots," one of Ferroki's sergeants yelled, pointing her people toward one side of the hold. "Strap everything down. We don't know how rickety this big box of a boat is." That earned a glower from the recruiter. "Dobbs, quit flirting with Fret. You know the doctor is taken. Let's go, everyone. Hurry up and settle in. We're going to war. Jinx, you're on duty to scrounge up some food and fill our bellies."

"Your sergeant is mouthy," Sorath said blandly to Ferroki as he drew even with her.

"I like it that way. Then I don't need to be."

"You've always seemed to prefer a quieter command style."

"It's true that I prefer it when I can walk past my troops, looking faintly disapproving, and they jump to do better, but sometimes, you need someone with a loud voice out on a noisy battlefield."

"She has that."

In the metal hold of the ship, the voice echoed.

"Thanks for the help back there," Sorath added. "Twice."

"No problem. I owe you a few." Ferroki held his gaze with dark eyes that never seemed frazzled. They reminded him of deep pools, barely stirring as they lay in the shady forest depths of his nearly forgotten homeland.

"You don't."

"Will I when I shove the medallion into your pocket and flee in the other direction?" Ferroki smiled, having no intention of doing that; he was positive.

"It depends on how long your hand lingers in my pocket. I might not mind."

She blinked, surprised at what might have been construed as flirting. Technically, it *had* been flirting, something he'd never done with her before, but she *had* called him her boudoir buddy. A joke, certainly, but she could have told the officer that he was something else. Her company's cook, perhaps.

But she looked flustered, a rare expression from her, and he regretted the remark.

"I better make sure everyone is settled in and try to find a bit more about our potential new mission." Ferroki patted his arm but then hurried away. Definitely flustered.

Sorath sighed. He couldn't seem to do the right thing today. He missed the days when his life had been simpler. Outthink enemies, lead troops into war, battle until bloody. Simple.

The faintest lurch was the only indicator that the vessel lifted off the ground. Sorath breathed out a sigh of relief. He knew better than to believe he was safe, especially since he'd just signed on to fight in a war against hugely powerful individuals with unlimited resources—and mercenaries—to throw around. But at least he and the transport vessel should be long gone by the time the zidarr figured out what had happened to the mages.

17

Morning found Jadora in Uthari's courtyard, getting her first good look at the ancient portal. Aboard the mageship, when Malek had been questioning her about the keyhole, she'd been too nervous to study it. Also, the light was better now, the sun rising over the courtyard walls and gleaming on the blue-black dragon steel.

Though she'd seen the artifact electrocute the drakur, she couldn't resist reaching out to touch it as she walked slowly around the ring. The flawless metal was slightly warm under her fingers, but it didn't otherwise react to her presumptuousness.

As she dug out a loupe to look for symbols beyond the writing that said, "Gateway to the stars," two older mages in red robes strode out to it. They ignored her and stopped in front of the keyhole near the writing. One produced a clumsy replica of the medallion from Jak's hat. Made from copper or bronze, it lacked the dragon emblem on the front and had likely been made from a mold. One mage thunked it into the keyhole.

Jadora highly doubted their efforts would work, but she watched curiously. It fit, but it wasn't a snug fit.

"Any chance it'll zap them with lightning?" Jak muttered, coming up to her shoulder with his sketch pad. He'd been taking measurements and drawing a blueprint of the portal.

"I don't know. They're not striking it with spears."

"They're shoving something in its orifice. If it were me, I'd be upset about that."

One of the mages attempted to turn the replica key, then poked it with a finger, and finally held his hand above it and tried some magic on it. The artifact didn't react.

Jadora wondered what would happen if the portal were activated as it lay on the ground. In the sketches of it in Loran's journal, sketches he'd copied from cave paintings and carvings in ancient stone pillars, it had always been depicted as standing upright. But the undulations of the linked dragons meant the ring didn't have a perfectly circular outside, so she couldn't imagine it staying upright for long without tipping over. She assumed it had either been braced or that its inherent magic had kept it upright.

When nothing happened, the mage plucked out his fake key, shrugged toward the shadows at one end of the courtyard, then led his buddy back inside. Malek was standing in those shadows, leaning his shoulder against a column as he observed the goings on. Or observed Jadora and Jak as they examined the artifact.

Was he reading their minds? In case they made a discovery?

Aware of his presence, Jadora had kept herself from clambering all over the artifact with her loupe to examine every inch of its surface. She *wanted* to do that, but if she learned something crucial, she preferred he not be there to witness it, to read her mind and learn alongside her. As long as she was clueless, so were he and his master.

But she doubted she could maintain that resolve if the guards marched her out here every day to study it. Nor did she think Malek would allow her to simply sit and stare at the artifact without doing anything.

One of Uthari's servants had brought the loupe and numerous other tools to their rooms the evening before. Malek had also come by, to make sure she'd received her husband's journal and politely ask if she needed anything else for her studies. She'd merely shaken her head, willing him to go away, worried that Jak would think things he shouldn't—about Malek's penis size or something else equally offensive—and that Malek would react. Fortunately, he hadn't stayed long, but before leaving, he'd scrutinized them both for long moments, as if they were some new puzzle to solve.

And here he was again this morning, scrutinizing them. Jadora had assumed he would disappear while she and Jak studied the portal, off on whatever loathsome missions he did for the king. But it was as if he were on vacation and had nothing better to do than loiter in the castle, in the same courtyard as she. At least he didn't undress her with his eyes the way the odious general did. She'd never caught Malek looking at anything other than her face.

As she slid her hand over the smooth metal, it occurred to her that it might be the archaeological mystery that kept him here. After all, he'd read Witiker's *Field Guide to Megalithic Artifacts of Eld*. Even if he'd implied it was the king who'd commanded him to study it, maybe he'd developed some personal interest. Archaeology *was* fascinating, especially the Dragon Era.

Well, he could stay if he wanted, but she wasn't going to encourage him or let him hold her tools.

She paused in her walk, letting her fingers linger on the head of one of the dragons. As with the first time she'd touched the artifact, a vibrant image popped into her mind. It showed her the portal erected in a grassy valley with patches of snow on nearby mountainsides. Dragons flew through that valley, hunting what she recognized from the fossil record and drawings by paleontologists as busaros, big creatures similar to modern bison. The dragons seemed playful, nipping at each other and having races, rather than serious hunters, and even though their eyes were yellow and slitted like those of reptiles, their scaled faces had an expressiveness that she'd never seen conveyed in artists' renditions. These were like the frolicking dragons from Iosako the Scribe's children's plays.

One flew toward the portal, and darkness with glittery silver lights appeared in the center, the rest of the valley no longer visible behind it. They were almost like stars in the night sky. The dragon folded its wings to its sides and dove to sail through the portal, disappearing from view. After a few seconds, the star imagery faded, leaving the center empty again.

Two more dragons landed in front of it, turning their backs to the portal and facing the rest of the valley—including Jadora's vantage point for this dream. If it *was* a dream. It was so vivid that she might have believed it a memory of something that had happened. But a memory from whose point of view? One of the dragon's? The portal itself? *Could* the portal have a memory? A sentience?

Two long-haired humans on horseback rode into the valley. Their clothes were made from fur and hide with bead decorations, and they rode bareback, using no reins or bit to guide their mounts. They stopped a few dozen yards from the dragons, facing them, and Jadora thought they might ask to be allowed to travel through the portal. But the dragons lifted their heads and roared, the noise reverberating from the valley walls. The horses shied and tried to bolt, but the humans patted their necks to soothe them and pressed forward. One raised a spear. Toward the dragons? Jadora couldn't believe they would dare. The dragons roared again but did not attack. The man threw his spear, not at them but at the portal itself.

The chiseled stone tip clattered against the metal ring, broke, and bounced off. Lightning streaked out of the portal, the same as it had done with the drakur on the beach, and it struck the men in the chests, knocking them from their mounts. The horses shrieked and thundered back the way they had come. The men lay unmoving on the ground. Dead?

The vision relinquished its hold, and Jadora drew her hand back, unease sending shivers through her. That had been a warning; there was little doubt. As she'd already seen, trying to damage the portal wasn't permitted. It could and would defend itself.

But why had those humans *wanted* to damage it? They must have hoped to destroy it, but why? And why with the dragons watching on?

"I don't destroy artifacts," she murmured, removing her hand from the surface, though it crossed her mind to wonder once again why the portal had been buried in the first place.

"You all right, Mother?" Jak was sitting cross-legged on the portal with his drawing pad out. If having his butt in contact with it was giving him any visions, he didn't mention it.

"As much as I can be right now." Jadora pointed to the drawing pad he'd brought out. "Are you getting all the dimensions? And anything else important? It would be good if we can continue to study it when we're locked in our rooms."

As they'd learned the night before, even though the suite they'd been given was luxurious, it was still a prison. The exterior door had been locked, and the guards on duty in the hall had stayed all night. Jadora had poked around in the suite's cabinets, collecting what materials she could that might be useful in an escape attempt, but she didn't know when they would get that opportunity. The only good thing was that nobody was loitering around reading their thoughts at night. They ought to be able to speak more freely then.

"Yes, already working on it." Jak lifted a pen.

"Good. Thank you." She stepped closer to him and lowered her voice. "Have you sensed anything strange when you've touched it?"

"The pen?" He raised his eyebrows.

"The *portal*."

"Uhm, sort of. It's a little bit like what I felt on the mageship, that I can sense its power. But it feels more alive than the ship. It's almost... I don't know how to explain it. Calling to me?"

"Has it done anything you'd perceive as a warning?"

"I don't think so. It's got this pleasant buzz." Jak slid his hand over the surface. "It makes me want to stay close and—"

He glanced up, lifted his hand, and widened his eyes in warning.

Jadora barely kept from jumping when Malek appeared at her shoulder.

"Do you require any assistance with your research?" he asked, his hands clasped behind his back.

"No, thanks," she said quickly.

"Unless you want to tell us what you feel when you touch the portal," Jak said.

Jadora shot him a quelling look. If they *engaged* Malek, he would stick around.

"We're comparing notes." Jak shrugged at her.

Maybe it would be good to have another data point. And maybe Malek would touch it too forcefully, and it would zap him into the next kingdom.

Malek regarded her blandly, and she remembered she was supposed to be guarding her thoughts.

He rested his hand on the portal—lightly—and gazed contemplatively toward the courtyard wall. A few guards were stationed at the doorways leading to other courtyards and eventually out of the castle. People who lived and worked there walked or drove their carts through the area, going about their daily business and only eyeing the artifact curiously as they passed. Jadora was surprised Uthari hadn't hidden it away in some vault where no one could see it. Surely, the other kings had spies in his city, and maybe even his castle, who would report its presence to their masters. Maybe Uthari was so arrogant in his belief of his supremacy that he didn't care. Or maybe he assumed the word had already gotten out.

"It doesn't fit through the doors," Malek said.

"What?" she asked.

"The artifact. It doesn't fit through the doors to any underground chambers—nor are there many of those in a floating city. Basements are problematic."

Jak snorted.

"He contemplated putting it in one of the large repair hangars in our shipyards, but his castle has more security." Malek pointed to the walls and upward at the open sky. "Not from the architecture but from dome-shaped shields that protect us. There is a magical barrier over the city as a whole and a second even stronger one over the castle. Can you sense them up there?" He had been talking to Jadora, but he looked at Jak as he asked the question.

In her mind, mallets struck alarm gongs. She shook her head minutely, hoping Jak was watching her, but he'd followed Malek's gaze upward.

"A little bit, I think," he said.

Jadora refrained from wincing, only because she was still in Malek's peripheral vision. *She* didn't sense anything, and she doubted any other terrene human would either.

"It is good to be aware of such barriers," was all Malek said. "Bumping into them in the night is painful."

Was that a warning that they couldn't escape because of the shields? How had they walked into the castle—and the city—in the first place if such defenses existed? Were they raised and lowered every time someone came and went?

"Does that mean we're safe from enemies here?" Jadora asked, thinking that a roundabout way to find out more about the shields. "That nobody can get in who isn't pre-approved?"

"For the most part," Malek said. "A few wizards are powerful enough to force them down, but that's rare, and everyone inside the castle would sense it if the shield disappeared. Also, the artifact that generates the shield would realize its defenses had been breached and alert King Uthari."

"Powerful like you?" Jak asked.

"I could do it, yes."

"You said the *artifact* would realize it?" Jadora asked. "Like a sentient being?"

"It is not thinking, but powerful artifacts have many abilities to react and respond in ways that are designed into them by their makers. Much as this portal, I assume." Malek had left his hand on it for the conversation, but he removed it now and told Jak, "It hums with magic, and I sense that it is aware of my presence."

"Yeah," Jak said. "That's how it is for me too."

"I have not yet received a warning." Malek regarded Jadora. "What did it show you?"

"Dragons flying around." She didn't want this confab with Malek, nor did she want him comparing notes with Jak when Jak's *notes* might condemn him, so she kept her answer terse and willed him to go away.

"And this constitutes a warning to you?"

"Dragons are large, powerful, and have fangs longer than your sword," she said.

"True. I've seen the fossils in the museums." Malek tilted his head to the side. "But that is not all you saw. You saw people die."

"Didn't anyone tell you it's rude to sift through people's thoughts?"

"Among mages, it is not considered rude. It is considered a failing of an individual not to develop mental defenses sufficient enough to protect one's mind against intrusion."

"*Non-mages* don't have that ability." She glared at him.

"Are you certain?" he asked, unfazed by her ire. "The monks of

Devaloryth have ways. Few of their kind have developed magical talents, but they can control their minds."

A twinge of curiosity distracted her from her irritation. She was aware of the stoic monks and their culture, but she hadn't heard that they could resist the power of mages.

"They also reputedly spend eight hours a day meditating," she said. "I don't have time for that."

"Perhaps a lesser amount of daily study would be required. I will bring you a book on the subject."

"Why? You don't enjoy reading my mind?"

One of his eyebrows twitched. "I gather *you* do not enjoy it."

No kidding.

"Regarding what the portal shows you versus what it shows us," Malek said, "perhaps it considers terrene humans to be enemies, or at least something of which to be wary."

"Why would it be wary of *us*?" She pointed at Jak, including him in *her* us, because it terrified her that Malek might have already figured out that Jak had some latent magical ability. "You're the one who would have the power to damage it if you wish. I've already seen that hurling spears at it doesn't do anything." Besides, she wanted to *use* the portal, not damage it.

"Perhaps it sees those with magical power as similar to the dragons, who reputedly had more power than even the greatest wizard has managed to develop. As I'm certain you're aware, some legends say that the dragons wanted allies among humankind and were the ones to help some of us evolve to use magic in the first place."

"Pindar the Great suggested he found proof that the dragons experimented on humans, giving some of them power so they could better *serve* dragons, not be aligned with them."

"I am, of course, aware of that hypothesis as well. Dioklesaz the Elder suggested that magical power was granted by the gods themselves, a reward for righteousness, and had nothing to do with dragons."

"Minosaurus the Druid wrote that the gods cursed some men by giving them power, which would more easily facilitate them destroying each other and wiping out the species, thus returning Torvil to the care of nature."

"That is an obscure reference," Malek said.

"Not if you've read the *Scrolls of Trees and Vines*, found in the Druid Temple of Southguard." Jadora lifted her chin, happy to dredge up every source she could think of to suggest that mages were a plague on humanity and the world, rather than superior beings who deserved the ruling positions they had taken by force.

"I am aware of the works, but they have not been translated into Wizards' Common or Dhoran. The druids, who have magical power of their own, have not allowed outsiders in to do the task."

"No, you have to visit their temple and read the scrolls in their native language."

"Which you've done?" Malek sounded more curious than skeptical.

"Yes. The druids study herbs like no other race, and their swamps and jungles contain many rare specimens. I spent two summers among them, learning from them."

"Fascinating."

Jak was looking back and forth from Jadora to Malek, looking a little stunned at the byplay.

Jadora took a step back, realizing she'd come nearly chest to chest with Malek as they'd been arguing, or debating was probably the better term. Who would the judges have awarded more points to if they'd been competing? And why were Malek's eyes glinting as if he'd *enjoyed* debating with her?

Uneasy, she took another step back.

"What are your thoughts on the runes?" Malek extended his hand toward the center of the ring.

"I..." She couldn't see any runes from where she stood.

"I was wondering that too." Jak scrambled from his seat to stand inside the ring and patted the inner side. "Did you see them, Mother? They're engraved in the metal but barely visible unless you're in here next to them. They're not like *anything* in Father's journal."

"Let me have a look."

As she scrambled over the portal and down into the middle, her curiosity made her momentarily forget about Malek and the probing he seemed to be doing with Jak.

"I'll copy them when you're done taking a look." Jak hopped back out of the center and waved her to take his spot.

"Good idea."

She had to crouch down and run her hands over the metal to detect the runes—her fingers found them first, dots and lines engraved in the surface. There wasn't any variation in color to make them stand out, and she had to lean close to see them. Making rubbings of them would be best. That would make them easier to study, but she grabbed the loupe so she could take a look at them in situ.

Groupings of dots connected by lines alternated with symbols or clusters of symbols. The symbols were all different, with none of them repeating. She didn't recognize *any* of them. Given how familiar she'd become with ancient languages in the past five years, that was surprising. *Were* they languages?

She counted thirty-two symbols or symbol groups, each alternating with the clusters of lines and dots. Those were all different too, though similar in style. She couldn't tell what they represented. Not words. They seemed more like maps. But maps of what? Some clusters had numerous dots, and others had only three or four. She thought of the molecular structures and how they were depicted in textbooks, but these didn't seem to be a match, at least not for anything she recognized.

"I don't know," Jak mumbled, making Jadora look up.

He was standing outside the portal and facing Malek, who had a hand on his shoulder as if they were good buddies. Jak's eyes were glazed as Malek studied him intently. Even though Jadora was as sense-dull as a rock, she could tell Malek was doing something to him—that energy he always exuded seemed to wrap around Jak.

Fear flashed through her, and she jumped to her feet. "What are you doing?"

Neither of them moved or acknowledged her.

She flung herself across the artifact, almost stumbling into them as she came down. She grabbed Malek's arm and pushed until his grip loosened and dropped off Jak's shoulder.

"That's my *son*," she snarled before she could worry about her safety and what might happen if she angered him. "Don't you touch my son."

Malek regarded her, his face a mask. She tried to shove him farther back, but she might as well have been pushing a rock wall. She was half-surprised she felt the heat of his chest through his shirt, and that he wasn't chiseled from stone—or pure cold magic.

Jak blinked and took a step back, putting a hand on the artifact for support. "I'm all right," he mumbled, not sounding *all right* at all. Had Malek *hurt* him?

"I will not do so again," Malek said, not noticeably perturbed by her interference. But he did look down at her hand, as if to point out that her daring to touch him was foolish and not permitted.

She yanked her hand back.

Malek took a step back. "I have learned what Uthari asked."

Her fear returned in full force. "What?"

"I must report to him," Malek said. "Find out what those symbols in the center mean and how to operate the portal. We will have the original key soon, and Uthari wishes to open the portal as soon as possible."

Uthari could shove his head up his ass. Or up Malek's. Still raging inside, Jadora barely managed to keep from blurting the thoughts out loud.

But it didn't matter. Malek's eyes narrowed.

"Do study the mind-protection methods of the monks," he told her. "You may live longer if you learn to wall off your thoughts. Not all mages are as indifferent to insults as I am."

"Thanks for the tip."

Malek inclined his head, as if her words of gratitude had been genuine, and walked out of the courtyard.

Trying not to think about what he would report to Uthari, Jadora rushed to Jak and gripped his arm. "Are you really all right? What did he do to you?"

"I'm... not quite sure. He asked if I could sense the power around us here in the sky city, and then... I don't remember. He touched me, and this weird flush of energy flooded me. It was overwhelming."

"Did he hurt you?" she demanded, though it wasn't as if she could do anything if Malek had. She was powerless here in this place, and she hated it.

She'd already lost Darv. What if Uthari found out Jak had power and was past the age when he could be claimed by the mages and trained as one of them? From all the stories she'd heard, they almost always *killed* people they found in the wild with power. Frustration welled up in her. Why was this happening to Jak?

"No, but the energy made me want to push against it, try to get it out so it didn't take over my body." His young face wrinkled in confusion. "Sorry, that sounds weird, but I don't know how to describe it."

"Did you push against it successfully?" She hoped he'd failed whatever the test was.

"I think I was starting to—he even said something, encouraging me to do it—but then you jumped in, and the energy disappeared."

"Don't do *anything* he encourages you to do." Jadora looked at the guards standing indifferently around the courtyard. "These aren't our allies or our masters. We're not here to serve them, no matter what they think."

"He was testing me, wasn't he?" Jak asked quietly.

"I think so."

"What does it mean? What was it a test for?"

She closed her eyes. "Nothing good."

"You have to tell me."

"I will, but not when others are around."

He frowned in protest and looked in the direction Malek had disappeared, as if he was tempted to ask *him*.

"We'll talk about it tonight," she whispered. "And I'll tell you everything I know."

Which wasn't much. If Jak's powers hadn't come from Loran, where could they have come from? Her own family had the magical aptitude of rocks. She'd married Loran young and had only been with one other man before him—more than two years before Jak had been born. There was no chance that he wasn't Loran's son.

Was it possible that inheriting magic wasn't the only way one could develop it? She'd never heard of anything to suggest that, but for terrene humans, much about the magical world remained a mystery.

How he'd developed this ability wasn't as important as what would happen going forward. What would she do if Uthari decided that Jak should be killed before he could become a threat to their kind?

Tears pricked at her eyes. She had to figure out how to activate the portal, not because Malek wished it, but so that she and Jak could escape.

Tezi sat against the wall, the mage transport vessel barely reverberating as its magic guided it through the skies. It was her first time off the ground, unless one counted her times being thrown by Sergeant Tinder, and it was hard to shake the uneasy feeling that she would be trapped in the sky city once they arrived. For so much of her life, she'd feared she would be selected and dragged up to one of the castles to be a king's bedroom servant. She never would have believed she would voluntarily step onto a mageship for a ride up to that world.

She drew her knees up and wrapped her arms around them. It was cold in the cavernous cargo hold, the area where the mercenaries had been told to stay. They shared the space with crates labeled *explosives, magelocks,* and—most alarmingly—*alchemical ingredients: danger, do not touch.* Straps bolted to the deck and walls kept the crates from moving around, but she didn't feel safe.

Nearby, others in the unit played dice and cards, unfazed by this rapid change in their plans. If anything, the mercenaries were excited, chattering about the possibility of *seeing action* and *combat bonuses.*

Tezi might have felt similarly, but she worried she hadn't had enough training to survive a serious mission. In the months since she'd joined, Thorn Company had been hired for a few skirmishes —raiding a bandit camp for stolen goods, chasing squatters out of a lighthouse, and exterminating giant tunnel rats that had moved into a mine east of Perchver—but nothing that could be called a war.

Was she ready for that? Were the others ready to rely on her?

The captain might be, after their incursion into the hotel together, but few others had seen her fight yet. On the mine-extermination mission, she hadn't been allowed to go down into danger. Sergeant Tinder had positioned her outside one of the tunnel exits, with orders to shoot any of the predatory rats that fled, but none had come in her direction. She'd ended up feeling worthless—if not deliberately placed where she couldn't get in the way.

Captain Ferroki finished talking to the leaders of two other small units who'd been recruited—Wrath Rangers, a squad of only ten who were supposedly experts on hunting and tracking enemies, and the Moon Guard, pale-faced northerners who might have come from Tezi's continent. Once done, she walked past her troops, checking in with the lieutenant and her senior sergeants, then surprised Tezi by coming over to sit down next to her.

"You doing all right, Rookie?"

"Yes, ma'am."

"Let's talk about today."

Tezi hid a grimace. Did the captain plan to berate her for disobeying the lieutenant and running to help in the hotel? None of them had been injured, and Tezi didn't think it had gone badly, but the captain hadn't truly needed her there, and maybe she would have preferred it if Tezi had obediently stayed on the highway with everyone else. It was hard not to feel disgruntled at the thought. Tezi doubted she would ever be a great hero featuring in a bard's song, but she couldn't stand back and take no action when people were being hurt. People suffering in the same way that *she* had once suffered.

"Yes, ma'am?" she asked quietly.

"First off, you should have stayed with the unit. Understood?"

"Yes, ma'am, but what if there had been more of them inside the hotel? What if you'd needed help?"

The captain grunted. "*I* should have stayed with the unit too."

"And left the, uhm, Vorzaz to get in trouble by himself?"

She sighed. "He should have stayed out of it too. I don't regret that we helped—at least not yet—but there will be repercussions. I've already talked to him, and he said that if he's ever questioned, he'll try not to let anyone know that you and I killed one of those mages. I don't like the idea of him taking the fall, but... I also don't want to see *you* with a warrant on your head." The captain gazed at the side of her face.

Tezi couldn't bring herself to meet that gaze, instead studying the gritty gray deck between her feet.

"Another one," the captain said.

Tezi jerked her head around. "You know?"

"I've had my guesses. You've been vague, but one reads between the lines."

"It's in Kingdom Darekarin where I'm from. I'd hoped that if I fled to another kingdom and a whole new continent that they wouldn't find me and they'd forget about me. And that if I learned enough, maybe I could protect myself if someday mages or bounty hunters *did* find me."

"And that you'd make new allies in our unit who would protect you?"

"No," Tezi blurted, looking in the captain's eyes, hoping she would believe her. "I don't want anyone to put themselves at risk for me. I just want to learn, like I said. I tried to sign up for a couple of other mercenary companies, but all they wanted was someone to cook and sleep with their men." She scowled at the memory of the leers and comments, though none of them had been as bad as the sanctimonious insistence of the mages, the certainty that they should and would be obeyed. "I want to be able to take care of myself, and I didn't have anywhere else to go." She lowered her voice and her gaze. "They killed my parents just because they tried to keep the mages from taking me. They'd already taken my brother, and I was all my parents had left. They didn't want to lose me. They were tired of losing everything to those *people*." It was hard to think of the mages and zidarr as people, as human.

"I understand. With luck, they'll be too busy with what might turn into an all-out war between multiple kingdoms, and they'll stop looking for you."

"I hope they forget about me forever," Tezi whispered.

"Then you probably shouldn't kill any more mages, not unless we're hired as a unit to do exactly that."

"Is it wrong to hope we are?"

"Probably not, but you need to know that any time we fight their kind, we have a lot of casualties. If I had my druthers, we'd never face mages, but the money is always much better. It's almost impossible to keep the company supplied and fed on what terrenes can afford to pay." The captain's gaze shifted toward a hatch that led deeper into the ship—the mercenaries had been told not to use it. "Bloody cactus."

A zidarr walked into the hold, and the conversations and dice rolls halted. Tezi's first thought was that it was one of Queen Vorsha's zidarr, but it was Zaruk's Stone Heart again. She'd *just* seen him on the magecart outside of the city. How had he gotten aboard? She was sure he'd been riding off to the south as the transport vessel had loaded up and taken to the air.

"How'd he get in here?" the captain murmured, echoing Tezi's thoughts.

Still clad in black, no hint of dust from the road on his garb, the zidarr only took a few steps before looking around at all the mercenaries. Searching for someone? Sorath? Tezi and the captain? Could he already know about the dead mages?

As he gazed in her direction, Tezi avoided eye contact and tried to shrink into the wall. The zidarr walked toward them.

The captain grumbled under her breath and pushed herself to her feet, standing in front of Tezi. Though Tezi wanted nothing more than to be ignored—or not noticed at all—she wouldn't hide behind someone else. She scrambled up to stand beside the captain. That earned her a quick glare rather than a nod of appreciation.

The zidarr stopped a few feet in front of them, his dark eyes as cold and hard as obsidian. "You assisted another in killing boys outside of Amuri."

It wasn't a question. He already knew.

Tezi licked her lips, afraid to say anything, not sure *what* to say. Was there any point in lying? All the stories said that these people —*beings*—could read minds.

"Boys raping women and tormenting their kin." The captain met the zidarr's gaze with a calm serenity that it was hard to believe she felt. "When the cruel sun dries up the desert springs, the rain must come and revive the earth so the world is once again in balance."

Her serenity didn't bleed over into the zidarr. Anger flashed in his eyes.

"It is not your *right* to balance anything, certainly not by *killing* our kind." The zidarr thumped a fist against his chest so hard it was a wonder his ribs didn't crack.

Where was Sorath? The captain had said he would take the blame for the hotel, but he'd disappeared.

The women of Thorn Company were watching this exchange, several on their feet now, hands on weapons. They glanced from the captain to the zidarr and back, waiting for a signal to try something. But what could they do? Even fifty armed soldiers couldn't best a zidarr if he was prepared for the attack.

The two other mercenary companies sat silent as they watched this exchange, and they didn't reach for their weapons. They wouldn't risk themselves to interfere. Tezi didn't see Sorath anywhere among them or among the crates strapped to the walls.

"Lord Stone Heart," the captain said, "it is the right of all men and women to stand up against injustice when they see it."

"Not with *murder*." Stone Heart thrust his hand out, and an invisible wave of power struck Tezi and the captain.

They flew back, slamming into the wall. Tezi hit so hard that the air in her lungs blasted out, and as she crumpled to the deck, she couldn't gasp it back in. The captain rose quickly to her feet, hands coming up, but surprisingly, she didn't draw a weapon.

Lieutenant Sasko and several others aimed their magelocks at the zidarr, and two people fired—or tried. The weapons clicked uselessly, their magical energy charges somehow depleted.

Stone Heart curled a lip at them and, without even making a hand gesture, used his power to flatten everyone to the deck. He stepped closer to the captain, his magic restraining her and keeping her from throwing a punch.

"Where is the man who attacked the boys first?" Stone Heart demanded, reaching for the captain's throat, as if he would strangle her if she didn't give the answer he wanted.

Tezi tried to stand, but the weight of a boulder pressed onto her back. She could barely turn her head to see what was going on.

The captain gagged, her face turning red as she struggled for air. He was constricting her throat with magic, not his bare fingers.

"Stop it," someone cried.

The captain dropped to one knee, but the zidarr didn't stop, not until something struck the deck behind him and exploded. The magic holding Tezi disappeared, but the shockwave knocked her against the wall again. The captain hit next to her, gasping for air.

Even Stone Heart staggered forward a step before whirling in time to face the cloaked man who'd come out of nowhere, landing in a crouch in front of him. Sorath. With his sword in his hand and the deadly pickaxe raised, he lunged for the zidarr.

His pick would have crashed through bone and muscle and into his foe's heart, but Stone Heart recovered quickly enough to raise his magical defenses. The weapon struck an invisible barrier inches from his chest, the zidarr not even flinching. Sorath swung his sword, trying to catch Stone Heart from another angle. It didn't work. The blade didn't make a sound as it bounced off the barrier, but it was as if it had struck a metal shield.

Sneering, the zidarr blasted raw energy at Sorath. He flew upward and backward, more than ten feet off the deck. Tezi expected him to land on his butt and skid all the way across the hold, but he twisted in the air like a cat and landed on his feet.

The captain sprang up and reached out, as if to grab the zidarr from behind, but another explosion blew less than two feet from them. Tezi jerked her arms up to protect her face, but pain blasted the side of her head as shrapnel struck. She hadn't even seen Sorath throw that—he must have flicked it toward the zidarr as he was in the air.

Either the explosive was strong enough to get through the magical barrier, or having it blow so close to him distracted Stone Heart, and for an instant, he was vulnerable. Sorath charged back in and slammed into him. Tezi rolled aside, but still received a hard kick in the ribs as the men struck the wall.

Somehow, Stone Heart had gotten his own sword out, whispering a quick command to make it glow a brilliant green, and he managed to shove Sorath back for long enough to bring it to bear. As Tezi scrambled out of the way, the men came together in an angry clash of weapons. Fire burned in both their eyes as they tried to kill each other. They struck so rapidly, steel clanging against steel, that Tezi couldn't follow the fight. A cut appeared on the zidarr's cheek, blood running down to his chin, and he roared in anger.

Sorath was fast, far faster than Tezi would have expected from a man of fifty, but he also bled from several cuts. He didn't have magic to help protect him.

On the other side of the battle, the captain drew her sword, but the men were lunging and dodging and slashing so quickly that she couldn't find an opening to help. Tezi drew her pistol, though she worried it would be as useless as everyone else's. Stone Heart must have used his power to drain the charges in all of them.

Footsteps thundered as armed men and women in green uniforms ran into the hold—Vorsha's troops.

Sorath dropped another explosive, disrupting whatever magic Stone Heart had been about to nail him with, but not for long. Even as smoke billowed in his face, Stone Heart thrust out his arms, and a blast of power struck everyone in the hold. Crates shattered as wood blew to pieces. The mercenaries *and* the soldiers who had been rushing to help tumbled backward.

From somewhere under his cloak, Sorath produced a throwing knife. He hurled it at the zidarr's chest.

Channeling his magic, Stone Heart moved inhumanly quickly and knocked the blade aside with his sword. It clattered to the deck inches from Tezi.

Growling, Stone Heart focused all of his power on Sorath, wrapping him in magic and hurting him with crushing pressure. Sorath's yell was as much one of rage as pain, and he never stopped glaring defiantly at his enemy, but he wasn't able to defend himself or throw any more explosives. Some power twisted his wrist, and his sword clanked to the deck. He followed, forced to his knees. His chest heaved as he sucked in air, the rage never leaving his eyes, never giving way to defeat. He looked like a caged tiger, tormented by his master, but believing that one day, the opportunity for revenge would come.

Tezi didn't see how that could happen. Now that Stone Heart had them, he would slay all three of them for killing those mages.

He prowled toward Sorath, his back to Tezi and the captain. Tezi wished she dared strike at him but doubted anything she could do would be effective. Besides, the green-uniformed mages were back on their feet, their weapons drawn as they eyed the mercenaries, ready if anyone moved against Stone Heart. Was he their ally? King Zaruk's right-hand man was working with Queen Vorsha's troops?

Sorath's eyes were tight, his face in a rictus of pain as Stone Heart's magic did more than hold him. Though he kept himself from crying out, his body kept jerking, as if electrical currents were coursing through him. Blood dribbled from his nostrils and one of his ears.

"Colonel Sorath," Stone Heart stated, no question in his tone. He knew who he had. "Imagine my surprise to find you in our kingdom. I thought you were dead, killed by an alliance of kings who banded together to get rid of a threat."

"Had to live," Sorath panted around the pain, "to write... my memoir."

"I'm sure the world would collectively experience an empty void if they didn't get to read the literature of a thuggish mercenary."

"If you... thought I was... a thug... you people... wouldn't have... tried so hard... to get rid of me." Sorath spat on the deck. His saliva was bloody.

"You *are* a thug." Stone Heart bent close to stare him in the eyes, no fear in his own. "You like killing mages, don't you?"

"More than you can know." Sorath glared back, also without fear, despite whatever pain the zidarr was inflicting on him. Maybe he'd already come to terms with his death and wasn't afraid of it.

"Good," Stone Heart purred.

For the first time, surprise flashed in Sorath's eyes. The captain's face held a similar expression as she looked over to Lieutenant Sasko, who could only shrug back at her.

Stone Heart must have released Sorath, for he pitched over sideways, his shoulder bashing onto the deck. He caught himself with his pickaxe hand before his head cracked down.

"Good," Stone Heart repeated. "You will lead the mercenary units that we are gathering. You will be flown to Uthari's sky city, where you will be unleashed against many, *many* mages." Stone Heart stepped forward to stare down at him. "If you're half as clever as your reputation suggests, maybe you and they will survive past the first hour of fighting."

Sorath glowered at the zidarr's knees but didn't say anything or try to rise. It looked like all the energy had ebbed from his muscles, stolen by magic.

"Find a uniform before you report to King Zaruk and his allies. And wash your face. You're scruffy as hell."

Stone Heart stepped past him and stalked through the hatchway, taking the uniformed troops with him.

Sorath rolled onto his back. For the first time, defeat lurked in his eyes.

"I was afraid it would be something like that," the captain murmured, walking toward him. "They're starting a war, and we're the cannon fodder."

18

Malek thought about *not* reporting to Uthari that he'd tested the professor's son, but as soon as the rebellious notion occurred to him, he quashed it and headed up to the king's suite. It would have been better for the boy if he'd shown no aptitude for magic, but it wasn't Malek's job to hide that he had. Besides, Uthari was expecting him to report in. He was curious about the progress on the artifact, and he would doubtless want to know if the boy—Jak—was a threat.

As he walked through the corridors, Malek's senses told him that he wasn't alone. He didn't look back but kept his defenses up, so no stray dagger would find his shoulder blades. Oh, he trusted his fellow zidarr, and knew most of them followed the Code as stringently as he did, but there was also a pecking order among them. Now and then, he sensed that Uthari's youngest zidarr, Yidar, had ambitions and would like to take Malek's spot as Uthari's right-hand man. He might not attack Malek directly, but he also might not hurry to assist Malek in a battle if he needed help.

Yidar and Gorsith, both dressed in black and bristling a variety of weapons from throwing knives to daggers to magelocks, trotted silently up the corridor and caught up with Malek, then fell in to either side of him. They were dirty, their short hair tousled, and their clothing wrinkled and stained, so they must have returned recently from a mission and also had reason to report to Uthari.

"Lord Malek," Yidar said, showing his empty hand, then touching it to his chest in the zidarr salute, a gesture Gorsith repeated. "It is good to see you well."

"Fellow zidarr." As the senior among them, tradition dictated that he not return the salute, but Malek nodded to each of them.

"We heard how three of Queen Vorsha's mageships attacked you as you returned from Zaruk's kingdom." Gorsith had a voice like gravel crunching under the wheels of a steam tractor. Scarred flesh across his throat served as a reminder of the garrote that had almost gotten him in the battle against Colonel Sorath's mercenary company. "How strange that her people were involved."

"Not so strange given the new intelligence we've gathered." Yidar waved to Uthari's double doors—they were already open ahead of them in invitation. "You'll want to hear this, Malek. War is about to find our sky city. Something I *relish*. A chance for honor and to prove myself."

"You proved yourself numerous times against that tree today." Gorsith smirked.

"I already told you. Vorsha's spies *hurled* that tree at me."

"You battled it nobly."

"They animated its branches!"

"I saw. Never has a dendritic foe caused so much trouble for a powerful zidarr."

"Stop laughing, Gor, or I'll tell your girl what *you* like to do with trees."

"Only the ones with strategically placed holes. And shut up about girls." Gorsith glanced warily at Malek. "You know that's not allowed."

"We can have girls, just not get married." Yidar frowned. "That's all the Code says about women. And men for that matter."

"Anything that divides your loyalties to the king isn't allowed. Right, Malek?"

"That's the rule," Malek murmured, glad his brethren subsided as they stepped into Uthari's suite.

Uthari sat at his desk by the windows that looked out over the castle and city wall and toward the clouds, though his gaze was on the three crystal communication nodes resting in front of him, each with a floating bust in the air above it. Malek recognized three other kings and waved for his fellow zidarr to fall silent and step off to the side with him, standing in a row in a rigid parade rest.

It was rare for kings to communicate directly and even rarer for so many of them to speak at once. This was about something important. The portal, Malek suspected.

If the doors hadn't been open for them, he would have led the others back outside, assuming Uthari would prefer privacy for such an important conversation, but Uthari glanced at them and raised a finger for them to wait there. He rarely kept secrets from Malek, at least not that Malek knew about, but a hint of surprise touched him that he would let the younger zidarr inside for this and speak openly in front of them. It wasn't, however, his place to question the king.

"Vorsha and Zaruk have gotten Dy and Dreter to agree to send troops, and they've been hiring mercenaries left and right," one of the kings said. "I trust your fortifications are stalwart, but you may want to send ships out and take the battle to them rather than waiting for them to come to your city."

"I'll take your advice under consideration," Uthari said, his tone suggesting he'd already had the information. "I appreciate you letting me know."

"Enough that you'll solidify that trade agreement we've been discussing? Your silver mines are overflowing with ore, and our alchemists use silver regularly in manufacturing headbands. The terrene population on my half of the continent is exploding, so we need more of them. You know how important it is to keep the dirt-lickers subdued."

"I certainly do, and I am open to trade, especially if you send a fleet of your ships to assist us in keeping Zaruk's minions from our walls."

"You wish us to assist you when you're so clearly in the wrong, Uthari? Everyone knows by now that you've stolen an artifact from Zaruk's kingdom."

"It was not originally built in his kingdom, nor was it ever used on land that any king claims today. Zaruk's predecessors were the ones to steal it from its original resting place. He has no right to it."

Malek raised his eyebrows. Was that true? *He* hadn't read anything to suggest that, and he thought he'd read more than Uthari—he'd certainly been assigned to read a lot. But it was possible that Uthari had been devouring all the same information on the portal over the years and had learned even more. It had been his main obsession for some time.

"An interesting hypothesis, Uthari. Have you run it past Zaruk?"

"I've attempted to do so, but he's refusing to answer my dome-jir." Uthari waved at one of the communication nodes. "Apparently, he's irked with me."

"Because you took his artifact *before* sharing your hypothesis about its provenance?"

"That's possible, but it would have been unwise to tip my hand. He should thank me, in truth. Had my ship not arrived in a very timely manner, the artifact might have been lost forever under the flows of that volcano. I understand it's erupted quite spectacularly."

"The ash has made it all the way to my kingdom," King

Wortalia said. "It's graying out the sky and worrying the farmers who depend on the sun for their crops. I suppose I'll have to send mages of my own to the source to do something about all that ash the volcano is still spewing. If Zaruk won't handle it himself. He seems distracted. What does that big circle you took do, anyway?"

"We're researching it now."

"Your kidnapped *archaeologists* are researching it is what I heard," King Jutuk said, smugness in his voice. Maybe Uthari hadn't shared that information, and Jutuk was rubbing in that he'd learned about it.

Malek didn't like that other kings knew about Professor Freedar and her son. When Uthari had suggested they might be targeted by enemies who wanted to keep Uthari from discovering the portal's secrets, Malek hadn't expected it to be so soon. How had word gotten out so fast about the portal? Malek still didn't know. They'd swept in and retrieved it so quickly, using the smoke from the volcano to hide their mageship, that nobody from the mainland should even have seen their approach.

Those mercenaries could have blabbed, but it was also possible someone from their side had been responsible. Someone from the crew of the *Star Flyer* or perhaps one of Tonovan's troops could have sold the information to another kingdom. Spies weren't uncommon, but they made Malek curl his lip in distaste. He preferred a straightforward battle among honorable opponents instead of skulking in the shadows and plotting treachery.

"We're researching it now," Uthari repeated, not acknowledging anything else. "Will anyone else commit troops? I am prepared to make it worth your while." He looked at each floating head in turn.

"What does the artifact do, and will you share what you discover?" Wortalia asked.

"We have only guesses at this point," Uthari said, "but if we gain valuable information, I will share it with my allies."

"Then we must consider if we wish to be allies with you in this."

"We've been allies before."

"That hasn't always been to our benefit."

"I've been fair."

"But reclusive."

"Are we not all reclusive?" Uthari asked. "That is the way of those who rule separate kingdoms."

"Send details of how much silver you're willing to part with and at what price, and we will talk further," Wortalia said.

"I have no need of silver," Jutuk said. "I believe my kingdom will watch and observe for now."

The other king grunted something similar and disappeared. Soon, all three heads were gone, and the light from the nodes dimmed.

"Come forward, my zidarr." Uthari rotated his chair to face them. If he was perturbed about the lack of commitment from his allies, he didn't show it. "Tell me about your mission and what you learned."

Since he was looking at Yidar and Gorsith, Malek did not respond.

"We verified that the mercenaries sent to invade the northern Sawtooth Mountains, and steal timber from our barges and iron from our mines, were paid by Vorsha. We stopped them before they got another load, and we sank their ships and questioned them." Yidar raised his chin, oozing the pride of youth at his accomplishments.

"They didn't know *why* she sent them," Gorsith added, "so we only have guesses."

"Either she wants us distracted while she and Zaruk prepare a raid on my city to steal my new acquisition," Uthari said, "or she thought we were already suitably distracted and she could get away with stealing resources without our notice."

"We noticed *and* stopped her, Your Majesty," Gorsith said.

"Excellent. You will be rewarded."

They bowed to him.

"Rest and prepare yourselves. There will be more fighting in the future. And I may have a special mission for one of you soon."

"Yes, Your Majesty," they said in unison.

"You are dismissed. Malek, remain."

Malek waited until the others were gone and the doors closed. He was about to share what he'd learned about Jak, but Uthari spoke first.

"You will continue to guard the professor," he said. "It is possible that our enemies will strike preemptively, before their forces arrive openly and en masse. They may wish to kidnap the archaeologists to gain their knowledge or kill them to ensure *I* do not gain their knowledge."

Malek understood the importance of keeping their guests alive, but the idea of missing out on a more challenging mission chagrined him. Between the castle defenses and the castle's own guard, Jadora and Jak ought to be safe. But there was much Malek could do out on the *Star Flyer*, firing upon enemies and keeping them from ever reaching the city. Even though he was intrigued by the mystery of the portal—and why it gave Jadora warnings and only hummed pleasantly for him and Jak— standing around all day while they read and copied symbols was not stimulating.

"I understand, Your Majesty, but perhaps others would be sufficient, and I could lead—"

"Nothing is more important than this, Malek." Uthari looked toward his medical apparatus. "My intelligence people have given me reports similar to the zidarr. I knew I might be starting a war by retrieving the artifact, and I *have* put into place measures, but I admit I'd hoped you would slip in and get it without anyone knowing."

It wasn't an admonishment, but Malek grimaced, feeling he'd failed.

"It is not your fault," Uthari continued. "I knew it might come to this, and I deemed the reward worth the risk. I thought we'd have more time before Zaruk retaliated, but... such is the way of the world. I will work on securing more allies while you pressure the professor to solve the mysteries of the artifact. I may send another to find that key. It doesn't look like we'll be able to afford to wait for treasure hunters."

Again Uthari didn't speak with accusation in his eyes, but Malek couldn't help but feel disappointed in himself. He should not have missed Jadora slipping that medallion to those mercenaries.

"I will do as you wish, Your Majesty." Malek turned toward the door.

"You had something else to report?"

Malek had almost forgotten. "I tested the boy."

"And?"

"He does not know it, but he has power."

Uthari's eyelids drooped dangerously. "Enough to be a threat at any point in the future?"

Possibly was the word that popped into his mind, but Malek paused to consider his answer. If he said that, Uthari would order the boy killed. He'd likely tell Malek to do it. It wouldn't be the first time.

Malek found himself reluctant to speak words that would result in the death of the professor's son. She'd already lost her colleague, and if they took her son, she would *never* be willing to work for Uthari—or Malek. She would fight them every step of the way and might be useless, resulting in Uthari's frustration and an order to kill her as well. Malek did not wish to see that happen. He rarely cared one way or another about the people Uthari ordered him to kill, but he'd been reading her papers and following her work for years, and had come to know her through them.

"I don't believe so," Malek found himself saying.

It wasn't exactly true. When Malek had used his magic to push at the boy's inherent magic, it had pushed back, a subconscious reflex with little thought from Jak. It had been a substantial push. If someone trained him, Jak could be turned into a powerful mage one day.

Even though it was almost unheard of to bring a terrene into the mage world at such an advanced age, it occasionally happened. Sometimes, normal humans longed for an easier and more luxurious lifestyle, with the promise of rewards never seen in the ground cities below, and they were eager to embrace the mage way. They didn't always need to be molded from childhood to be loyal to the mage community. Malek had no idea if Jak could ever develop such a loyalty, but perhaps if he could be brought into the fold, his mother would be less inclined to fight them and try to escape.

"Hm." Uthari scrutinized him thoughtfully.

Malek was too practiced to let his thoughts seep out for any mage to read, but the small dishonesty bothered him. He met Uthari's gaze, hopefully without artifice, though he was tempted to correct himself.

"I will trust your assessment," Uthari spoke before Malek could make his decision. "It would be difficult—even more difficult—to win the professor's cooperation if we killed her son."

"I agree."

"Return to your bodyguard duty, and do whatever you can to hasten their studies along. As I said, I will send another to retrieve the key. If the wheel of war has already been set into motion, we cannot wait for opportunists with no loyalty to us to find it."

"Understood. Are you sure you don't want me to go?"

"You have your duty." Uthari smiled faintly. "Have you won her trust yet?"

"It has only been one day."

"That is a no then."

Though Malek believed the teasing held no reproach, he felt the urge to imply he'd made progress. "We had a charged debate on the origins of mages."

"You mean you argued with her? That is not how you win the trust of women, my friend."

"We cited sources. It was a debate."

"*Sources.*" The faint smile turned into a full-on smirk with eye-crinkling. "Surely, her heart is bursting with interest."

"You said I had to win her trust, not cause any of her organs to erupt."

"Yes, this is true. Carry on, my scholar-zidarr." Uthari inclined his head and gestured toward the door.

Malek shook his head as he walked out. What did it say about him that he would rather go into battle than attempt to win the trust of a woman?

A twilight breeze rustled the papers stacked on the side of the portal, and Jak slapped a hand down to keep them from flying away. He'd spent an hour taking rubbings of all the symbols and collections of dots on the inside of the ring, and he didn't want them to sail out of the courtyard and over the city wall. He wondered how often that happened, that people lost notes, love letters, and cracker wrappers to the wind. Forever.

One of the omnipresent guards looked over at him. So did his mother.

"It's getting breezy and dark. Maybe we could take our notes and continue inside." Jak hoped she would catch that he wanted to talk without observers present.

"Have you finished the rubbings?" Mother asked.

"I have one more to go."

"Maybe our captors will let us go inside then."

None of the four guards in the courtyard said anything. It had been hours since Malek left to speak with his boss, and Jak was trying not to worry about what they were talking about—and if it included him.

He couldn't believe he'd let Malek stroll up and start diddling with his mind. It wasn't his fault—thanks to the magic, he'd barely been aware of what was going on—but he was disappointed in himself for not grasping the significance earlier. The fact that Malek had used the word *us*, categorizing Jak with *him*, had been telling, and even before that, there had been the conversation in the cell of the mageship where Mother had admitted she didn't sense the magic emanating from the walls and floor. He should have realized sooner that his ability to do so was atypical. But how could he have gotten stuck with this when neither of his parents could use magic? It didn't make sense.

Since two of the guards stood close to the portal, one pacing a slow circle around it, Jak hadn't yet had a chance to speak with his mother in private. He longed to know if she had some secret that she hadn't told him. That thought disturbed him. He and his mother didn't keep secrets—at least he hadn't thought so. They were friends, to the extent that it got him mocked by the other boys at school, but since Father had died, they'd only had each other. They had to stick together and watch out for one another.

Two of the guards left, muttering something about dinner to the two remaining, and the courtyard felt less stifling. The remaining two stood at the exits instead of pacing around the portal. Maybe Jak and Mother could speak without eavesdroppers now.

She must have thought similarly, for she climbed across the portal and slid down into the center with him.

"I'll help you with the last rubbing," she said loudly enough for the guards to hear.

"Right. Hold my crayon."

"Did he really give you crayons?" She sounded bemused. Maybe archaeologists didn't think colored rubbings were professional enough.

"There's charcoal, too, but these are more vibrant." Jak pressed the blue one into her hand, then knelt down, grabbing tape to affix the paper to the last collection of dots he needed to capture.

"My team usually uses charcoal."

"That's because they're boring old fossils."

"You know I'm *on* my team, right?"

"I think of you as more of the leader or director."

"The director of fossils."

"Your words, not mine." He waved for the crayon.

She crouched down beside him, careful not to block the courtyard lights—little daylight remained to see by.

"So, what's the hidden curriculum that nobody bothered to give me at the start of class?" Jak asked quietly as he adjusted the paper. "Father was secretly a mage?"

"No." She shook her head vigorously, her ponytail flopping against the side of the ring. "He hated mages and all things magical. I knew him well for years. He never showed any aptitude for magic."

"Then how could I have it? My grandparents?"

"Nobody. Not that I know of." She rested a hand on the side of the ring, acknowledging the hum of energy against her palm. "This is so powerful that even I can tell it's magical. I've never encountered anything like it."

Jak frowned, worried she was changing the subject. He wanted to get to the bottom of his mysterious abilities.

"There's a pillar made from dragon steel on Agathar Island in the Tarnished Sea," she said. "Thousands of years ago, sailors, pirates, and explorers all learned to avoid the island because the inhabitants didn't like strangers, and they reputedly had great power and could call down storms to destroy their ships. For centuries, nobody visited until a natural storm stranded a whaling vessel there. The inhabitants had all disappeared, leaving behind only the dilapidated remains of their village, evidence of a war, and the undamaged pillar. The whalers left as soon as they repaired their vessel, swearing the island was cursed. The archaeologists who later studied the ruins believed the inhabitants squabbled and killed each other with their great magical power, eventually not having enough people remaining to keep their civilization going."

"And this has some relevance to our conversation because...?" Jak turned his palm upward.

"Mages exist all over the world, so I'm not sure it ever occurred to anyone to question the power of those on Agathar Island, but now I wonder..." She removed her hand from the portal but didn't take her gaze from it. "I wonder if the *pillar* could have, over time, altered their blood in such a way that the humans there developed magical power."

"Because it was dragon steel and dragon steel is magical?"

"That's my line of thinking, yes. Since dragons came to Torvil so long ago, there's a lot we don't know about them, but it's agreed by most historians that humans didn't leave behind anything to suggest they had magical abilities *before* that time. We believe that dragons either deliberately gave some of our kind power like theirs, or that it rubbed off or was somehow a byproduct of their interaction. There are hypotheses about mating between the species too, but serious scientists agree that's implausible. However it happened, magic became a part of those affected, and they were able to pass along the ability to use it to their offspring."

"But I've been able to sense magic since long before we found this artifact." Jak waved at the portal.

She considered him. "*How* long?"

"It started after Father's death. Not right away. Maybe a year later. So, I guess, about four years now."

"You've worn his hat almost every day since his passing."

"Yes, but that's not..." His fingers twitched upward to the spot the medallion had rested until recently. The medallion that they believed was the key to the portal and was likely also made from dragon steel. He lowered his voice. "You think *that* could have given me power?"

"I don't know. It's just a thought. If dragon steel *can* convey power to humans, it must be slowly with exposure over time, or someone else surely would have made the connection long before this."

"There aren't that many dragon-steel artifacts in the world, are there?"

"No. Most that have been found are locked away in museums or are too large to move, such as the Agathar Island pillar."

"Maybe, if this *did* come from the medallion, it will fade in time."

"I wish that were true, but the number of magic-using humans running around today, thousands of years after the dragons left, suggests it may be a permanent change."

"Great." Jak stared at his paper, barely seeing it. The thought that Malek and Uthari could be discussing whether they would kill him or not sauntered into his mind.

"I'm sorry I didn't notice and couldn't warn you earlier," Mother said quietly. "You never seemed... weird to me."

"I didn't seem *weird*?" Jak gave her an incredulous look. "You didn't find it odd when I drew a clinometric map of the living room and furnishings? Or flooded the bathroom because I wanted to practice doing hydrographic surveys for my toy boats?"

"You did those things at age five," she said dryly, "not fifteen."

"Because you can't get away with flooding the bathroom when you're older." He waved away the idea that magic might have been to blame for his precocious childhood. "Father said so."

They shared a wistful smile of remembrance, and Jak's heart ached. It seemed wrong to wish his father were alive and here in this mess with them, but he would have loved to see the portal. And he would have had some kooky ideas about how to escape. He'd regularly gotten out of traps set by ancient peoples intent on keeping their treasures untouched—he could have escaped some stinking wizard's castle.

"I better prove to our captors that I'm indispensable. Until we can figure a way out of here." Jak took the crayon and rubbed it sidelong over the paper. "We *are* still figuring a way out of here, right?"

"Yes." Mother nodded firmly, then lifted her head, probably worried someone had overheard that.

Jak eyed the collection of dark-blue bumps against the lighter-blue background of his rubbing. There were about a dozen of them, and something tickled his mind, some familiarity that he hadn't felt when he'd done any of the other rubbings. On each of them, the dots had been arranged differently, sometimes just a few of them scattered on the page and other times dozens. The urge to flip through atlases came to mind.

"That's odd," Mother murmured, not ducking back down.

"What?" With the rubbing finished, Jak stuck his crayon in his pocket and stood to add the page to the stack.

"Our guards left." She waved to the two main exits to the courtyard, the ones where two guards had remained after the other two left.

"Maybe they went to dinner."

"And left us here alone?"

Jak folded his stack of rubbings and stuffed them in his shirt. "I was going to suggest we request a trip to a library later, but, uh, maybe we should try to escape?"

"Even if there weren't guards at the main exit of the castle, I doubt we could stroll out into the city. What about that dome shield Malek said surrounds this place?"

"Maybe that was a lie."

"Do you sense it?" Mother eyed him. "You told Malek you did."

Yes, and that had been a mistake. Jak should have realized it immediately. Maybe Malek had already been fuzzing his mind.

"I can sense *something* up there. I don't know how to tell what it is or if it encompasses the entire castle. But maybe we should risk—"

Mother gripped his arm and pulled him back into a squat.

As he dropped, Jak glimpsed a dark figure leaping over a wall and landing in a deep crouch in the courtyard. Three more figures followed, hoods hiding their faces, but they all carried weapons.

Mother sank even lower, pulling his head below the portal. Did she think they could *hide* from whoever the intruders were? Jak doubted that would work, not that he had a better idea. Was it silly to hope they'd come for some other reason and were just passing through the courtyard on the way to their destination?

Mother dug into her pocket and pulled out a vial. Jak might have rolled his eyes—when had she found the time and resources to concoct something *else*?—but with new enemies in the courtyard, he only hoped that whatever it was could be used as a weapon. Neither Malek nor their mage guards had been thoughtful enough to return *Jak's* weapons.

A faint rustle sounded as a shadow fell across their hiding spot. One of the figures jumped onto the portal just above them. He emanated power, the same way Malek did. Another zidarr?

Somewhere behind the zidarr, weapons clashed, the first real noise in several minutes. Maybe the guards had come back from dinner and discovered the intruders.

The zidarr, a hood shrouding his face, looked down at Jak and Mother. He wasn't pointing a weapon at them, but that didn't mean they were safe. He might have come to kidnap them, but he might have come to kill them and keep them from helping Uthari.

"If you're looking for the king," Jak said, his back pressed against the side of the portal, "I believe his suite is upstairs. You'll like it. It's posh. Nice chairs. Servants. I bet they'd give you a massage if your muscles are achy after scaling the walls and bursting through that magical shield thingie."

Mother shot him a quelling look.

Power gripped Jak like a vise, pinning his arms to his sides. It hefted him into the air, his mother rising right beside him. Jak could kick his legs, but it didn't matter; the zidarr was too far away to reach with a boot.

"I've got them," he called softly over his shoulder.

Another dark figure in the courtyard crouched above the body of one of Uthari's guards. He didn't radiate as much power as the man lifting Jak into the air, so maybe he was a normal mage and not a zidarr. Unfortunately, Jak didn't see how that helped him. One zidarr was formidable enough.

Another quick skirmish was happening in a doorway to the courtyard. Elsewhere in the castle—up on one of the exterior walls?—light flashed and weapons clashed. Were there *two* incursion parties?

Their captor turned his back to spring down from the portal. Though the power gripping Jak and Mother and keeping them dangling in the air didn't subside, Jak could squirm a little. He wished he had something he could throw at the zidarr. The blue crayon wouldn't defeat a mage with godlike power.

But when the zidarr turned back to guide them down, Mother threw something. Her vial. She'd taken the lid off, and she was close enough to the zidarr that he didn't have time to erect magical defenses. It bounced off his cheek, splattering a clear liquid on his face, before clattering to the ground.

Whatever the stuff was, he gasped and reared back. The vise of power disappeared, and Jak landed on the edge of the portal.

Before he could think better of it, he kicked the zidarr in the side of the head. The man reeled back, but only for a second. He flung out a hand, and magic slammed into Jak like a battering ram. It flung him all the way across the portal, and he struck down on the other side, his breath exploding out.

With his solar plexus spasming, Jak leaped up, afraid the zidarr would spring after him and attack again. He couldn't speak, but he waved for his mother to follow him and ran toward the nearest exit from the courtyard, one that led into a garden. If they could get away from the area and find weapons, they might not be so defenseless.

But as he ran, he realized the zidarr hadn't flung Mother across the courtyard. He glanced back, and his heart plummeted into his boots.

The zidarr had grabbed her, pulling her to his chest, and he stood now with a dagger to her throat. His hood had fallen back, revealing a man younger than Jak had expected—they looked to be about the same age—with red splotches on his face from Mother's attack.

Surprised the zidarr hadn't called out for him to halt, Jak stopped and lifted his hands. But Mother's captor wasn't facing him or even looking in his direction.

Someone else had entered the courtyard through another gate. Malek.

His sword and main-gauche glowed white, throwing eerie highlights across his hard features. Blood spattered his cheek and forehead, though he didn't appear injured. He must have been the one dealing with the other fight.

"Come any closer, and you'll lose your king's scholar," the younger zidarr said, facing him.

Mother's eyes were round with fear, but she didn't shout or cry out. She gripped the zidarr's arm, her knuckles white as she tried to pull it and the dagger away from her throat, but he didn't budge. He might not be as experienced as Malek—Jak didn't even know for certain that he was a zidarr—but he was fearsome and fit and powerful.

A bead of blood dribbled down Mother's throat. The urge to sprint over and fling himself at the man coursed through Jak, and he took three steps before he caught himself. The zidarr glanced over for the briefest of seconds, enough to let Jak know he was aware of him.

"Didn't you come to kill her anyway?" Malek prowled forward, not sounding like he cared one way or another if Mother died.

Jak cared. He backed toward the courtyard wall, hoping he could circle behind the zidarr and do... he didn't know what. *Something.*

The intruder's allies were fighting in a wide stone tunnel leading into the courtyard—even with a diversion, the stealthy incursion hadn't made it far before Uthari's people noticed. But the only thing that mattered to Jak was getting Mother out of her captor's grip.

Power thundered across the courtyard like a hurricane wind. It railed against Malek's clothing and riffled through his hair, but it didn't stop his advance. Even though Jak wasn't the target, some of it clipped him, knocking him into the wall hard enough that he lost his footing. He pitched down, knee cracking against the ground. Pain lanced up his leg. These people could accidentally kill him by throwing their power around.

Malek advanced several steps, rounding the portal toward his enemy.

"Stop, damn it," the younger zidarr snarled. "You went to great lengths to get this woman. I can't believe you'd throw her life away."

"We went to great lengths to get the *artifact*," Malek said, though he did slow his approach, pausing ten feet away. The dagger was even tighter against Mother's throat, slicing in, drawing more blood. "You'll find it's impervious to any attempts you make to damage *it*."

Yes, the portal could take care of itself. Mother, on the other hand...

The memory of the drakur being slain by the portal jumped into Jak's mind. Was there any way to channel that power and use it against the intruder? He was standing right next to the portal. But unless his dagger slipped and he nicked it, Jak doubted the ancient artifact would lash out. Unless it could be convinced the zidarr was a threat to it. Was it possible to communicate with the portal? Mother had said it had been giving her visions.

Jak found himself crawling toward the artifact, though he had no idea how to do what he was thinking, or if it was even possible. But all day, they had been discussing how it seemed to have some sentience, that it was more than a lump of metal. Far more.

"The portal is useless to you unless you figure out how to use it." The young zidarr sounded calm and sure of himself, though he had to be nervous about Malek's approach, about being in an enemy stronghold.

Jak eased closer to the portal. It blocked his view of Mother, the zidarr, Malek, and the fighting in the tunnel, but that meant none of those people could see him. He touched the cool blue-black metal, feeling the familiar buzz of energy against his skin.

"Perhaps we've already figured out how to use it," Malek said.

"In a day? The mystery of the millennium? Oh, I'm sure." The zidarr's tone grew sharp as he barked, "Stay back!" He growled. "Take another step, and she's dead. You'll only have the boy. Does he even know anything?"

I know a lot, Jak thought, and focused on the portal. He pictured the zidarr in his mind, that dagger and his magic, how he was close enough to stab the weapon into the metal, shearing off a piece of it and damaging it.

A tingle of energy went up his arm, and a new image formed in his mind. It was of Malek facing the zidarr, and Mother being held prisoner—exactly what was happening. Had the vision come from the portal? Was it responding and showing him what was truly going on and conveying that it wasn't worried about being damaged?

Jak replaced the image with another of his own, of the portal shooting out lightning and striking the zidarr while leaving Mother alone. Another tingle ran up Jak's arm, but no lightning shot out. Damn it. The artifact seemed to be listening to him, but it either couldn't or wouldn't obey his suggestion.

"He knows enough to take over, should you kill the woman," Malek said.

Jak doubted there was any chance Malek was monitoring his thoughts while he was busy facing an enemy, but just in case, he thought, *Get him to threaten the portal,* booming the words loudly in his mind, willing Malek to hear them.

Faint rustles and murmurs came from the wall above the courtyard. Numerous guards were now up there, aiming mage-locks down at the zidarr. Jak winced, terrified for his mother. She could die to friendly fire as easily as to the zidarr's dagger. Not that anyone here was truly a friend.

"Not another step, Malek," the zidarr growled.

Jak lifted his head to peer over the portal. Malek had closed the distance to six feet.

"If you don't value the woman, then what about *this*?" The zidarr lunged to the side, dragging Mother with him, and slapped something down on top of the portal. "With a thought, I'll blow this thing to the stars."

An explosive? Jak touched the portal again.

Now, will you attack him? he silently urged it.

He needn't have bothered. Before he'd finished the question, yellow lightning shot out, three branches slamming into the zidarr's side, leg, and head.

The deadly energy must have brushed Mother, for she cried out.

Jak ran around the portal to get her, but Malek reacted first. He sprang forward, tore the dagger out of the zidarr's hand, and pulled her away.

The zidarr screamed as lightning wrapped around him, his body convulsing and spasming. With Mother out of the way, the guards on the wall opened fire. Blue charges from magelocks slammed into the zidarr, pummeling him as mercilessly as the lightning. Malek narrowed his eyes, focusing on his enemy, and the zidarr's head exploded.

Jak halted, gaping. Had Malek done that—did he have the power to *blow up a man's skull?*—or had the portal?

The zidarr's headless body slumped to the ground, the lightning disappearing.

Malek didn't release Mother, but he pointed his sword toward the tunnel in case another threat approached. The battles in there had subsided. The king's guards and another man in black—not one of the intruders—walked into the courtyard, dragging two prisoners. The body of the final intruder also lay back in the tunnel.

"You're welcome, Malek," the black-clothed man said.

"Thank you, Yidar."

"Where's Gorsith? Don't tell me he was eating dinner and missed all the fun."

"I ordered him to guard Uthari," Malek said. "The first incursion team went for his suite."

Jak crept closer, wanting to check on Mother, though Malek

hadn't released her yet. Or maybe she hadn't released *him*. Relief stamped her face, but fear lingered in her eyes as she stared at the portal. If it had brushed her with that lightning, she had a reason to be wary of it.

"I wondered what took you so long to get here," the other zidarr—Yidar—said.

"*I* wonder who bribed some of our people to conveniently disappear." Malek looked at the uniformed men, though they weren't the same ones who'd been guarding the courtyard earlier.

Yidar shrugged. "It might have been a magical compulsion. Such as you were trying to use on Coxen there." He sniffed. "*Most* zidarr aren't susceptible to such tricks. I wonder why Vorsha sent such a young pup." Yidar himself didn't look that much older.

Malek shifted his attention to Mother, seemed to realize he didn't need to hold her close anymore, and released his grip on her. "Are you all right?" He eyed the blood on her neck and lifted a hand as if he might touch it or try to staunch the flow.

She stepped away, her hand going to her neck. "I think so. It's just a cut. The buzz I got from the portal was more rattling." She shook out her hand as if she'd been stung by a jellyfish.

"I apologize for not being as timely with my arrival as I should have been." Malek's tone shifted from formal to curious. "What did you do to his face?"

"You saw that?" she asked.

"I saw the result. The last time I saw Coxen, half of his face wasn't burned off. Or peeled off?"

"Burn is the more accurate term. I made an acid in case I needed to defend myself."

"There's not a laboratory in your suite."

"There's a kitchen."

Jak, who'd seen Mother make things from all manner of unlikely liquids and powders, wasn't surprised. Now that she was free, he quickened his pace toward her, but he paused when he came even with the explosive the zidarr had planted. The portal might appreciate having that removed. But when Jak reached for it, he paused in puzzlement.

It was... a mitten. At least it *looked* like a mitten. Was this some strange mage tool designed to appear innocuous but actually be a weapon?

"He won't need that now." Malek walked over, picked it up, and tossed it onto the smoking corpse.

"I don't understand," Jak said.

"No? It was your idea."

"Convincing him to threaten the portal? You were reading my thoughts when I, er, *thought* that?"

"I wasn't, but you projected." Malek's eyebrow twitched, reminding Jak of the other threat lurking. He lowered his voice to add, "I suggest you not do that around other mages if you wish to avoid notice."

"You manipulated him?" Mother looked back and forth from Jak to Malek. "Into what? Believing his own mitten was an explosive?"

"And that the only way he would get out of the situation was to use it to threaten to blow up the portal," Malek said. "I admit I wasn't sure if the *portal* would believe it was being threatened."

"I hope it's not mad that we tricked it." Jak regarded the artifact uneasily. In case it made a difference, he sent soothing and apologetic thoughts toward it.

"Let's hope ancient artifacts don't experience anger," Mother said, though she was also eyeing it again. "I am a little chilled to learn that it may be able to read minds. It had to have been reacting based on the zidarr's thoughts, his belief that he was threatening it, rather than having a mitten plopped down on it."

"Powerful mages can read minds," Malek said, "so I'm certain the dragons were able to."

"And they were able to pass that ability into the tools they made?" Mother sounded skeptical.

After watching the portal fry the zidarr, Jak had no trouble believing it could read minds. It had heard his attempts to communicate with it. He was certain of that.

A guard captain came up and saluted Malek. "My lord, we'll have the bodies removed and take these prisoners to the dungeon for interrogation. Is there anything else you wish of us?"

"Sweep the castle for any more intruders, and find out how these got in."

"Yes, my lord."

Malek looked at Jak and Mother. "I'll have someone escort you back to your rooms, and I'll check on you later."

"That's not necessary," Mother murmured.

"The escorting or the checking?" Malek asked.

"I wouldn't object to an escort right now." She grimaced as two guards dragged the dead zidarr's body away.

"I see. It's the checking," Malek said dryly, unaffected by the bodies around the area. "I'm afraid the king wants an update at the end of each day, and I'm the one he's put in charge of that, so you'll have to report to me and endure my odious checking in on the progress."

Mother touched her bloody neck and didn't respond to his words. She nodded to Jak. "You have your rubbings? We'll look at them in better light inside."

"Is there any chance we could use a library tomorrow?" Jak asked Malek. "Is there one in the city?"

"There are many," Malek said, "including one in this castle."

Jak wouldn't have minded getting *out* of the castle. "Does it have lots of atlases?"

"And linguistics reference books?" Mother lowered her hand. "I want to see if I can find a match for the symbols."

"Yes. King Uthari's collection is extensive. If it will help your

research, I will request his permission for you to visit his library."
Malek looked toward the courtyard entrance.

General Tonovan was walking in with several of his uniformed
men. Mother groaned, but he barely glanced at her, instead stopping in front of Malek.

"We've got new trouble. You better come with me as I report to
Uthari."

"It's begun?" Malek asked.

"If by *begun* you mean did two of Queen Vorsha's mageships
strike at some of our barges gathering food from farms, then yes.
They didn't even try to hide their identities. This is an open decla-
ration of war. I sure hope this was worth it." Tonovan kicked the
portal, scowled at Mother and Jak, and strode toward a door
leading into the castle.

Jak watched, wishing the portal would electrocute him in the
ass, but the foot must not have been threatening enough. Too bad.

19

It wasn't Lieutenant Sasko's first time in Zarlesh, the cloud city of three hundred thousand where the grumpy middle-aged King Zaruk ruled, but she didn't have fond memories of the last time, so she pretended this was a new experience. She also pretended, as usual, that she wasn't awed by the towering structures or alien architecture defying the laws of gravity. They were mage buildings made by mages showing off their magic, nothing more. The balls floating at the apexes of the great stone arches lining the wide main street weren't impressive, even when they spun and occasionally bounced to a different arch, bumping an existing ball out of the way and causing it to bounce to another and so on down the line. Someone who liked puzzle games must have built that.

Captain Ferroki walked at her side, with Sergeant Tinder, Dr. Fret, Rookie Tezi and the rest of their mercenaries marching in neat squads of fifteen behind them. The other mercenaries who'd departed from the transport vessel came behind Thorn Company, also marching in tidy formations.

A few pedestrians on foot, bicycle, or magecart glanced at

them as they passed, but the citizens didn't seem alarmed by armed troops striding down their main street. Nor did any of them take interest in the newly appointed mercenary leader, Colonel Sorath, now walking with his hood back at the front of the formation. The white-haired zidarr, Stone Heart, strode in front of *him*, leading the procession, with a few green-uniformed officers from the ship marching in his wake. Thorn Company had been told they were being taken to the local garrison, where they would wait while more mercenaries arrived.

A chilly breeze made Sasko wish she'd opted for the sleeved version of her uniform. They were now thousands of feet above sea level, the temperature notably cooler than it had been in the desert. Sorath must have felt it, too, for he pulled the sides of his cloak around his shoulders to drape down the front of his body.

"Are you going to have a problem with this, Captain?" Sasko tilted her chin toward Sorath's back.

"With what?"

"Taking orders from a former nemesis."

"We were rarely nemeses, and I respected him even when we were pitted against each other." Ferroki looked over. "Are *you* going to have a problem with it?"

"You know how I feel about taking orders from men."

"Unless it's under the covers?"

"*Especially* if it's under the covers. Someone tries to boss me around, and I'll put a death grip on his dick."

"A move that must make you popular on shore leave."

"That and my great tits."

"You're a soldier through and through, Sasko." Ferroki nodded toward Sorath. "We always have to work for men, either when our units are joined with others for larger missions or when we take jobs they assign. It's the way of the world."

"Yeah, but they order *you* around, and then you order me

around. That works for me." Sasko didn't go into her past or the reasons for her feelings—the captain knew it all.

"Nothing will change."

"What if he thinks that because we've spent a couple of days together, he can boss us around? You followed him into a brothel to deal out carnage."

"It was a hotel, not a brothel. And don't remind me." Ferroki lowered her voice. "Don't remind *anyone*." She looked at the back of the zidarr's head.

"Sorry." Sasko had been useless in that situation, busy chasing her camel and dodging lightning bolts. Knowing Ferroki had gone off and risked herself without Sasko annoyed her to no end. That mages could wave a hand and flatten an entire company of soldiers to the ground was infuriating. "Do you think we'll be punished?"

Sasko didn't nod to the zidarr's back; she trusted Ferroki knew who she meant.

"He's either forgotten that we played a role in that—" Ferroki tilted a thumb back toward Tezi's squad, "—or he's lumping us in with Sorath as people who might be useful in his impending battles."

"The rookie is going to be useful?"

"She shot one of them." Ferroki shrugged. "It's also possible he believes we'll die and that the mages will be avenged."

"That seems likely. I could see the zidarr knowing about Sorath and believing *he* could be useful, but our reputations aren't nearly so vaunted."

"My reputation isn't bad," Ferroki said dryly.

"Yeah, but it's not vaunted."

"As my second-in-command, it's not your job to batter my ego into the ground."

"Are you sure? Vanity can get a commander and her troops killed. That's in Ostark's *Way of the Soldier*, isn't it?"

"He mentions overconfidence, not vanity."

"Practically the same thing. My point is that I don't know if having Sorath in charge is a good idea. Yes, he won a lot of battles, and he's smart under that punched-in-the-nose-fifty-times face, but he got his entire unit killed. There were what, five survivors? Ten? Out of hundreds."

"Because three kings colluded to pretend to hire his company, then turned their combined forces on them to take them out. They weren't even kings known to be aligned with each other—the opposite. They'd been enemies sniping at each other for decades. I'm sure that's the only reason he was led into that trap."

"That's one version of the story. There are a lot. There's one that says they paid him a fortune to lead his people in there for massacre."

"That's ridiculous. Does he *look* like a man with a fortune?" Ferroki waved at Sorath's forgettable clothing, as travel-stained as their own. "Besides, *he's* the only one the kings would have cared about. His men were well-trained, but they weren't the thinkers, the leaders. They weren't the ones the wizards feared might one day be turned against them..."

Sasko dropped the subject. She didn't truly believe the other versions of the story she'd heard, but she hoped they wouldn't end up under his command. Betrayal or not, Sorath *had* lost his unit. The man was cursed by the gods.

Their leaders turned down a side road, taking them toward a walled fortress within the greater walled city. Zaruk's castle-and-lightning-bolt crest hung on giant blue banners to either side of a fortified gate. Magical and mundane weapons were mounted on the crenellated walls.

"This isn't his castle, is it?" Sasko asked.

"No, his garrison," Ferroki said. "I've been in it before. The castle is over there. You can see the golden walls glinting in the light."

"Of course you can."

Guards waved their unit through the open gate, a raised portcullis leering sharp wooden teeth down toward them. On a parade field inside, the ground made from some strange textured gray stuff that served as a reminder that this city wasn't built on land, numerous mercenary companies already waited. There were far more soldiers than Sasko had expected, troops lined up in formations facing the center of the gray field, with little separation between the units. In some spots, only the colors of the uniforms served to delineate one company from the next. Some were small, like the Wrath Rangers they'd ridden up with, and others had fielded hundreds of soldiers.

"Form them up, Sasko," Ferroki said, then pressed something into her hand. The damn medallion wrapped in a kerchief.

Feeling the thing was even more cursed than Sorath, Sasko almost thrust it back at her, but Ferroki was already jogging after Sorath. They were being waved toward a meeting of commanding officers in the center. Sasko stuffed the medallion in her pocket, hoping a few dozen yards was enough to keep the mages out there from sensing it. That and the fact that everything in this place had to be made from magic. Hopefully, with all that around, nobody would notice a little old ancient medallion.

Two zidarr in dark clothes without ornament, save for their weapons, waited, and the white-haired Stone Heart joined them. Ten unit commanders were in the group—twelve if Sasko counted Sorath and Ferroki—as well as several officers in the uniforms of Zaruk, Vorsha, and King Dy. A couple of them glanced toward a central tower on the garrison's main structure, as if receiving telepathic instruction.

People stood up in that tower, watching the proceedings, but Sasko couldn't make out faces. She wondered if the three kingdom leaders were here or if they'd sent minions. It wouldn't be that surprising for Zaruk to be in his own city, but it was rare for the kings to leave their sky castles. Vorsha and Dy might be attending through communications nodes.

There weren't many open areas left on the parade field, so it took some finesse for Sasko to march Thorn Company into formation without breaking rank. But she maneuvered them into a corner and took her place up front, waving Corporal Jinx out with the guidon.

Then came the waiting, standing in a silent parade rest while the higher-ups decided their fate. The rest of the troops had to be patient until their commanders returned and relayed what information they wished. At least, that was how it usually went. But Sasko was close enough to the group meeting that she could overhear some of the louder voices.

"I *know* who he is. My people aren't following him... got his whole unit *killed*."

Ah, some of the other commanders had the same objections that Sasko had. Sorath stood next to Ferroki, his jaw clenched as he stared up at the tower. He'd been wearing a scowl since his confrontation in the transport vessel, since learning his fate. Sasko wondered if he would have preferred death to working for the kings and with the zidarr again.

Stone Heart kept pointing to Sorath while he spoke to the twelve mercenary commanders in the gathering.

"...happy to listen to his advice but... Colonel Ramhorn should be in charge." One of the commanders pointed out another.

"Colonel Sorath is known for his effectiveness against mages." That was one of the zidarr, his tone as dry as sandpaper. "You'll be battling almost nothing *but* mages."

"Fantastic," someone muttered.

"Mind your tongue in our presence."

"You said you wanted us to be blunt."

"To be blunt, *my lord*." The zidarr lifted a hand, and the

offending commander gasped and dropped to one knee, gripping his forehead as if someone had thrust a dagger into it.

Nobody else reacted, though Sorath didn't conceal the cool stare he slid toward the zidarr.

"And I wish bluntness regarding our military tactics and the planned raid, not your feelings on mages." The zidarr released the commander, who gasped again at the cessation of the pain. "Is that understood, Captain?"

The commander pressed his knuckles against the gritty ground, and a long moment passed before he could push himself back to his feet.

"Yes, my lord." This time, there was no disrespect in his tone. His face was ashen.

Sasko was glad the second-in-commands hadn't been called up for the meeting. Working for mages was hard to avoid in this world, but she preferred to interact directly with them as infrequently as possible.

"Is there a chance of a surprise attack?" Sorath asked.

"Several of our allied mageships attacked theirs as they were stealing an item from King Zaruk's land, and there was a battle," Stone Heart said. "Thanks to their trickery, our ships were destroyed. Uthari will be able to guess that we'll retaliate."

"You're going to retaliate because they defended themselves adequately?" Sorath asked.

Stone Heart squinted at him. "Because they *stole* something priceless from our land. Do not assume that because you could possibly be useful that your crimes will be forgotten and that we won't kill you."

"The urge to serve you adequately is building up in me like flatulence."

Ferroki elbowed Sorath to shut up, but it was too late. Stone Heart or one of other the zidarr used magic to force him to his knees, and his face twisted with pain.

Ferroki's fingers twitched toward him, as if she wanted to help. All three zidarr glared at her, and she clasped her hands behind her back.

"If you punish everyone who speaks up," Ferroki said—damn it, why was *she* speaking up?— "we will not have time to plan a campaign and catch them off guard."

Her voice held little accusation or censure, just her usual calm, as if she were quoting from one of her fables. Even so, Sasko cringed, anticipating she would be the next one struck down. But maybe the zidarr felt less threatened by a woman. They released Sorath.

He stood up, as wan as the other commander, but he drew a steadying breath and continued where they'd left off. "Is the primary goal to utterly defeat Uthari and take over his kingdom? Or to get this *item* that his people have taken?"

Sasko didn't know why they were being vague about the artifact. By now, gossip about it must have spread throughout the kingdom—maybe *all* of the kingdoms. She wagered everybody here knew what they were talking about.

"We would love to take over his kingdom," one of the zidarr said with a snort, "but reacquiring the item is the primary goal. Damage done to his city *while* it's being reacquired is encouraged. His theft was an act of war. He brought this on himself."

"Where is this item located?" Ferroki asked. "Do you know?"

"In a courtyard in his castle," Stone Heart answered.

"Ah," Sorath said, "a simple place to infiltrate."

Stone Heart squinted but didn't otherwise react to the sarcasm. "Someone sent in a team prematurely to attempt to retrieve it, hoping to make a full-on assault force unnecessary, but they were not successful." Stone Heart gave a significant look to the men in Vorsha's green and also one of the zidarr.

"Since you've already given up the element of surprise," Sorath said, "we should attempt to make a diversion work. They'll know exactly what we're doing, since what you're trying to get is obvious to all, but if we threaten enough of his prime resources—such as the food that's brought up to feed his city—he'll be forced to send out troops, lessening the number left in his home skies to defend his city."

"We can handle that." One of the commanders lifted a hand.

"Sure, take the easy job, Kal," another said. "Let the rest of us storm his fortress and face Malek and his other zidarr."

"The zidarr will handle the zidarr," Stone Heart said coolly. "I am not afraid to fight Malek."

"I would be," another of the zidarr muttered.

Stone Heart gave him a scathing look, but all he got was an unapologetic shrug in return.

"Half of the units will attack at strategic points in Uthari's kingdom to draw his mageships away," Stone Heart said. "Once his forces are split, the rest of you will fly at his city from varying directions under the dark of night. Colonel Sorath will lead those mageships, and you'll defer to him."

"With all due respect," a new voice said, "no, my lord. Nobody's trusting his judgment against mages."

"We'll only follow Ramhorn," the commander who'd objected to Sorath earlier said. "We want to *survive*."

Sorath returned to gazing at the tower and said nothing to argue for himself as leader. He hadn't wanted to be here, but if nobody was willing to follow him, would Stone Heart kill him? As punishment for his crime? Ferroki would object to that, which could mean trouble for all of Thorn Company. Sasko shook her head bleakly when Ferroki looked over at her, a troubled expression on her face.

"With so many of you engaged in this," Stone Heart said, "the survival rate should be high. Sorath has fought and won against mages before, as you all know. His first loss came when he was set up, by some of the people he now has a chance to fight against." Stone Heart looked at Sorath. "You should be delighted."

"Queen Vorsha was also among those who arranged that," Sorath said without hint of delight. "*Last* year, she was an ally to Uthari. Are you sure she can be trusted not to tattle your plans to him?"

The zidarr who must have been one of Vorsha's loyalists surged up to Sorath. "The queen is *not* allied with that thief. The truce they formed against you was temporary, to rid the world of terrene soldiers who try to build their careers by targeting our kind." He curled a lip. "Too bad they failed. I hope you sleep poorly, haunted by the deaths of all those who died while you walked off the battlefield alive."

"Actually—" Sorath lifted his pickaxe to scratch the side of his nose, "—I crawled off the battlefield, almost bleeding out after using my belt to make a clumsy tourniquet."

Ferroki, who might not have heard that part of the story before, turned sympathetic eyes on him. A few others eyed his pickaxe as he lowered it to his side, grim-faced and maybe also sympathetic. But none of them changed their minds and said they would follow him into battle.

Stone Heart glared around the group, probably reading their minds and debating if it was worth threatening them into compliance. All of the commanders except Ferroki studied the ground to avoid his gaze.

Normally, Sasko would be proud of her captain for holding his gaze, but since *she* didn't want to follow Sorath, either, she would prefer Ferroki throw her vote behind the other colonel. Sasko had never worked with Ramhorn on a campaign before, but she'd heard he was solid. Admittedly, they would need brilliant over solid to have a chance on this mission. Launching an attack at a known target when the enemy was most expecting it was ludicrous.

"Fine," Stone Heart finally said, after what looked like a telepathic consultation with someone in the tower, "Colonel Ramhorn will lead the main thrust to attack Utharika from multiple angles and keep them so busy they'll be spread too thin to adequately defend the item."

Several commanders nodded. Others looked bleak, like they were rethinking whether they wanted to sign on for this. Sasko had a feeling that nobody had been told what this mission would involve before being allowed onto the transport vessels. Doubtless they'd only been told that the pay would be good.

"You're providing the majority of the troops," Stone Heart continued, "but we'll provide the transportation, well-armored and well-armed mageships fast enough to allow you to escape if you need it. And as I said, we'll send zidarr and highly trained mages along to assist you. Also magical explosives that you can lob into their city." Stone Heart smiled at this imagined carnage. "This isn't a suicide mission, gentlemen. And upon its completion, you will be rewarded."

Stone Heart took a few more minutes to detail the pay the units would receive, along with bonus rewards that would go to anyone who brought him the head of Uthari or any of his zidarr. No matter what he'd said, this sounded like an all-out war, not just a grab for an artifact.

Sasko thought the meeting was wrapping up, but Stone Heart turned to Sorath and pointed a finger at his chest. "*You*, my mage-hating colonel, will still play a vital role."

"I'm so relieved," Sorath said in a deadpan voice.

"I'd threaten to kill you, but there's little need. You're the type to lead the charge. You'll end up dead on Malek's sword point."

Ferroki frowned. "What's his role?"

"Actually, it's *your* role." Stone Heart wiggled his finger at Sorath *and* Ferroki, then pointed over to Thorn Company.

Sasko sighed. Why couldn't Ferroki have volunteered them to attack a silo somewhere?

"While the *diversion* is happening—" Stone Heart waved at the rest of the units, "—you'll slip in on a fast small mageship, abseil into their city without being noticed, and find a way into the castle to get the artifact. You'll secure it while also finding and destroying the mage tool that creates a defensive shield over Uthari's stronghold. Once you're ready, you'll signal the ship to come pick you up. The mage crew should be able to levitate the artifact out of the castle once the barrier is down, but if necessary, you'll throw hooks around it so it can be hefted out. *If* you return it here, where it belongs, King Zaruk has agreed to pardon you for your crimes, providing you leave his kingdom and never return again."

Judging by the distasteful twist to Sorath's lips, he didn't find the deal that appealing. Or maybe it was the task he'd been assigned that he objected to. Sasko couldn't remember hearing of any mercenary companies ever breaching one of the kings' castles. Their kind were usually used for ground attacks in wars of attrition. In all her years as a soldier, Sasko had *never* been flown into battle on a king's mageship.

"I trust you won't have trouble following Sorath's commands, Captain." The frown that Stone Heart leveled at Ferroki said she had better not.

"I acknowledge that Colonel Sorath is a capable leader," Ferroki said, "but I have not yet signed a contract or verbally agreed that we will partake in this mission."

"Nobody has," Stone Heart said, waving at the other commanders, "but if they know what's good for them, they will. As will you."

Ferroki opened her mouth, but he cut her off.

"There are not unlimited people in the world with the wealth and interest necessary to hire mercenaries." Stone Heart leaned in and towered several inches above her. "It would be a simple matter for the word to get out that you and your girl unit were too cowardly to take what is a more than fair offer from a king. World leaders speak with each other. If you do not want your Twig Company to be blacklisted, you *will* take this assignment."

"Thorn Company," Ferroki said without batting an eye. "Why does it matter to you if we take the job or not? You have others here who will do it."

"Because *you* will follow Sorath."

"And you think he's the only one who can get your object?"

Stone Heart eyed Sorath who was eyeing him back. They radiated distaste at each other, but Stone Heart's tone was almost respectful when he replied. "I think he's got the best chance. And your female soldiers won't be seen as threats, so you're more likely to be able to slip in with him. Do it and succeed, and I'll see to it you receive triple pay."

Ferroki took a deep breath before answering. Money wasn't everything to her, but Sasko knew she'd grown weary of the struggle to earn enough to keep everyone paid. Having full coffers for a while would appeal to her—to any mercenary captain.

"Very well," Ferroki said. "We'll sign a contract."

Sorath turned a bleak expression on her, but he didn't object. Maybe he no longer cared if he lived or died. It was hard to imagine that he believed they could succeed. He didn't look like a man who thought he would earn a pardon and be allowed to escape Zaruk's kingdom without a legion of mages hunting him down.

20

THEIR LAVATORY HAD A FIRST-AID KIT WITH BANDAGES, AND AS SOON as Jadora and Jak returned to the suite, she cleaned the cut on her neck. It stung, the wound deeper than she'd realized. Had she been back at home, she would have gone to Dr. Petrosni for stitches. Her heart rate, which had finally slowed to normal after they'd returned to their suite, took another zag upward as she realized how close that bastard had been to slicing her jugular.

With a tremor to her hands, she wrapped a bandage around her neck, then took a deep breath and tried to calm her mind enough to contemplate the future, not the past. If the kings were starting a war with each other, and preemptively sending people in to kill her and Jak, they needed to escape more than ever. Tonight was proof that they couldn't rely on the supposed castle defenses to keep them safe. Even Malek couldn't watch over them every second of the day, and if enemy zidarr could manipulate the minds of the guards watching over them, who knew when they would disappear again? Or turn on her and Jak with weapons more deadly than a mitten?

A part of her wanted to laugh at that trick, to appreciate what

Malek had done, but she worried that with new threats, she would forget to think of him as an enemy. She reminded herself that she was only here because of him, because he was King Uthari's loyal man and would do whatever his master wished. She shouldn't feel gratitude toward him or anything at all.

But... he'd showed up in time to save her life. What if he hadn't?

She rinsed her hands and splashed cool water on her face, trying to wash away those thoughts. He was as dangerous to her and to Jak—*especially* to Jak—as any of them. It would be easier to remember that if he were more like Tonovan, but she was glad he wasn't.

"I've been thinking, Mother," Jak called from the kitchen, odd thumping noises punctuating his words.

Was he preparing their dinner? If so, that would be a delight—nothing like a dagger to the throat to stir one's appetite—but he hadn't mastered much more than sandwiches and had to be reminded to prepare even those.

"Thinking is something that I feel like I should, as your supportive mother, encourage," Jadora said, walking out, "but usually, what you mean when you say that is that you've been *scheming*."

"They're very similar words."

"Yet not adjacent to each other in the thesaurus."

"Would it make you feel better if I'd been ruminating? Or contemplating? Or cogitating? Those are thinking-adjacent."

"I'm not sure I would believe you." She found him *next* to the kitchen, stomping on the floor tiles. The counter was devoid of sandwiches or anything else resembling a meal. "For some strange reason."

"Malek said the shield around this castle protects everyone inside from intruders." Jak walked into the parlor, stomping along the way. The thuds sounded solid. "So how did enemies get in?"

"Bribing or compelling the guards to lower it long enough for them to come in?" Jadora asked, though she remembered Malek saying the shield hadn't gone down.

"I don't think so."

As Jak stomped around the room and into the bedrooms, Jadora found a ham, carrots, and potatoes in the magical icebox and drew them out to prepare a meal. There was something surreal about groceries appearing in the kitchen—or even *having* a kitchen—in the rooms that were their prison. As she sliced the vegetables and heated a pot of water to boil—the flames that powered the cooktop came on with a touch—she thought of the farmers who'd worked hard to grow the food, only to have their crops taken by mages who never had to work hard to produce anything. Admittedly, Jadora didn't produce anything either, unless one counted the papers she wrote for publication and the classes she taught, but she paid for the groceries she consumed.

"Nothing." Jak sighed as he walked out of his bedroom and flopped down on the couch. "I guess that would have been too much to hope for, but we *are* on the bottom floor of this place."

"Were you searching for secret passages?"

"Maybe not anything as obvious as that, but I thought there might be ducts or maintenance shafts or *something*. I know magic keeps these cities in the air, but I doubt twenty mages are sitting in a room somewhere holding hands and concentrating around the clock to keep it aloft. They must have built tools that do the job. Remember that glowing engine on the mageship? And how it had tendrils that stretched out all over the hold and through the walls to other parts of the ship? There has to be a power infrastructure like that for the city too, most logically built into the platform that everything rests upon." He pointed at the floor. "And if we assume that it sometimes needs maintenance, then there have to be crawl-spaces down there all over the place so mages can get to the different sections. Oh, I suppose with their power they could repair things remotely, but those intruders had to come from *somewhere*. Maybe they came up through the floor."

"Is that why you want to go to the library? To see if there are schematics for the city's infrastructure?"

"That wasn't my original reason, but do you think there would be? I'd expect those to be somewhere more private, like the architect's office or maybe a room where the maintenance people work. Still, if it's the king's private library, maybe he's not worried about the riffraff wandering in."

"What *was* your original reason? I don't object—it's a good idea—but you've roused my curiosity. You said something about atlases."

"Because of that last rubbing." Jak brought his stack over, unfolded them, and smoothed the wrinkles out of the topmost one. One corner was ripped, and the wrinkles defied smoothing.

"When my team makes rubbings in the field, we usually store them in folders to preserve them for travel."

"Is your team usually hurled against walls by mages?"

"More so now than in the past." Jadora shook her head, wondering again if the rest of her team had made it home, and also wondering what she would tell them—and the entire faculty of the university—about Darv if *she* ever made it home.

"We live in treacherous times." Jak held up the collection of dots. "Does this look like anything to you?"

"My mind went to chemistry and started looking for patterns related to science, but no. Although with your choice of a dark-blue crayon, it reminds me of a night sky."

"Exactly. That's what I think it is. The dots are stars. This is a constellation."

"You knew that when you picked the blue crayon?"

"I had a hunch from the dots. Last semester, I took astronomy, and we made star charts."

"Which constellation is it?" She tilted her head to look at it sideways, then reached out, turning the paper in Jak's hands. Once it was in the new direction, it was more familiar. "The Dragon's Tail?"

"That's my guess."

"The Dragon's Tail constellation is only visible from the Southern Hemisphere. I've only traveled down there and had the opportunity to see it once." The druid civilization she'd brought up with Malek lived on Zewnath, the Jungle Continent, and she'd been invited on an expedition early in her career to research and gather rare herbs that grew only at altitude there. The druids, and the terrene humans that lived there, had been sparse, and her team had only interacted with a few traveling merchants and nomadic herbalists.

"I've only seen it in books," Jak said. "And I want to verify it by looking at a star chart. Hence the library request."

"What about all these other rubbings?" Jadora waved to the stack. "Did you recognize any other constellations?"

Jak frowned. "No. None at all. That's what has me doubting myself and wanting to verify this one. It's possible this is a coincidence and that the dots represent something else..."

"Which symbols were next to that grouping of dots? Do you remember?" Jadora shuffled through his stack, but he'd done the rubbings, so he would have a better chance of recalling.

"That one, I think." Jak slid a page out of the stack. "It was on one side, and this is the one that was on the other." He pulled another page out and set it next to the first. "I have no idea what these symbols are. Father mostly studied the dragon language and didn't put notes about many of the ancient human tongues in his journal. I've been surprised the portal isn't covered in runes from *their* language, at least not that we can see."

Jadora placed her elbow on the counter and gripped her chin as she studied the papers. One wasn't familiar at all, having strange hashmarks that could have been made by a drunken chicken doing pirouettes in the dirt. The other one...

"Maybe the books in the library will help," Jak said. "I was thinking the star charts, if that's what all of the groupings of dots are, could be a clue as to where the portal must be placed in order to work."

She looked at him. "You think it has to be placed in a certain location? I don't remember that in Loran's notes." The vision she'd had—that the portal had given her—came to mind of a valley with the ancient artifact in use in the center.

"There wasn't anything specific, but he made a lot of references to it being located in a remote location and people and dragons having to travel long distances to use it. If it could work from anywhere, why wouldn't they have moved it to a central and more populated location? We've seen that it's not hard for mages to move it around, and dragons were a lot more powerful than even the most talented humans."

"That's an interesting point. If you're right, then even if Uthari gets the key, he wouldn't be able to activate the portal from his courtyard." Dare she hope that was true? "And these symbols could be crucial in figuring out where it *does* work."

"That's what I'm thinking."

Jadora shuffled through the symbols again. "The thing is... I don't think these are languages of our world. There were only so many ancient civilizations that developed written languages, and after five years immersed in archaeology—not to mention all the years Loran would share his findings with me—I'm familiar with a *lot* of extinct languages. The probability of there being thirty-two that I don't recognize having been placed on this ancient artifact is low. Especially when the portal is supposed to *pre-date* written languages altogether."

"I thought that was weird too. Is it possible they're from the dragon world? All of them?"

"Wait. Here's one that's somewhat familiar." Jadora turned one of the papers that he'd singled out upside-down. It featured a grouping of symbols with little feathers—or were those leaves?—as accents on the curving lines. "I've seen another language on Torvil with leaf and branch accents. It belongs to the druids I was just thinking about. Their people have maintained a close link to nature throughout the millennia that they've lived on their continent Zewnath. Their continent Zewnath in the *Southern Hemisphere.*"

A thrum of excitement ran through her. They had no proof that the dots pointed to places where the portal could be placed to work, but the possibility was enough to tantalize her.

"But where would we start to look once we arrived in Zewnath?" she mused, assuming they could figure out a way to travel thousands of miles with the portal. She couldn't envision it, except by working with Uthari's people. The idea of getting the portal to work so the arrogant *mages* could go through it first and make contact with dragons... It didn't bother her any less today than it had five years ago.

"You could spend a lot of time searching," Jak said. "It's the smallest of the continents, but that doesn't mean much. It's five million square miles, not to mention the chains of islands stretching off in two directions."

"I have some contacts down there—there's a team of archaeologists from the Temril Kingdom with a permanent base of operations there, and I made a good impression on the local herbalists, so—"

The door opened.

Jadora swore and shoved the two rubbings to the bottom of the stack as Malek walked in. "Do zidarr not knock?" she blurted, hoping to distract him before he could start reading their minds.

"Rarely." Malek looked blandly over at them, glancing at the papers.

"What if we'd been in here naked?"

He quirked an eyebrow at her. "Then my evening would have grown more interesting."

"Gross." Jak made a face, either at the thought of his mother's nudity—or of a man finding it interesting—and took his stack of rubbings into the parlor.

Jadora hoped he was keeping his mind free of thoughts. The last thing she wanted was to share their suppositions with Malek. Just because he hadn't found the key yet didn't mean he wouldn't, and once he had the key, the portal, and knew where to take it...

She shoved her own thoughts aside, doing her best to blank her mind, and stirred the forgotten potatoes and carrots boiling on the stove. Instead of trailing Jak into the parlor to look at the rubbings, Malek strode toward the kitchen. Even though she didn't *want* him showing an interest in the rubbings, his approach unnerved her.

Malek set a book and a small blue clay jar on the counter. "This cream is made by a local alchemist and can heal simple wounds so that they leave no scar." He gestured toward her bandaged neck. "Only a small amount is needed. Do you wish assistance in applying it?"

"Are you offering to rub my neck?" she asked, startled.

He cocked his head, as if puzzled by the question. "I am offering to rub healing cream into your wound, since it is in an area you may find difficult to treat yourself."

"I think I can manage it. Thanks for bringing it." Feeling oddly flustered, Jadora turned the book so she could read the title. "*The Mind Way* by Divine Patriarch of the Sacred Monastery Dok Fran. You brought me a book to teach me how to keep mages out of my mind? Won't you find it inconvenient if you can't read my thoughts?"

"It takes many years of meditation and practice to learn the ways of the monks. I will have accomplished my mission long before you master the techniques."

"Your confidence must excite your king."

"He expects my competence and is indifferent to my confidence."

"Does he punish you if you fail him?" Jadora wondered how close Malek was with Uthari.

In the literature, the zidarr were always depicted as supremely loyal, owing their training and in some cases their existence to the powerful wizards who trained them from an early age, but maybe those stories were exaggerated. Was there any way one of his kind could ever be loyal to, or at least sympathetic to, a terrene human? Maybe she ought to be nicer to him and try to...

Try to *what*, Jadora? Win his loyalty for herself? Little chance of that happening. Still, the thought made her wishful, if only because it would be much easier to achieve her goals with the portal if she and Jak had some powerful help.

"He rewards and punishes his people suitably to incentivize them." If Malek was reading her mind, he didn't comment on her thoughts.

"That sounds like a yes." She pulled the vegetables off the heat.

"People are also rewarded and punished in your society."

"Not with pain."

"That is untrue. If you're a homeless boy on the streets and you steal because you're starving and have nothing to eat, you'll be punished with a lashing, if not by having your hand chopped off."

"In some less progressive cities, perhaps. But I doubt you were ever a homeless boy on the streets or that you speak from experience." She eyed his face, imagining him long ago turned over to the zidarr for training and indoctrination by what must have been mage parents as powerful as he. From everything she'd read, such power—or at least the potential to develop it—was largely hereditary. He'd probably been coddled from birth as some future great warrior-wizard to serve his king.

"If you need nothing further, I will leave you to dine." Malek headed for the door.

Jadora blinked, surprised by his abruptness. She hadn't offended him, had she? Not with her words, but maybe with her thoughts. If she truly had a notion of winning his sympathy, she would have to try harder to keep her mind still around him.

"Wait," Jak said, "what about the library? Can we go?"

"Tomorrow." Malek departed, closing the door firmly behind him.

Jadora picked up the monk book, wondering if she could find any useful tips that she could employ right away. She didn't have years to spend studying.

Blue and red dragons soared out of the portal as if they were flying out of the stars. They entered a lush green jungle with a great waterfall tumbling hundreds of feet into a deep blue pool. Huge colorful birds flapped out of trees, cawing and screeching as they took up more distant perches. A monkey chattered from a branch, then fled higher up into camouflaging fronds.

But the dragons had not come to hunt. Their wings flapped in ways Jak wouldn't have dreamed possible—no bird had ever twisted its wings so—and performed aerial acrobatics over the trees. A few dove down to the water like ospreys, but they didn't catch a fish and fly back up. They plunged into the depths and disappeared for several seconds before emerging to roll on their backs, flapping their wings in the water and splashing it about.

Playing. It had never occurred to Jak that dragons might play.

Something thundered in the distance, the noise reverberating through the jungle. Birds fled from trees, and animals scurried into burrows. The dragons climbed out of the water to stand on the side of the pool with their taloned feet gripping moist black rock half-buried in green undergrowth. With slitted reptilian eyes, they peered at each other and all around, and then one looked toward the portal—its starry center had disappeared after they'd flown out.

Another boom sounded, and the dragons sprang into the air. The portal came to life again, a field of stars appearing in the center, and they flew through it and disappeared.

Several quiet moments passed before a tree tumbled down, half blocking Jak's view of the pool and the waterfall. He found he couldn't move to change what he was able to see, but soon humans with chains and axes clambered into view. They wrapped the chains around the tree and harnessed them to a team of pokran and horses so they could pull it out of the way. More minutes later, carts appeared on a road freshly made in the jungle, wooden wheels rolling through the mud and smashed vegetation.

Men and women in togas and moccasins rushed forward with ropes and crude grappling hooks made from copper. They hurled the hooks toward the top of the portal, some missing but others catching.

Were they going to pull it *down*? Jak tried to yell a protest, but he had no ability to communicate with them. He could only observe as the scene played out on the stage.

Once the hooks were secured, the men and women attached the ropes to their team, just as they had with the tree. A feeling of uncertainty came to Jak. From the people? No. They were determined and had no doubt about their mission. From the *portal*? It seemed to wonder if these people were a threat and if it should defend itself.

Before it decided, the humans toppled the portal, the ground trembling as its weight struck down. The view started fading, going from lush greens and blues to gray. A man leaped atop the portal and pointed at the cart, then pointed off into the jungle or to some even more distant point. Commanding his people to move it someplace far, far away? As far away as a distant volcanic island on the other side of Torvil?

The vision faded into blackness, and Jak woke up.

He stared around the dark room, half-expecting to find himself back in that lush jungle. The vision had been so vivid that it took him a moment to remember where he was, his bedroom in Uthari's castle. All was quiet; all was dark.

"Just a dream," he muttered.

But something told him it had been more than that. Jak left his bed, padded to the window, and opened the shutters. From his room, he couldn't see the entire courtyard, but he had a view of a corner of it. One side of the portal was visible, still lying on the ground, still guarded.

Two of those guards were talking in low voices and pointing at the portal. It was glowing a faint blue, highlighting the entwined dragons that made up its frame. Jak had never seen it do that before.

Had the guards done something to bring the portal to a higher level of wakefulness? Could that even happen? Or maybe this was some residue of magic from the battle that had taken place hours before. But if so, it should have come out *then*.

Can you hear me? Jak asked, though he doubted the portal would be able to understand him even if it could. He doubted even more that he had the ability to reach out to it without touching it directly.

The blue glow pulsed once, and the guards skittered back. One man pointed at the portal, then to an exit from the courtyard. The other guard ran off, to report this oddness, no doubt.

Is there something you want me to do? Jak asked, though he didn't know if the portal had singled him out to share that dream—

dream or memory of the past?—or if everyone in the castle had received the same vision.

Another blue pulse of light.

Do you want to be returned to that place? So dragons can fly through again? For the first time, it occurred to Jak to wonder *why* humans had gone to great lengths to topple the portal in the first place. And move it far, far away from the place it could be activated. If that was truly what had happened. Maybe his subconscious mind was making up stories that had nothing to do with facts. How often did his dreams actually make sense? Still, there was a magical portal glowing at him in response to his questions.

He received two more pulses of blue in response to those last questions. *I've been separated from the key. Can you work without that?*

The portal dimmed.

You need the key for us to open a portal back to the dragon home world?

Another pulse.

That's what we thought. We'll try to figure something out. I'm not sure if we can get you out of this castle though. That's... a challenge. We're prisoners here. Unless you can help us escape?

Jak didn't know how that could happen, short of the portal hurling lightning bolts at everyone in the castle and blowing the doors open for him. How much power did it actually have? If it hadn't been able to keep itself from being toppled, it wasn't infinite. Or at least it couldn't be used in infinite ways. So far, he'd only seen it act to defend itself.

Instead of pulsing at the question about escape, the portal fell dark. Once again, it was only blue-black metal under the lamps of the courtyard, appearing as lifeless as when they'd first dug it from the earth.

A few seconds later, someone walked into view—Malek. The

guard who'd run off to tattle on the portal was trailing him, speaking and pointing at it.

Jak watched to see if Malek would be able to stir it to life—if he would try to.

Malek stopped, hands clasped behind his back as he regarded the portal, then turned his head to look straight at Jak.

Even though Jak hadn't been doing anything wrong—at least he didn't think so—fear clutched his heart, and he skittered out of view. He lay back on his bed, imagining scenarios where Malek stormed into his room and demanded to know what he'd been doing. Or ordering Jak to try to communicate with the portal on his behalf. On Uthari's behalf.

But surely, Malek could speak with the portal as easily as Jak had. There was no reason to believe it preferred him over anyone else. He wondered if it was only that nobody else had *tried* to communicate with it.

Long minutes passed as Jak looked up at the ceiling and worried, but Malek never came to his room. He didn't dare return to the window to see if he was still out there.

After what seemed like hours trickled by, Jak silently asked the portal if it was still listening. He didn't get a response, nor did he see a blue glow through the window he'd left open. Tomorrow, he would try again to communicate with it.

21

SORATH'S STUMP ITCHED AS HE DID PUSH-UPS IN THE OUT-OF-THE-way spot he'd found on the open deck of the *Dauntless*, the optimistically named mageship that was flying him and Thorn Company to Utharika.

He grimaced at the annoying tickle, but it was better than the pain that had been a constant companion the first few months after his hand had been severed at the wrist. That he could now put weight on the stump and wield his pickaxe like a weapon was a boon, a far better result than he'd once expected. He refused to feel bitter about the loss since so many men had lost their lives. *His men.*

Stone Heart had been right, the bastard. Sorath *did* have nightmares in which he relived that battle over and over with all the creative variety that his sleeping mind could conjure. The only things that never changed were the accusations on the faces of the dying. No matter how bad the nightmares, waking up and remembering that the battle had really happened was always worse.

Afterward, he'd tried alcohol, mushrooms, magebands—all manner of things to rob a man of his aspirations and take the edge off his pain. But it hadn't lasted long. Everything had seemed a cheat. It was fairer that he remember, that he have the clarity to think of the men he'd lost and say apologies to their ghosts as he burned offerings under the full moons.

Now, as Sorath headed for another battle, he feared a repeat of his last. What if he once again survived while the women of Thorn Company were killed? He'd hoped exercise would keep him from dwelling on that possibility, but it was a distraction for his body, not his mind.

Sweat slithered down his jaw and his spine as he switched from push-ups to squats, hefting a heavy coil of rope he'd found over one shoulder. His stump kept itching. He gritted his teeth and ignored it, making a note to wash it well before he put the harness back on that kept his pickaxe head tightly affixed.

His thighs soon quivered, a reminder that he'd been lax with his exercises lately. Anyone looking at his lean frame would still call him fit, but he'd once carried twenty pounds more of muscle.

Once he'd retired—been forced out of the mercenary business by his failure—and become an infrequent artifact hunter and full-time memoir writer, he'd seen little point in putting his body through the grind of fitness and weapons training. If he'd known he would end up here, sailing through cloudy skies the day before a battle that might be his last, he would have kept it up.

"There you are," Captain Ferroki said, rounding the cabin on the deck that had been creating his private spot.

Startled, Sorath fumbled the big coil of rope, and it slithered off his shoulder. Though he caught it with his elbow, it was heavy enough to threaten damage to his joints, so he let it thump to the ground. He grabbed his pickaxe head and harness, so he could strap it back on. Since he usually only took it off to sleep and bathe—and perform the exercises that were hard to do with a tool for a hand—he felt naked without it.

No, that wasn't accurate. *Nudity* didn't bother him. Being seen without a hand—with nothing but the pink of his ugly stump visible—bothered him. He wasn't even wearing a shirt with a sleeve that he could yank down. Because he had limited attire, he'd taken it off to sweat.

"I didn't mean to startle you." Ferroki lifted an apologetic hand.

"It's fine. I didn't expect anyone to come looking for me." Sorath faced her, atypically clumsy as he buckled the straps of his harness.

She only watched for a moment, then looked off into the gray mist beyond the railing. Being polite. It was the usual response from adults. Only children gawked, their responses less practiced, more honest. He wouldn't have minded if Ferroki wanted to look, but he would have preferred to be whole in front of her.

"I wanted to make sure you weren't drinking yourself into a stupor somewhere," she said.

"If my reputation suggests I do that frequently, then I'm aggrieved."

"It doesn't, but people change." She glanced at the harness as he finished buckling it on. "Things change people."

"Yeah."

"And I wouldn't blame you if you felt the need. I'm certainly having regrets about getting on that transport vessel. I should have demanded more details beforehand, but I'd assumed we would have the option to leave if the mission wasn't to our tastes." Her mouth twisted. "I don't know why. Having the kings—or their zidarr—bully mercenaries into accepting contracts isn't without precedent. Negotiations with the fox never go well for the chicken."

"Chickens have to eat. When the foxes are in control of the feed, it's hard to find a way to win."

"Yes. It has been that way for a long time. The entire time I've been a mercenary. Sometimes, I question why I'm still doing this, leading a company and risking our lives day in and day out, but it's all I've ever known. My parents were both soldiers, and it was what they taught me. I don't have any other skills to offer the world."

"Have you ever thought of being a caravan guard or body-guard? It would be less dangerous, and the lives of others wouldn't rely on your decisions." Sorath grimaced, admitting that thought might bother him more than it bothered Ferroki.

"It's not that easy. I learned early on that being a woman working in a world where the prevailing opinion is that men are more qualified means it's harder to get a job. Even if you can, your employers don't want to pay you as much. It's better to work for yourself. It's not necessarily an easier path, but you make the rules, and eventually, you can get regular clients who appreciate your worth and pay you fairly."

"So you started your company from scratch?" He hadn't known that. Most of the large mercenary outfits had been around for generations. Usually, one was promoted up through the ranks of an existing company. He'd done that and been second-in-command for Fang and Talon when the old commander died.

"I did. With four other women who were tired of working for oppressive employers. I enticed them to join me with tales of chickens outwitting foxes."

"Cunning. Most people have to use money for enticement."

Ferroki smiled but only for a moment. "The company grew over time, but I've lost all of those original four now. One retired from the mercenary business to have a family, but the rest were killed in battle."

"You know what it's like then," he said softly, though he'd always sensed she did. Most mercenary commanders did, even if few had endured the debilitating number of losses he had.

"Yes." Ferroki leaned against the railing. "I've had a look at the map of Utharika and have some thoughts. Do you want to join Sasko and me for a chat? We should have a plan of action."

"I agree." Sorath grabbed his shirt and tugged it on. "I'm ready."

But Ferroki held up a hand. "Before we join the company… there was another reason I came looking for you." She cleared her throat and looked at the deck. "The real reason."

"You didn't truly think I was drinking myself senseless? I'm flattered."

"I came to apologize," she said quietly.

Sorath studied her profile. With rich brown skin and warm dark eyes, a strong nose and jaw, Ferroki had always struck him as a handsome woman. Not necessarily beautiful in the classical sense but handsome. Today, with the gray mist from the clouds they were flying through softening her features, he noticed that she'd aged well, despite the arduous career, and he thought of the times their paths had crossed before. Of times he'd thought about asking her for a drink or a walk—or a kiss.

Being the commander of a company was lonely. One was always expected to have the answers and never show weakness. Unlike many of his men, he'd never married, never felt he should have a woman back home, not when the odds were so good of him dying and never returning to her, of leaving her with children to care for by herself. But he occasionally felt he'd missed out on the opportunity for companionship and regretted that he'd never had someone to confide in, someone to care for—and be cared for by.

"I'm sorry," Ferroki went on, "that I came to your shop and got you involved. I'm sure you were enjoying your retirement, or at least enjoying not being shot at on a regular basis."

"I wasn't. There's no need to apologize for that. Besides, I didn't have to come after you or play hero at the hotel. I got myself into this."

"Because you wanted to help us." Ferroki lifted her gaze to meet his. "To help me. Honestly, I appreciate that you did." She touched his arm, her eyes gentle.

It wasn't the arm with the pickaxe but the healthy one that had all of its nerves functioning and had no trouble feeling the warmth of her touch through his shirt. For a moment, he regretted that he'd put it back on. Her touch on his skin would be even nicer.

"If I tried to take advantage of your guilt and gentle feelings toward me and kiss you, would you allow it?" Sorath raised his eyebrows and attempted to look appealing—and kissable—though he expected her to yank her hand back and step away.

She didn't step away, but she hesitated before answering. "Yesterday, I would have, but today, you're my commanding officer."

"Ah." Sorath wanted to rail at the world—why was she taking to heart that idiot zidarr's suggestion that he be in charge?—but he forced a smile. "Hell, what was I doing yesterday?"

"Getting into trouble. The same as me."

"Busy work."

"Yes." She lowered her hand and nodded toward the rest of the ship. "Shall we?"

"Lead the way, Captain."

Malek arrived during breakfast to escort them to the library. Jak hadn't had time to share his dream or the portal's late-night blue throbbing with his mother. He'd asked if *she'd* had any dreams, and she'd gotten a haunted look in her eyes. He had a feeling that meant whatever nightmares had plagued her had been different from his. The mystery of why humans had toppled the portal—if that had indeed happened—was concerning but not haunting, and the dragons playing had been cute.

Jak stuffed a pastry in his mouth, grabbed his rubbings and the drawing tools he'd been given, and didn't comment when he glimpsed his mother slipping a few vials into her pockets. More of whatever acid she'd thrown at the intruder? She'd never said exactly what that had been, but he'd caught her macerating some of the chilis from the icebox and scraping the seeds into a concoction the night before. Jak hoped they could get through the day without being attacked, but their chances seemed poor here.

As Mother gathered her books, Malek's gaze lingered on her pockets, and Jak realized he must have seen her slipping the vials into them. He didn't miss much. Jak waited for Malek to step forward and remove them, as he had with other things she'd pocketed, but he smiled faintly and stepped into the hallway to wait for them.

He couldn't *approve*, could he? Not of Mother using her little weapons against him or any of his allies certainly, but maybe Malek believed she was more likely to use them on possible intruders and didn't mind that. Still, his willingness to leave either of them with a weapon, however minor, was surprising.

Jak no longer knew what to think of Malek. To believe him an ally would be asinine, but since he'd apparently been tasked with protecting them as well as keeping them here, it was growing harder to loathe him.

As Jak stepped into the hallway with Mother right behind, he reminded himself that Malek may have been the one to kill his father. Just because these people were being decent to them for the moment didn't mean that would continue. They wanted something, and once that had been accomplished...

"Malek," a cool voice said as their group started down the hall.

A zidarr from the night before—Yidar, Jak remembered— jogged to catch up with him. He jostled Jak as he passed, not glancing his way or apologizing before falling into step beside Malek. Jak glowered at the back of his head, wondering if he should ask his mother if he could hold her vials.

Though he didn't speak, his face must have given away his irritation, for she lifted a finger to her temple. The zidarr also looked back, his eyes slitted. Jak hurried to push any thoughts of attacking him out of his mind, realizing belatedly that he would read thoughts as easily as Malek.

"Yes, Yidar?" Malek asked, not looking back, not drawing more attention to Jak.

"The king's spies have verified that enemy ships are flying toward our city, and a farm barge was destroyed outside of Jominar down below. The mage crew was killed."

"I am aware. King Uthari has sent mageships to protect our resources and attack those of Zaruk, Vorsha, and Dy, the now-confirmed alliance that seeks to acquire Uthari's artifact for themselves."

"Rumor has it that it was originally *their* artifact."

Malek looked sharply at him. "The portal was buried on that island millennia before any ancestor of Zaruk's put a castle in the sky. He has no claim on it."

Jak looked at his mother, wondering what she thought of the zidarr arguing, if it was anything they could use to their advantage. She only shook her head, touched her temple again, and nodded at Yidar's back.

Another warning to watch his thoughts. She must have had a reason to believe Yidar was more dangerous than Malek. Or more likely to do something to Jak if he learned about Jak's potential? A chill went through him as he realized that must be exactly what she was worried about. And what *he* should worry about. He emptied his mind of thoughts and gazed at the back of Malek's head as they passed through an intersection and took a turn.

"Of course I agree with King Uthari," Yidar said. "I have only been trying to reason through their alliance and determine how concerned we should be."

"About three powerful wizards marshaling their forces against us?" Malek asked. "Concerned."

"I believe so too. I suggested to the king that you and I should be the ones to go out with the mageships and do battle with those who approach. We could keep them from ever reaching our walls and doing damage to our people and our city."

"Gorsith and General Tonovan left with the interceptor ships early this morning."

"He is only one zidarr. And those three will send zidarr of their own into the war. The battle will be *glorious.*" Yidar clenched a fist as the group turned into a wider, more ornate hall, passing two soldiers positioned to guard it. "But Uthari refuses to send us all out of the city at once. Perhaps you should speak with him."

"His priority is guarding the portal and those who can figure out how to make it work. As you saw last night, they are targets for our enemies. The *main* targets."

They entered a wide chamber with marble columns supporting friezes of warriors, mages, and dragons below a gilded dome-shaped ceiling. Two towering doors stood closed on the far side. For a change, they were made from wood instead of gold, but the rich colors and whorls promised they'd been sourced from some rare and exotic species of tree.

Yidar looked back at Jak and Mother again. "It does not seem that babysitting scientists is a task worthy of a zidarr such as you, Malek. Does this one even have a use?" He pointed at Jak, his finger in the air in front of his nose.

Jak didn't allow himself to contemplate biting that finger, not for more than a second. But maybe it was a second too long, for the zidarr held his gaze, his eyes flinty, his body radiating tension like a coiled spring.

"You do not like us, do you, boy?" Yidar whispered.

"They are our prisoners," Malek said dryly, though he watched Yidar intently. "Would you not find it suspicious if they had warm thoughts toward us?"

"They should have *respectful* thoughts toward us, else they should be punished."

Yup, that fleeting finger-biting thought had definitely gotten through. Jak didn't even know what respectful thoughts would look like—should he imagine himself on his knees kissing Yidar's boots?—so he attempted to think of nothing again.

"As you were pointing out," Malek said, "we have larger concerns than what our insignificant and unarmed prisoners are thinking about us. Did you have a reason for searching me out?"

"Yes." Yidar stopped and faced him, causing their procession to halt. "Uthari will listen to you if you argue that we should be allowed to go into battle. A high-level mage can babysit his artifact and archaeologists. This could be the battle of a lifetime, Malek. For us to sit it out would be intolerable."

"I suspect we will see action."

"If we were out there, we could keep that action from ever arriving on the king's doorstep." He lifted a hand and clenched a fist again. "You *know* our power, Malek."

Malek appeared indifferent to their power. "Did Uthari give a reason why you aren't allowed to go? There is little need for both of us to guard the artifact."

"He believes that with so many ships being thrown against our city some will get through. He's unwilling to be without us." Yidar pointed at Malek, then his own chest. "But if you talk to him, he will listen. He confides in you in a way he doesn't with Gorsith or me." He sneered with bitterness that he didn't try to hide.

"He will one day confide in you as well. In my first ten years serving him, the only thing he ever told me was that I wasn't applying myself enough and that I needed to stop projecting my attacks."

"As he says to me now. But I beat out nine other candidates for this position. I have applied myself every step of the way."

Malek spread a hand. "He sees that, but he does not wish to foster arrogance in us, lest it lead to our downfall. When you earn it, his praise will mean more than if it had been given freely all along."

The sneer sprang back to Yidar's lips, but he tamped it down and sighed. "You are correct, of course."

Yidar looked toward a painting of a mage on a flying chariot hunting elk in a forest, but his gaze was speculative rather than accepting. His abrupt shift to acquiescence didn't feel authentic to Jak.

"I accept that I must serve for more years before I'm considered as zidarr as you, but I still believe he is wrong about stationing us both in his castle. I believe that you especially could make a difference out there." Yidar looked back to Malek. "What if I were to guard the artifact and the archaeologists while you joined Gorsith in the sky? Should not at least one of us get to fly out into this magnificent battle?"

Alarms sounded in Jak's mind. When he looked at his mother, he found an equally worried expression on her face. For some reason, this zidarr was trying to get Malek out of the castle.

The question made Malek's expression turn wistful. Even if he hadn't admitted it, he must long to be out there in battle. Not, as Yidar said, stuck here babysitting archaeologists.

"That is not Uthari's wish," Malek said.

"If you asked him, he would let you go. I may not be as powerful a wizard and warrior yet as you—" was it only in Jak's mind that Yidar's voice oozed flattery? "—but I am capable of guarding a hunk of metal and two people. We *easily* defeated their incursion teams from last night. They sent a boy zidarr barely old enough to have gained the title and too weak-minded to keep from being manipulated. He was probably on his proving mission. Our enemies can't want that artifact very badly if that's what they fielded."

"Perhaps those teams were largely sent to gather and send back information on the portal's whereabouts and were not intended to succeed. A communications gem was found in the zidarr's pocket."

"One does not throw away a zidarr, however young and inexperienced. We are too valuable for that. Just as you are too valuable to stay here while a battle rages in the clouds."

Malek gazed thoughtfully at Yidar. Realizing the man was trying to manipulate him? Or contemplating his offer? How badly did Malek want to be out there? And what happened if Jak and his mother were left behind with Yidar? For that matter, had Malek and the others ever figured out how that incursion team had gotten into their highly secure castle? Maybe Yidar had let them in. Maybe he'd been bought off by the other side.

Worried by Malek's long silence and thoughtful expression, Jak caught himself willing Malek to read his mind, to grasp how suspicious this setup was.

But it was Yidar who spun toward him, eyes wide with incredulity. "This boy has magic." Moving so quickly that Jak didn't have time to react, Yidar lunged in and grabbed him by the shirt. "You are a wild one! And you've hidden it. He is past the age, Malek. He must be slain."

Fiery pain erupted in Jak's chest, and he cried out, back arching as he tried to pull away from the zidarr. It felt like his heart was being torn out. His vision blacked, and his pulse pounded in his eardrums, wild and erratic—and in danger of being halted forever.

As abruptly as the magical attack started, it stopped, leaving him gasping. Malek twisted Yidar's wrist and jerked him away from Jak.

At the same time, Mother yelled, "Let him go, you bastard!" Something splashed against Yidar's flesh. The contents of her vial. It shattered as it hit the marble floor.

Yidar roared, stumbling back. "What is *that*?"

He wiped at his face and lifted a hand, fingers curled like

claws. Jak stumbled in front of his mother, hoping he could protect her from an attack. If only he knew how to use his supposed magical power.

Malek stepped in to keep Yidar from hurting them again, not by stopping Yidar from trying, but by raising a magical shield. Jak couldn't see it, but he could sense it. If he hadn't been gasping and trying to recover, his chest raw from whatever the bastard had done, he would have worried that he could sense such things now.

"You *protect* them?" Yidar roared.

"As I was commanded to do." The dry humor had disappeared from Malek's tone, but it remained calm, unperturbed in the face of Yidar's rage.

Jak hoped he knocked the other zidarr on his ass.

"The king doesn't know that he's a wild one, does he?" Yidar pointed past Malek's shoulder at Jak but only for a moment before snarling and wiping his sleeve vigorously across his face. "Gah, that burns like alcohol on fire. Did you know they have weapons?"

"The king is aware that he has potential," Malek said, ignoring the second question. "I tested him. It is insignificant, and he will not be a threat."

"The laws of the sky kingdoms say to slay *all* terrenes who develop power too late to be brought into the fold." Yidar lowered his arm, his face incredulous—and ridiculous since one of his eyes was squinted closed as tears leaked from it. "It does not matter how significant. You know that."

"We need them to decipher the secrets of the artifact. After that, the boy can be slain."

Jak hoped he was appeasing the other zidarr and had no intention of killing him. It was hard to tell with his flat and indifferent tone.

"You play with fire, Malek."

Malek snorted. "An untrained boy is no threat." A hint of amusement crept into his voice. "He's not the one who stung you."

"*Stung* me? That bitch burned my eye half-out. What if that shit damages my vision?"

"You will recover. Go wipe your face, and then bring your weapons for a sparring match. You can take out your aggressions on me."

Yidar looked scathingly at Jak, making it clear who he wanted to be aggressive with. Jak did his best to appear unafraid and defiant, but his chest still ached. Why had Malek invited Yidar to *return*?

The zidarr backed toward the exit but warned, "Do not listen to his thoughts, Malek. He seeks to trick you. I heard him."

"I am not easily deceived," was all Malek said, not moving until Yidar left the chamber.

Malek eyed the shattered vial on the floor and the moisture around it. Whatever Mother had made from ingredients in the suite, it wasn't enough to steam a hole through the tiles and reveal the secret ducts or tunnels Jak still hoped to find. Malek flicked a finger, and flame—or pure molten magic—incinerated the evidence and dried the liquid.

"Professor Freedar," he said.

"Yes?" Mother gripped Jak's shoulder and stepped up beside him.

"I suggest you study *The Mind Way* with your son. His thoughts are dangerous to him." Malek looked at Jak. "He didn't have to read your mind to hear your accusations. You projected them telepathically."

"I..." Had he? Crap.

Mother's face grew bleak—bleaker.

"The book." Malek walked around them, waving to open the double doors, then nodding for them to go in while he waited outside. Were he and Yidar going to spar out *here*? It was more of a foyer than a gymnasium.

"We'll read it together," Mother said firmly and walked into the library.

But Jak hesitated, worried Yidar would keep trying to convince Malek to leave the castle while he stayed. Jak had little doubt that if Malek left, he and Mother would be dead before sunset.

"Is what I thought possible?" Jak asked quietly.

They were alone in the chamber, the guards too far down the corridor to hear, but Jak felt like he was suggesting something that could get him killed.

"That Yidar means to betray us?" Malek asked. "The zidarr are trained from childhood to follow the Code and loyally serve their king."

"So there's no chance he could have been the one to let enemies in to try to kill us?"

"He would gain nothing from doing so."

"What if he's been subverted by your enemies? Offered a higher position or a bunch of money?"

"Any king who managed to *subvert* a zidarr would then know he could not trust the zidarr himself. We are loyal and incorruptible, some of our power coming from the wizard who early in our training infuses his into ours." Malek touched his chest. "Yidar is young and not diplomatic, but he is not a traitor."

Jak bit his lip, worried that Malek's faith in his Code and his own loyalty would make it impossible for him to believe someone else could be corrupted.

"Stay away from him if you can," Malek added, "and keep your mind still when you can't. It would not be treasonous for him to kill a wild one. He is right that it is the law, for the safety of our people."

"Your people hardly need extra safety measures."

"Once we did. Mages were feared, cast out, and hunted because they were different." Malek gazed into his eyes. "You must know this, even if you are young. The history textbooks explain how our kind were forced to band together and learn to defend ourselves."

"Uh. That wasn't in my textbook."

"If that is true, the faculty and curriculum used for teaching at your university are due for an audit." Malek waved Jak into the library and shut the doors behind him.

22

TEZI SAT ALONE ON THE DECK, THE MIST DAMPENING HER COPY OF Thanok's *The Teachings*. She kept reading the lines about how those who chose the righteous path over the easy one would be rewarded, if not in this life then in the next. Her father had been a big believer in working hard and selfless sacrifice and had quoted often from the book, and he'd died to a zidarr's blade for trying to keep his daughter from being taken. She hoped he truly was being rewarded now in the afterlife.

The captain and Sorath walked into view, waving for Lieutenant Sasko to join them. Some of the other mercenaries who were out on the deck, braving the weather to sit together in groups instead of being closed off in the tiny cabins they'd been assigned belowdecks, looked over at them. But it was a private meeting, and nobody else was invited. A planning meeting.

"Rookie," Sergeant Tinder called from where she sat cross-legged next to Dr. Fret and two other women. "Come over here."

"Yes, Sergeant." Tezi closed her book, walked over, and stood in an uncertain parade rest in front of them. "Do you need something, Sergeant?"

"Yeah. For you to sit down and stop looking so glum. And like you're praying that you won't die tonight." Tinder slapped the deck beside her, careful not to disturb the fuses and canisters she had lined up as she assembled explosives.

Seated on her other side, Fret was knitting something that looked like a fancy bag. Whatever it was, it was less destructive than explosives. Corporal Basher leaned against the railing, smoking a fat cigar that smelled like burning foot fungus.

"You don't think praying for the success of this mission would be useful?" Tezi sat cross-legged, emulating Tinder and careful not to bump anything laid out before her. Were this a sailing ship, she couldn't have done such fine work out on the deck, but other than the occasional breeze sweeping across the mageship, there was no movement to worry about.

"Divine intervention would be useful," Tinder said, "but I doubt that you muttering passages in *The Teachings* will cause it to occur."

"My father used to sing the passages."

"I'm sure that made a huge difference."

"He had a nice voice." Tezi swallowed and stared at the deck, trying to push aside the memories of her family. She accepted them when she was alone, and it didn't matter if she cried, but she didn't want to show any of these hardened warriors her weaknesses.

"He gone, kid?" Basher asked.

"Yes." Tezi hesitated. "Mother too."

"Figured it had to be something like that. Most little girls with loving, supportive families don't run off to join mercenaries."

"They *were* loving and supportive," Tezi murmured.

Tinder swatted Basher's boot. "Quit getting her weepy."

"She arrived like that."

"No, I didn't." Tezi hadn't shed a tear, and she didn't intend to.

Maybe her eyes were filmed, but she blinked away any moisture that might give her away.

"Get pissed at whoever or whatever killed them," Tinder advised Tezi. "You're supposed to build up your aggression before going into battle, like a tea kettle with the lid on and the water boiling. Then when you're on the field, you let it blow against your enemies."

"Is that what Dr. Fret is doing?" Tezi pointed to the balls of yarn slowly transitioning into a bag.

"Yeah. See how quickly she thrusts and stabs with those needles? You can feel her aggression building."

Fret, who even during weapons training seemed no more aggressive than a recently fed cat lounging in a sunbeam, lifted her eyebrows. "I have defeated enemies with these needles, you may recall."

"Rats nibbling on the yarn in your knitting bag don't count as enemies," Tinder said.

"I was referring to the handsy sailor at the tavern last month who was determined to get me to sit in his lap. Though the rats were also large and offensive."

"With equally foul breath."

"Indeed."

Tezi smiled, feeling for the first time like a part of the company. Tinder and Fret were engaged in the same banter as usual, but they were acknowledging that she existed.

Lieutenant Sasko, who'd finished her meeting with the captain and Sorath, approached the group. "Tinder, you know the mages gave us a huge pile of magical explosives, right?"

"I do."

"Did you check them out? It's probably not necessary for you to waste your own materials making black-powder grenades."

Tinder gave her a frank look. "The *magical* explosives glow pink and are shaped like mushrooms."

"It's more of a red glow."

"With all due respect, LT, you're colorblind. They're *pink*. I'm not throwing pink glowing mushrooms at my enemies. We may be women, but we're also mercenaries. We have standards."

Fret nudged her. "Do you want tassels on your grenade cozy?"

"It's an ammo pouch, not a *cozy*."

"Of course. Do you want tassels on it?"

"Yes, please."

The lieutenant rolled her eyes and walked away.

Tinder reached over and thumped Tezi on the shoulder. "Give us the story of the hotel, kid. The captain hasn't said anything, and Sorath isn't that approachable, but it was clear from what that zidarr said on the transport vessel that you all killed some mages."

Ah, that was why Tezi had been invited over. For gossip. Well, it was better than being ostracized.

"I've been instructed not to..." Not to what? The captain hadn't said she couldn't talk about it, just that they shouldn't admit to anyone they had killed a mage. That did seem wise, but was there any point to hiding it when that zidarr had figured it out? Besides, the idea of letting Colonel Sorath take all the blame didn't sit well with her. "Incriminate myself," she finished with a helpless shrug.

"Incriminate yourself? Does that mean you killed someone?" Tinder gaped at her, then elbowed Fret. "Our rookie killed someone."

"I didn't say that." Tezi's cheeks warmed.

"It was one of the mages, right? Not some poor innocent that you were trying to save."

"Nobody innocent died. I mean, not by our hand." She was flustered and stumbling over her tongue. Maybe she should have kept reading and ignored the invitation to come over.

Tinder scrutinized her. "Yeah, I believe you. You're actually not horrible with a magelock." Tinder elbowed Fret again. "She hit one of those cranky guards in the shoulder when that skirmish broke out in the magistrate's office, remember?"

"I remember," Fret said calmly, continuing her knitting and sounding far less intrigued with the story of the hotel than Tinder. Maybe as a healer, she didn't like hearing about people being killed. Even mage people.

"You might be all right when we storm the king's castle, Rookie. Just get used to everyone there having a way to defend themselves from bullets and magelock charges. Unless you can break their concentration first by blowing up a grenade in their faces." Tinder smiled and patted her ceramic shells lovingly.

"For most people, that would just blow off their heads," Basher said around her cigar.

"Mages aren't like most people."

"No kidding. Explain to me again why we accepted this mission?"

"Because it's a war, we're mercenaries, and we don't get paid if we don't fight," came a voice from the side—the captain.

Basher yanked out her cigar and scrambled to her feet to salute. "Sorry, ma'am. I know that."

Everyone else started to stand to do the same, but the captain patted the air for them to stay seated. She particularly looked concerned that Tinder might rise and accidentally kick a grenade down the deck to explode.

"At ease," the captain said. "I just need Rookie Tezi."

"Rookie Tezi the *sniper*," Tinder said with a grin.

The captain raised her eyebrows. Tezi knew it was a joke but still had to fight the urge to bury her face in her hand. She hoped the captain didn't think she'd been bragging about her role in the hotel incursion. She'd barely *done* anything there.

"We might make that true," the captain said.

Surprised, Tezi stood up at attention. "Ma'am?" she asked uncertainly.

The captain held up her finger. "Tinder, you know there are magical explosives, right?"

That earned another eye roll from the sergeant. "They're pink mushrooms, Captain."

The captain arched her eyebrows. "They have a handle that you chuck them by, like a throwing axe, but I wouldn't consider that a mushroom stem."

"They have stems and caps. They're either mushrooms or penises. I think some mage with a disrespectful sense of humor made them that way on purpose to mock the female mercenary unit." Tinder shook her head. "Even if it was accidental, nobody will take pink grenades seriously."

"They're more of a red," the captain said, "and if they're not taken seriously, all the better. They'll be more effective when they blow up."

"I trust mine more." The ceramic shells got another loving pat. "They're proven effective, they're made from reliable chemical ingredients, not magic, and they're gender neutral."

"Gender-neutral grenades are important?"

"Damn straight."

The captain must have decided to end the conversation, but she scanned the rest of the group before leaving. "Nice tassels, Fret."

"Thank you, Captain. They're for Tinder's grenade cozy."

"It's an *ammo pouch*." Tinder glared at Fret, who only smiled as she continued knitting.

"See if you can work in some pink thread," Basher said, drawing a similar glare.

"I don't have that many colors, sadly," Fret said. "If we survive and get paid well, maybe I can pick up some new yarn in one of the cities."

"The reasons mercenaries risk their lives," the captain murmured, then crooked a finger toward Tezi. "Come with me."

"Yes, ma'am."

"The glowing grenades weren't the only armament the mages supplied us with," the captain said as they headed belowdecks, passing the grumpy captain of the ship along the way. Toggs, a mage loyal to Queen Vorsha, he'd introduced himself as. "It's somewhat reassuring," she added, "that they gave us extra tools and actually want us to win, not simply be annihilated while they send their own troops in."

"I'm glad, ma'am." Tezi kept herself from asking if it would make a difference against such powerful foes. What were the odds that their ship would be able to sneak in and get that artifact?

The captain led her to an armory with a green-uniformed mage standing guard out front, one of the crew that had come with the ship. He nodded and let them in.

Numerous magelock rifles hung from racks, shelves held crates of cannonballs and shells for the ship's weapons, and bags of netted material held what Tezi could now only think of as pink glowing mushrooms. The captain ignored those and patted the long metal barrels and sleek wooden stocks of magelock rifles in a small rack by the door. They were the most impressive weapons in the armory. Their sights, trigger mechanisms, and other ornamentation were made from silver and highlighted with gold, including flying dragons engraved into the barrels and stocks.

"Those are the fanciest magelocks I've seen, ma'am."

"And highly accurate. They're enchanted with magic for superior aim and durability. Or so I was told." The captain shrugged, acknowledging that since terrene humans were sense-dead, they had to take the word of mages when it came to how magical things were. Until the mercenaries actually used the weapons, they had no way to know how reliable or good they would be. "Pick one. Let's try it out."

Tezi blinked. "You want me to take one of the special magelocks?"

"Let's see how good you are with one."

"But it's got *gold* on it," Tezi whispered, afraid she would damage the thing or make it less valuable somehow.

"Everything mages make for themselves has gold. You may have noticed how many things in their cities are gilded."

"I did. It was a little…"

"Ostentatious?"

"Especially the drinking fountain with the golden spout. There was a kid spitting in it when we walked past."

"Mage kids aren't any different from human kids until they get old enough to fling magic."

"Is that the age they mature and stop spitting on things?"

"If that hotel was any indication, they never mature."

The captain frowned, pulled two magelocks out of the rack, and thrust them into a charging box mounted on the wall by the door. It hummed, emitting soft *thwumps* as compact magic blasts of power similar to black-powder bullets were stored in the weapons. A glowing yellow tendril snaked from the bottom of the box through the deck and connected into the energy source that powered the mageship. When the *thwumps* stopped—far more than the usual ten or twenty charges had filled the weapons—the captain handed one of the magelocks to Tezi.

Thanks to the gold, or sturdier and higher-quality materials overall, it weighed much more than the short pistol Thorn Company's armorer had issued Tezi when she joined. It was easily ten pounds, so doing long marches with it over her shoulder would be noticeable, but if it was a more accurate and longer-range weapon, the tradeoff would be worth it.

"The ship's not large enough to test its accuracy over distance, but I want to see how you do with something better than that lizard plugger." The captain waved to Tezi's holstered magelock, then led the way out of the armory.

The crewman standing guard whistled as Tezi passed. The

captain paused and frowned back at him. Tezi caught him checking out her butt.

"Sorry, ladies," he drawled, winking at Tezi before looking at the captain. "I was admiring your assets."

"There's an old poem," the captain said, "that goes: he who treats the dune crawler as a potential meal instead of acknowledging the power of its jaws and the sharpness of its teeth may find himself a macerated bloody pulp left beneath the desert sun for the vultures."

The crewman's forehead creased. "That's a poem?"

"The poem of life," she murmured.

"It didn't rhyme."

"I don't think he got the point, ma'am," Tezi murmured.

"They rarely do."

The mist had grown thicker up on deck, with twilight encroaching, and Tezi could barely see from one end of the ship to the other. Maybe the pilot was deliberately keeping them in cloud cover in the hope of hiding their approach to Utharika. It was hard to believe that clouds could keep the mages from sensing the magic of the ship, but if the diversionary vessels were making a more blatant approach, maybe Uthari's people wouldn't think to look for the *Dauntless*.

Earlier, some of the women had set up a shooting range with a couple of wooden targets with crudely painted red bullseyes, and the captain led Tezi to a spot thirty yards from one. At such close range, Tezi knew she could hit the target without trouble, but having the captain next to her made her nervous.

"You've practiced with a rifle since you joined?"

"Yes, ma'am. Sergeant Tinder introduced me to a lot of weapons my first month."

"Good."

The captain readied her own rifle and fired first. Her practice charge thudded into the center of the bullseye, and red wood splintered off. Tezi wondered if she should point out that Tinder had taught them to fire the rifles from a prone position with their elbows propped on the ground for support. Given the height and closeness of these targets, Tezi would wrench her neck trying to fire that way now. She would have to keep her arms steady without support.

"Go ahead." The captain rested the stock of her weapon on the deck and nodded encouragingly.

Tezi lifted the magelock, grimacing at the weight but relieved she could hold it up and steady—at least for long enough to shoot. When she'd first joined, she might not have been able to, but she'd made progress, even if the others didn't see it.

She pressed her cheek to the stock, lined up the sights, exhaled and found her point of stillness, then fired. The blue charge of energy surged away, striking the target in the center and blowing away wood. She fired twice more at the adjoining targets, more because she worried she wouldn't be able to hold the heavy weapon up and steady for much longer than out of a desire to show off, and she hit the bullseye on those two.

"We might have found your special gift, Rookie," the captain said. "When we finish our mission here, we'll do some long-distance training with moving targets."

"Yes, ma'am." Tezi decided to find it encouraging that the captain said *when we finish* rather than *if we survive*.

"You taking her on the incursion team?" Sorath asked.

Tezi hadn't realized she had more witnesses than the captain and blushed.

"She needs more training first," the captain said. "But what do you say to having her up here shooting over the railing and protecting our backs while we try to get that artifact out of Uthari's castle?"

Sorath nodded. "I'd feel better about that than about your

sergeant hurling explosives down all around us. A magelock is a pinpoint weapon."

"Sometimes explosives are handy," the captain said.

"True. Give them to her." Sorath pointed at Tezi.

"How do you feel about pink mushrooms, Rookie?" the captain asked.

"I'm not above using magical weapons, ma'am."

"Good. You and Tinder can stand side-by-side and compare results."

"Who will go in on the incursion team?" Tezi hadn't expected to be chosen and told herself she was more relieved than disappointed about being left behind on the ship, especially since it sounded like she would still have an important role.

The captain looked at Sorath.

He shook his head. "They're your people. You should pick. Let's keep it to eight or ten though and put together a backup team in case we fail."

"An optimistic thought."

"I prefer logic and meticulous preparation to optimism," Sorath said.

"I'm not opposed to those things, but the troops respond well to a butt pat now and then."

"Interesting. Your command style is different from mine."

"My troops are probably different than yours were."

"True. Few of my men put tassels on their ammo pouches." Sorath tilted his head toward the front of the ship. "The helmsman says we're less than an hour out. Better get ready."

Nerves fluttered in Tezi's stomach. Would the unit truly survive this mission? Would *she*?

23

THE MAGNIFICENCE OF THE LIBRARY COULDN'T MAKE JADORA FORGET that another zidarr had figured out Jak had magical power. Or the potential to learn it.

Though she was trying to do research, she couldn't keep from fretting and frowning in his direction. None of this was his fault, but that didn't make it any less distressing. Oh, how she wished she hadn't brought him along on her dig. He would have resented her, but he wouldn't have been in danger.

Thump, thump, thump. Jak stomped past, checking the floor tiles again.

In the first five minutes they'd been here, he'd found a star chart and verified that the dots on his rubbing matched perfectly with the Dragon's Tail constellation. Now, he was back to searching for hollow spots under the floor.

As far as Jadora could tell, they were the only ones in the private library—Malek had shut and possibly locked the door after waving them in—but that didn't keep her from wincing at his noise.

"Must you be so suspicious?" she breathed.

"Yes," he whispered back. "I'm trying to find a way out."

"Are you reading that book?" She'd foisted *The Mind Way* into his hands as soon as he'd finished with the star charts.

He needed to master the teachings of the monks even more than she did. He was toting it around, but she hadn't seen him spend much time reading.

"Yes, but it's full of fables. If they teach anything, it's vague."

"I saw them as lessons."

"Vague lessons."

"Read the third one," she said. "*The Serenity of the Turtle.*"

"Oh, I'll be sure to. Such scintillation cannot be missed."

"Would you take this seriously? That zidarr almost killed you."

Jak stopped at the table between rows of bookcases where she sat with atlases and linguistics tomes open before her. "I know, Mother. I'm aware. I'll try to do better at not letting them into my head, but I want to focus on escaping, so we don't have to worry about them picking up on stray thoughts."

"I do as well, but we may not get an opportunity until..." Jadora looked toward the door, worried Malek or someone else would walk in on them.

It was also possible someone inside would overhear them. Before grabbing all the useful books she could find and sitting down, she'd peeked down all the aisles to look for people. She hadn't seen anyone, but the library was vast, including two mezzanines that were roped off. When she'd touched a rope, contemplating going under it, a warning buzz had shot up her arm.

"The war starts?" Jak asked softly.

She nodded. "If there's fighting and the zidarr are called away or distracted, that could be our opportunity to slip out, sneak to the harbor, and stow away on a cargo ship flying off to pick up cabbages."

"We need to *steal* a ship, not stow away. We can't give them time to catch up—you know they'd come after us. Besides, who sends barges to collect cabbages while the city is under fire?"

"Hungry mages."

"Ha ha. Did you see that little winged ship in the harbor? It looked like a bird. I bet it's fast. But we have to get out of the castle first." Jak returned to stomping on the tiles.

Jadora ran her finger down the page of the book she'd dug out on the ancient druids of Zewnath. The distinctive leaf flourishes and curving lines made her certain that she'd been right with her guess, that the one familiar grouping of symbols from the portal was in their language. The book was on culture and history as much as linguistics, but there were examples of the druidic written tongue that had been translated. If she could find a match, that might be the clue they needed about where the portal had to be located for operation.

"Mother?" Jak stopped stomping and came to her table again. "Did you hear what Malek said before closing the door?"

"For you to stay out of trouble?" She flipped another page, running her finger down the columns.

"No, about mages being hunted long ago. That's not true, is it? I didn't sleep through my history class—I may have doodled a lot during it, but I *was* listening. We didn't read many chapters from our textbook—it was mostly Professor Colindun giving lectures— but I don't remember anything about that."

Jadora paused, leaving her finger to mark her place. "He didn't have you read Gorazar's *History of the World*?"

"Just a few chapters here and there. It wasn't so scintillating that I felt compelled to read pages that weren't assigned."

"What did he say about the Magic Wars and how the mages came to establish their cities?" Jadora didn't like the thought that professors at the university—her own colleagues—might be teaching revisionist history.

"That the reason some people developed magical powers and

others didn't was debated but that those who did came to think highly of themselves and soon used their superhuman abilities to amass followers, take over governments, and coerce people into militaries and under their rule. Our people didn't realize the threat until it was too late for our numbers to be an advantage. They started the Magic Wars, but by then, our failure was inevitable. Not only did the mages win, but the most powerful among them declared themselves wizards and rulers, and built the sky castles that eventually grew into entire cities in the skies. None of us terrene humans could reach them to attack even if we dared to."

"Hm. The part after the wars is correct, but Malek's version of how the schism first came about is closer to what I've read in Gorazar's and in other texts from different cultures around the world. In the beginning, when people first started developing power, they were feared and shunned and often killed. Some believed dragons gave them their power, but at the time, it was also popular to believe the slavemasters in Hell created them to serve their needs. Supposedly, if you mated with one of their kind, you would lose your soul, and your children would be born demons. Back then, mages hadn't refined their powers and learned to do the great things they're capable of today. They were mostly clairvoyants who could do a few tricks. Killing them wasn't as difficult, and humans did a lot of that."

"So they banded together for protection?"

"And made a concerted effort to learn how best to channel their abilities and use them against any who threatened them. It's not impossible to imagine that we would have ended up in this situation eventually anyway—" Jadora waved at their surroundings to indicate the city and their rulers, "—but it's believed that one of the reasons they're driven to keep us subjugated is fear that we'll find a way to rise up again and destroy them."

Clangs sounded on the other side of the doors. Yidar and

Malek sparring? Hopefully, they would wear each other out and be too tired for mind reading.

"We just want equality, right?" Jak asked softly. "I know that's what Father wanted, why he was looking for the portal and help from another world."

"To have an equal say in government or to have them give us a piece of the world and leave us to govern ourselves, yes. For them to have to farm their *own* crops." She snorted at the thought of one of the robed elitists in the castle pulling up weeds in a field. *Malek* might be unfazed by the idea, filing it under his zidarr duties, but he seemed rare among them.

"When Father used to talk about the dragon world, I wished we could all go live there with them." Jak smiled. "I was only ten and wanted to explore."

"I've had similar wishes."

Jadora returned to studying the page, though it was a moment before she could focus again. She skimmed down the columns, the symbols barely registering until she spotted a match for the one in Jak's rubbing.

"That's it," she whispered. "The translation is 'waterfall pool in the jungle.'"

Jak sucked in a breath. "I dreamed about that place."

"You dreamed? Or you touched the portal, and it gave you a vision?"

"I'm sure the portal gave it to me, but I was sleeping in bed at the time. I meant to tell you about it this morning, but Malek showed up early."

"I haven't dreamed about the portal, but I saw it in a vision when I touched it." Jadora couldn't believe she was talking so casually about visions, as if they were something that usually existed outside of psychedelic experiences.

Jak didn't tease her. He was staring down at the translation.

"For me, it wasn't a jungle or a waterfall," she added. "It was an open valley."

"Were there dragons in your vision?"

"Yes. Until the portal killed people." She frowned at the memory. "Did you get a warning like that in yours?"

He shook his head and explained what he'd seen. His description of a waterfall tumbling into a pool in a lush jungle sounded exactly like what the ancient words etched on the portal implied.

"If that's where it can be set up and activated," she said, "why would it have shown me a different place? On what seemed like an entirely different continent? In another vision, the first one it gave me, it showed me dragons in an icy landscape with a sky that didn't look like anything on Torvil."

"Maybe those are *all* places it can operate, but they're not all on this world. Mother." Jak gripped her arm. "What if the portal wants us to take it someplace it can work, so the dragons can return to Torvil? Maybe it misses them. Maybe it's been *lonely* buried under a volcano all this time."

"I'm not ready to ascribe human emotions to an ancient artifact, but I *can* believe it's trying to communicate something to us."

"That it wants us to take it home."

"Let's not forget the warnings in our visions," she said. "Humans died in one of mine."

"Because they attacked it, right?"

"Yes, but *why* did they attack it? And why did they tear it down in your vision? Jak..." Jadora scowled down at the page. "It's possible the dragons weren't our allies, and the people who attacked the portal and tore it down did it because they were afraid of it. Or because something bad had come through it to our world."

"Not the dragons. We wouldn't have a whole religion with a benevolent dragon god if we'd believed that."

"There's a religion on Yorakka Island where they worship

ferns. Humans can conjure up strange notions to help them make sense of a tumultuous world."

"But are they *benevolent* ferns?"

Jadora sighed and leaned back in her chair.

"Look, it's asking for our help. I'm sure of it. If we take it there and set it up, and something bad happens—" Jak jerked his head toward the library entrance. "Did you hear something?"

"Besides the clash of swords through the door?"

"Yeah." He lowered his voice to a whisper. "I think someone's in here with us."

He left the table to peer into nearby aisles and out the tall windows in the back of the library.

Jadora hadn't heard anything. She closed the book and debated whether or not to stuff it behind a row of books where it would be difficult for someone to find again. If she'd found the translation, Malek could too. And who knew if the portal was giving him visions? Maybe he would be able to connect the translation to a dream and figure out where the portal needed to go to be activated.

But someone with magic might be able to easily find a book out of place behind a shelf. She could take it with her, but it was old and heavy, and as soon as Malek saw her carrying it, he would know she'd found something in it.

"You wish to leave this place?" a woman asked from behind her.

Jadora almost fell out of her chair.

"I knew it," Jak blurted, rushing back into view. He carried a bust from a pedestal, as if he meant to use it as a club.

But the woman was familiar. This was one of the servants who'd delivered their belongings to them on the first day. Altrucia. Her lank brown hair hung limply under a mageband circling her head, but her eyes weren't glazed today.

Jadora turned to face her. "What did you say?"

"You know a way out?" Jak added.

"I know the castle well. I have served here for many years. I have also seen what happens to those the king brings here for advice or because they have knowledge that is useful to him." Altrucia looked pointedly at Jadora. "He never wishes their knowledge to fall into the hands of his enemies, so once they deliver it to him, he makes them disappear."

"I feared that might be true," Jadora said.

"Come." Altrucia waved. "I will show you a way out." Steel screeched beyond the doors, and she winced. "But we must hurry. If they catch me helping you, I will be punished."

"Won't they punish you anyway?" Jak asked. "When they realize we're gone and had help getting out?"

"No. Because we will all escape together. I have a husband I have not seen in more than ten years." Altrucia pointed to the floor—or to the land thousands of feet below the city. "Even though I know of all the hidden passages in the castle, I've never dared use them. But you have friends coming. They will retrieve you, and you will take me with you, yes?" Her eyes gleamed with hope.

"Uh," Jak said.

"We'll take you with us as far as we can," Jadora said, "but I'm afraid we don't have any friends coming to help. We'll have to steal a ship from the harbor and hope we can figure out how to fly it."

"Only someone with magical power can operate their vessels, but are the king's enemies not your allies?" Altrucia frowned. "I overheard the king say that mercenary companies would be sent in to try to retrieve you and the artifact."

"That's possibly their intent." Not because of friendship but because King Zaruk also wanted Jadora, Jak, and the portal. If they succeeded in kidnapping them, it would be jumping from one imprisonment to another. Jadora was about to explain that but paused as a new thought bloomed. Mercenary companies? If the kings working against Uthari had hired mercenaries, was it possible that Thorn Company was among them? If so, would there be a chance to join up with them? Maybe the women could once again be convinced to help. Maybe they even still had the key.

Horror jolted Jadora as she realized that they might, if they truly were on their way here to fight, bring the very key Malek and Uthari were searching for and inadvertently drop it in their hands.

"We might be able to get a ride from some mercenaries," Jak said. "But it's also possible I could fly a craft. I have... knacks."

Jadora blinked and looked at him. "You don't know how to *use* any of your knacks yet."

"Maybe there are tips in this book." He held up *The Mind Way*.

"About flying mageships? I doubt *The Serenity of the Turtle* has a lot of advice on aerial navigation."

"Mother." Jak rolled his eyes in exasperation. "Let's get out of here and figure it out later."

Altrucia nodded firmly.

"I'm just worried that we'll trade one master for another," Jadora said, "and that our next babysitter won't be as even-keeled as Malek."

Altrucia shook her head and whispered, "Malek is not cruel or prone to outbursts like some of the others, but if his master orders him to torture or kill you, he will. He is completely Uthari's man. Do not believe you are safe with him. He is a weapon without feelings, without remorse."

For some reason, Jadora wanted to object to that, but what did she know? Nothing. She barely knew Malek, and if Altrucia had been here for a decade, she had to be familiar with all the zidarr.

Jadora tore out the page with the translation, stuck it in her pocket, and put the book back on the shelf. "Let's go."

～

The drizzle dampened Tezi's cheeks. She could have believed they were sailing across the ocean on a foggy night instead of through the clouds. The mageship's exterior lamps had been turned off and all the hatches closed, so that light from the magical devices that powered the craft wouldn't seep out. They had orders not to speak or make noise. "Running quiet," Captain Toggs had called it.

The other ships in the allied fleet must have been doing the same, because Tezi didn't see or hear sign of others in the clouds. Even so, she sensed they were getting close to their destination. Tension mingled with anticipation, hanging in the air like the mist. Though she couldn't see them, Tezi was aware of Sergeant Tinder to one side of her and Lieutenant Sasko to the other. Occasionally, one of the mercenaries stirred, armor and weapons clanking faintly, but someone had mentioned that enemy ships could already be out here among them, and since then, everyone had been careful to obey Toggs' call for silence.

A distant boom drifted to them. Thunder?

"That's it," Tinder whispered. "Our fleet has encountered the enemy. Too bad we're in the rear."

Not thunder. Explosives.

Tezi rested her hand on her rifle, her thumb tracing the dragons engraved in the silver plating above the trigger mechanism. She hoped the imagery didn't have any religious connotations, since the teachings of Thanok said it was sacrilegious to believe any of the dragons of eld had been gods. Making idols in their likeness was forbidden. She was less certain about drawings —or images engraved in magelocks—but she did not want to upset Thanok, not on the eve of battle. Thorn Company might need his favor tonight.

"We'll see plenty of action when we slip into their well-defended city," Basher whispered from Tinder's other side.

"I look forward to it," Tinder said.

"You're fondling your grenades, aren't you?"

"Usually."

"Cut the chitchat," Sasko growled, and the group fell silent again.

A white flash from the same direction as the boom penetrated the clouds, eerie and strange in the mist. Tezi sank to her knees and rested the barrel of her rifle on the railing, nervous but ready to do her part.

Thorn Company's orders were to hold tight when the enemy was spotted and let the mages start the action. They would encase the *Dauntless* in a protective barrier until it was time to drop it so the mercenaries could fire. Tezi trusted someone would let her know when to shoot, since she didn't otherwise know how to tell if magic surrounded them or not.

A cloud darker than the rest caught her eye. Or *was* it a cloud? Could there be other ships out here running dark, trying not to be seen? And if so, was it one of their allies? Or one of their enemies? It seemed to be moving parallel to the *Dauntless*.

"Lieutenant," Tezi whispered.

"I see it. Be right back." Sasko jogged toward one of the mage crew.

An instant later, a boom rang out as orange light flashed from the dark cloud, revealing that it was a ship.

"We're under attack!" a mage crewman yelled. "We've got a barrier up. Hold fire, *hold* fire."

An orange fireball flew toward them, and Tezi ducked below the railing. It grew larger and larger, threatening to slam into the side of the ship. At the last second, it struck their invisible barrier and bounced off, dissipating.

"The barrier is down," a calm voice said. "Mercenaries, return fire."

Someone behind Tezi reacted more quickly than she, the blue blast of a magelock charge sailing away. It struck a barrier around the enemy ship instead of hitting a target.

"Fire the artillery weapons," Sorath barked—that had been him shooting. He, the captain, and Sasko had the other special magelocks. "We've got to whittle down their shield, boys."

"*And* girls," Tinder corrected, leaning back to use her *arm* like an artillery weapon.

Tezi wouldn't have thought they were close enough, but Tinder heaved one of her grenades toward the dark shape paralleling them. It arced through the clouds and blew up when it struck the barrier, never reaching the ship.

Tinder swore at the waste. The *Dauntless*'s big weapons opened up, pummeling the enemy with cannonballs and magical charges ten times the power of what magelocks could fire. Tezi fingered the trigger of her rifle but didn't shoot, not able to tell if the attack was doing anything to *whittle down* their defense. She didn't want to waste her charges on an impervious shield.

During a pause, the enemy ship lowered its barrier to return fire. Tezi sank lower as bolts of yellow and orange light streaked toward them.

"Barrier up!" one of their mages cried.

An order or a warning? Tezi couldn't tell. Most of the projectiles exploded before reaching them, and she breathed a sigh of relief, but something that had been lobbed high and slow tumbled *over* their mages' defenses and descended toward them. A grenade from a counterpart of Tinder's on the other ship.

Tezi lunged to her feet and pointed her magelock in the air, trying to track the dark shape against the gray clouds. She fired at the same time as someone else—the captain. Their blasts struck simultaneously, and the grenade exploded dozens of feet above the ship.

"Take cover!" the captain yelled as shrapnel rained down on them.

It pinged off the deck and railing, and someone cried out in pain, but it could have been worse. The ship itself wasn't damaged.

"Get a barrier up *over* us," Captain Toggs yelled to his crew.

"This is foolish." Sorath glanced toward the navigation cabin. "We're in a three-dimensional environment, and we're broadsiding each other like warships firing cannons on the sea." He'd been speaking to Captain Ferroki, but he didn't wait for an answer. He ran to the navigation cabin and disappeared inside.

"He's not going to have any luck getting the mage crew to listen to him," Sasko said.

"They will if they know what's good for them." Tinder had another grenade in hand, but both ships had their barriers up, so she didn't throw it. "And us."

"Mages *never* know what's good for us."

Tezi tried not to feel useless as the ships lowered their defenses only long enough to fire upon each other, then raised them immediately after, so they wouldn't be vulnerable to the volleys. Weapons from both sides bounced off, with nothing getting through the shields. Tezi could now make out red-uniformed people on the deck of the other mageship, and might have tried to pick off an officer, but she worried about the ramifications of mistiming and hitting their own barrier.

"Be ready to fire," Captain Ferroki said. "We might be weakening the mages maintaining their shields enough that they'll be forced to drop them."

"That happens, ma'am?" Tezi rested her magelock on the railing again, looking for an important target. She settled on one of their cannon operators.

"Mages eventually get tired when their shields are under attack. It takes effort to maintain them. These battles are often of attrition."

Smoke from the black-powder weapons filled the air, and Tezi could no longer see the deck or even the other ship. So much for targeting an individual.

A faint vibration hummed through the deck. It took her a

moment to realize the *Dauntless* was descending—the other ship remained on its straight-ahead route, at least for the moment. Their craft was descending *and* angling toward it.

"Won't they just change their path?" Not only was it Tezi's first major battle, but it was her first time on a mageship. She had no idea what the normal combat tactics were.

"Depends if they think this will give us an advantage or not." The lieutenant shook her head. "I'd rather get above them and have the high ground than... whatever it is we're doing."

The *Dauntless*'s mages lowered their defenses, and the crew fired off the largest volley of weapons yet. Cannons and magical charges boomed and flashed, filling the air with the stink of black powder. Tezi still couldn't see what they were firing at. Maybe that was the point. Would the crew of the other ship fail to see them sliding underneath them? Would that tactic *work* against mages? Maybe if the mages were busy shoring up their defenses, they would be distracted for a moment.

"What can we do from below?" Tezi asked.

"I've got ideas." Tinder hefted her grenade.

"Won't their defenses wrap all the way around their ship?"

More flashes appeared in the air above the *Dauntless*, and projectiles streaked away into the clouds. The enemy ship hadn't adjusted where it was firing yet.

Through the smoke and the clouds, its black hull grew visible above and slightly behind them. Tezi aimed her rifle toward it but hesitated. Would firing at the hull do anything? Even without magic, it ought to be sturdy.

"Adjust your aim, gunners," Captain Ferroki said quietly. "Our mages should unload all they've got to try to burrow an opening in their defenses."

She'd no sooner finished the words than the ship's magical guns fired. The first charges struck a barrier under the hull and did nothing.

A shout reached their ears from the enemy ship: "They're *under* us. Adjust targets!"

"We can't shoot them *through* our ship," someone else up there yelled. "We've got to move. Move!"

"Keep firing," Sorath ordered, patting a mage at one of the cannons. "We're wearing them down."

False optimism or truth? Tezi didn't know how he could tell. Their projectiles kept bouncing uselessly off the invisible barrier or exploding against it, too far from the enemy ship to do any damage.

But mere seconds later, that changed. A fiery orange ball cast from a mage's hands made it through the air where the barrier had been. It slammed into the hull of the enemy ship. More weapons fired, magical charges smashing through the hull and exploding inside.

Tezi shot once, not sure her smaller magelock would do anything. The blast put a dent in the hull. It didn't do much. Fortunately, the *Dauntless*'s more powerful weapons continued to punch through the hull and blast into the interior of the ship.

The enemy craft veered to the left and rose in elevation, trying to get away from them.

"Stay with them," Sorath ordered through the hatchway to the navigation officer.

A fireball shot off the deck of the ship above and curved, arching through the mist toward them. It was the first one to do so, and the defenders weren't prepared to raise a barrier again. It slammed into the side of the *Dauntless*, tearing through the hull. The jolt knocked Tezi into the railing.

She grimaced, imagining an enemy attack blowing up the magical engine that powered the craft. What would happen then? Would they fall out of the sky and plummet to their deaths thousands of feet below?

"Raise shields to the sides," Captain Toggs yelled. "Keep it open above."

"Can they do that?" Tezi pushed back to her feet.

"I think so," Tinder said. "I've heard that creating a bubble all around something is harder than a simple flat shield."

More fireballs curved down toward them, and Tezi braced herself. One streaked straight toward the top of the ship—toward her and the other mercenaries. Several swore and flattened themselves to the deck. Tezi crouched down beside Tinder.

But the fireballs blasted against a renewed shield a dozen feet from the ship. Feeling sheepish, Tezi rose up again.

"All fire on the engine compartment." Sorath pointed upward toward a specific spot on the enemy ship's hull.

"And Uthari's people," Ferroki added.

Their hull had been torn open in numerous places, huge gaps revealing the innards of the craft, including the glowing magical artifact that powered it. But snipers had run down to their engine compartment, crouching next to the holes in the hull, raising weapons to fire upon Tezi and the others. There was no barrier above the *Dauntless*, no magical protection from that direction.

As blasts and bullets pounded their deck, Tezi darted behind the corner of the navigation cabin. Scant feet away, someone screamed as they were hit.

Tezi leaned out and fired at Uthari's red-uniformed defenders. The *Dauntless*'s mages focused on the magical engine itself, hoping to blow it up as the other vessel zigzagged its course, trying to get away from them. But the big mageships did not move quickly, and as soon as they changed course, the *Dauntless* followed. A defiant whoop came from the navigation cabin as Captain Toggs' helmsman successfully stuck with them. He sounded young.

Tezi spotted an enemy soldier aiming for Captain Ferroki and fired before he could. Her charge struck him in the chest, and he tumbled out through one of the holes in the hull. He fell past the bow of the *Dauntless*, screaming as he disappeared below.

Though chilled, Tezi made herself fire again. If they didn't survive this battle, or if their ship was incapacitated, their part in the war would be over before it started.

She tried *not* to focus on the mercenary—Corporal Jinx—lying unmoving on the deck five feet away, blood pooling under her body. This was what she had signed up for. She couldn't expect anything but horror and death—maybe her own.

"I'm out of charges," someone barked.

"Me too," someone else responded. "No time to recharge. Here."

One of Tinder's grenades sailed toward the enemy's vulnerable engine compartment. Tezi didn't have many charges left either and tried to make them count.

Sorath appeared, his arms full of the glowing red mushroom explosives. He thrust a few at Captain Ferroki, then started hurling them himself. They struck the hull and blew. One landed squarely on the pulsing engine.

With a flash of white light, an explosion ripped from the bottom of the enemy ship, blowing huge chunks of the hull in all directions. A piece the size of a house slammed into the deck, almost taking out two more mercenaries. Smoke filled the air again, stealing Tezi's ability to find targets. But it didn't matter. With its engine destroyed and no magic remaining to keep it aloft, the enemy ship gave way to gravity and plummeted downward so fast the breeze stirred Tezi's hair.

A ragged cheer went up from the mercenaries and the mage crewmen. The captain and the doctor rushed to the downed corporal, but Fret soon shook her head. They'd lost her.

Tezi leaned her forehead against the cabin, worried that Jinx wouldn't be the last.

24

As Jadora and Jak trailed Altrucia across the library, the sounds of swords striking beyond the double doors faded, and silence fell. If the zidarr sparring session was over, they might not have much time. Altrucia must have had similar thoughts because she sent nervous glances toward the exit and broke into a run to lead them under one of the mezzanines.

Jadora told herself that they weren't yet doing anything condemning, so she didn't need to be scared, but she also propelled her legs more quickly, her vials clinking in her pocket. The tiny noises echoed like peals of thunder in the cavernous library. She flattened her hand against the pocket to keep them quiet.

They stopped before reaching the back wall, and Altrucia tugged at a shallow bookcase that stood ajar. She must have come in that way to avoid being seen by the zidarr.

Jak let out a soft, "Hah!" at this confirmation of secret passages.

After a last glance toward the library entrance, Altrucia slid behind the bookcase and onto a small landing less than two feet by two feet. The nook had been built between two bookcases that were shallower than those around them. She had to step carefully to avoid falling into a square hole in the floor, the rungs of a metal ladder just visible, thanks to the lamps lit in the library.

"Follow." Altrucia didn't hesitate to start down the rungs, but she paused and removed her headband. "Take no magic with you or the zidarr will be able to track us." She slid it out, leaving it on the floor, and waved again for them to follow.

Jadora frowned at Jak, worried *he* was magical enough that Malek would be able to track him. All they could hope was that they could get far enough away that tracking like that wouldn't be possible.

Jak must have thought the headband on the floor would be an obvious clue, for he picked it up, ran it back up the aisle, and stuck it between some books.

As soon as Altrucia had descended far enough, Jadora climbed down after her. It was so dark that she had no idea how far they were dropping, and she worried she would step on their leader's hand. But Altrucia must have been as eager to escape as they, for when she called up, "Last person, close the bookcase," her voice came from well below Jadora.

"Got it," Jak replied.

A faint grinding sound came from above, and the vestiges of light from the library disappeared.

Jadora placed her hands and feet carefully, having no idea how far she might fall if she slipped. Logically, she knew the platform that supported the city couldn't be *that* deep, but her mind conjured images of plummeting into an abyss for a few eons before landing hard enough to die instantly.

Jak's boots rang softly on the rungs—they sounded alarmingly close to her fingers.

"Don't step on me, please," Jadora said. "I'm taking my time."

"Enjoying the scenery?"

"Something like that."

Soft rasps came from below, followed by the appearance of a tiny orange flame.

"There are mage lamps," Altrucia said, "but I fear using their tools will lead them to us. I brought torches."

"Torches are fine." Jadora's foot came down on something with a broader base than the rungs, though it didn't sound like a solid floor. "We appreciate your help."

Altrucia lit a second torch from the first, the faint stink of kerosene filling the still, dark air, and handed it to Jadora. She bent to shed light on the floor. It was a grate with normal-looking pipes under it and un-normal-looking tendrils with a faint green glow to them. They didn't emit enough light to see by, so Jadora was glad for the torches. And a guide. They'd come down in a dead-end, but she wagered there was a maze of tunnels down here.

"This way." Altrucia headed down the tunnel.

As they hurried away from the ladder, Jadora lamented that they couldn't take the portal with them. Leaving it in Uthari's hands felt like such a failing. But if there was a chance they could reunite with Thorn Company and get the key—and take *it* far from here—maybe that would be enough for now.

Their long narrow tunnel was almost painfully straight, and Jadora was glad. The more steps they put between themselves and the castle the better.

Her light played over something fuzzy, damp, and gray on the wall, and she paused. Mold would have been her first guess, but tiny sprouts came from the variegated lump. Not a fungi then. But what plant could grow down in this dark tunnel with no notable substrate on the hard walls?

Jadora brushed her finger over it. Even the texture was strange. Was it some blending of magical and natural? Or a species endemic to the sky city?

She fished in her pockets for an empty vial and her small spatula sampler.

"*Mother,*" Jak whispered from behind her. "Don't tell me you're pausing in the middle of our escape from megalomaniacal mages to take a sample of something growing on the wall."

"I wasn't going to tell you. Hold this." She thrust the torch at him, scraped a few spongy blobs off the wall, making sure to get the sprouts, and slid them into the vial and corked it.

"Other people's mothers aren't like this."

"Their home lives must be stultifying." Jadora put her vial away in a different pocket from the others, grabbed the torch, and said, "Thank you," as she hurried after their leader. "If you want to draw a map later, I'll hold your torch for you."

"That's fair." Jak glanced back.

She lowered her voice. "You don't hear anyone following us, do you?"

"I hope not."

The answer did not reassure her.

"I heard a clank a little while ago," Jak admitted, "but it might have been whatever machinery operates down here."

Or it might have been someone opening that hidden bookcase access?

Grimacing, Jadora caught up with Altrucia and wished she would go faster. If Malek had figured out where they'd gone, he could sprint through these tunnels and catch up with them quickly.

Could zidarr see in the dark? She wouldn't be surprised. Would he be annoyed with them for trying to escape? Or dryly amused? So far, he'd trended toward the latter, but if he had to chase them through tunnels for miles and got in trouble with his master for letting them out, Malek might feel differently this time.

A hint of light came from up ahead, and Jadora slowed down.

"Is that something magical?" she whispered.

It wasn't the same yellow as Altrucia's torch—not natural flame. The glow was orange this time.

"Yes," Altrucia said. "But it is nothing to be alarmed about. It is... the sewage treatment box."

"Just what I was hoping to see on my trip to a sky city," Jak muttered.

Altrucia's pause made Jadora uneasy. Their guide wouldn't have a reason to *lie* to them, would she?

She looked back at Jak, the flames of her torch throwing his face in shadow, and she belatedly wondered if they'd made a mistake. Her feet slowed. The light was coming from around a corner up ahead, so she couldn't yet see the source, but it was growing brighter. Nothing in this tunnel so far hinted—or suggested via smell—that they were in a sewer channel.

Altrucia noticed that they'd fallen back and waved. "Hurry. Do not slow now. The way to the surface is just up ahead."

"Problem?" Jak murmured.

"I'm not sure," Jadora murmured back.

They passed something else on the wall, not plant matter. It was the remains of a broken fist-sized dome that had been mounted there. The shards had fallen through the grating, and a few pieces were visible on the pipe and green glowing tendril they'd been following.

The air buzzed as Jadora stepped past the broken dome, but whatever it was didn't hurt her. As soon as she took another step, the sensation went away. Had that been a more formidable barrier before the dome—the device that operated it?—had been broken?

Altrucia stepped over a large dark lump on the grating and stopped in a four-way intersection. Whatever was responsible for the orange glow was off to her right side. It painted her face in warm light and didn't appear to alarm her.

Jadora had almost convinced herself it truly was a sewer box or other piece of infrastructure when the light moved, shifting the shadows on the wall. And on the grating. Jadora halted. The large lump Altrucia had stepped over was a man wearing the red uniform of Uthari's militia. It *had* been a man. His throat was slit.

There was no way Altrucia had done that.

Jadora halted. "Who—"

An invisible force pushed her from behind. She whirled, trying to lunge away, but Jak smashed into her. The force was pushing him too.

"Can't fight it," he snarled in frustration as he kept stumbling forward, bumping her along ahead of him.

Jadora thought about screaming—or *threatening* to scream—but to whom would she cry?

"Well done, Altrucia," a male voice rumbled.

A man in green clothing stepped out of the side tunnel as the wall of power forced Jadora and Jak into the intersection. Altrucia backed up and avoided her eyes when Jadora shot an accusing glare at her.

The man in green wasn't carrying a light—whatever was making that glow came from farther down the tunnel behind him. It provided enough illumination to see him nod at Altrucia. His long hair was back in a ponytail, and he lacked a military mien, nor were his green tunic and trousers a uniform, but that shade was reminiscent of the uniforms Queen Vorsha's people wore. Two magelock pistols hung in holsters on his hips.

Jadora couldn't tell if the man was a zidarr, but she hoped not. Malek and the other zidarr she'd seen didn't bother with projectile weapons—why would they when they could fling their power around like bullets? Maybe if this was a mage of middling power, she and Jak had a chance of overpowering him.

"I wish you could have brought the artifact as well," he continued, "but I suppose it would not have fit down a ladder."

"No, my lord." Altrucia kept her gaze downcast.

The man stepped forward and rested a hand on the side of her head. Whatever he did caused her face to relax and the tension to ebb from her body. "You have done well. As promised, a place on a barge called the *Field Drifter* awaits you in the harbor." He pressed a glowing fob into her hand. "This will direct you to the right berth. Tell the captain the sun sets on the castle, and he will let you aboard. He loathes Uthari and is loyal to my master."

Jadora found she couldn't step forward or back but that her arms weren't immobilized. She slid her hand into her pocket, fingers wrapping around a vial of the mild acid she'd made earlier.

"Yes, my lord. Thank you." Altrucia bobbed her head.

As the man stepped back, still focused on Altrucia, Jadora uncorked her vial and threw it at the side of his head. He whirled and caught it, but without a lid, some of the liquid spattered his hand and face.

He snarled and lunged for Jadora, his fingers snapping in the air. He was several feet away, but it was as if they snapped around her neck—and squeezed.

Altrucia might have helped, but she fled in the direction the mage had indicated, and she didn't look back. Wheezing for breath, Jadora couldn't help but feel betrayed. If terrene humans couldn't stick together, how would they ever change the world?

Jak rushed past Jadora. She wanted to stop him—to protect him—but the invisible fingers tightening around her neck stole her breath and kept her from moving.

Their grip released as Jak plowed into the mage, surprising him. They tumbled to the grating together. Jak tried to snatch free one of the holstered pistols, but the mage knocked him back, half with power, half with a punch. The weapon clattered off the wall and bounced onto the grating.

The mage snarled and rose to his feet. Jak sprang up at the same time. The weapon had landed closer to Jadora than to either of them, and she crept forward, hoping Jak's body blocked the mage's view. She picked up the pistol.

Jak crouched to spring at the mage again, but a blast of energy knocked him backward. Jadora ducked low a heartbeat before he would have crashed into her. Instead, he sailed *over* her. From her belly, she found the trigger and fired at the mage.

He hadn't yet recovered from his attack on Jak, and the charge blasted him full in the chest. Shock and pain flashed in his eyes as he staggered back, gaping at her. Jadora fired again and again, terrified he would recover and kill both of them.

Only when Jak rested a hand on her shoulder did she stop. "Not that I don't support shooting people who are tormenting us, but I think we'll need the rest of the charges in that magelock to get out of here."

Their enemy lay on his back on the grating, holes blown in his chest. No magic would cause him to rise again.

Jadora's hands shook—no, her whole body shook—and she dropped the weapon, barely noticing as it clattered onto the grate. She sank to her knees, numbly aware of the hard bite of the metal through her trousers.

She was a scholar, not a murderer. How had she ended up in this situation? She hated this place and all these people. The idea that she might never be able to return home to her normal life filled her with almost as much distress as the mage's death.

Jak picked up their torches, the pistol, then went to the body to pull the second firearm out of the holster. He returned to her side and patted her shoulder. "Do you want one?"

Still numb, Jadora shook her head slowly. She wanted to escape, but she didn't want to kill anybody else. He handed her one of the torches. They were lucky they hadn't gone out.

Jak spun, as if he'd heard something, and peered back down the tunnel they'd originally come from. He wrapped his arms around her and helped her to stand.

Afraid Malek was on their trail, Jadora locked her knees and forced her legs to support her weight.

"To the harbor?" Jak whispered, pointing one of the magelocks in the direction Altrucia had gone.

"For all we know, that leads to an incinerator, and she's running into her fiery death."

"I've studied infrastructure maps. It's rare for incinerators to be included among the pipes that provide power, water, and sewage treatment for cities."

Jadora *hoped* there was an incinerator somewhere for the sewage, and that it wasn't simply dumped out of the bottom of the city onto the land below, but this wasn't the time to wonder about it. She waved for Jak to lead the way.

They walked softly, trying to keep their shoes from making noise on the grating. The glow grew brighter, and faint thunks came from an alcove that opened to one side of the tunnel. Magical machinery several feet tall and wide occupied the space, with an orange orb in the center, feeding power into green tendrils as well as a pumping system. Several types of pipes and conduits ran up through the ceiling, as well as into the wall at the back of the alcove, and down under the grating and into the tunnel.

Altrucia had continued past, and Jak started doing the same, but his head jerked around again. He peered back toward the intersection, then pointed into the alcove.

Jadora opened her mouth to question him, but he held up a finger and shook his head. He darted behind the machinery, the tangle of magical and mundane equipment large enough to provide a hiding spot, and waved for her to join him.

Though Jadora would rather run than risk being caught back there, Jak seemed certain that someone was coming. They ground out their torches on the grating, the magical machinery providing enough of a glow to see by. They had weapons now, so maybe they could defend themselves if they needed to. In the alcove, at least they could put their backs to a wall. Not that such tactics mattered much against mages.

She squeezed behind the machinery with him. There was barely room between it and the wall, and a lever thrusting out mashed her in the breast. Maybe women weren't meant to go on adventures such as these. Her elbow brushed against a glowing piece of metal as hot as a branding iron, and she jerked it back, clunking it against the wall and barely avoiding cursing. Maybe *nobody* was meant to go on adventures such as these.

Jak found a spot where he could peer through a small gap. Jadora let him have the watch duty and shifted, trying to make herself less uncomfortable. A pipe dug into her hip, reverberating with magical energy or whatever it was that flowed from the station out into the rest of the city.

Long seconds ticked past, the machinery drowning out any other noise, and she was tempted to ask him what he'd heard. *She* hadn't heard anything, but it was possible some other sense—this magical sense that he was learning about—was guiding him. She didn't know what to think about that but continued to fear it would get him in trouble with the zidarr. The thought of losing him almost brought tears to her eyes.

Maybe she sniffed, for Jak held his finger to his lips again, then pointed through the peephole between two pipes. She leaned over in time to see someone walk into view of the alcove from the direction of the intersection. Someone in simple clothes and a brown jacket. Malek. The orange glow highlighted the hard angles of his face. He looked pissed.

Certain he would sense them watching him, Jadora wanted to pull back and close her eyes, but she didn't dare move. He looked toward their hiding spot. Since they were behind the glowing light, it *should* be hard for him to make them out in the shadows, but she doubted he used only his eyes to track people.

He squinted toward the machinery and took a step into the alcove, and she was sure they were about to be dragged back to the castle by their collars. Then the grating shook. *Everything* shook.

Memories of earthquakes she'd experienced sprang to mind. It was over in seconds, but it left her shaken. Jak's eyes were wide, but he hadn't budged. He wasn't moving, maybe not even breathing, as if afraid to draw Malek's attention.

She understood that, but Malek was looking toward the ceiling now. Using his magic to sense what was above it? Or above the city?

A woman's scream came from the tunnel, from the direction Altrucia had gone. Malek's head swiveled toward it, and he ran off.

Jadora sagged, exhaling the breath she hadn't realized she'd been holding. Her head thunked against the pump housing.

The grating shook again.

"What's going on?" she murmured, though she feared she already knew.

"I think the war has started," Jak said. "The city is under attack."

25

JAK STOOD UP AND CREPT OUT FROM BEHIND THE PUMP MACHINERY. At least fifteen minutes had passed since the last quake rocked the tunnels. It had been even longer since Malek ran off to check on Altrucia's scream. Jak also hadn't heard anymore explosions or cries of pain. Hopefully, that meant the defensive shields were now in place and further attacks wouldn't reach the great floating structure.

But if the city wasn't in danger now, where had Malek gone? Jak had assumed he would, once he realized Altrucia wasn't Mother, come back the same way. He might have been called back to the castle to defend it. Or he might be in the tunnels searching for Jak and his mother.

"Hope not," he muttered.

"Let's try to get to the harbor." His mother stood, shaking out her legs. "The attack and the diversion it's creating may be our best chance to escape."

"I'm worried we'll run straight into Malek if we go the way he went. Should we go back to the intersection and pick a different direction?"

"And end up lost down here for hours?" She surprised him by relighting their torches by touching them to a glowing piece of metal on the back of the pumping machinery.

"I have an excellent sense of direction. I don't get lost."

"If not lost, then unable to get out. We haven't passed any other ladders or ways up. If that mage was telling the truth, there's at least one ship waiting in the harbor. It's that way, right?" She pointed down the tunnel in the direction Malek had gone.

Jak considered the route they'd taken since the library. "More or less."

"That may be our only option anyway. Remember that broken dome on the wall of our tunnel at the four-way intersection? There were domes in the two tunnels that we didn't take that weren't broken. I think they may create barriers that you can't pass unless you know how to unlock them. Or break them."

Jak had forgotten about it but nodded at the reminder.

"All right." He took one of the torches and peeked both ways before stepping out of the alcove. "But if we run into Malek, you get to take the brunt of his wrath while I cower behind you."

"Your bravery warms my heart."

"I think he likes you more than me." Jak jogged off down the tunnel.

"I don't know about that. He's keeping other mages from annihilating you for being cheeky and magically gifted."

"It's just been one other mage—that zidarr."

"And maybe Uthari. He went off to report to him, remember."

"Maybe they had more interesting things to discuss than me." The tunnel curved, making Jak doubt that it would truly take them to the harbor.

A boom came from somewhere above them, but the ground didn't shake. There was some proof that the defenses were in place. Good. *After* Jak and Mother escaped, the invasion fleet could destroy the place. Not before.

Another intersection lay ahead, and he raised a hand as he slowed down. A body was crumpled in it, face-down with arms and legs sprawled out. The clothing was familiar. Altrucia.

Jak crept forward to see if it was possible she'd only been knocked out. It occurred to him that she might have been left as bait to draw them out. He gripped one pistol tightly, the other jammed in his waistband until his mother wanted it. If she ever did. She'd seemed shaken after killing that mage. Understandable, but Jak would have done the same thing to protect her.

He missed seeing a shard of glass on the grating and kicked it with his boot. It clacked against the wall before tumbling between the bars and shattering against the pipes running next to the glowing tendril. The body didn't stir, but Jak froze, worried Malek was lying in wait around the corner.

"Another broken dome," Mother whispered, pointing past his shoulder to the wall.

Queen Vorsha's mage must have originally come this way, destroying those devices—and knocking out the barriers—as he went. Jak eased toward the intersection and peered around the corners. Nobody was waiting to pounce. To the right, another broken dome on the wall suggested the mage had come from that direction. It was the way most likely to lead to the harbor. A good thing, because more domes were mounted to the tunnel walls ahead and to the left. They hadn't been broken. He thought he sensed a buzz of magic from both directions, either from the working domes or from barriers blocking the way.

"Check her, please," Mother said from behind him.

Jak didn't think Altrucia was alive, but he knelt down to roll her over. He braced himself in anticipation of her neck having been slit by one of Malek's blades, but she'd screamed before Malek had gotten to her. Her face was charred beyond recognition, her skin burned off and the muscle beneath blackened to a crisp.

He jerked his hand away, letting the head fall back. His stomach churned. That was worse than a slit throat.

"Did you see?" he rasped without looking back.

"Yes," Mother said grimly. "She either ran into another mage or..." She looked toward the tunnel straight ahead, the dome glowing softly.

Jak stuck a hand in his pocket, looking for something he didn't need. He found a pencil that had been sharpened down so far that it didn't have much use left and tossed it down the tunnel.

A little burst of light flashed as it struck an invisible barrier, then tumbled through the grate to land on the tendril. As blackened as Altrucia's face, it wafted smoke upward.

"We're not going that way," he said.

"She must have been running full out and didn't realize she had to turn." Mother pointed to the right.

"Yeah." Even though Jak believed the barrier was down in that direction, he poked the air with his pistol before committing to walking through. Nothing happened.

"Wait." Mother held up a hand and crouched by the body. She grimaced as she patted Altrucia's pockets.

"I doubt she has any extra vials you can commandeer."

She gave him the flat look the comment deserved, then drew something out. The glowing fob the mage had given Altrucia.

"Maybe it can guide us to the ship he mentioned—and the captain who doesn't like Uthari. Such a person might be convinced to give us a ride out of here."

"Didn't the mage say its captain was loyal to his master?"

"Yes. But it could be an option. We can't grow wings and fly out of this place on our own."

"Right."

As they continued onward, Jak worried about coming to a dead-end or a barrier they couldn't get through.

"We've gone far enough that we should be close to the city wall by now," he said after they'd passed through a couple more intersections, the broken domes leading the way—and unbroken domes ensuring they didn't deviate.

"I hope you're right and that we can get out."

Light ahead made him slow down again. Some daylight trickling through? *Was* it still daylight? They'd spent a long time at the library and in the tunnels.

It was another alcove, the machinery inside similar to the setup in the first, steady hiss-thumps emanating from it.

A boom thundered somewhere above—closer than the last one had been—and Mother eyed the ceiling warily. By unspoken agreement, they hurried past the alcove. Sooner or later, they had to come to a way out of here.

"There." Jak pointed toward a dead-end with metal rungs fastened to the wall. They led up into a vertical shaft.

He rushed forward, glancing up to make sure the way was clear as he grabbed one of the rungs. But he halted, then swore.

Ten feet up, a promising hatch appeared to lead out of the tunnels, but halfway up the shaft, one of the domes was mounted to the wall. This one wasn't broken. It glowed an ominous orange, and he sensed a tiny buzz of power stretching across the shaft.

"Either the mage didn't truly want her to escape," Mother said, peering up, "or he didn't come in this way and didn't realize there was one at the exit."

"Or..." Jak handed her his torch and climbed a few rungs so he could look more closely at the dome. The glow from within made it hard to tell, but he picked out cracks in the glass. *Sealed* cracks. It looked like the dome had been broken and the pieces fused back together. "Malek fixed it on his way out."

"Ensuring we were trapped down here?"

"Probably. Maybe he got called off to do something and wanted to make sure we couldn't wander off before he came back to find us."

"Come back down here, get behind cover as much as you can, and try shooting it." Mother waved to his pistol as she backed up. "He wouldn't have expected us to have magical weapons."

"Good idea. That might work." Jak dropped back to the ground.

The blast from a magelock ought to be as powerful as whatever energy the mage had personally channeled into the domes, right?

There wasn't anything to hide behind, but he backed under the ceiling of the tunnel as much as possible for protection, then leaned out to make the shot.

"Careful." Mother set his torch down on the grating and kept hers, though there was enough light from the glowing dome that they didn't need them. "If it doesn't break, the charge will ricochet back toward us."

"I know."

"That might happen even if it *does* break."

"I know that too."

"Good. You're my only child. I'd prefer you live."

"I assumed that, but it's nice to have verification. Can I make the shot now?"

"Yes." Mother gripped the back of Jak's belt, as if she planned to yank him to safety if there was trouble.

Maybe she'd seen mage artifacts blow up before. He hoped this one was weaker than usual since it had been broken and repaired.

Jak aimed, thought a quick prayer to Shylezar, and fired.

His shot hit the dome squarely and ricocheted off. It bounced to the opposite side of the shaft, then to another side, and another. Mother tugged Jak back even as he scrambled out of the way. The charge bounced off another side of the shaft and zipped into their tunnel.

They dropped to the grating as it whizzed past, scant inches above their heads, and disappeared around the last bend. Only when the sound of it bouncing off walls faded did Jak dare lift his head.

"Note to self: firing magelocks indoors isn't a good idea."

"*Especially* in tunnels." Mother let go of him and sat up with a sigh.

She'd dropped her torch, and it had gone out. Jak's still burned where she'd set it on the grating.

Jak rose and checked on the dome, hoping the shot had knocked it out of commission. The sides of the tunnel were chipped and blackened where his charge had struck, but the orange dome continued to glow cheerfully. The buzz of the barrier remained.

"That bastard must have reinforced it," he grumbled.

"That's possible."

"We can't get out of here if we can't break it." Jak thought back to the various intersections they'd passed through, trying to remember if any other tunnels hadn't been guarded by domes and barriers, but the only route open was back to the library.

"Wait." Mother held up a finger. "I have an idea."

She trotted back down the tunnel. Puzzled, Jak wondered if she truly wanted him to wait or come with her. He had their only weapons—unless she had more vials of acid to fling at people.

He took a few steps after her, but she turned into the last alcove they'd passed. A faint *ker-clunk* came from the machinery, and the hiss-thumps faded, as did the dim light in the tunnel. The glowing tendril under the grating went dark. Only their single torch burned on the grating by the shaft.

Barely visible in the gloom, Mother stepped out from the alcove. "I pulled the lever in the back. I'm hoping that turned off the flow of magic to the domes as well as this section of the city. And that an alarm doesn't ding to summon dozens of maintenance mages responsible for keeping the city's plumbing working."

"I doubt anyone is worried about running water while the city is under siege." Jak patted his way back to the shaft.

"If their fancy water closets stop working, they may worry. Biological functions can't be set aside just because it's a time of war."

"Funny, Mother." Jak leaned into the shaft, and his heart lightened. The dome was dark, and the barrier was gone. He spun and hugged her. "It worked. I can't believe Malek didn't think of that."

"I doubt zidarr spend a lot of time in the bowels of the city contemplating how the infrastructure works. I wouldn't have thought of it if my chest hadn't come to grief on the lever at the other machine."

"Let's see where we come up." If Jak's sense of direction wasn't lying to him, they ought to be next to the harbor. He hoped there really was a barge waiting that they could cadge a ride on.

Though he believed the barrier down, he proceeded cautiously and poked at the air overhead with the tip of his pistol. It didn't encounter anything, and he didn't get zapped. He stuck his tongue out at the dome as he passed it.

When Jak pushed up on the handle on the hatch, it didn't budge, and he worried that his triumph had been premature. But it twisted, letting him spin it a couple of times, so he could ease the hatch open.

It was dark outside, and fog further muted the view, but thanks to light from lampposts, he could see damp pavement and grass beyond. Hope roared through him. For the first time, their escape seemed plausible.

"Don't get ahead of yourself," Jak muttered, carefully raising the hatch a couple more inches, so he could see around the area.

The booms were much louder now, and the shouted orders of soldiers came from somewhere above them. Jak worried he'd come up right under the city wall, with the hatch in plain view of men and women up there defending their homes.

He spotted the docks and the grassy lawn to either side of them. What he *didn't* spot were any ships.

He swore under his breath. "Where did they all go?"

When they'd arrived, there had been dozens of, if not more than a hundred, vessels of all types. Some had been military mageships and had doubtless been ordered into the skies to defend the city, but what about all the transports, barges, and personal yachts and schooners?

"Jak?" Mother hung on the ladder below his feet.

"There aren't any ships."

"None?"

A mageship sailed past the end of the docks, a dark shape against clouds that were hugging the city, making it feel like a dense fog had them in its grip. Jak had no idea if it was natural or had been magically created by Uthari's enemies, but it made it so he could barely see the people manning the weapons on the deck of the mageship. He hoped it also made it hard for the soldiers on the wall above to notice that this hatch was up a few inches.

"All the nonmilitary vessels must have been told to beat it at the first sign of trouble." Jak could see why, since the harbor was outside of the walls—and possibly outside of the city's protective shield—and more vulnerable. "And all of the military vessels must be out fighting. There's nothing for us to stow away on."

Mother slumped, her arm hooked over a rung. "I needn't have memorized the pass phrase the mage gave to Altrucia."

More shouts came from overhead, from a watchtower on the wall. With everything going on, the soldiers inside would be paying close attention to everything around them. That meant sneaking to the city gate was out. Not that it was likely to be open in the middle of a siege anyway.

Jak and his mother were stuck.

"We're going to have to come up with another plan," he said.

"I'm not sure if there's anything we can do but wait and hope."

"Yeah." Jak tried not to think about the fact that Malek knew exactly where they were and would, sooner or later, return to get them.

Sorath was pacing the deck of the *Dauntless* as they flew close enough to see one end of the floating city of Utharika, a fifty-foot-high wall hiding all but its tallest buildings from sight. Watchtowers and weapons dotted that wall, the city gates were closed, and the extensive dock system that poked out from a peninsula was devoid of ships.

All of Uthari's mageships were in the air, flying in front of, above, and to the sides of the city. A few of the allied craft were harrying them, hurling magical and mundane projectiles at the city, then flying off, trying to lure the defenders out into the clouds.

The explosives blew before getting close to the structures, thanks to shields protecting the city. Sorath's experience told him they were created by powerful artifacts and would be much more difficult to wear down than those conjured by individual mages.

He leaned through the hatchway of the navigation cabin and ordered the young helmsman to halt the *Dauntless* while they assessed the scenario. The cloud cover remained dense, with drizzle further reducing visibility. It had been a boon for the attackers who'd managed to get close without being seen, but it didn't look like that advantage had helped much. The city had clearly been ready for the invasion force. At least the clouds made it difficult for the artillerymen on the walls to target the allied fleet.

That didn't keep them from trying. Booms thundered from all

corners of the city. The clouds muted the noise somewhat, making the danger seem farther away than it was, but Sorath had no delusions. Even here, they could be in danger as the weapons on the walls launched projectiles more than a mile.

Ferroki came up to his side, her rifle in hand. "Any thoughts on how we're going to slip in without being noticed?"

"I'm working on it."

"I foresee a formidable task."

"That's a tactful way of saying we're screwed," her lieutenant said, walking up to join them.

"You know I'm famous for my tact," Ferroki said.

"We always knew this would be difficult." Sorath never would have accepted this mission if he hadn't been forced into it. He had no doubt that if he hadn't said yes, Stone Heart would have killed him. "We'll have to be crafty."

"*You'll* have to be crafty," Lieutenant Sasko said. "We're just here to be the muscle."

"Your people are mouthy," Sorath told Ferroki.

"You've observed something similar before."

"It must be true then."

Knowing they couldn't loiter out here forever without being noticed—and fired upon—Sorath turned away from them and gripped his chin to consider their options. They had to get the ship close enough for him and his party to sneak in and find that portal, but to get inside the walls, they would have to find a way to breach the shields.

He leaned through the hatchway again. The helmsman, a young mage in his twenties who kept complaining about how much slower mageships were than the snow chargers he'd grown up racing, was looking in his direction expectantly. His own commander was out overseeing repairs of the giant hole that had been blown in the side of the *Dauntless*. Fortunately, the fireball that had hit them hadn't struck any of the ship's magical components and didn't affect navigation or propulsion.

"Don't take us any closer, killer," Sorath said, "but drop us down a couple hundred yards, so we can look at the bottom of the city."

"Will do, Colonel." The helmsman saluted even though mages usually scoffed at the rank structures of terrene military units.

Sorath had already decided he liked the kid.

"They'll have defenses down there," Ferroki said.

"True, but I've gotten in through the bottom of a city before. Granted, it was one of King Jayzar's colonies and not a kingdom capital, and they didn't have their shields up, but we were able to knock out the weapons in the middle of the night. We cut our way into the platform, crawled through the infrastructure, and made it to the royal residence to rescue a kidnapped princess. This isn't my first infiltration."

Of course last time, he'd had the element of surprise, something these idiots had given up as soon as they'd started attacking Uthari's farm barges. For that matter, as soon as they'd attacked Malek's mageship and failed to get the portal that first night. If they'd asked Sorath for advice, he would have told them to wait a few months—or at least weeks—to try a sneak attack.

As the *Dauntless* descended below the city, the relatively flat bottom of the platform coming into view, Sorath groaned. Not only were there copious large weapons mounted around the rim and on an inverted pylon at the center; there were no fewer than five massive mageships lying in wait under the city's shadow. The mist kept Sorath from seeing all the way to the far side. There could have been more.

"And during this previous infiltration of yours," Lieutenant Sasko said, "was there a fleet of warships waiting to pummel you mercilessly with huge mage weapons?"

"No, that didn't come until we were fleeing *from* the infiltration."

Two of the ships opened fire on them.

"Barriers up!" mages in the forecastle shouted.

Fireballs and cannonballs sped toward them, blazing orange through the night sky, and slammed into their defenses.

"Take us back up, killer," Sorath ordered.

"Good idea, Colonel," the helmsman replied, already piloting the craft higher.

Their defenses held, but Sorath worried that some of those ships would fly out from under the city and give chase. Earlier, they'd survived an encounter with a single vessel, but he didn't have delusions about winning against five of them. Their whole objective was to avoid notice while the rest of the fleet kept Uthari's ships occupied.

As they rose back even with the city and above, Sorath walked to the railing. He tried to radiate calm for the sake of the mercenaries and mage crew watching him, but he worried he'd made a huge mistake. He barely breathed as he stared at the edge of the platform, expecting those ships to sail out, weapons blazing.

In addition to lifting the *Dauntless*, the helmsman navigated them farther away from the city, back out into the clouds. Booms came from all around them as Uthari's mageships clashed with the invading fleet, but none of the vessels lurking under the platform gave chase.

Sorath exhaled a relieved breath. They must have had orders to stay put and make sure nobody got close to the semi-vulnerable belly of the city.

"Close call. That's twice we've gotten lucky today." Ferroki waved toward the side of the *Dauntless* that had been damaged.

"What's Plan B?" Sasko asked.

Sorath gazed toward the damaged part of their ship, though

the hole wasn't visible from the deck. "It's coming together for me."

"Oh?" Sasko and Ferroki asked together, both with equal wariness.

"We're already damaged," he mused. "Maybe I can keep Toggs from repairing it."

"Uh, why?" Sasko asked.

"And I'm sure your sergeant with the fondness for fondling grenades could create some realistic smoke to billow out of the hole in the hull."

"You think they won't attack us if we're close to their city but visibly damaged?" Ferroki asked skeptically.

"I think they won't attack us if it's clear we're out of control and going to crash on that lovely lawn beside their harbor."

They stared at him as if a few cogs had fallen out of his machinery.

"I only mean for us to *pretend* to crash, of course."

"My experience with sailing ships and flying ships," Sasko said, "is that it's hard to pretend to crash without *actually* crashing."

"We have a good helmsman. I have confidence in his abilities. He kept us under that other ship like a tick on a dog's belly. That takes talent."

"Sure," Sasko said, "all the bards tell tales of the magnificence of the talented tick."

"Ticks *do* feature in Su Dom's fables," Ferroki murmured, "in lessons on tenacity."

"Talented and tenacious. That's our helmsman. I have faith. Find your bomb-loving sergeant and have her report to me." Sorath patted them on the shoulders, ignoring their dubious expressions, and returned to the hatchway.

He considered getting permission from Captain Toggs, who'd finished barking orders at his crew and was standing up on the forecastle deck, his hands clasped behind his back as he gazed out at the battles. Instead, Sorath pulled aside a junior officer and told him to delay the repairs for now, that the mercenaries had a plan. Though puzzled, the officer went off to relay the message.

It was a foregone conclusion that the captain of the *Dauntless* would say no to crashing his ship, even a *pretend* crash. If he could manage this, Sorath wouldn't tell Toggs until it was too late to turn back.

Flashes and booms came from a battle in the clouds above the *Dauntless*. They would have to do this quickly, or they would end up more grievously damaged, and crashing five thousand feet below instead of on the city's peninsula.

"Nobber," Sorath addressed the helmsman, "give us ten minutes to prep some smoke, and then I need you to pretend to crash the ship on that grassy stretch beside their docks."

The kid looked back at him, blinking a few times. "*Pretend*, sir?"

"Yes. Make it look realistic but not *too* realistic. If we take some more damage on the way in, fine, but we need to be able to fly away afterward. With a huge artifact strapped to our deck. I don't know how much it weighs, but it could be tons."

If Sorath succeeded in getting to the portal and attaching hooks and ropes to it, he hoped the ship's mages had enough energy left to levitate it up to the deck. But he had better not get ahead of himself. A lot needed to go right before they could lift anything.

"Did Captain Toggs say this is all right, sir?" Since he was a mage, Nobber could have telepathically asked the captain for confirmation himself. Interesting that he hadn't.

"I'm sure he'll agree that it's an excellent plan once we get away with the artifact. Maybe you'll get a medal for incredible flying." Sorath had no idea if mages gave medals for prowess in flight, but they liked to give out sparkly awards to their military troops, so it was a reasonable bet. Mercenaries preferred time off and combat pay to medals, but the higher-ranking mage officers always had decorations all over the chests of their pretty uniforms.

"A very realistic pretend crash." Nobber nodded to himself. "I think I can do it, sir."

"Good." Sorath resisted the urge to watch and pace as Nobber flew the *Dauntless* closer.

Usually, the main defensive shield over a sky city protected what was inside the walls, leaving docking areas outside open for ships to come and go during a battle, under the assumption that any mages in the watchtowers could put up temporary shields to protect the area if enemies attempted to land. But it had been a long time since Sorath had been to Utharika. It was possible this sky city did things differently, extending its shield, when activated, over its docking area. It was also possible the mage defenders had temporary shields up over the area now—and would keep them up as a crashing ship plummeted down.

Better not to watch. Besides, he had more to do before they arrived.

"Ten minutes, killer." Sorath thumped Nobber on the back and left the navigation cabin.

Lieutenant Sasko had rounded up Sergeant Tinder.

She saluted him. "You need something blown up, Colonel?"

"Eventually, I have no doubt, but first, I need smoke. A *lot* of smoke. I want it to billow out of the hole in the hull, dark and tarry and stinking of death and desperation."

Tinder leaned close to Sasko. "I know the stink of death, but what's desperation smell like?"

"Fleeing camels, stale cigars, and Sergeant Basher drinking too much and realizing she's been flirting with a pretty boy claimed by a zidarr."

"Oh, I remember that night. The zidarr threatened to melt her tongue with magic and file her nipples off with his sword." Tinder scratched her jaw. "I'll see what I can do."

"Make as much heavy smoke as you can," Sorath said, worried he should have been more prosaic with his description of what he wanted. "And make it last. Our chances of getting over their wall or cutting through their front gate without being noticed are slim, but if there's enough smoke and we're extremely lucky, maybe we can make it work."

"Our allies better keep them busy," Sasko said.

"Our success was always going to rely upon that," Sorath said.

"A fact that makes me all kinds of warm and cozy." Tinder trotted off to hunt for smoke-producing materials.

"Are you going to take some mages from the crew with you?" Ferroki asked Sorath.

"Yes. I've picked out five that are open to taking orders from me —it would be suicidal to go without magic users."

"It'll be suicidal anyway."

"True. Who did you choose from Thorn Company to send with me?"

"Are you planning on stealth or blowing your way into the castle with all the power and ferocity that you can muster?"

"Stealth for as far as it'll get us. Eventually, they'll spot us, and we'll have no choice but to resort to blowing our way through things and hoping for the best." Sorath hoped they could get to the castle before that, else they would find platoons of mages and zidarr waiting for them, but this whole mission was predicated on luck and more than a few things going their way.

"So, a mix of people. Tinder and Basher, for the blowing-things-up part, and Majirra and Uti for their knack for sneaking up and overpowering people before they know what's going on. If you need a sniper, Poker and Yuvay can pick sentries off a wall at five hundred yards."

"What about the kid you just gave the nice magelock to? Tezi."

Ferroki hesitated. "She's just a rookie. I was going to keep her here to help defend the ship."

"She's got a level head from what I've seen, looks to be a good shot, and if we get into the unlikely scenario where flirting with a guard could distract him long enough for the rest of us to bash his head in... she's your prettiest merc."

"I didn't realize flirting was one of your preferred military tactics."

"I'm not too proud to use subterfuge and diversion. Any tactic that gets me into the enemy stronghold. I would flirt with the guards myself, but I don't find that as effective as it used to be."

Ferroki eyed his oft-broken nose and scarred face. "Strange."

"Isn't it?"

Tinder lumbered past, carrying a barrel, sacks of black powder, and a container that, judging by the scent, held either rotten eggs or sulfur. She'd put that collection together with impressive speed. Dr. Fret trailed after her, carrying matches and grenades in a yarn sack, and kept wrinkling her nose at the odor wafting back to her.

"Give us five minutes, Colonel," Tinder said, as they headed belowdecks.

Sorath stepped into the navigation cabin to monitor their approach. The city was no longer in view—wisely, Nobber had backed them farther away from the action for their musing moments—but flashes of light ahead and to the right promised they were still close. Outside, the rain picked up, and rivulets ran down the glass windows of the cabin. Sorath hoped that wouldn't affect Tinder's ability to blow a suitable amount of smoke into the sky.

Ferroki stepped inside. "I've let everyone we chose except for Tinder know they're going in with you. They're grabbing their gear. Tinder is starting her smoke-making fire, but I'll tell her as soon as she's done. Another minute or two, and we can head in."

"Thank you." Sorath lifted a finger before she stepped back out. "A word?"

He stepped back from the helmsman's seat, so they could have a moment of privacy.

"Are you having doubts?" Ferroki asked.

"By the minute." He smirked. "But I wanted to tell you, in case you wondered, I didn't pick you for my team for a reason."

"Because captains aren't supposed to be expendable and don't get sent on infiltration teams?" she asked dryly.

"Usually, that's true, but you won't be any safer back here."

"I know."

"In part, I wanted you here because we'll need someone smart who can direct a brilliantly targeted assault in order to get this ship in to retrieve the artifact from the heart of an enemy city."

"And you think that's me? I'm touched."

"I've seen you fight. And you've been in the game as long as I have, and you haven't lost your company—or your life—so that's a testament to the rest."

"We lost someone today," she said grimly.

"I know. I'm sorry." He shouldn't have brought that up and wished he could say more to console her—it was always awful to lose men—but there wasn't much time. "I have a small request. I'm hoping you'll agree to it, given that you're still toting that medallion around even though it's akin to being marked for death."

"Yes?" Ferroki didn't even look wary, the gods bless her.

"I left my manuscript in a secret nook under a flagstone in the curio shop. If I don't survive today, will you retrieve it the next time you're back south and figure out a way to get it published? Maybe some of those archaeologists will feel grateful that you hauled them away from that volcano and have contacts in academia with a press. The manuscript is incomplete, but maybe you'd know a good way to finish it off. You like your words as much as I do."

"And yet have never been tempted to tell tales of boudoir buddies."

"Give it time. That fine turn of phrase will grow on you."

"I don't think it's any more likely that I'll survive the day than you, but if I somehow do and you don't, I'll find a way back there and get it published for you."

"Thank you." Sorath had been fairly certain she would say yes, but her agreement still warmed his heart. Since they'd already discussed kissing, and why it wasn't appropriate, he hugged her. That might not be appropriate either, but the moment required *something*.

She hugged him back. "Good luck down there. Don't get all of my people killed."

"I'll do my best."

"We're blowing smoke like a charred pig in a pit fire, Captain," Tinder said, leaning in. Her eyebrows rose at their embrace. "Oh, sorry. I didn't know you two were having a tender moment."

Sorath released her.

Ferroki patted him on the back before stepping away. "We're done. Give Fret instructions on how to keep the smoke going, and gather your weapons and explosives. You've been picked for the incursion team."

"Have I? Well, that's a joy."

"You'll get to blow things up," Ferroki said. "You know you love that."

"This is true."

"It's going to be tense," Sorath told Tinder. "Any special weapons or methods of attack you and the others can bring would be appreciated. We're probably going to end up facing zidarr."

"Zidarr?" Tinder grimaced. "I may wet myself."

"That's not the kind of special attack I had in mind."

"Pee power." Ferroki smiled.

Sorath grunted. "Female mercs aren't as different from male mercs as I imagined."

"Uh, sir?" came Nobber's worried voice from the wheel.

He'd navigated the *Dauntless* closer to the city again, and they looked through the rain and clouds down upon the wall and docks. He'd raised their craft to a higher elevation, maybe so it could convincingly plunge down to "crash" from above.

Before, the docks had been empty. But now, a black mageship was gliding toward a berth near the city gates.

"This could be a problem," Nobber said. "I think that's the *Star Flyer*. Malek's ship. Any ruse we try... He's going to see through it."

True, but Sorath found the approach of the other ship promising. It suggested that there wasn't a shield protecting the docks—or at least that it was down for the time being.

Booms came from behind the *Dauntless*. *Close* behind it.

Sorath leaned out the hatch and spotted two ships firing at each other less than a hundred yards back. One of their allies and one of their enemies. Fiery blasts streaked from ship to ship, and Sorath couldn't tell who was winning, but if Uthari's vessel came out on top, its crew might turn its attention to the *Dauntless*.

"We don't have the option to back away again," Nobber said.

To the side, black plumes of smoke caught Sorath's eye. Tinder's smoke. It billowed out of the hole in the hull, reminding him of the Dragon Perch volcano as it had been about to blow.

"That won't burn indefinitely," Ferroki warned from behind him. "We've got limited time during which this might work."

"I know." Sorath stepped back into the navigation cabin. They would have to chance it, even if it meant crashing under Malek's nose. "Tinder might get an opportunity to use her *special attack* earlier than expected."

"Hell," Tinder said.

"Go get your gear, join the rest of the team, and be ready." Ferroki thumped her on the back.

"Look, sir." Nobber thrust a finger toward the viewing window as a man in tan pants and a brown leather jacket leaped down from the city walls, dropping fifty feet to land in a crouch without hurting himself, and sprinted for the now-docked mageship.

If not for that move and the blazing main-gauche and sword he carried as he ran, the smoke, dark, and rain would have kept Sorath from being certain he was a zidarr. But he was not only certain of that but knew those were Malek's favored weapons.

There was no gangplank extended, but Malek ran down the docks and vaulted across the gap to the deck of his ship. Crewmen out in the rain raised their arms in a cheer. As the vessel lifted into the air, Malek joined a uniformed officer on deck. General Tonovan, most likely.

Maybe things were getting bad for the defenders, and Uthari was sending out his best. Sorath hoped that was the case.

The *Dauntless* rocked, startling him.

"Fire from behind!" one of the mages out on deck called. "Raising our barrier."

"We're out of time," Ferroki said quietly.

"Actually, we've waited until the perfect time." Sorath jogged to Nobber's seat. "Take us in, killer."

More fire streaked toward them from the victorious ship behind them—Uthari's victorious ship. Fortunately, the mages of the *Dauntless* were ready now and had their defenses up.

Captain Toggs, a graying crust of a mage who wasn't nearly as polite as Nobber, stomped into navigation. "What's going on? We're being fired on." He thrust his arm back through the hatchway. "You're going the wrong way, Nobber."

"He's taking us in for our mission," Sorath said, wishing the *Star Flyer* were rising faster. Malek's ship was still above the docks, rotating slowly toward a battle being fought off to the side of the city. "Tell them to let a couple hit us, Nobber," Sorath said quietly, trusting that the mages could give telepathic commands to each other. He didn't want to explain his reason to the captain.

"*Hit* us?" Captain Toggs had better hearing than Sorath would have guessed. "Are you insane?"

"Yes, sir," Nobber said vaguely—it wasn't clear who he was responding to, but he grinned as he started zigzagging, inasmuch as the ponderous ship could manage such maneuvers. He must have relayed the message to the mages responsible for keeping the barrier up, for a fireball made it through, slamming into the rear of the hull.

Toggs swore and ran outside, yelling at his men to get the barrier back up and for others to prepare to return fire.

"Here we go," Nobber whispered, pushing down the altitude lever.

"Should I hold on to something?" Ferroki asked quietly.

"Respectfully suggest your ass, ma'am." Nobber spun the wheel hard, and the ship tilted far more than should have been possible for one of the steady mageships, then descended so fast Sorath's stomach pitched into his boots.

He grabbed a beam on the ceiling—and Ferroki before she could go flying. This was it. No turning back now.

26

MALEK CROSSED HIS ARMS AND GAZED OVER THE RAILING AS THE *Star Flyer* rose away from Utharika and the docks. He peered at the hatch that led into the infrastructure under the city, half expecting Jadora and Jak to pop out of it, though that shouldn't happen. When he'd passed through, he'd fixed the barrier there, ensuring they couldn't escape if they found their way to the exit shaft. But they were resourceful. He imagined Jadora flinging a chemical concoction at one of the door-domes and somehow knocking out its power.

Malek hadn't wanted to leave the tunnels, not until he found them, but Uthari had summoned him, warning that Zaruk had secured more allies and scrounged more forces than expected. He'd ordered Malek to join Tonovan in defending the city and said Malek could search for the missing prisoners later, reminding him that they were on an island in the sky—there was nowhere for them to go.

Fortunately, Uthari hadn't made any snide comments about how Malek had let them escape out from under his nose in the library. Typically, Uthari was too measured and mature for snide comments. *Yidar* had been the one to make one. Yidar, who had been pushing to get Malek out of the castle and join the battle earlier. Malek hadn't wanted to entertain Jak's suggestion that Yidar was up to something fishy, but the more he thought about it, the stranger his words seemed. And now Yidar was back in the castle with Uthari and the artifact. They weren't alone, by any means, but with Malek and Gorsith off in ships defending the city, Yidar was the only zidarr there.

Booms and flashes of orange in the night sky drew Malek's attention to the east. Two ships had come out of the clouds and were descending rapidly toward the city. One was familiar—one of Uthari's mageships captained by a reliable man—and the other belonged to an enemy, the hull painted green in Queen Vorsha's colors. There were as many of her ships out here as Zaruk's, and Dy's brown-and-gold vessels were rare.

Malek lifted a hand to hurl magic at Vorsha's ship, since it was barreling along a trajectory that would take it perilously close to the city. But its lights were out, fires burned in several spots in the back, and black plumes of smoke roiled from a gaping hole in the hull. He didn't see any crew members left on the deck. Maybe they'd evacuated on lifeboats.

He squinted to gauge its path. Would it zip right past and crash thousands of feet below? If so, there was no point in bothering with it. Or would it crash into the docks? The latter would do damage and be a pain in the ass for someone to clean up later.

As it flew closer, Uthari's ship chasing it and lighting up its backside with fire, Malek started to raise a shield over the docks to ensure it would bounce off instead of crashing there. But Tonovan jogged over, jabbed him in the shoulder, and pointed off to the port side of the *Star Flyer*.

A hulking blue-and-silver mageship—one of King Zaruk's— was out there in the clouds, its crew aiming magelocks and cannons toward the city. No, toward the *castle*. The enemy ship was angling past the *Star Flyer* and toward Uthari's headquarters. A fit figure in black stood atop the forecastle with his arms raised, rain plastering his short white hair to his skull.

"Stone Heart," Malek growled.

"That's why Uthari sent you out here," Tonovan said. "He's taken out the shield on the west side and obliterated two of our watchtowers. He'll have his eye on the castle now."

Malek had no love for Tonovan, but when it came to defending Uthari and the city, they were on the same side. For this battle, they would fight as brothers.

"Take us up to him." Malek narrowed his eyes and channeled a gust of wind to slam into Stone Heart's side and distract him from whatever magic he was about to hurl. "Get me on that ship. I'll deal with him."

"Good. The bastard smashed a hole in our deck earlier when we opened fire on him. He can cut right through our defenses." Tonovan touched a gash leaking blood down his jaw to mingle with the rain and drip onto his uniform. "Then he disappeared back into the clouds before we could chase him down. This is moon-cursed weather for defending against a siege." He sneered upward at clouds that were growing darker as the night deepened.

When Malek's attack hit Stone Heart, surprise flashed on the other zidarr's face. He dropped his arms and wheeled to face Malek across the distance.

"You should have expected me, old nemesis," Malek said quietly.

The other ship was too far away for Stone Heart to hear the words, but Malek didn't try to hide the thought in his mind. The cool glare that replaced the surprise suggested his enemy had heard.

Stone Heart tested him next, sending a stream of raw power toward the deck under Malek's and Tonovan's feet. Their mages were ready and had bolstered the ship's defenses, but several of them grunted and staggered back under the extreme onslaught. Malek channeled his own magic into their barrier, ensuring Stone Heart's attack didn't get through.

The *Star Flyer* ascended higher, leaving the harbor and the city below, and veered toward their enemy. Malek glanced down in time to see the smoking mageship smash onto the grassy lawn near the docks. Fortunately, the island's sturdy engineering held up under the onslaught, but he frowned at the mages in the watchtowers. They should have kept that from happening, but they were busy gaping up at Stone Heart's ship, worrying the zidarr would blast them to oblivion.

Malek wouldn't let that happen.

He readied another attack as their ship closed on the enemy vessel. He knew, just as Stone Heart knew, that their magical attacks wouldn't get past each other's defenses, but once they faced each other from the deck of the same ship, with blades whirring in a flurry of physical attacks that would come too quickly for one to concentrate on magic, a winner would be decided. Malek intended to be that winner.

Jak waited with his hand on the handle of the hatch, his arms aching from hanging on the ladder for so long. He wanted to look outside, but the last time he'd raised the hatch a couple of inches to peek out, what he'd seen had nearly made him pitch off the rungs. Malek had appeared out of nowhere, leaping down from the towering city wall, as if it were a five-foot drop instead of fifty. He'd run toward a familiar mageship that had docked for him.

Jak had pulled the hatch back down so quickly, he'd hit himself on the head. Then he'd waited, holding his breath, afraid Malek had heard the thump and would turn around. But nobody had lifted the hatch; as far as Jak knew, nobody had seen him yet.

Between the rain and night's darkness, the hatch shouldn't be that noticeable from the towers atop the wall.

"Should I check again?" he asked, noticing Mother gazing up at him, the waning light of their torch showing the concern in her eyes. "If Malek's ship left—with him on it—we could take a stab at finding a hiding place out on the docks. Maybe some other ship will land, and we can stow away. By now, you'd think some of Uthari's mageships would be damaged enough to force them to come home for repairs."

"Go ahead and check. I'll—" She broke off and peered into the dark tunnel.

The nearby machinery was still off, but she looked like she'd heard something. Or *someone*?

He frowned. What if a city maintenance worker had come to see why the machinery had gone off? Did people worry about such things while their city was being bombed? Mother's joke about water closets came to mind. Maybe it hadn't been a joke.

When she looked up again, she held a finger to her lips, her eyes grave. "Voices," she mouthed.

Jak tightened his grip on the handle. They were going to have to take their chances and hope they could find a bolt-hole out there.

A thunderous smashing and wrenching of metal reached his ears, almost startling him into losing his grip again. That hadn't been one of the ubiquitous booms of explosives hitting the city's defenses.

He lifted the hatch to peek out and almost ended up coughing and giving away his position. Great plumes of black smoke billowed toward him, the acrid odor assaulting his nostrils.

His first thought was that someone had lobbed explosives at the docks and they'd caught fire. But there was enough light from street-lamps to make out the hull of a mageship out in the grass. The wrecked vessel was tilted dramatically to one side, a huge hole in its hull pointing upward. Clouds of black smoke flowed out of it so thick and tarry that it reminded Jak of the time he'd seen—and smelled—a vat of molten rubber catch fire in one of the university chemistry labs.

Strangely, there weren't any flames leaping from the hole, but small fires burned on other parts of the ship. If any of the crew had survived the landing, they must have been too injured to worry about putting them out. Or maybe they were too afraid that if they showed their faces, the guards in the watchtowers would open fire on them.

Jak wished he could see up to the wall and towers to catch the reactions of the defenders, but he hadn't dared open the hatch more than a couple of inches, and he didn't do so now. Two uniformed guards appeared, running out from the gate to check on the downed ship. They carried magelocks and wore kerchiefs over their mouths and noses to protect against the noxious smoke. Jak, with his eyes watering, wished *he* had a kerchief. If he sneezed as they ran past, he would give his position away.

If he'd been wiser, he would have closed the hatch, so there was no possibility of that happening, but he couldn't help but think this could be their opportunity. They couldn't stow away on the wrecked ship—it could blow up at any second—but the smoke made an impressive screen. If the guards had left the gate open, he and his mother might be able to sneak into the city and find a place to hide until the battle ended.

He leaned down to wave for her to come up but found she'd already climbed the rungs and was right below him. She held a finger to her lips again, then pointed downward.

This time, Jak also heard the voices.

"It couldn't have turned off on its own," a man said from back in the tunnel. "Someone was down here monkeying with it."

"No kidding, genius. It was that dead woman. She broke all the domes."

"How would a servant from the castle break the door-domes? It's not like you can beat them with a wrench."

Or even shoot them, Jak thought.

Mother pointed upward, silently asking if they could go out.

Jak checked again and barely stifled a groan. For some reason, the two soldiers had stopped right in front of his position instead of continuing to the wreck. They weren't looking at the hatch, so he didn't think they'd seen that it was ajar. The backs of their black boots were to him as something in the sky beyond the docks had them riveted.

Jak pressed his nose to the rim of the hatchway trying to see what. He could just make out a battle between two mageships, one blue and one black. The latter looked like the *Star Flyer.*

Surprisingly, the mageships weren't firing at each other. Two swordsmen came into view on the deck of the blue vessel, their glowing white blades slashing at each other so rapidly it was impossible to track the fight. *That* was why the ships weren't attacking each other. Malek, and who knew how many others, had found a way onto the enemy ship. Jak didn't recognize his opponent, but he carried two scimitars, each glowing as brightly as Malek's blades, and Jak had no doubt this was another zidarr. Blue was King Zaruk's color, so maybe that was his right-hand man, Stone Heart.

As the zidarr fought, blades striking as fast as lightning, Jak found himself as riveted as the two guards. Who would come out on top? Even though Malek had kidnapped him and been his captor these last few days, Jak found himself cringing any time he seemed to be at a disadvantage and breathing a sigh of relief whenever he recovered and pressed his opponent back.

Mother tapped the sole of Jak's shoe and pointed upward urgently. That knocked him out of his trance. If the maintenance men found the problem and flipped the lever back on while Jak and Mother were hanging there, they would be as dead as Altrucia.

He pushed upward on the hatch. He had to hope the guards were too busy watching the fight to notice him and his mother crawling out.

But as he put his hand down to climb out, the guards spun. Not toward him but toward several figures rushing through the smoke toward them with their weapons raised.

Jak almost jumped back down into the shaft. But the newcomers had come from the wreck, not the gate, and they were angling for the guards, not for him.

As Jak hung partway out of the shaft, the group of men and women sprang for the two guards. With efficient and deadly slashes, they downed their opponents before the men could yell a warning.

The thick smoke made it hard to make out uniforms or faces. All Jak knew was that they'd come from the downed ship and were therefore working for Queen Vorsha. They could be allies of the mage who'd sent Altrucia to lead Jak and Mother out of the castle, from one prison into the next.

"Look out," a young blonde woman whispered and pointed at Jak.

When they'd first met, she'd made such an impression on him that he had no trouble identifying her now. Soot smeared her face, her uniform was frayed and burned on one side, and she carried a long magelock, but she still looked more like a fellow university student than a fierce mercenary.

"Thorn Company girl," Jak whispered, waving. "We need to get out of here. Can you help us?"

Maybe it was an inane thing to ask—all of the mercenaries turned to gape at him—given that their wrecked ship was burning behind them.

"Uhm." She glanced uncertainly at the others. "We're on a mission."

"Is that a way in?" A big man with a scarred face strode toward Jak, then peered into the shaft.

Mother, who'd been trying to get out, almost bumped into him.

"Do you still have my medallion?" Jak whispered to the blonde, not sure who any of the other people were. The women had to be from Thorn Company, but there were also five mages in the uniforms of Vorsha's people. Would they try to kidnap them?

"I—" she started to answer.

But the big man pointed into the shaft and whispered, "Down, down," in an authoritative voice.

Just as Mother pulled herself out and crouched next to Jak, the big man—their leader?—sprang into the shaft, not bothering with the rungs.

"There are mages down there," Mother whispered as more mercenaries piled in after him.

The blonde woman lingered until a stout older mercenary slapped her on the back. "Get moving."

"Our medallion?" Jak looked toward the wreck, wondering if it might yet be salvageable.

Was there any chance they could fly it out of there? Even if they managed, the guards might shoot it down. Those on the wall were just as riveted by the battling zidarr as the other two had been, but they would surely notice an entire ship taking off from under their noses.

"I think the captain has it," the blonde girl said.

"Where's she?"

"Rookie," the older woman barked from halfway down the rungs. "Get down here."

Jak gripped his mother's arm and nodded toward the ship.

Before they could take a step, a guard up in the closest tower shouted, "There's someone down there!"

Jak almost sprinted for the wreck anyway, thinking the guards might not be able to fire at them through the city's defensive barrier, but blue charges from magelocks blasted into the ground. One slammed into the hatch, half ripping it from its hinges.

"Back in," Mother whispered, sliding down the rungs. "And hurry. Don't forget about the barrier."

The barrier he expected to be activated any second. The mercenaries had already run off down the tunnel, so they may have distracted the maintenance men.

"I think our medallion is on the ship." Jak crouched, hiding his body behind the hatch as much as he could. "We don't want to go back down there."

More magelocks fired. A charge hit inches from him, blowing away pavement. Pieces slammed into his shoulder and the side of his face. Pain blasted him, and he stumbled into the shaft. Mother tried to slow him as he fell past her, and her grip kept him from crashing all the way to the bottom. He managed to hook an arm around the rungs. More charges slammed down up above, and Mother pulled the hatch shut and descended again.

Jak sagged against the wall at the bottom. He was almost glad that the mercenaries hadn't waited for them, since they might blame him for the fact that the guards now knew people were down here... and would doubtless relay the message. True, Malek had already known, but he probably hadn't been that worried about Jak and Mother sabotaging things. If the guards realized enemy troops had come out of the wreck, they would send teams down right away.

"What do we do?" Jak whispered, glancing up. Mother hadn't been able to close the hatch all the way, not with its now-warped hinges, and shouts and booms echoed down to them.

"Ask her for information, I think." Mother nodded toward the dark tunnel.

He'd thought all of the mercenaries had gone ahead, but the blonde girl was waiting for them.

"I'm Professor Jadora Freedar," Mother told her. "I didn't catch your name before." She spoke so calmly and formally, as if guards might not yank open the hatch at any moment.

Worried about that possibility, Jak waved for them to get out of the shaft.

"I'm Tezi. The captain has your medallion, Professor. It's caused... a lot of trouble."

Mother winced. "I was afraid of that. Is she back on your ship? Did she survive the landing?"

"This way, Rookie," the gruff mercenary called.

"Bring your friends," the big man added. "Especially if they know the way to the castle."

The mercenaries reached the alcove and lit lanterns, providing enough light for Jak to see a red-uniformed maintenance man crumpled on the grating at their feet. Blood dripped from a short pickaxe the leader gripped. Or was that something fastened to his arm in place of a hand?

"She survived," Tezi said as she jogged ahead, gesturing for them to follow her. "But we're on a mission. Help us, and I'm sure we can take you to her."

"What's the mission?" Mother asked, though she could probably already guess.

Jak could.

"We're supposed to get the artifact and take it back to Zaruk and his allies. They hired our company to help fetch it."

When they reached the others, Jak counted eleven total in the group. The other maintenance man lay dead in the alcove, his neck broken.

Jak stared numbly at the bodies. Even though Uthari had

kidnapped him, these were presumably innocent people who happened to live in his city. Mages, undoubtedly, but they'd never done anything personally to Jak or his mother. To kill them simply because they were in the way...

"This is war, kid," the leader said, making Jak wonder if he'd mumbled his thoughts aloud. Maybe the horror on his face was easy to interpret. "And why is your rookie telling this boy our plans, Sergeant?"

"She probably likes him. He's kind of cute."

"*Sergeant.*" Tezi shook her head in vigorous denial, something Jak might have found disappointing in another time and place. But now, he was standing next to two dead people. "These are the archaeologists from the volcano," Tezi added. "The ones Malek kidnapped."

"The ones who pulled that artifact out of the earth after ten thousand years and started this whole war?" the big man asked.

"Uh." Tezi looked helplessly at Jak.

He didn't know what to say. Until that moment, it hadn't occurred to him to think of things that way, but the mercenary wasn't wrong.

The sergeant grunted. "The wizards all hate each other and are all always vying to gain power. A pin dropping on the wrong side of a border could have started this war. I say we take these two along so they can show us to the artifact."

Jak looked at Mother, who was looking back at him, her expression as grave as his. The portal was supposed to be for terrene people to use, to find a solution to the oppression of living under all these wizards. They didn't want Zaruk to have it any more than Uthari, and it was very possible that Zaruk's plans for it would be even more detrimental for humanity than Uthari's. If Uthari was to be believed, he wanted to find a longevity plant. What if Zaruk wanted to raise an army of dragons to take over Torvil and enslave everybody, mages and regular humans alike?

"What were you two doing in that shaft?" the big man asked.

"Escaping," Mother said and introduced herself again. "Who are you?"

"Colonel Sorath. I'm in charge of this incursion."

A clang sounded—someone throwing open the hatch.

"Noncombatants out of the way," Sorath said, pushing Jak and Mother into the alcove. "Rookie Tezi, guard them. Keep them alive at all costs. Mages, mercs, with me."

As boots rang out on the ladder rungs in the shaft, he charged back in that direction with his team behind him. Tezi pointed for Jak and Mother to step into the alcove. She didn't have a lantern, so they were left in the dark. During the climb out—and rush back in—they'd lost their torches.

"Are we prisoners again?" Jak whispered to Mother, wishing they'd been left alone instead of with a guard. Even if Tezi wasn't menacing, she was one of them and would likely report back what they said.

Mother sighed. "I don't know, but trying to go back to raid that castle with a small group of mercenaries sounds like suicide."

"For them or for us?"

"Both."

27

JADORA WANTED TO TALK TO THE MERCENARY LEADER, BUT THE grim-faced man was pressing forward without pause. In the twenty minutes she and Jak had been with him, he'd led his people to kill two groups of Uthari's guards, mages sent down into the tunnels after them. The fast, efficient way the mercenaries dispatched their enemies chilled her. They threw small explosives to distract them from using their magic and then attacked with deadly determination.

But what choice did she and Jak have but to follow them? Jadora had little doubt that they would find legions of castle defenders waiting for them in the library if they returned, but the dome barriers were still up in the other tunnels along the route back, funneling the mercenaries in that direction. And now that Uthari's people knew there were intruders in the tunnels, it wouldn't be safe to hide out down there. Further, if Malek finished his fight with the other zidarr, he would also come looking for them here. She and Jak had few options.

The group passed Altrucia's body without comment, but the leader—Sorath, she reminded herself—halted when they reached the intersection where the green-clad mage who'd started this lay crumpled.

Jadora braced herself. Since the mercenaries were on the same side as the dead man, they would want to know how he'd died. Sorath directed his mages and soldiers to guard the four tunnels and waved for Jadora to join him in the center of the intersection. With the space tight in the underground labyrinth, they had to stand inches from the dead man.

"Professor Freedar," Sorath said. "I'm sure you regret that you ran into us, and that we drew attention to your escape attempt."

With the harbor empty of everything save the wrecked ship, they hadn't had anywhere to go, but she nodded in agreement.

"I assume your goal is to return to your home?" Sorath pointed downward and raised his eyebrows. "With your medallion?"

Uh, Ferroki had told him about that? Jadora hadn't sworn the mercenary captain to secrecy but wished she hadn't said anything.

"To return to land, yes. As for home?" Jadora spread her arms helplessly. "King Uthari wants us for what we know. It would be dangerous to our friends and family if we went back to the university."

"Us?" Sorath pointed at Jak, eyebrows rising higher. "Both of you?"

Though he was bedraggled with a bruise swelling on his cheek, Jak lifted his chin. "I'm very desirable."

"I'd ask the women if that were true if we had more time. Look, we could use your help finding the artifact and any intelligence you have on the layout of Uthari's castle. Oh, and if you have any idea where the magical device is that keeps the barrier over their city, or at least the castle, we'd love help finding that too. We'll handle getting the artifact onto our ship. We don't want you caught in the crossfire or anywhere that there will be combat." Sorath grimaced at the dead mage. "And if we all get out of here alive, I'll find some way to get you back to land before we take the artifact to our employer."

"Your employer, another king."

"Yes."

"I appreciate your offer," Jadora said, "but we don't want Zaruk to have the portal any more than Uthari."

"The whole point is for *humanity* to have it," Jak added. "Terrene humans who need what it offers."

A couple of the mages in the mercenary party frowned over at him. Jadora lifted a finger to her lips to remind him not to speak negatively about mages. Maybe she shouldn't have admitted she didn't want Zaruk to have the portal.

"It came from King Zaruk's territory, didn't it?" Sorath asked. "He claims that it's rightfully his."

"We were on a joint archaeological mission with permission to dig there by the Perchver magistrate and university heads," Jadora said. "It wasn't originally from that area though, so there's a question of who the rightful owner is. If the dragons who made it, or their descendants, returned to Torvil, it would belong to them."

Sorath waved a hand. "We don't have time to discuss the politics." His tone said he didn't care much about them. "Will you help us find it? If we take you back to land afterward?"

"Even if you can get it through their defensive shield," Jak said, "what *ship* are you going to escape with it on? Yours crashed."

"It's only partially crashed. With luck, Captain Ferroki is using the cover of smoke and battle to get the *Dauntless* repaired so it can lift off as soon as I give her the signal." Sorath patted a compact tube tucked into his belt.

"Some noise down this way, sir," one of the mercenaries whispered, pointing her magelock in the direction they'd come.

"Of course there is," Sorath grumbled. "Tinder, Davrosh, watch our rears. Everyone else, this way."

Sorath glanced at one of the destroyed domes and nodded for

his team to continue on toward the castle. He must have been familiar with them or figured out the significance of the broken ones.

"We'll help," Jadora said, walking behind him. "As long as you keep your word and find a way to get us back down to land—with the medallion."

He glanced back. "It's key to getting the portal to work, isn't it?"

It crossed her mind to lie, but he was her only way out, and he seemed to already know the answer to the question. "We believe it is quite literally *the* key."

"They'll hunt you forever to get it. Why not let them have it?"

"They have everything else," Jadora said bleakly. "My late husband believed—and *I* believe—that this could lead to a change." She kept the words vague, since the mages might still be paying attention, but Sorath's eyes sharpened as he looked back at her again. Did he grasp what she meant?

He lifted his arm, the pickaxe tool where his hand should have been. "I'd like to see a change."

Dare she hope Sorath would abandon his current contract if she could convince him that change might be possible? Assuming terrene humans were the ones to gain access to the portal. And assuming it still worked and led somewhere with dragons, dragons who could be convinced to become allies against the mages. All that assumed a lot, and she knew it, but her husband had been so certain it could work, that it was worth fighting for. Worth dying for.

"I'll be happy to tell you about our plans if we survive and get out of here." Jadora would wait until later to try to convince him to... fail to return the portal to Zaruk.

Sorath started to reply, but a boom came from the city above, and the tunnels quaked, pitching them into the walls and each other. Snaps came from the ceiling as the grating trembled under their boots. Jadora's shoulder struck the wall hard, and she barely kept her footing. The light from the glowing tendril under the grating flashed twice and went out, leaving them in the dark.

"That was a lot worse than the other attacks," Jak said.

One of the mages leading the group conjured an orange ball of light.

Something clattered onto the grating, and dirt trickled down onto Jadora, brushing her cheek. No, not dirt. The aggregate material the mages had used to build these tunnels was crumbling. She looked grimly at the ceiling. A long jagged crack had appeared, and chunks were still falling out.

"I think that means the city's defensive shield is down," Sorath said. "That will help us complete our mission, but we're going to have to hurry."

If they didn't, they would be annihilated right along with the city.

Sorath charged into the lead. Jadora allowed herself to be swept along in the rush of mercenaries. Though she worried they might be buried if the mages didn't get their defenses back up and the city took numerous direct hits, for the first time she felt some hope that they might be able to get the portal away from the kings. If Sorath and the mercenaries could be convinced to help her instead of turning it over to their employers, that could be the key to success.

Another powerful jolt rocked the tunnels. More snaps emanated from the ceiling, not overhead this time but in the darkness behind them. The cacophonous crashes and thuds of a rockfall echoed to them. Shouts of anger and pain and orders to "raise your defenses" came from the mages who had been trying to catch up with them.

"We better get off this island before it falls out of the sky," one of the mercenaries muttered.

"We're almost back to the library," Jak said.

"A library in the castle?" Sorath asked. "That's where you escaped from?"

"Yes," Jak said.

"Any chance the portal is waiting on the floor in there?"

"No, it's in the courtyard. It's too big to fit indoors."

"I hope it's not too big to fit on our ship," one of the mercenaries said.

"If we have to," Sorath said, "we'll fly it out of here on a rope hanging from the wastewater pipe."

"There are ladder rungs ahead," the mage creating the light said.

The group picked up their speed, but another shock jolted the city. Cracks and snaps rang out ahead, and a huge chunk of the ceiling tumbled down in front of them, throwing up rock dust that left them all coughing. If they'd wanted to make a stealthy incursion, the probability of that had just plummeted further. Though the mages defending the city had more to worry about than intruders in their tunnels now.

It would be the perfect time to get the artifact, but the way was now blocked. Rubble lay piled up to the ceiling. Pipes were visible above, and the sounds of combat were much louder now, but it didn't look like enough of the ceiling had fallen away for them to get out that way. Too bad. Jadora guessed they were inside the castle grounds now. There was no reason they needed to go up through the library, except that those shouts made it sound like half of Uthari's soldiers might be right above them.

"Start digging," Sorath said. "Quietly."

"Our pursuers are coming," someone in the back said. "They must know we're here."

Sorath stepped past Jadora and Jak, joining the mercenaries in the rear. There was only room for two of them to stand shoulder to shoulder in the tunnel, but they formed a wall of grit and weapons.

"We'll keep them back." Sorath drew his magelock. "The rest of you dig and clear the way as quickly as possible."

They already were, men and women kneeling on the rocks, dragging chunks down from the top. Jadora could hear Uthari's people running, boots ringing on the grating, and doubted the mercenaries would clear a way to crawl through in time. She hunkered down, hoping not to be hit in a firefight. There was no room for them to help dig *or* defend.

Jak had a hand on one of the pistols he'd gotten from their would-be kidnapper, and he pointed at the other one as he met Jadora's eyes.

"Do you want it now?" he whispered.

"No." She waved for him to squat down with her and make as small a target as possible. "And don't you jump into shooting people." She lowered her voice, not wanting the mercenaries to hear. "If we're all captured, they might be more lenient if it's clear we weren't *helping* the intruders."

Jak scowled. "I'm worried less about how things look than saving our butts."

"You waving a magelock around won't save any butts." She pointed for him to stop touching the weapon and get down, then started pushing some of the rocks that had come from the pile into cover they could hide behind.

"I was going to shoot it, not wave it."

"Don't do either. As long as we're just innocent academics, nobody needs to feel compelled to kill us."

"Innocent academics can be caught by stray bullets, the same as anyone else."

"Then rub your lucky compass and pray to Shylezar."

"Are you going to rub your vials?"

"Every chance I get."

～

In the back of his suite, in a room full of magical devices that were connected to the energy sources throughout the city, King Uthari closed his hand on a crystal and channeled his power into it. It flowed through conduits in the castle walls, down into the underground infrastructure of Utharika, and to one of the central generators that kept the city's defenses up. He sensed two of his mages at the generator, already hurrying to repair damage that had knocked out the shield, and Uthari willed his magic to mingle with theirs, lending them the power they needed to quickly repair the device.

The shield had only been down for a minute, and Uthari's mageships were keeping the invading fleet from getting close enough to land many attacks, but some were getting through. He was well aware of damage being done to his city and his citizens being harmed. Fortunately, the talented mages knew how to use his power, and they telepathically let him know when they had enough and gave him an estimate as to how much longer it would take to get the shield back up. Five minutes.

Uthari frowned—it was a long time for the city to remain exposed—but accepted that they were doing the best they could. He reached out telepathically to General Tonovan and several other officers captaining his fleet and ordered them closer to the city to keep enemy ships from dropping explosives and magical attacks at vulnerable targets.

Once that was done, he returned to the office in his parlor to check on Malek. A magical viewer he'd long ago created for the wall next to his desk displayed an overview of the numerous battles going on around the city, including the one between the *Star Flyer* and Zaruk's flagship. Through the window over the desk, Uthari also caught glimpses of the two vessels in the clouds not far from the city wall. On the deck of Zaruk's ship, Malek and Stone Heart were fighting, as they had been since before the shield went down.

Uthari knew Stone Heart was a powerful wizard and as good a fighter as any, but he'd expected Malek to best him, especially after they'd gone to swords. Worried for his most loyal and capable zidarr, Uthari was tempted to order his personal mageship to come pick him up so he could go assist Malek. He'd had the vessel readied before the enemy showed up, and it was docked to the roof in the back of the castle.

These days, Uthari wasn't as spry with a blade, but his power had not waned over the years. If it had, someone would have tried to take his throne from him long ago. Only the need to keep an eye on the city to ensure the safety of the citizens who trusted him kept him in the castle. From here, he could see everything on the viewer and more helpfully direct his officers inside and outside of the city walls.

Still, the urge to go out there and fight called to him. If he had trusted Yidar more, he might have left the young zidarr in charge of the castle and his command, but Yidar was no Malek. And the magistrate, second in command after Uthari, would put the needs of the city far above the need to utterly destroy their enemies. When last Uthari had checked in on him, he'd been sending soldiers and maintenance men into the tunnels after intruders who had sabotaged the infrastructure. Hopefully, the magistrate's people would find their wayward archaeologists while they were down there.

Malek and Stone Heart were riveting as they tried their best to slay each other, mixing sword attacks with magical ones. As blasts of energy ricocheted off their personal shields, they smashed into the ship all around them. The mages on the craft, clearly intimidated by the two zidarr in their midst, were staying out of the fight, even though it was undermining their ability to protect their vessel. Their shields were meant to defend it from *outside* attacks, not those coming from their own deck. Since it was one of Zaruk's ships, Uthari hardly cared. Let them crash it, so long as Malek got off first.

He adjusted the viewer to see the area around that battle, hoping no other ships from Zaruk's fleet were flying in close to assist Stone Heart. He paused, frowning at one of Queen Vorsha's mageships. It was crashed in the park beside the docks and appeared out of commission, but he surveyed the deck, checking for enemies who might open fire on Malek. Dense black smoke made it hard to see, but his senses told him people were alive in the cabins and belowdecks.

A number of magical devices were also still operable on the ship. There was nothing wrong with the engine or power source. Strange that the crew hadn't tried to fly the ship away. It wasn't as if hull integrity mattered overmuch with a magical airship. Was it possible this was some ruse? He squinted through the cloudy gloom and thought again of the intruders that had been reported knocking out power in the tunnels under the city. Maybe they weren't merely trying to damage the infrastructure. Maybe they were sneaking in to—

"Get my portal," he growled. "The bastards."

He'd known that was their objective. He'd just assumed they would come in mageships from above. What did they intend to do? *Fold* it so they could sneak it out through the tunnels?

"Idiots."

As Uthari further scoured the suspiciously crashed ship, an exotic piece of magic tickled his senses. An exotic but *familiar* piece of magic. It had the same signature as the dragon steel of the portal.

"The key," he breathed. "They brought it here?"

Uthari was about to order a platoon of soldiers to storm that ship and search the hands for the key when he sensed Yidar approaching his suite. What did he want now?

Yidar had a great deal of potential, but he spoke too much and had too many ambitions. More than once, he had hinted that he intended to prove himself and one day earn Malek's place as Uthari's first zidarr. A lot would have to change for that to happen. Uthari trusted Malek above all others. He made a mental note to warn Malek to watch his back.

As soon as Yidar entered, Uthari sensed that something was wrong. The young zidarr moved with his usual easy, athletic gait, no hesitancy about him, but something about him—about the magical energy he projected—twanged at Uthari's senses. After all these years, Uthari trusted his instincts. Yidar was up to something, possibly a betrayal. At the least, some plot to further his ambitions. Did he have plans to get rid of Malek? He wouldn't dare move against *Uthari*, would he?

Though he no longer wore weapons, at least when he was within his own suite, Uthari could take care of himself. If need be, he could make an energy lance to defend himself against blades that might be capable of slicing through a personal shield.

As Yidar approached, Uthari clasped his hands behind his back, keeping his attention on the viewer. Instead of speaking, he waited for the impatience of youth to betray itself.

"Your Majesty, I've checked on the artifact again. It is undisturbed, and the guards remain in place in the courtyard." Yidar's voice didn't hold the bored tones that it had earlier in the evening when he'd been pleading to be permitted to go out and join the battle. Actually, he'd been pleading for him and *Malek* to go out. And if not himself, then at least Malek, so he could use his skills where they were needed most.

Belatedly, Uthari realized he'd done exactly what Yidar had asked. He'd forgotten that Yidar had made the request. When more ships than his intelligence people had led him to believe were coming had shown up, Uthari had sent Malek out to help Gorsith. It had been the logical action since the power of a zidarr could turn the tide of a battle, and Malek was the best.

"Thank you, Yidar," Uthari said.

Yidar glanced toward a corner of the office, one with a table that held the generator carved from purple dylorian crystal that Uthari had long ago imbued with enough power to maintain the shield around the castle. It was separate from the city's defense grid. As always, it hummed softly with power, proof that it was working.

Uthari eyed Yidar, but not before the younger man returned his gaze to the viewer on the wall, as if he'd never looked anywhere else. "Stone Heart has come? Zaruk has sent everything he's got, hasn't he?"

"So it would seem."

"All that for some ancient artifact?"

"So it would seem," Uthari repeated. "No doubt it is only an excuse for the war that Queen Vorsha has longed for for decades. She saw the opportunity to turn Zaruk into an ally, Zaruk who once studied with me and has been an ally more often than an enemy in the past."

"He must truly want the artifact."

"If that were true, he would have been searching for it. He is surprisingly disgruntled, considering he did not know it existed a week ago."

"Is it true that it can open a portal to the world where dragons live?" Yidar asked the question casually, as if he cared little about the answer, but Uthari sensed this was at the heart of what had brought him here and debated if he should answer.

"Who told you that?" Uthari asked equally casually. He'd asked Malek to do this research in secret.

"I saw some of Malek's notes. He'd surmised that humans wanted it so they could go to the dragon realm and, if they still exist, bring them back as allies for a war they would launch against us. If there is truly evidence to support that dragons still live, and they *could* be won as allies, one would think a king could also reach out to them. If such powerful creatures were won to his side, it would ensure that nobody *dared* plot against him. He might even use them to take over the other kingdoms and unite the world under one ruler." Yidar grew a little breathless as he rapidly laid out the scenario. He caught himself and shrugged as if indifferent. "I presume that is why you want the portal."

Uthari squinted at him, surprised he was admitting to reading Malek's notes, notes that Uthari had little doubt hadn't been carelessly left out for anyone to find. Yidar must have sneaked into his room when Malek was off on a mission and rooted around until he found the research.

Maybe Yidar sensed Uthari's suspicions for he waved at the viewer and changed the subject. "Stone Heart is older than Malek and very powerful. Do you believe Malek will win?"

"Yes. When did you read Malek's notes?" Uthari wouldn't allow himself to be diverted. He lowered his voice to add in a dangerous tone, "And for *whom*?"

Instead of answering, Yidar squinted in concentration. Uthari braced himself to defend against a magical attack, but Yidar was still focused on the viewer.

Stone Heart succeeded in knocking Malek back, his main-gauche flying from his hand, and Uthari's breath caught. He wouldn't have expected his first zidarr to be disarmed.

Yidar watched intently, and Uthari wondered if he was trying to manipulate the battle from here, over a mile away. Just in case, Uthari channeled some of his own energy across the void, reinforcing Malek's shield before Stone Heart could rush in to take advantage. Uthari spotted several of Zaruk's mages creeping in to help Stone Heart and launched a mental attack at them. They jerked, lifting their hands to their heads, losing their ability to use magic of their own.

Yidar spun, pulling out a magical dagger, and hefted it to throw.

Uthari's attention snapped back to the office, and he lifted a barrier more impervious than diamond all around himself. But *he* wasn't Yidar's target. The dagger sped across the room and slammed point first into the shield generator. Purple lightning branched from it, and its power disappeared. Uthari gaped, sensing the shield that protected the castle disappearing. With the city's shield still down, that left them defenseless.

Uthari whirled as he raised his personal defenses, expecting Yidar to attack him next. He wasn't wrong. A rush of power battered at his shields, and Yidar lunged in with another blade—his magical zidarr short sword. Surprisingly, he didn't aim for Uthari's heart but for his thigh, as if he only wanted to put him out of commission.

It didn't matter, for Uthari's shield, practiced and refined countless times over the centuries, halted the blade as surely as dragon steel.

"What have you done?" Uthari demanded, hurling an attack of his own, though he couldn't put everything behind it, not when this was one of his zidarr, fostered and trained since boyhood to serve the kingdom.

Yidar stumbled back under the assault, but his own defenses protected him from the brunt of it.

"Why would you leave our people defenseless?" Uthari added.

"You'll protect them. They'll be fine." Yidar glanced toward the window, toward a mageship taking the opportunity to fly close to the castle. It wasn't from the enemy fleet; its hull was black with red trim—Uthari's colors. "But the portal will be mine."

"You didn't know it existed a week ago. Why do you care?"

Was that ship coming to help Yidar steal the artifact? Fury erupted in Uthari's chest, replacing the shock and betrayal, and he launched another attack.

His magic overwhelmed Yidar's defenses, and the zidarr staggered back, almost dropping to a knee. But Yidar found some reserves and maintained his shield. He threw something at the floor, an explosive that boomed, flashing white and filling the air with smoke. As if he expected such an amateur tactic to distract Uthari, Yidar followed it with a blast of his own power and several rapid slashes from his sword. Did he expect to cut through?

Uthari shook his head, wrinkling his nose at the smoke in the air, and prepared to restrain his wayward zidarr with magical bonds.

But the door flew open, distracting him more than the explosive had.

"Your Majesty," one of his officers blurted. "The castle shield is down, and mageships are encroaching on our position."

Yidar threw another wave of power at Uthari, then raced around him, his blade raised. Uthari ignored the officer and turned, expecting an attack from behind. But Yidar kept going and sprang for the window, his magical sword shattering the enchanted glass. He leaped out onto the rooftop below and ran, no doubt to get to the courtyard and the portal.

Though he was still puzzled about why Yidar wanted it, Uthari reacted quickly. He crunched across the glass on the marble floor in time to wrap his power around Yidar as he tried to leap off the roof. Coils of magic ensnared him in midair. Uthari squeezed his fist, willing his power to squeeze Yidar. Guards in the courtyard looked up and raised their firearms, pointing them uncertainly toward the zidarr.

Yidar screamed as power crushed him. He launched a mental attack, but Uthari deflected it, the shields around his mind as solid as those that guarded his body.

The price for betrayal was death. It was stated no fewer than ten times in the Zidarr Code. As he squeezed tighter, Yidar crying out, Uthari could have crushed every organ and bone in his body. But he was reluctant to kill the man he'd trained from boyhood. Even if Yidar was no Malek, and not even as dependable as

Gorsith, didn't he deserve to be heard? At the least, Uthari wanted to question him and find out what his plans had been—and who else he'd suborned into helping him. Also he wanted, if not to give Yidar a second chance, to understand.

"Get every available mage out to raise personal shields to protect us until I can repair the crystal," Uthari told his officer as he concentrated on restraining the still struggling Yidar. "Everyone wants the artifact, but *nobody* will take it from me."

"Yes, Your Majesty."

Uthari reeled Yidar back toward his broken window like a fish on a line. There wasn't time to ask the questions he wished answered now, but there were cells in the castle that could hold even a zidarr. Yidar was about to find out what it was like to spend time in one—and if the city was destroyed because of his betrayal, he could plummet to the earth below, the same as everyone else living here.

28

Lieutenant Sasko joined Ferroki in the navigation cabin, her eyes watering and lungs raw from the smoke outside. The deck was tilted so far sideways that she had to grab the beams on the low ceiling to keep from falling over. The mageship's crash landing had been convincing. At least she believed so. And the guards in the tower also believed so—or they were too busy watching the zidarr battle on the other mageship to worry about the *Dauntless*. She peered through a window, but the wind had shifted, and the smoke kept her from seeing if it was still going on.

The young helmsman who'd been responsible for the crash was frowning over the instrumentation. The wheel, altitude lever, and various gauges appeared undamaged, but a pulsing magical doodad that probably powered something important was cracked and smoking.

"I think we have a replacement *orboxitor*," he said, then flung himself down to the deck to open cabinets under the wheel.

"Good," Ferroki said. "We need to get this ship ready to lift off again. It'll take Sorath some time to find the artifact, but if we're not ready to pick him up when he signals us, the whole mission could fail."

"Dr. Fret is keeping the noxious fire going," Sasko reported. "The rest of the mercenaries are putting out the fires in the back and patching up anything that's crucial for flying. I told them to be quiet and stay belowdecks as much as possible so the guards don't have a reason to pay attention to us."

"I doubt we'll be that lucky." Ferroki glanced out the windows, several of them cracked. It was still raining, and the rain beaded up along the cracks and dripped into the interior. "They were on the way over here when they spotted our incursion team."

The cabin's hatch opened, bringing smoke inside along with the very angry Captain Toggs.

"Nobber," he growled. "You idiot. That was on purpose, wasn't it? You crashed because that ludicrous mercenary told you to."

"Uh." From his hands and knees, the helmsman looked hopefully at Ferroki and Sasko, as if they could help him.

"*He's* not your commander. *I am.*" Toggs thumped his chest, then stretched his hand toward the helmsman.

Pulses of crackling energy shot from his fingertips and slammed into the young officer, knocking him away from the cabinet he'd been opening. He curled into a ball on the deck as the captain's magic pummeled him.

Ferroki lifted a hand, as if to grab his arm and try to stop him, but Toggs glared icicles at her.

"We need to get the ship repaired, Captain," Ferroki told him calmly. "He who saves the fox hunt until after the eggs have been collected from the coop and stored safely in the farmhouse is less likely to lose his breakfast."

Sasko eyed the mage captain, wondering if he was a fan of fables or would think Ferroki a kook that he should ignore. Or zap with magic.

Nobber writhed on the deck, gasping as he squinted his eyes

shut, his legs twitching and fingers spasming. Even though Sasko preferred to leave mages to handle their disputes between themselves, she felt sorry for the kid and wished she could help. The urge to crack Toggs on the back of the head while he wasn't looking came to her, but then she might end up on the deck writhing beside the helmsman.

It wasn't Ferroki's words but the sound of something slamming down outside of the navigation cabin that made Toggs release his officer. He frowned through the hatchway and stepped outside.

Ferroki rushed to help Nobber to a sitting position. His hair was sticking out in a thousand directions and his fingertips were blackened. He wobbled, blinking uncertainly—or was that spastically? Maybe his eyelids weren't working right now.

"Can you go back to repairs?" Ferroki asked him gently. "We'll try to distract your captain."

"I—I'll t-t-try," he stuttered.

"Zidarr Stone Heart?" Toggs asked, only a step outside the hatchway.

Remembering the fight they'd been witnessing, Sasko peered past him. The white-haired zidarr who'd almost killed Sorath in the transport vessel was sprawled on his back on the deck, as if he'd fallen there from a great height.

Sasko stepped outside and twisted her head to peer up at the sky. That was exactly what had happened.

The mageship that he and the zidarr Malek had been fighting on had disappeared. Had it been so damaged that it lost its power and crashed out of the sky? She didn't see the blue hull of Zaruk's craft anywhere, but the other mageship, the *Star Flyer*, was still up there. Someone had thrown a rope over the side, and Malek was hanging on to the end, swaying with its movement as he looked down at Stone Heart.

Toggs didn't see that. He was creeping toward the zidarr, a

hand raised, as if he wasn't sure if Stone Heart was dead or would leap up at any moment, striking down anyone nearby.

Malek started climbing up the rope to his ship. A uniformed officer came to the railing and looked down at him. Sasko had seen General Tonovan a few times and recognized him.

A groan came from Stone Heart.

Toggs rushed to his side. "My lord, do you need help?"

"Yes." Stone Heart's eyes fluttered open. "I need someone to kill that asshole," he snarled, pain lancing his voice.

"Thought he was supposed to handle that," Sasko muttered.

Stone Heart rolled into a sitting position and glared up at the *Star Flyer*—Malek was almost up to the railing, and the craft was coming about.

He swore. "They're going to come try to finish me off." He glanced around at Sasko as well as Toggs. "And he'll blast this ship to pieces to do it. Is Sorath here? This is the ship on the incursion mission, isn't it?" He gaped through the smoke toward the watchtowers. "Are we on the *ground*?"

"The grass next to the city docks," Toggs said. "It was Sorath's idiotic idea."

"Crashing?"

"Pretending to crash. But we've taken so much damage that—"

"Every- everything's b-b-back powered up," came Nobber's call from behind Sasko. "Tell the captain."

As Stone Heart struggled to rise the rest of the way—Toggs didn't look like he dared offer help—the ship carrying Malek flew closer.

"Do we get out of here before he arrives or keep playing dead and hope they don't obliterate us?" Sasko asked, glancing at Nobber and Ferroki.

"Even if we managed to get in the air," Ferroki said, "there's not time to get out of here. They would pin us against the city walls."

"Mages, defend the ship," Toggs bellowed.

His crew had been swift to react in their earlier battles, but they glanced uncertainly at each other and at the *Star Flyer's* approach. Malek had made it to the deck and stood by the railing with his glowing sword in hand as his ship carried him closer.

Stone Heart staggered to his feet, his face twisted with pain. He must have fallen more than fifty feet. No normal human could have survived that. He was lucky he hadn't missed the peninsula altogether and plummeted thousands of feet. That would have killed even a mage.

The *Star Flyer* fired weapons at them. Their mages had gathered and raised a barrier around the *Dauntless*, but the long looks they exchanged with each other suggested they believed they were doomed.

Booms came from the castle walls—the men in the watchtowers had realized the crashed ship had people on it and was worth targeting.

"We may have to surrender," Ferroki said. "This won't end well."

Toggs glared over at her. "We have a mission. The king ordered us to get that artifact, and we will." He coughed, the wind shifting and blowing the smoke across their deck, then wiped his eyes. "Our people don't *surrender*."

"Mercenaries do," Sasko muttered.

She didn't like it, but they got paid to fight, not to die, and none of them cared one way or another which king ended up with the damn artifact.

"I don't think anyone is going to give us a chance to surrender." Ferroki found a spot where she could fire from cover and aimed her magelock at Malek. With both ships shielded, there was no point in shooting, but she would wait for her chance.

Reluctantly, Sasko joined her.

"Uhm," Nobber said, left alone in navigation. "Do we lift off? Or...?"

Magical attacks assaulted them from both sides, flashing as the energy blasts struck their barrier. One of the mages keeping those defenses up crumpled to the deck.

"Lieutenant Maskert," Toggs yelled, his arms raised as he presumably contributed to the defenses, "get back to your feet and help out."

The mage had passed out and didn't hear him. Stone Heart staggered back, his own hands thrust outward toward Malek. Were they still trading blows? Mental attacks instead of physical ones?

Sasko aimed at Malek, itching to squeeze the trigger, waiting for someone to let her know when she could fire. Stone Heart dropped to one knee, his face tense with concentration and pain.

Abruptly, Malek's ship stopped attacking. Two big blue mage-ships flew out of the clouds on the other side of the *Star Flyer*. More of Zaruk's people. One ship opened up on the *Star Flyer* and one fired at the watchtowers, at the guards who'd been targeting the *Dauntless.*

"Scoot us out of here," Ferroki yelled through the hatchway to Nobber. "Don't go straight up, or we'll be in the line of fire, and don't go down, since those other ships may still be skulking under the city. Try to take us horizontally out of here. Make it look like we're fleeing and not coming back."

"*Can* we flee and not come back?" Sasko asked wistfully while keeping Malek in her sights.

He was still focused on Stone Heart, barely aware that his ship was shifting its attack to the vessels on the other side, the ones actually firing back. Stone Heart kept glowering at him, his lips twisting and flexing as he concentrated on whatever magic he could send through defensive barriers. Malek's frosty face didn't show as much emotion.

The smoke coming from the hole in the *Dauntless*'s hull increased, as if the fire had spread. Even though Sasko knew it should only be the carefully controlled blaze that Tinder had built in a metal barrel and that Fret was monitoring, she worried that it had escaped and was burning everything belowdecks. The smoke increased so much that she could no longer see Malek's ship, or even the city wall and watchtowers.

A wrenching noise came from below and reverberated through the ship as it attempted to ease away from its crash site. Sasko winced, afraid the guards would hear the noise and resume their attack, but they were busy fending off the onslaught from the new ship. A couple of brown-hulled vessels lurked farther out in the clouds, cannons firing over their ally ships and toward the city.

One slammed into the wall, knocking a crenellation off the top. That startled Sasko—it was the first weapon she'd seen get through the city's defenses and damage anything.

A cheer went up on King Zaruk's ships, and more cannons opened up.

Malek flung a final attack toward Stone Heart that knocked him on his back even though the *Dauntless*'s defenses were still up, but then turned his attention toward the new arrivals. He and the other mages on the *Star Flyer* focused further attacks on the vessels firing at the city.

Toggs helped Stone Heart get to his feet. "The city defenses are down."

"Then fire at them." Stone Heart raised his voice to repeat the order to the mages on the deck.

"No," Ferroki said. "This is our chance to sneak out of sight, recover, and wait for Sorath's signal."

"To Hell with his signal." Stone Heart strode into navigation, limping but not slowing down. "If their defenses are down, we can fly in and get that artifact without him."

Sasko doubted it would be that easy. Ferroki also shook her head, but Stone Heart had taken command of their ship, and he ignored them.

"Go check on Fret," Ferroki told Sasko. "Make sure we aren't burning down from the inside out while we attempt this."

Sasko nodded but before leaving asked, "Think we can get in there and get it without Sorath's help?"

"I'm not sure we can get it even *with* his help. There's also the possibility that this is a ruse, that Uthari or whoever is in charge of the city defenses is letting us believe they're more damaged than they are."

"Why would they do that?"

"To get us inside the city, raise their defenses again, and trap us?"

Sasko frowned. "And why would they do *that*?"

Ferroki slid a hand in her pocket and held up the medallion. "We have something they want, don't forget."

"I was hoping they didn't know that."

"It's possible they don't. But I wouldn't count on it." Ferroki returned it to her pocket before Stone Heart glanced back at them.

Sasko left navigation, wishing she were far away from here and wondering if she would survive this mission.

Tezi lacked the strength to hurl rubble off piles, so she ended up shoulder to shoulder with Colonel Sorath, facing down the tunnel toward the last intersection as the city defenders encroached, their angry voices echoing off the walls. There was nothing to hide behind, so she hoped the others cleared the rockfall before their enemies showed up. But the voices rang out clearly now, so she doubted they had much time.

"Take a couple of the pop-bangs out of my pocket, killer." Sorath stood with his pistol pointed down the tunnel and his pickaxe hand up in case someone made it within melee range.

"Throw them as soon as those mages poke their heads into the intersection up there."

"Yes, sir." Tezi felt weird sticking her fingers in his pocket, but it wasn't as if he had a free hand to grab them for her. She withdrew three smooth spheres and juggled them awkwardly in her left hand until she found a grip that still let her support her rifle. "Will these keep them from using their magic on us?"

"Probably not, but they can be distracting to mages, especially less-experienced ones. They've probably got their best people defending the castle walls, especially now that it sounds like the city shield is down."

Another boom erupted nearby, the tunnels quaking. The shield was *definitely* down.

The voices stopped, aside from an uncertain squawk as pieces of the ceiling clattered down. Behind Tezi, even more rocks thudded and clattered as the rest of the team worked on clearing the way. The professor and her son crouched between Tezi and Sorath and the others, looking like they wished they could disappear into the new cracks in the tunnel walls. Tezi wished she could think of something comforting to say to them. These last few days couldn't have been pleasant for them, not as King Uthari's prisoners. Not as *Malek's* prisoners.

A woman in a red uniform stuck her head around the corner and threw something. Tezi fired at her, afraid it was an explosive. At the same time, Sorath's black-powder pistol cracked in her ear. Tezi's charge caught the woman's shoulder as she leaned back, and she cried out, but if she fell, it was out of sight. Sorath's bullet slammed into the projectile—something similar to one of Tinder's grenades—and it exploded twenty feet from them.

The blast brought down a portion of the ceiling and blew holes in the walls. It also roared down the tunnel at them, wind knocking Tezi back several steps. Sorath spun, catching her under the armpit with his pick before she could fall over the professor.

"Thanks," she mumbled, embarrassed by her scrawniness, since it meant power could easily toss her about. At least she'd kept hold of her weapon. She hurried to get back into position beside Sorath and aim it in the right direction. He'd returned instantly to his position, his pistol aimed at the intersection. "I'm sorry you're stuck with me."

He glanced at her. "Is there someone else I should be stuck with?"

"The others are more experienced and stronger."

"Experience comes with time. You'll get it too one day."

"I know. I'm just... never mind." This wasn't the time to complain that the unit didn't seem to find her that useful. They'd invited her to sit with them on the way over. That was enough.

"You thought quickly and made the shot. You're doing fine, killer. Do you want to follow a crazy man down a tunnel?"

"Is that rhetorical? Or do you mean now?"

"Rhetorical is a good word. I'll use it in my memoir." He winked at her. "But I mean now. They're right around the corner plotting something." He pointed at her hand. She still held the little spheres. Dropping his voice to a whisper, he said, "Cover me."

Keeping his weapon raised, he trotted soundlessly down the tunnel.

Tezi realized he meant to crash their party. Did he even know how many were lurking around the corner? She gripped her magelock and one of the spheres and hurried after him.

Someone else leaned around the corner, a male mage this time, with his hand raised to throw another explosive. His eyes widened in surprise as Sorath charged at him, firing before he could throw. The blast hit his wrist, and the explosive tumbled to the floor. As it detonated, Sorath turned his shoulder and raised his arm to protect his face. Before the smoke had cleared and the rubble had stopped falling, he holstered his firearm, drew a short sword, and charged around the corner.

Clashes and thuds erupted as he attacked.

"Get him!" someone cried. "Shoot!"

Instinct told Tezi to be careful about charging blindly around the corner, but she had to help him as much as she could. If he died after telling her to cover him, the others would never forget it. *She* would never forget it.

She crouched low and pointed her weapon around the corner, gulping at the eight mages facing Sorath. One of his explosives hit the ground between them, startling a few in the back as he slashed and cut with his weapons. Someone aimed a magelock at him, but he anticipated it and twisted, pressing his back to the wall in time for the charge to whiz harmlessly past.

It almost shaved *Tezi's* eyebrows off as it zipped into the intersection, but she didn't let it scare her into retreating. She used the opening to fire at one of the mages closest to her.

The uniformed man had been focused on Sorath and didn't have his defenses up. Her charge struck him in the side, hurling him back into one of his allies. She got off two more shots before the mages realized she was there and they had to split their attention.

Sorath rammed one of his enemies into a wall before the man could fire at Tezi, but one in the back shot over their heads and almost got her. With her heart pounding, she jerked back around the corner. She longed to plaster her back to the wall and stay there, but with Sorath fighting fearlessly in the midst of so many enemies, she couldn't. She made herself lean around the corner and fire again.

Several of their enemies lay bloody and unmoving on the ground, and one had even been decapitated. But Sorath still had a lot to handle. One gripped him in a magical hold, but he managed to drop another of his spheres. The boom startled the mage just enough for Sorath to pull free, grab him, and slam his pickaxe into his chest.

Tezi ignored the sickening crunch of bone and fired again, picking her target carefully in the confusing morass of battle. This time, the mages were expecting it, and her charges ricocheted off their defenses. One almost struck Sorath, and she gulped. If he were killed by friendly fire, it would be even worse than being slain by enemies.

Remembering the spheres, she threw one over the heads of everyone to land behind the mages at the back of the group. It blew at the same time as another explosive hit the city from above. The tunnel quaked as smoke filled the area, and two of the mages toward the front jerked their arms up, using magic to shield their heads in case a rockfall tumbled down.

But their deaths came from another direction as Sorath plowed into them, using the distraction to his advantage. He cracked the two mages in the skulls with his deadly pickaxe.

As he closed on those in the rear of the group, a mage who had only been stunned and not killed pushed to his knees and hurled power at Sorath's back. Sorath stumbled and pitched against a wall.

Tezi fired, shooting his attacker in the back. His defenses weren't up, and the blow knocked him face-first into the grating. Sorath whirled and finished him off with another mighty chop from his pickaxe.

Tezi grimaced at the crunch of it breaking the mage's spine, but he'd been the last of their enemies, at least for the moment, so they had a reprieve. She leaned back around the corner and slumped against the wall. Her legs were rubbery, and she was tempted to let them give way and sit for a moment, but Sergeant Tinder appeared beside her. She locked her knees and feigned nonchalance at the battle.

"There's a law among mercenaries that you better learn,"

Tinder said as Sorath walked back around the corner, blood dripping from a dozen cuts on his face but no worse wounds bothering him.

"Yes, Sergeant?" Tezi braced herself for a reprimand. She thought she'd done all right, but maybe Tinder had seen her firing from the cover of the corner and thought it cowardly, especially when Sorath had charged right into the fray.

"Never run into battle with someone crazier than you are," Tinder said.

Tezi blinked and looked at Sorath.

"Really, Sergeant," he drawled. "Nobody would *ever* watch my back if they followed that rule."

"That would be a shame." Tinder grabbed Tezi and tugged her back toward the rockfall. "Don't get our rookie killed. We like the way she sucks up to the captain."

Tezi's cheeks warmed. Why was she saying that in front of the colonel?

"All mercenaries suck up to their commanders." Sorath wiped the blood off his pickaxe and sword and followed them. "That's how a hierarchical system works."

The rockfall had been cleared enough that the team could scramble over the top and down the other side.

"Those with dignity," Tinder said with a sniff, "don't deign to sucking."

Sorath nudged Tezi with his elbow. "She's the one who was getting a little yellow yarn bag with tassels made for her ammo earlier, right?"

Tinder leveled a dark look over her shoulder at them.

"Yes." Tezi managed a smile. "But I think they were dignified tassels."

"Oh, I'm sure."

29

"THERE ARE PEOPLE UP THERE WAITING," ONE OF THE MAGES SAID.

They'd reached the rungs up to the library, the shaft dark, meaning the hidden door at the top was shut. Jak didn't hear any noises coming from above, but he didn't doubt that a mage could sense castle guards stationed to defend the entrance. He and his mother stood with their backs against the wall at the bottom of the shaft, trying to stay out of the way.

"I'm sure Altrucia wasn't the only one who knew about this door," he said.

"Who?" a mercenary asked.

"The woman who helped us escape. We, uh, stepped over her body earlier."

"Huh."

"If she helped you, I'm sorry she died," Tezi said quietly.

It was the first time she'd spoken directly to Jak and made eye contact. He wished he were less sweaty and bedraggled, and that they weren't in the middle of a city being bombed. Chatting with her over coffee at the cafe by the horticulture department's gardens on campus would have been much nicer.

"She tried to turn us over to the dead mage we also stepped over," Jak said, "so I wasn't that attached."

"Oh." Her forehead wrinkled. Maybe he shouldn't have been flippant. But if he started acknowledging emotions and how he was feeling about the night—the deaths they'd seen and the mage *his mother* had killed—he might collapse in a weepy mess. That rarely impressed girls. Even his mother was frowning at him.

"Sorry," he muttered, not sure if that was the correct response, but it rarely hurt.

"How *many* people are up there?" Sorath had climbed last over the rubble pile, making sure no more mages were coming from behind. He straightened his uniform and brushed off pulverized rock as he joined them.

"It's hard to tell for sure, sir, but at least twenty." It was strange hearing a mage call a terrene human *sir*, but the five magic users detached to the incursion unit must have accepted Sorath as their boss.

"All mages, I suppose," Sorath said.

"Most of the populace of the city, except for the servants, are mages."

"No chance servants are guarding the library?" one of the mercenaries asked wistfully.

"Don't worry," the one who'd introduced herself as Sergeant Tinder said. "We'll send Colonel Sorath in first. He likes charging a room."

"Charging tunnels is doable. Rooms, especially library-sized rooms, aren't so appealing. There's too much space for people to flank you. You have to move fast."

"You seem decent at that."

Sorath shook his head but reached for the rungs to go first. "Just charge up after me. Someone bring grenades."

"I've always got grenades." Tinder patted an oversized ammo pouch clasped to her belt.

"You're not going to throw explosives in a library are you?" Mother asked.

"It's the only way to have a chance against mages." Sorath climbed to the top, his pickaxe clinking as he hooked it on the rungs.

"The city is being bombed anyway, Mother," Jak pointed out.

"I realize that, but destroying books... seems sacrilegious."

"Only if they're sacred books."

"*All* books should be revered."

"Quiet down there." Sorath grunted as he pushed the lever to open the door. No light seeped in. Were the mages waiting in the dark to surprise them? "And put out the light."

"I'm not certain I like him," Mother murmured as their mages made their magical illumination disappear, leaving the tunnel in darkness.

"Because he's ordering us around?" Jak murmured back. "Or because he's going to blow up books?"

"The latter is more egregious, though you know how I feel about the former."

The mercenaries brushed past them to climb up after their leader. Sorath hadn't made a sound, and Jak wasn't sure he'd stepped off the ladder until shouts came from the library, echoing oddly down their shaft, and the first explosion went off.

"Wait for us to handle it," one of the mages said, patting Jak clumsily on the shoulder in the dark, then climbing past him.

"Gladly." Jak leaned his head back against the cool wall, shivering at the drafts that whispered in from the destroyed portions of the tunnel.

He tried to listen for more mages coming after them from that direction, but it was hard to hear anything over the clamor of the battle that raged up above. It sounded like entire armies clashing, not a ten-man squad of mercenaries against however many were defending the library. Maybe there *was* an army up there.

Mother must have also worried that the sheer number of weapons firing, explosives detonating, and battle cries sounding meant that their team was overwhelmed, because she asked, "What are we going to do if they don't survive?"

Jak had no idea. If the mercenaries lost, would the castle defenders close the hidden door and deem their duty completed? Or would they come down here to see if anyone was lurking in the tunnel?

"You're older and wiser," he said. "You're supposed to know."

"I'm afraid I haven't had answers since this all started."

"With the defenses down, maybe there's a chance the portal really can be taken. Even if this team fails... it sounded like the crew of their ship would be along to try to get it."

"I doubt they *can* get it without the mercenaries distracting the mages that will be guarding it in the courtyard."

A more distant explosion sounded, and the tunnels shivered in sympathy. Jak almost asked how much damage one of these floating cities could take before it fell out of the sky, but he didn't want to know.

As the battle continued in the library, the hairs on the back of his neck rose. The faintest scraping sound came from the tunnel, back where the rockfall was. In the pitch darkness, he couldn't see if anyone was coming. The noise was so soft that it might have been made by a rat, but why would a rat be roaming around in the middle of a bombing?

Jak pointed his magelock in that direction and squeezed his mother's shoulder to warn her that he was stepping past her. Maybe she also sensed something, for she didn't ask what he was doing.

Seconds passed, and he didn't hear another noise, but his sixth sense told him that someone was coming. Should he shoot into the dark and hope to get lucky? What if it was an ally instead of an enemy?

He almost snorted. *What* ally? He and Mother didn't have any allies here. Even the mercenaries would turn on them if someone paid them to.

Something seemed to stir in the darkness. Maybe it was his imagination, but... he fired.

Blue light flashed as the charge sped from his magelock. It only lasted a split second, but that was enough to see the face of an armed man in Uthari's red uniform approaching with a sword raised. The charge slammed into his chest, and he flew backward, crashing into someone else who'd come over the rockfall after him. The man Jak had hit dropped to the ground.

Jak fired again, panic welling up as he realized the situation was even worse than he'd feared. The second uniformed man wasn't caught off guard and twisted to the side before the charge hit him. It struck the rock pile behind him. Jak shifted his aim to fire again, but the man moved too quickly. He rushed Jak, slamming him against the wall and clamping down on his wrist with an iron grip. He smashed Jak's hand against the hard wall until he dropped the magelock.

In the dark, Jak heard rather than saw the man drawing a dagger, the faint whisper of it leaving its sheath. Before the blade could slice into Jak, the man jerked away, releasing him as he gasped. A droplet of fire struck Jak's cheek. Mother must have thrown one of her vials.

Jak squatted down, patting around for the magelock he'd dropped. But another weapon buzzed right beside him, and blue light flashed in the tunnel again, highlighting the man as he flew backward. Mother stood with the fallen magelock in hand, her eyes grim, her jaw set. That was the image of her that was burned into Jak's mind as the light from the charge faded.

"Thanks, Mother," he whispered, shaking out his hand. It hurt from being slammed against the wall, but it could have been much worse.

"You're welcome. We'd better go up. There could be more coming." She patted around in the dark, found him, and hugged him fiercely before pushing the weapon back into his hand. "There are only a couple of charges left. And that was my last vial."

"I'm glad you put it to good use." Jak rubbed his cheek where the droplet of acid had splattered him, then followed the wall to the rungs.

"I almost grabbed the one with the sample in it."

"That might not have been as effective." His cheek would burn for a while, but he didn't complain. He was still alive. "Going up."

Jak climbed carefully and slowly, listening for more intruders and trying to figure out which way the battle above had gone. The sounds of weapons clashing and grenades exploding had stopped, but he didn't hear any voices that would have let him identify the winners. The possibility that he was climbing up into the arms of waiting castle guards weighed on him with each rung he ascended.

At the top, he felt around until he found the back of the bookcase. It was only ajar a few inches, and he peered through before pushing it open further.

There was *some* light, the yellow of lanterns burning near the library's entrance, but nothing was lit in this aisle under the mezzanine. He could barely see two bodies on the floor several feet away. Mercenaries? Guards? The dim lighting made it impossible to make out the details of their clothing.

Beyond the end of the aisle, books, pieces of cases and shelves, and shards of marble tile lay scattered across the floor. The entire library hadn't been destroyed, but it had taken damage. Mother wouldn't be pleased. As much as he liked books, Jak was more concerned about the blood spattering the floor. Whose people did it belong to?

Faint rustling and low voices came from the direction of the entrance, but Jak couldn't see the speakers through the bookcase. He wanted to wait until someone stepped into view, so he would know whose side had won, but Mother tapped his ankle.

"More people are climbing over the rock pile," she whispered up.

There would be no waiting. Jak pushed the hidden door open enough to clamber out. He crouched, the nearly spent magelock in hand, until Mother made it out behind him. They closed the door and crept toward the bodies. Identifying them should tell them who won before they committed to leaving the aisle.

But when they reached the bodies and could see well enough to discern uniforms, his heart sank. One wore Uthari's colors, but the other was one of their mages—the one who'd patted him on the shoulder and offered encouragement.

A boom rang out, startling him. It wasn't another explosion, but it echoed almost as loudly through the library, especially when a second and third boom followed.

"That sounds like a battering ram," Mother breathed.

"Why would *mages* need a battering ram?" Jak eased past the bodies toward the end of the aisles.

He breathed a sigh of relief when he spotted his blonde friend —admittedly, Tezi had only spoken to him once and might not consider *him* a friend—behind an upturned table, her long rifle balanced on the edge as she pointed it at the closed double doors. The body of a red-uniformed guard lay a few feet behind her. *Numerous* guards were on the floor, all dead or unconscious. Jak didn't see any more mercenaries among them and was amazed Sorath's team was faring as well as it was. Though there were fewer guards than Jak had expected. Uthari's forces had to be split, their focus in a dozen directions.

Another *bam* sounded as something struck the doors, the stout wood quivering only faintly. The rest of the mercenary team was fanned out with their weapons pointed at the doors, using whatever they could find for cover. Only Sorath crouched out in the open, a couple of his spheres in hand and ready to throw. Clearly, he meant to charge whoever came in.

"There's a lot of magic in those doors," one of the team's mages whispered.

"Will they hold?" Sorath looked over at Jak and Mother, though they hadn't made a sound. He raised his pickaxe weapon.

Jak hoped that gesture meant *stay where you are*, not *come out and join us in battle*. If he could find a way to help without flinging himself into danger, he would, but he'd had enough battles for the night.

"Not indefinitely," the mage said.

"Should we charge out to meet *them*?" Sergeant Tinder hefted one of her explosives.

"There are a lot more guards out there than we faced in here." The mage looked toward Jak—no, toward his fallen comrade on the floor in the aisle.

"Someone go check the windows." Sorath tilted his head toward the far wall, though the curtains were drawn on whatever view lay beyond them. "See if we can climb out. We want to get to the portal, not fight the entire contingent of castle guards."

"I'll do it," Jak said, immediately liking the idea of climbing out of here before being forced into a battle.

Was it possible that they could reach the portal from here? The library was on the third floor, and he knew from the way it faced and their walk here that it wouldn't be near that particular courtyard, but perhaps they could find a route around the exterior of the castle to it.

An explosive dropped so close it sounded like it had landed inside the castle. The floor quaked, bookcases rattled, tomes flew free, and a chandelier in the ceiling smashed to the floor behind the mercenaries. Several booms answered, seemingly from right overhead. Artillery weapons mounted in the castle towers? Or were mageships up there, trading fire with each other?

As Jak drew closer to the windows, Mother right behind him, he wondered if Malek had survived his battle with the other zidarr. And if so, would he stay out there and keep fighting, or would Uthari call him back to the castle? What was the likelihood that a bomb would drop on Uthari's suite and take out the old wizard?

They reached the windows, but as Jak parted the curtains, a vision charged into his mind so forcefully he almost tripped. In it, he was lying on his back in the courtyard that held the portal, looking up toward the bellies of three mageships battling each other under a cloudy night sky. It took him a moment to realize he was seeing the world as if he *were* the portal. As in his dream, it was sharing its perspective with him. This time, it wasn't some ancient memory but a vision of the present. And he wasn't dreaming; he was awake and standing in the library, somehow seeing this even though his eyes were open.

Two of the three mageships were painted green, one of the colors of the intruders, and one was the black of Uthari's forces. At first, Jak thought the black mageship was defending the artifact against the others, but ropes with grappling hooks dangled over the railings. Was someone on Uthari's side trying to steal the portal? Or was that a ship that had been painted to *look* like it was on Uthari's side? Surely, such a simple ruse wouldn't fool mages. Maybe, now that the castle's defenses were down, Uthari's people had been ordered to move the portal to a safer locale. But why use rope and grappling hook when the mages could levitate the big artifact around?

Cannons fired from the other ships, keeping the black vessel too busy to fly down close enough to hook the artifact. From the fingers of mages standing at the railings, fireballs and crackling blue electricity streaked across the dark sky. A sense of disgruntlement filled Jak. Originating from the portal? It had to be, but what did it mean? That the portal was unhappy to have people fighting over it? Maybe it worried they would damage it in their battle.

Jak sucked in a sharp breath as a new thought occurred to him. Maybe if he could reach the portal and touch it, as he had the other night in the courtyard, he could convince it to attack the ships up there. Or somehow help the mercenary ship that had crashed, the mercenary ship that held their captain and Jak's medallion. Unfortunately, he didn't see it in the sky, not from the portal's perspective. Maybe it was too damaged and hadn't been able to get off that peninsula.

Someone gripped Jak's shoulder, shaking him until the vision snapped, and he found himself staring at the window again, the curtains now open. His mother stood beside him, her brow creased with worry.

"Are you here with me?" she whispered as another boom thundered through the library. Something snapped. A door hinge?

"Yeah, sorry. I, uh, got a message from the portal."

She stared at him as if he'd failed his favorite cartography class. "It... spoke to you?"

"It shared a vision. I think if I could get to it, I could convince it to help."

"Help how?"

Good question, since he hadn't seen the ship the mercenaries wanted to get the portal on. But maybe one of their ally ships would work. That wouldn't get Jak back his medallion, but at least they could escape the city under siege. But to what end? Whatever ship got the portal would be chased by Uthari's remaining forces. Malek himself would personally come for it; Jak was sure of it.

"It'll defend itself," he said when Mother squeezed his shoulder again. "Like before, remember?"

"You think you can get those ships to throw mittens down on it?"

"No, but they're attacking each other right above it, and there's shooting going on all around. If we could get out into the courtyard, and I could touch it, maybe I could convince it that it's in danger, and it would take action."

"Get out into the courtyard with a battle going on all around? We'd be better off staying in the library." Despite the words, Mother unlatched the window and pushed it open, so she could lean out and take a look.

Jak's fingers twitched toward her as he envisioned some stray charge blowing her head off. But the fighting wasn't taking place on this side of the castle. Other than a few flashes of light off to the side, they couldn't see much, except for the city wall. There was a roof two stories below and a gap of ten feet between its wall and the castle wall. They might be able to run through that alley and find a way to the courtyard.

Bam!

"It's about to give," one of the mercenaries said. "Do we try the windows?"

Mother leaned back in and called to them. "There's a big battle going on at the courtyard."

"We'll make it bigger then," Sorath said grimly.

But before the mercenaries could charge back to the windows to join them, a final bam sounded, flinging the doors open with a crash. Explosives detonated and magelocks blasted. Men and women shouted, and someone cried out in pain.

From their spot, Jak and Mother couldn't see the battle. She hunkered down, holding a finger to her lips. But Jak peered out the window again, thinking they would be better off sneaking to the courtyard. They wouldn't need to run all the way out into it, not until things quieted down, but—

He jerked back as the black hull of a mageship flew past only ten yards away. Its belly skimmed just above the castle wall. This close, someone on the deck could easily glance in the library window.

Jak squatted low next to Mother, only his eyes above the sill. Uthari must have called more of his people in to help with the battle over the courtyard.

He could see up to the railing, but nobody stood within view. The crew was probably focused ahead, toward the other ships. The vessel passed by as weapons fire and sword clashes filled the library. Jak started to rise, but a second black mageship came right behind the first. He squatted back down so quickly his butt hit the floor.

Its hull was burned and peppered from cannonballs and magical attacks, revealing the wood beneath the paint. A gaping hole showed the inner workings of the craft, including a faint glow from the magical engine that powered it. Mages stood at the railing, their arms raised or weapons in hand, their determined faces pointed toward the courtyard.

Jak sucked in a startled breath as a familiar face came into view. Malek.

His clothing was ripped and singed, and blood that might have been his or some enemy's was dried on his jaw. He carried his blazing sword, the blade resting on his shoulder as he waited patiently to put it to use.

The urge to belly crawl away from the window filled Jak, but he dared not move. Unfortunately, the crack of a weapon firing in the library nearby drew Malek's attention to the open window. His gaze locked on to Jak and Mother.

Jak swallowed, afraid he would lash out with his power, that he would be furious about their escape attempt and everything that was happening tonight. Malek's angular face gave away nothing of his thoughts.

The mageship continued flying past, opening fire on another vessel that had to be coming in over the main part of the castle.

Malek faced forward again and strode out of view. Jak doubted that meant they were safe, just that Malek would deal with them later.

"I don't know whether to feel relieved or distressed that he's still alive," Mother murmured.

"I think the probability of success for the mercenaries' mission just got that much more improbable."

After the ships had passed, Mother leaned out the window again, peering upward instead of down. She leaned farther out, so far that Jak grabbed her arm, afraid she would fall. Especially when a thunderous boom came from the entrance to the library, followed by a cacophonous rockfall—a *ceiling* fall. Wood shattered as more bookcases toppled, and magelocks fired amid the slabs of ceiling tumbling down. So much dust clouded the air that it traveled all the way under the mezzanine to their window.

Mother barely seemed to notice. "There's a ship up there. *Way* up there."

"There are ships all over the place." Jak eyed the hazy aisle behind them warily. If the mercenaries had been overrun, they would have company soon. The shouts that trickled back were muted, and he couldn't tell which side was voicing them.

"Ships with huge holes in the hull leaking black smoke?" Mother asked.

Jak frowned and leaned out beside her, craning his neck to peer past the eaves of the library. The ship was so far up that he could barely see it through the hazy cloud cover, but... "That does look like the same hole that was in the crashed ship. And the hull is the right color."

"If those are our mercenaries, your medallion should be up there. And maybe a way for us to get out of this."

"I need to get to the courtyard so I can try communicating with the portal, not into a ship a hundred feet above us."

"It's fifty, sixty at most, and I'm not letting you run out into the middle of a battle to try talking to an ancient artifact."

"I wasn't going to *talk* to it. I was going to communicate telepathically with it."

"That's not any less strange. Listen, Jak. There's no way *we're* going to get out of here with that portal, and I'm skeptical any mercenaries are either. But if we can escape with our lives and the medallion, that'll be enough, at least for today. Let me have one of the magelocks." She plucked the spare pistol from his belt. "I'm going to try to get their attention. Maybe they'll come down and get us."

"Oh, sure. We're as priceless and valuable as the portal. They'll be sure to risk their ship and themselves to come down."

"If the mercenary commander is up there, she'll recognize us —and our value." Mother pointed the magelock at the dark sky and fired so that its bright blue charge soared upward and past the railing of the mageship.

"Let's hope the commander of every other mageship out there doesn't recognize our value," Jak said, "and come kidnap us for it."

Admittedly, the library window was no longer in view of the other ships—they'd all flown past to join in the battle over the courtyard. Still, they might see that shot as the signal it was and come investigate.

Mother waved upward—was someone looking down?—and fired again.

Jak rubbed his face. "They're going to think you're firing on them, not signaling them."

He envisioned cannonballs raining down onto the roof of the library—or mage fireballs.

Someone thundered into the aisle behind them, and Jak spun, pulling out the other pistol. But it was Colonel Sorath.

"Is someone shooting at you?" he asked as he raced toward them, the other mercenaries pounding after him.

Only then did Jak realize the sounds of battle near the doors had fallen silent. "Did you beat all of them?"

He'd envisioned hordes of mages flowing in after they bashed down the door.

"They're temporarily delayed."

A groan came from the entrance.

"Under a pile of rubble," Sorath added.

Sergeant Tinder patted her ammo pouch.

"Your ship is up there." Jak pointed out the window.

"They'll want us to have the artifact ready to lift off then." Sorath leaned past Mother, taking Jak's spot, though he only glanced upward and then peered toward the courtyard. He waved for his people to follow him, then shoved the window open farther so he could climb out. "We've got to clear the way so they can fly down and get it."

"I might be able to help," Jak said.

"No," Mother said sharply, frowning at him. "We're escaping."

"Not if they don't come down to get us." Jak doubted his mother's shots to the stars would convince the crew up there that they were allies who should be given a ride.

Sorath prodded him. "How can you help, killer?"

"I've communicated with the portal before and have gotten it to defend itself. Vigorously."

"He doesn't know if he can do it again," Mother said.

"Vigorous defense?" Sergeant Tinder glanced at her comrades. "From an artifact?"

"A *dragon* artifact," Jak pointed out.

"Please." Mother gripped Sorath's arm. "You can't take my son into that battle. Malek and who knows what other zidarr are over there, along with five mageships whipping magical attacks everywhere. Not to mention the guards in the courtyard and the towers."

Sorath hesitated, then nodded. "You better stay with your mother, kid. But not in here. It's not going to be safe for long."

A gust of magical wind whistled through the library doors. Jak couldn't see the entrance, but he heard the activity there as huge pieces of rubble clunked and thudded off the pile. More mages had come to dig out their buddies.

"Definitely not safe in here," Sorath muttered. "They'll have that cleared in a minute. Everyone goes out. We'll take that alley to the courtyard."

Mother looked wistfully up at the mageship, but it had given no indication that its crew had noticed her shots.

"We'll be all right, Mother," Jak said as Tezi and several others climbed past them, out onto the roof and down the side of the building. "So long as your rappelling skills are in order."

"When I *rappel*, I usually use rope." But she climbed out the window ahead of him as more mercenaries skimmed over the edge of the roof and down to the side yard. She paused, looking hopefully up at the sky.

Jak shook his head. They weren't going to get out of here until the battle over the artifact was resolved, one way or another.

30

LIEUTENANT SASKO LOOKED OVER THE RAILING AS THE *DAUNTLESS* flew high over the city, hugging the clouds and trying to avoid notice as they navigated toward the castle. A half-dozen other ships from both sides battled below, their magical attacks and incendiary rounds lighting up the night.

Smoke still wafted from the side of the *Dauntless*. Tinder's fire had died out, but whatever she'd concocted to burn was effective, the lingering black clouds continuing to help camouflage their ship. Sasko wouldn't have believed it possible they could get this close without being fired upon, but she also hadn't known other vessels would be angling for the artifact.

"They're fighting each other," Ferroki said, coming up beside her. "One of Uthari's ships is firing on two others. I don't know why, but this would be the ideal situation for us if they weren't right above our goal."

"Descend," Stone Heart barked from the deck. He'd recovered sufficiently from his attack, though he was still limping, to stalk about and make it clear that he'd taken over the *Dauntless*.

Captain Toggs relayed the order to the helmsman and didn't question the zidarr.

Ferroki did. She stepped away from the railing to face him and asked in her quiet, nonchallenging manner, "My lord, you want us to drop down into the middle of their firefight?"

Stone Heart glowered over at her. "We're getting that portal. All of *this*—" he waved to the city, the other ships, and a gash in his temple, "—was for the portal. We've lost numerous ships. Zaruk and the others will be furious if we don't come back with it."

"I understand, my lord, and I don't disagree about our mission. I just wondered if there's a way to get it without jumping into the middle of everyone shooting at each other. If we try to lift the artifact out in front of them, won't they all attack *us*?"

"Some of those are our allies. They'll help us. And I'll handle a diversion for the rest." Stone Heart lifted his chin. "Don't worry about it, mercenary. Just shoot your magelock when ordered to do so."

"Yes, my lord." Ferroki managed to keep her tone neutral, but Sasko knew how much she hated arrogance—and tactics that a five-year-old could poke holes in.

"What happens if Malek is down there and beats the stuffing out of him again?" Sasko whispered.

Corporal Dicer ran up to them, giving the zidarr and ship's captain a wide berth. "Ma'am, someone fired two shots from below. The blasts flew past us and straight up, and the crew didn't react, but I think it may have been a signal."

Ferroki looked sharply at her. "Sorath and our team?"

"It could be, ma'am. It wasn't the flare that the colonel took, but maybe they lost that." Dicer held up a spyglass and pointed beyond the railing. "There are people down there climbing out a window and across a roof."

Ferroki grabbed the spyglass and rushed back to the railing. Sasko peered down at the castle, its large courtyards, and the cluster of ships battling each other. Fire in other parts of the city drew her eye. Several of their ally vessels were hurling flaming projectiles at structures outside of the castle walls. Targeting infrastructure and government buildings, Sasko hoped, and not the homes of innocent people. Inasmuch as she considered mages innocent people.

"That's our team," Ferroki said loudly enough for Toggs and Stone Heart to hear.

A group of ten or twelve people was climbing down the side of a large building inside the castle to a narrow side yard. Sasko spotted Tezi's blonde head standing out in the haze and darkness. One other woman with darker hair kept glancing upward.

"Is that the professor?" Sasko wondered. "Did they find her?"

"It might be." Ferroki's hand strayed toward the pocket where she'd been keeping the medallion.

Toggs and Stone Heart crowded around them at the railing, and she lowered her hand.

"They don't have the artifact yet," Toggs said. "We should wait until they put the hooks around it so we can drop rope and lift it up here."

"Hooks?" Stone Heart curled a lip. "*I* can lift it. What we need is people distracting all those who will oppose me and make the task difficult." He squinted toward one of the black-hulled ships floating over the courtyard. "Malek is down there. I can sense him. And another zidarr. Damn it."

Malek's ship was firing on two other ships as they fired back. Oddly, as Ferroki had pointed out, one of its targets also had a black hull.

"Are they firing on their own side?" Captain Toggs asked.

"It looks like it," Ferroki said. "But why? Betrayal from within?"

"This could be our opportunity to slip in." Toggs glanced at Stone Heart. Maybe he also hadn't fancied the idea of descending into the middle of a firefight.

Stone Heart gripped his chin as he stared down at Malek's ship. Scheming about how he could come out on top if they had to fight again?

"Take us down," Stone Heart said. "Not directly over the courtyard but back where the mercenary team came out of that building. By the time we're ready to make our move, maybe our enemies will all have destroyed each other."

"Hopefully not taking out our team at the same time," Ferroki murmured, her gaze toward their mercenaries.

Sorath's group had reached the ground and was advancing through the shadows toward an expansive garden along the castle wall. On the other side of it, gates led into the courtyard where the portal rested. And where dozens of lamps glowed and magical attacks blasted through the sky like fireworks. There would be no shadows to hide in down there.

Reminded that Ferroki seemed to have feelings for Sorath, Sasko patted her on the shoulder. "They've gotten this far," she said as the *Dauntless* descended, the events below coming into sharper focus. "Odds are that they can survive another twenty minutes."

"I hope so."

"I don't know who knocked out the city defense shield," Sasko said, "but it's a bit of luck that it looks like they've been able to take advantage of."

"Yes. Our employers may have an ally on the inside."

"The real challenge will come *after* we get the artifact, if we indeed manage that." Toggs mopped sweat from his brow, as if he'd been engaged in a battle himself instead of simply yelling orders at his crew. "Every ship left in their fleet will give chase."

"Yes, but there are a lot of green and blue ships among them." Ferroki pointed out a few ally vessels. "If we're blessed with the hare's luck, they'll buy us enough time to get a head start, so we can make it back to Zaruk's city. At that point, if Uthari's people follow and there's another war to fight, Zaruk and his allies will have to draw up another contract for us to sign."

"And pay us again?" Sasko smiled, though she'd had enough of this battle and would prefer to go back to simple missions down on the ground, missions that didn't pit them against mages.

"War is the best chance mercenaries get to line their coffers," Ferroki murmured. It sounded like she was quoting some old saying, but Sasko doubted that one came out of her favored fables.

"Money can only be spent by the living."

"True."

"Ah," Captain Toggs muttered, concern in that single note. He wasn't looking toward the courtyard as they continued to descend but up toward the sky.

Stone Heart peered in that direction too. Sasko didn't see anything, but the two men exchanged long looks with each other.

"What is it?" Ferroki asked.

"The city defensive shield is still down, but the one that's over the castle, the one that let all these ships get in close, including ours, is back up." Toggs pointed to the sky overhead. "We can sense it. It just re-formed up there."

"Does that mean it'll be harder to get the portal?" Sasko asked.

"It means that even if we get it, we won't be able to escape afterward. Unless someone can knock the shield out again, we're stuck in their city."

Sasko hoped for a cocky comment from Stone Heart about how he could easily knock it out, but for the first time, he looked daunted. "That's going to be problematic."

Why did Sasko have a feeling that was a huge understatement?

Jadora kept glancing up at the mercenary ship as she followed Jak and the others through the side yard, fireballs and other magical attacks casting aside shadows as they lit up the night ahead. When the vessel had started descending, her spirits had risen as she envisioned them swooping in and lowering ropes, so she and Jak could climb out of this mess and leave the battle for the mercenaries. But the vessel had stopped descending. Since it hovered more than forty feet above them, ropes wouldn't likely be lowered.

"Sir." One of the mages near Sorath held up a hand. "Wait."

Sorath, who'd led the way into every battle Jadora had witnessed, paused. "What is it?"

"I sense..." The mage looked up, not at any of the ships but toward the clouds above them.

"The castle's defensive shield is back up," one of the other mages said grimly.

"Meaning that even if we're able to get to the portal and secure it, our ship won't be able to pick us up?" Sorath asked.

"Oh, picking us up won't be the problem. But escaping afterward will be impossible." The mage pointed toward the sky. "The shield is a dome that extends from there to there and peaks right over our ship. The *Dauntless* is caught inside. All of these ships flying low over the castle are trapped."

"If they're trapped inside, they can still do damage to it and each other. Maybe they'll knock out the shield again." Sorath continued forward, as if the revelation had changed nothing. He had a mission, and he was determined to fulfill it.

The mages, who understood the defenses and the magical system more thoroughly, exchanged worried looks with each other and lingered in the back as the mercenaries stuck with Sorath. They weren't the only ones to stick with him. Jak was right at his side, even slightly ahead.

What was he *doing*? Jadora charged after him, squeezing past two mages and grabbing his shoulder.

"Let them go first," she whispered. She didn't want to *go* at all.

Jak didn't look at her. His eyes were glassy as he stared toward the courtyard. She snapped her fingers in front of his face. Was the portal putting another vision in his head? If she'd known the artifact had the power to lure her son to what might be his death, Jadora never would have dug it up.

"I have to convince it to help," Jak mumbled, pulling against her grip.

"What's it trying to convince *you* to do?" she demanded.

At first, he didn't answer, but after a pause, he said, "It's afraid."

"*Afraid?*"

"That this is the end, that the magic being thrown around will be enough to destroy it. That's why I don't think it will take much to convince it to help." Again, Jak tried to pull away and keep walking.

Jadora grabbed his other shoulder but struggled to hold him back. She almost stepped into a thorny rosebush next to a burbling stone fountain, the serenity of the garden a ridiculous contrast to the chaos of the night.

Jak didn't yank hard, but he pulled away from her with steady determination. She found herself stumbling along after him, still gripping his shoulders.

At least the mercenaries had drawn ahead, passing more fountains and trees and benches that lined the path. At the end of the garden, an open gate to the courtyard was visible. Red-uniformed guards inside launched magical attacks at the ships twenty feet above.

An explosive streaked from one of the vessels and struck a castle wall, blowing a hole that sent rubble flying all over the courtyard. Clanks and clinks sounded as several pieces hit the portal.

Maybe Jak was right; maybe it *would* defend itself. But who would it target? Every ship in the sky, including the one that was supposed to pick them up? Was an ancient artifact capable of distinguishing ally from enemy? Her stomach churned as she imagined its power destroying the mercenaries as well as Uthari's people.

Sorath continued to lead his people through the garden, the air thick with pollen knocked from flowers by the rattling of the ground, and stopped at the entrance to the courtyard. Jadora tightened her grip on Jak, trying to keep him from weaving through the group to the front again. Sorath studied the situation ahead.

The portal was in the same place as it had been before, but no fewer than forty guards stood around it, half shielding it and themselves with their magic, half flinging attacks at the intruder ships. On the walls and in the guard towers, more of Uthari's people fired cannons and magelocks. The green-hulled ships seemed to mostly be defending themselves, knocking aside the attacks targeting them and keeping the defenders distracted from the mercenary ship.

Sorath waved Tinder up to his side and pointed at her grenades.

Jak tried to walk up to join them—or walk straight out into the courtyard where he would surely be blasted down. Jadora released his shoulders and wrapped her arms around his torso, leaning back and digging in her heels. His face was slack, eyes still glazed. Even if communicating with the portal had been his idea, she didn't believe that he was acting of his own accord now.

A burst of magical power came from the deck of Malek's ship —maybe from Malek himself—and slammed into one of Zaruk's vessels. It tore away the defenses around it, leaving it open for attack from others.

"Open fire!" Malek yelled, the cry for his allies as well as the defenders below.

Tinder pointed toward the artifact and raised her eyebrows. Sorath held up a finger.

With the cacophony of noise, Jadora couldn't hear their words, but he seemed to be saying to wait. She hoped so. Maybe the two sides would blow themselves up, and their team could sneak in afterward.

She glanced at their getaway ship, still wishing it would lower a rope for her and Jak, though she wouldn't be able to convince him to climb it right now.

One of the mages tapped Sorath's shoulder and pointed behind them. More ships were flying in from the rear of the castle —more ships that had been caught inside when its defensive shield went back up. They were blue-hulled and green-hulled. More allies of the mercenaries.

"Help is coming, Jak," she whispered, shaking him, hoping to knock him out of the trance. "We may have a shot after all."

The newcomers opened fire on the back of Malek's craft. Its mages had defenses up, but with so many enemies focusing attacks on it, could the mages onboard sustain their shields? Even with Malek's help?

Jadora stared upward, strange feelings of bleakness filling her as she imagined him dying during this battle. He'd been the one to kidnap her, to start her down this awful road, but he'd also been... oddly polite to them. He'd even protected them. As strange as it seemed, she didn't want to see him die. It would doubtless be better for Jak and Jadora and their quest if he did, but she couldn't wish that end for him.

Not that it mattered. As one of the new ships joined in with the others, Malek's fate seemed inevitable. She tried to feel cheerful since it meant that she and Jak might not only escape but escape with the portal.

Then, strange streaks of red lightning came out of the castle, from a window on an upper floor. They branched and blasted into the ships of Uthari's enemies, the two over the courtyard and the others approaching. Screams came from the decks as the lightning branched and branched again to wrap around the vessels. Their shields were torn away by the raw power. It burned in the sky so brightly that Jadora had to lift her hands for protection and close her eyes. The brilliant red still flashed against her eyelids.

Even as a mundane human with no ability to sense magic, she felt the raw power. Was the portal responsible? If so, this was like nothing she'd seen it unleash before.

"Stay back," one of the mercenaries warned. "It's Uthari."

Jadora had lost her grip on Jak when she lifted her hands, and she hoped those words weren't for him. She pried her eyelids open to make sure he hadn't moved, but the brilliant lightning made it hard to see anything.

"I was afraid he'd show up." Sorath's voice was calm despite the screams coming from the ships above them, and she found that slightly reassuring.

Squinting, Jadora saw one of those ships crash into the street on the other side of the castle wall. Another careened off toward the city walls, its entire frame blackened and smoking, no sign of life on the deck.

"Jak?" she called softly, searching for him among the mercenaries, with her eyes watering. "Someone grab him, please."

Sorath swore. "He's in the courtyard."

Jadora surged toward the gate, imagining one of Uthari's bolts striking him down, killing him instantly.

Sorath caught her by the shoulders and stopped her. "Stay here. I'll get him."

As he ran into the courtyard, weapons at the ready, a shout of, "There they are!" came from behind the mercenaries.

The defenders they'd eluded in the library had caught up with them.

"Behind," Tinder barked as Uthari's lightning continued to pummel ships, razing them with power that the mages on board couldn't defend against. She threw something at the group of twenty guards running toward them—a grenade.

One of them spun a fireball into the air to intercept it. The grenade blew up between the groups, the power sending them all stumbling back.

Jadora thudded off the wall, Tinder hitting right beside her with a grunt. Something bashed against Jadora's wrist—Tinder's clunky bag of grenades. The flap hung open.

On impulse, and before the mercenary sergeant moved away, Jadora grabbed one and crept toward the courtyard. Let the others deal with the defenders. She had to get Jak—and to drag him to a safe spot and sit on him.

The mercenaries clashed with the castle defenders as she crept through the gate and into the courtyard. Several charred bodies lay dead on the ground inside. But where had Jak gone? The mages were still protecting the portal, save for four who had charged out to meet Sorath, but she didn't see Jak anywhere. She hoped he'd come to his senses and found a hiding spot.

More red lightning streaked out of Uthari's window and slammed into another ship. She swallowed, afraid he might have already struck down Jak for daring to get close to the portal. His power might have been enough to char him beyond recognition.

That thought almost paralyzed Jadora, and she scanned the bodies as she backed toward a wall out of some vague self-preservation instinct. Until she figured out where he was, she should stay out of the line of fire. She halted, remembering how they'd hidden in the opening in the center of the portal to talk. Maybe he'd somehow sneaked past the mages to climb inside it.

A shadow falling behind her made her jump. A hand landed on her shoulder, and terror lurched through her. She whirled with the grenade in her hand, her thumb on the plunger. But the hand shifted from her shoulder to her wrist with lightning speed, halting her throw.

"That's not your usual projectile," Malek said, his face almost unrecognizable through dried and fresh blood, soot, and other grime.

She gaped at him, then glanced upward at the *Star Flyer*. What was he doing down *here*?

"Keeping you from getting killed," he said, reading her mind—or her face. Exasperation was the predominate emotion on his, but surprisingly, he didn't sound angry. Didn't anything faze the man?

He pulled her back toward the wall, pressing her into the slight cover offered by a support column. "Stay."

"I came for Jak," she blurted.

"I know." Malek turned and took a step toward the portal, as if he knew exactly where Jak was, but someone else dropped down from above, as if it was perfectly normal for people to jump thirty feet and land without killing themselves.

The man—the *zidarr*—came down on the portal itself, startling the guards around it, some of whom had been busy gaping at Malek. That looked like Zaruk's Stone Heart.

He crouched on the side of the portal, sneering in Malek's direction as he drew his scimitars. His face was as grimy and bloody as Malek's, his white hair matted with sweat and soot, his dark eyes reflecting the red glint of Uthari's continuing lightning attacks.

"You've stolen something that belongs to my master," Stone Heart called, "and as I told you before, I intend to take it back."

"Let us finish what we started before you fled our last battle." Malek drew his own weapons.

"You knocked me over the side, you bastard."

"An attack that was meant to be fatal. This time, I'll drive my blade into your heart."

"You can try," Stone Heart growled.

As Malek strode toward him, a familiar hat poked up from the center of the portal, Jak's wide eyes visible between Stone Heart's legs.

"Shylezar save him," Jadora whispered, terrified.

Her fingers tightened around the grenade—Malek hadn't

taken it from her—but she couldn't throw it, not with Jak in the middle of the battlefield.

Helpless, she could only watch as Malek sprang up on the portal to join Stone Heart, their weapons clashing as they came together in a flurry of furious blows.

31

Tezi used one of the rosebushes in the garden for cover as the defenders who'd chased them from the library encroached. Some hurled magical attacks, which the mages on Sorath's team deflected, and others skulked through the shrubs, fountains, and statues to get closer.

Aware that the rosebush wouldn't stop bullets or magical blasts, Tezi tried to avoid notice as she searched for a target that might not have his or her guard up. But everything the mercenaries threw at the other party bounced off. The defenders had their magical shields up as they strode forward, trying to push the mercenaries through the gateway and into the courtyard—where they would be in the middle of the chaos of the other battle.

Sergeant Tinder threw a grenade, not straight at their attackers but above them, hoping it would fly *over* their defenses. Tezi watched it, worried it would tumble back toward them. But the lob carried it over the shield in front of the mages, and one of them had to rush to form something new over their heads. It exploded ten feet above them. Though they'd gotten their defenses shifted in time to prevent anyone being harmed, they were startled by the close call.

One of the mercenaries took that moment to pepper the ground in front of them with some of Sorath's exploding spheres. That rattled them further, especially when bushes and a stone bench blew up all around them.

Tezi aimed at a mage on the end, one who didn't look like he was concentrating effectively to defend himself. Her shot took him in the shoulder, and he flew back.

"Their defenses are down," one of the mercenaries barked. "Fire."

A magical blast knocked back the defenders as several charges flew in, pegging them in the chests. Tinder hurled another grenade, this time straight at the group, but someone in the back had recovered enough to spread a barrier in front of his people.

The grenade bounced back toward the mercenaries without detonating. Tinder swore and lunged for it, but one of the mages wrapped her in a blanket of power, holding her fast.

Terrified, Tezi dove in from the rosebushes. She caught the grenade before it hit the ground, cradling it gently so it wouldn't blow, and threw it into the air over the garden wall. It exploded ten feet up, taking out two guards who'd been running along the wall toward their battle.

Chunks of the stone wall flew, several smacking her, one in the side of the head and one hard enough to send her rolling into the rosebushes. Thorns clawed at her face and hands, and warm blood dripped down the side of her cheek.

Before she could scramble to her feet, mages from her team ran past her, with several mercenaries right behind them. Someone had forced down the defenders' barrier again, and the two groups came together, weapon to weapon, fist to fist.

As Tezi rose, wobbly after the strike to the head, someone reached out and grabbed her, helping her up.

"Good thinking, Rookie," Tinder said and slapped her on the back. "We might just let you stick around."

A quick, "Thanks," was all Tezi managed before Tinder charged off to join the others in the fray.

Tezi patted around, found her magelock, and rushed off to help. She had no idea if they would survive the next ten minutes, but at least she'd gotten praise from Tinder.

Jak came fully back to his senses in the worst spot imaginable. He crouched in the center of the portal, keeping his head below the surface, as Malek and Stone Heart battled scant feet away. Metal rang out, the noise deafening this close, and their boots moved in a blur as they lunged and retreated, parrying, thrusting, and slashing, the entire sword fight playing out on the side of the portal.

They knew Jak was there—both men had glanced down at him—but they were too busy with each other to attack him or spare him another glance. He still had a couple of charges in his magelock and thought about trying to shoot one of the zidarr, but he didn't even know which one he would target. They were *both* enemies, both wanting the portal and to keep Jak and his mother against their wishes. He vaguely wanted Malek to win, but it would be best for him if they killed each other. Not that he and his mother would have freedom even then.

Red blasts of lightning continued to fly from an upper window, Uthari's dark silhouette just visible in a dim room. He'd taken down one of the black mageships—the one whose crew had seemed to be working against his people—and three of his enemies' ships. Jak had never seen such power in his life or imagined it was possible.

A streak of lightning shot toward the most distant green vessel —the mercenary ship that had crashed on the lawn. The ship that was supposed to take the artifact and get it out of here. The ship that held the mercenary captain who had Jak's medallion.

Damn it. If that one went down...

Jak gripped the hilt of his magelock, tempted to shoot Uthari. Would it work? If the wizard was busy attacking, maybe there weren't any defenses protecting him. But he was up in his suite. Chances were some artifact there would protect him even if he wasn't consciously thinking about defense.

Besides, Jak would only get one shot before the mages guarding the portal spotted and shot *him*. There were dozens of them, though they'd backed away slightly to ensure they didn't lose their heads to a stray sword swipe from the powerful zidarr. He had no idea how he'd gotten past them. The last thing he remembered was his mother gripping his shoulder, and then he'd woken, as if from a dream, here in the middle of the portal.

The *portal*, he realized, staring at the blue-black dragon steel in front of him. It had done it—taken control of him.

Later, he would find that alarming, but now, he remembered his original intent and pressed his palm against its cool metal.

A low sword slash whizzed near his ear, and he jammed his hat lower on his head and sank to his knees, huddling down as much as he could with his hand still on the portal. As the men battled above him, flecks of blood and sweat spattering the back of his neck, Jak did his best to focus on communicating with it. Before, he'd tricked it, but he didn't want to trick it again. Something told him the portal was intelligent enough to come to resent that.

We're stuck in this place together, he told it, sharing an image of him and his mother locked in the cell on Malek's ship even as the portal had been imprisoned on its deck. *I know you've only acted to defend yourself before, but won't you help us to escape? We'll take you with us.*

He formed the imagery of the jungle, the pool, and the waterfall in his mind, trying to replicate what it had shared with him in that dream.

We'll take you back to that place, to the pool and the waterfall where you were set up before. Is that where you belong? Where you need to be placed for dragons to use you again? Afraid the ancient artifact didn't understand his language, Jak tried to convey his meaning with images as well as words. He had no idea how he would convince the mercenaries and whoever commanded their ship—one of Vorsha's—to fly off to Zewnath in the Southern Hemisphere instead of back to Zaruk's city, but he would do his best.

Screams came from above, breaking Jak's concentration. A blast of red lightning struck someone on the deck of the mercenary ship, and the charred body flew all the way to the far side and over the railing. It tumbled down to splat sickeningly on the castle wall.

Stop Uthari, he pleaded silently to the portal, realizing the king was the greatest threat here now. Stone Heart and Malek would also do their best to keep Jak from getting the portal, but for the moment, they were busy with each other.

A grunt of pain came from above, followed by the clatter of a sword hitting dragon steel and bouncing to the ground.

Jak wanted to ignore the battle above him and focus his efforts on the portal, but he couldn't keep from lifting his head enough to see who'd been hurt. Stone Heart stumbled back, gripping a gash in his chest, blood streaming through his fingers. He sneered at Malek, who advanced with deadly intent, and kept his other scimitar up.

The lightning halted abruptly, the sky going dark.

Jak peered up at Uthari, and his entire body clenched with fear. The wizard was looking straight at him. He must have spotted Jak for the first time, maybe even realized what he was trying to do. Surely, Uthari could read his mind as easily as Malek could.

Uthari lifted his palm, his eyes narrowing as he focused on Jak.

Seeing his death in those eyes, Jak silently cried, *Help me!* to the portal. *Please.* He envisioned it lashing out at Uthari to protect Jak.

Red lightning sprang from Uthari's palm. Jak ducked low, though he was certain it would arc and have no trouble reaching him. But the portal responded with an attack of its own, and blue lightning streaked out from its surface. Blue and red met, sizzling and writhing angrily in the sky ten feet above the portal, as if fighting their own battle.

Meanwhile, Malek paid no attention. He lunged in with his main-gauche, knocking Stone Heart's scimitar aside, then followed up with his long sword. The glowing blade swept through the air as red and blue lightning danced overhead, casting his face in a demonic light. As Malek's magical blade cut through Stone Heart's neck, severing his head, the blue lightning from the portal advanced across the sky, driving the red back.

Uthari lurched back from his window, and the red lightning disappeared completely. The blue flowed through the window, and a startled cry came from the king's suite. More lightning sprang from the portal, striking guards all across the courtyard with enough power to throw them twenty feet into the walls.

Malek must have realized he was in danger for he sprang away from the portal. But lightning struck him, wrapping all around his body as pure power flung him through the air. He bounced off a wall and landed on his back, not moving.

"Don't hit my mother," Jak blurted, spotting her still crouching by a column with a grenade in hand.

The portal blew more defenders off the castle wall as lightning branched along it and into the guard towers. Jak had no idea if it was killing everyone or just knocking them down, but he worried about what he'd unleashed.

Then the portal shifted, startling him. It wobbled on the court-yard ground, and it took him a moment to realize what was happening. A dozen mages were levitating it into the air. They were up on the mercenary ship, all lined up at the railing, their faces tight with concentration. The mercenaries on deck were throwing ropes over the side to their teammates in the courtyard and garden. Jak spotted Tezi's blonde hair before the portal rose higher, blocking his view.

Realizing he was about to be left behind, he sprang up, catching the portal and scrambled onto the side.

"Mother," he yelled, waving for her to join him.

But before she'd taken a step, Sorath rushed to the wall and grabbed her, somehow hoisting her over his shoulder with his pickaxe arm. He ran back across the courtyard and sprang, catching one of four ropes dangling down. Beside him, more mercenaries climbed up the others. He merely held on, concentrating on keeping his grip on Mother.

As the portal kept rising, Jak sprawled on his stomach. It wobbled and tilted, the mages' grip on it tenuous.

Thankfully, nobody fired at him. The portal had knocked down everyone left who might have done so. Fresh smoke wafted from the mercenary ship, and there were so many holes in its hull that it would have sunk if it had been in the ocean. Would it truly carry them out of here?

A thought jolted Jak. What about the defensive shield protecting the castle? They would all be stuck here if that was still in place.

He flattened his hand against the portal, groping for a way to ask if it could knock out the defenses so they could escape. An image came to him of a purple crystal lying on a carpet inside the king's suite, not far from Uthari himself, who was groaning as he clutched his chest. The top of the crystal had been blasted off, shards littering the floor around it, and smoke trickling upward.

"Was that the device that kept the shield up?" he asked. "Did you do that?"

A faintly smug feeling emanated from the portal.

"Uh, good work." Jak patted it, having no idea if it would appreciate it or not. All he knew was that it would be wise to stay on its good side.

They came even with the railing of the ship, then rose above it as the mages directed the portal toward the deck.

Jak peered over the side and down to the courtyard. A couple of the guards were moving, grabbing their chests and groaning the way Uthari had been. Maybe the portal hadn't struck to kill. Normally, that would have filled Jak with relief, but then he focused on Malek. He lay on his back where he'd landed, his arms and legs wide, completely still... until his eyes popped open.

Jak gulped, worried they would have to deal with him again. As powerful as Malek was, they might have to deal with him right away if they didn't get out of the city quickly.

He scrambled off the portal, his legs wobbly, as it came down on the deck. Sorath made it to the railing, pushing Jak's mother over before him. She thanked him, then ran to hug Jak. He hugged her back, relieved she hadn't been killed because he'd let himself be taken over by an artifact.

"That's everyone," the mercenary captain—Ferroki?— called, helping Tezi over the railing. "Fly us out of here."

"Get us out of here, Nobber," someone else barked, an older man wearing one of Vorsha's green uniforms and a lot of rank. The captain of the ship.

Mother looked over at him, and Jak could guess her thoughts, that if they couldn't figure out how to sway the man or take over the ship, they and the portal would end up prisoners in another king's castle.

"Malek's still alive," he whispered to her. "Should we ask someone to..." He couldn't finish the thought. If anybody was ever going to be able to kill Malek—and ensure he couldn't give chase —now would be the time.

Jak peered over the side. Their ship was gaining altitude and veering away from the castle and toward the city wall, but he could still see the courtyard. Malek had rolled onto his elbow and with a shaky hand was reaching for his fallen weapons. He wasn't likely defending himself—a charge from a magelock might take him out.

Mother slumped against the railing beside him, following his gaze. "I don't think we can. He was trying to protect us."

"For his master, not because he cares about us. And he'll follow us. He'll—"

Jak broke off, for Malek had found his feet and drawn a magelock. He pointed it at their ship—looking for a target on the deck. The ship's captain? The mercenary leader? Jak and Mother? They were sailing away, but they were still within range, still close enough for him to shoot. Jak and Mother were the only ones at the railing, the only ones he could see from down there.

Jak jerked back, flinging himself to the deck. To his horror, Mother didn't move. She just stared down at Malek. Jak lunged back to his feet and grabbed her, pulling her back from the railing, but not before he saw Malek lowering the magelock.

He could have fired but hadn't.

"How did you know?" Jak asked, knowing Mother had been certain.

"He's been protecting us all along."

"Not for any altruistic reasons."

She shrugged and sank down to the deck. "It doesn't matter."

"He'll come after us. I'm pretty sure Uthari isn't dead either."

"Let's worry about one problem at a time." She looked toward the ship's captain, who stood with Sorath and Captain Ferroki, studying their prize as the vessel sailed over the city walls and into the cloudy night sky beyond, a few of their ally ships staying behind to lay down fire to distract the remaining defenders. "First, we have to convince them to take us to Zewnath."

"I know. The mercenaries outnumber the crew—it looks like

by a lot—but I doubt they're going to turn on their employers for no reason. Even if that wasn't bad for their business, who would dare cross a king? Besides, it's not like we have the money to outbid Zaruk and hire them away." Jak patted his pockets, as if some priceless ancient coins might be lurking in them. He still had his lucky compass and a few writing utensils, but that was it.

"No, and I agree that they wouldn't cross a king, even if they knew us and cared enough to want to help us. I do wonder if they might be convinced if they knew what we hoped to do. The colonel—Sorath—seemed intrigued by the idea when I alluded to it." Mother patted her own pockets, no doubt also looking for coins. But what she pulled out was the vial containing the smudgy substance she'd sampled in the tunnels, along with a few small vials of samples that she'd somehow managed to keep since the Dragon Perch Islands. Another pocket contained Father's journal and *The Mind Way*.

Jak would have laughed at the size and number of her pockets if he hadn't been so exhausted. "I'm glad you have that." He pointed to Father's journal. "If we'd left it behind, Malek might have been able to figure out where we want to take the portal."

"He read it thoroughly. He might already have pieced it together."

"Even we didn't know until we saw the star chart."

"True," Mother said, "but it's possible it could have been sending *him* visions too."

"Let's hope it has better taste than to make friends with the enemy."

Captain Ferroki walked toward them, and they fell silent.

"We're out of weapons range of the city, for what it's worth. I'm sure Uthari will send pursuit if he survived. Is there any chance he didn't?" Ferroki lifted her eyebrows, asking Jak directly. Maybe she'd seen him hunkered in the middle of the portal and guessed that he'd been responsible.

"I think he and Malek were injured but are alive." Jak glanced at the portal but didn't explain further.

Ferroki reached into one of her own pockets and withdrew the familiar medallion. She handed it to Mother, the ornament looking no worse for the wear.

"Thank you," Mother said. "I'm sorry we don't have any money to pay you for keeping it for us. We've been detained until recently."

Ferroki snorted softly. "I can imagine. We didn't negotiate a contract. There's no need for payment."

She started to turn away, but Mother stopped her with a lifted hand. "Wait."

"Yes?"

"Is there any chance..." Mother looked at Ferroki but paused as Sorath walked up to stand at the captain's side. Mother pushed herself to her feet, faced them, and took a deep breath. "Is there any chance you'd be willing to convince the captain of this ship to take the artifact to a different location?" She didn't tell them where, but she quietly summed up what they believed it could do if they took it to the right location and activated it—and also what that could mean for mankind. Terrene mankind.

Sorath's eyes grew wistful as she spoke of the powerful dragons possibly being talked into an alliance with mankind, one that could end the rule of their wizard overlords. Then people would be free from oppression, free to carve out their own destinies. Ferroki seemed more skeptical as she listened, but she didn't interrupt and let Mother finish.

Sorath was the one to answer. "We signed a contract to work for Zaruk and his allies and return the artifact to them. To do anything else would be breaking our contract and going back on our word. If we did that as mercenaries, we could never find work again." Interestingly, he didn't say anything about being afraid of being hunted down by angry kings, but Jak imagined that also figured into the equation. "Besides," Sorath continued, "we aren't in command of the ship and have no say in where it goes." He tilted his head toward the captain of the vessel, the man still studying the portal. "That is Captain Toggs."

"Where did the lightning shoot out of?" Toggs was asking one of his mages. "That was *amazing*. It doesn't even look like a weapon."

Maybe it was Jak's imagination, but there seemed to be some significance in Sorath's eyes when he looked toward the ship's captain and back again. Ferroki's eyebrows rose, but she said nothing, and they walked away together.

"Is it just me," Mother murmured, "or were they implying that if we convinced the *captain* to turn his ship to the south, they wouldn't stand in the way?"

"I'm not sure that expression said all that, but it definitely sounds like the captain is the one we need to deal with for matters related to the ship's direction."

"Do you think you can convince the portal to help you sway him?" she asked curiously.

Jak hesitated. *Could* he? No, probably not. The captain was studying it from several feet away and hadn't so much as touched a finger to it since his people landed it on the deck. None of the crew had. They must have all seen what it was capable of.

"I don't think so," Jak said slowly, though it seemed like he should be able to find a way. The portal *wanted* to go home; he was certain of that. "It didn't do anything during the battle until Uthari decided to fry me. I'd spent several minutes before that trying to convince it to lash out."

Mother shook her head, moisture glistening in her eyes. "In that moment, I thought I was going to lose you. I'm relieved but surprised it protected you."

"Me too."

"Maybe we need to convince the captain to attack you, ideally while you're sitting in the middle of the portal."

"Funny, Mother."

"You could insult his shoes. Or perhaps the size of his drawing utensil."

"Thanks so much for these brilliant ideas."

She smiled, then lifted a finger. "Are you willing to bluff?"

"I..." Right away, Jak realized what she was asking. "I could try."

"You can do it. Just think ferocious thoughts."

"You know that's not natural for me."

"Imagine he dumped an ink pot on the map you spent a hundred hours working on for your end-of-year project."

"All right, that's got me suitably riled."

"Good. Try to make yourself believe the bluff, in case he's talented enough to read minds."

"I'll try." Jak removed his hat, the air cool against his damp hair, and held out his hand. It might be best to return the medallion to the spot where it had gone unnoticed for years, nobody guessing that it was the key to operating a powerful artifact.

Mother handed it to him, and he smiled, pleased that she trusted him with it. But then, she always had. She'd known long before he had that it held some significance.

After returning the medallion to its place and the hat to his head, Jak pulled the brim low, hoping it shadowed his eyes and made him look ferocious—or at least older than his age. He pushed himself to his feet, strode to the portal, and hopped up on it. Facing the captain from the higher ground seemed wise, especially since he looked like an old grump.

"I appreciate you helping us escape from the vile clutches of King Uthari," Jak said, deciding it couldn't hurt to butter up the officer before threatening him. "And I'm delighted that our portal is now aboard a ship sailing quickly away from his city."

"*Our* portal?" Captain Toggs asked, then looked at Ferroki and Sorath. "Who is this kid?"

"Your guests are Professor Freedar," Sorath said, "and, Jak, wasn't it?"

"Yes," Jak said. "Jak Freedar, cartographer extraordinaire."

"Jak," Sorath said without commenting on the rest, "and Professor Freedar, this is Captain Toggs, leader of this ship and crew."

"And transporter of this artifact back to its rightful owner," Toggs growled, "King Zaruk."

"We're archaeologists." Jak waved at Mother, who'd come over to support him in this. Too bad she hadn't had time to replenish her vials with some acid concocted from whatever chemicals one could find aboard a mageship. "We're the ones who dug up the artifact. Our team had signed documents from Perchver University and Zaruk's personally appointed magistrate giving us permission to search for and excavate any artifacts discovered on the Dragon Perch Islands." True, though he had no idea where those documents were now. Probably incinerated by lava flows. "Though we've been researching the artifact extensively for years, we didn't realize until recently that it's sentient and has desires."

"It has desires," Toggs said in a flat tone.

"Indeed. After being buried for millennia, it wishes to be returned home." Jak didn't give the spiel about how it could perhaps be used to gain allies against the mages, since he was addressing a mage. All the captain needed to know was that the portal wanted to take a trip to the Southern Hemisphere—and would object to anyone trying to take it somewhere else. "It has no desire to be held by King Zaruk or any other king."

"Darn."

"Since I've been elected to speak on its behalf, I must request that you change course for the Southern Hemisphere. The continent of Zewnath specifically." Jak wished he knew *where* on that continent the pool and waterfall were, especially since it was five million square miles in area and Malek was sure to come looking for them soon.

"Oh, sure. We'll set course right now."

"Excellent."

"Sit down, kid, before I throw you overboard. It's a *long* drop to the ground from here."

"Uh, sir." One of the crewmen stepped forward, lifting a finger. "That artifact is what roasted Uthari's people with lightning."

"I have eyes," Toggs said. "I'm aware of that."

"That kid was touching it. I think maybe he was responsible."

"Don't be stupid."

"I wasn't responsible for the lightning," Jak said. "The artifact was. I only encouraged it."

"Uh huh."

This bluff wasn't going well. Jak wished Toggs were as impressionable as the mage standing to his side.

"As I said," he pushed on, hoping the captain was bluffing about throwing him overboard, "I am grateful to you and these fine mercenaries, so I have no wish to threaten you, but I must insist—the *artifact* insists—that you change course."

To his surprise, the portal pulsed blue, the way it had the night it had shared that dream—that memory—with Jak.

Toggs stumbled back, the sarcastic sneer leaving his face.

"I don't think he's joking, sir," the crewman said. "I think he can control it."

"How? He's just a kid."

"Jak has been studying the portal for more than five years," Mother said. "He's young, but he *is* an expert, and when we were locked up in Uthari's castle, he had time to establish a rapport with it."

"A rapport?" Toggs protested. "It's a piece of metal."

The portal pulsed blue again. Somehow, that pulse managed

to convey indignation. A faint hum of energy ran through it, tickling the bottoms of Jak's feet. He didn't know what that felt like to a trained magic user, but it must have been something impressive, for the eyebrows of every mage on the deck flew upward, and they backed farther from the portal, Toggs included.

His face turned ashen. Maybe the portal had conveyed some additional message to him.

"It was crafted long ago by dragons," Jak said. "I assure you, it's far more than a piece of metal. Your master wouldn't want it if it were not very special. And very powerful."

Another pulse.

"Shit." Toggs looked around at his crewmen for help, but they all avoided his eyes. When he looked toward Sorath and Ferroki, they didn't break eye contact, but they also didn't offer any assistance. "Are you going to let them bully me?" Toggs demanded.

"I'm not doing anything to piss off that ring," Sorath said.

Ferroki nodded in agreement.

Toggs swore again, then raised his voice and yelled through the hatchway into navigation. "Set a course for Zewnath, Nobber."

"Uh, yes, sir. Which port?"

Toggs gave Jak a scathing look, but all he said was, "Which port? It's a big continent."

That was, of course, the problem. Jak closed his eyes, envisioning some of the maps that he'd studied, and tried to guess where that pool might be. Unfortunately, great swaths of the landmass were full of mountains and lush green vegetation, so that alone didn't help to narrow things down. And those stars in the star chart would be visible from anywhere on the continent.

"Port Toh-drom," he said, opting for something central and hoping they could find a guide in the most populous city who might have been to that pool before.

"Right." Grumbling, Toggs walked into navigation and relayed the destination.

A faint hum went through the ship, and it hiccupped as it shifted course. Jak hoped the damaged craft could *get* them all the way to the Southern Hemisphere.

"You better watch your back, killer," Sorath warned. "You've made an enemy today."

"I doubt it'll be the last." Jak decided that he would sleep on deck, maybe even in the center of the portal, and pray that it protected him if Toggs sent someone after him with a knife.

"Probably not."

EPILOGUE

MALEK'S ENTIRE BODY ACHED, BUT NOTHING STUNG SO MUCH AS HIS chest. It felt like the blast from the portal had seared his very heart. He was certain it had stopped beating as the raw power had blown him across the courtyard and only resumed again when he'd thumped down onto the courtyard ground, startling it back into its rhythm.

Others who had been struck by the power of the portal hadn't been so lucky. Before leaving the courtyard to find Uthari, he'd checked on the other castle guards and found many of them dead. Later, Malek would see a healer, but others needed their services far more than he.

His only satisfaction, after watching that smoking wreck of a ship escape with the artifact, had been seeing Stone Heart's decapitated head and lifeless body on the ground. If Zaruk's zidarr hadn't been sent along to harry Malek, the archaeologists never would have gotten away. The artifact would still be in the courtyard, and the castle would still be protected by its magical shield. Probably. The boy Jak being able to call upon the portal's power to channel as a weapon had been unexpected and—from what

Malek had read of Freedar's notes—unprecedented. Malek couldn't have anticipated that.

Not that he would utter these excuses to Uthari. He would give no excuses, only accept whatever punishment his liege deemed necessary for this disgraceful failure.

He still didn't know why one of their own ships had slunk in and attempted to get the artifact for itself, but that craft and its treasonous crew were now wrecked, smoldering in a street outside the castle. Those who survived would be questioned later, if not by Malek, then by Uthari himself.

Malek, having been summoned by his liege, stepped into the windowless dungeon in the center of the castle. Little damage had been done to this part of the compound, and mage lights glowed from the walls. A strong barrier stretched across a cell in the back, the hum of its significant power crackling against Malek's nerves.

Uthari stood in front of the cell, leaning subtly on a staff. The chest of his tunic was charred, the same as Malek's own shirt; he'd also taken a lightning bolt to the heart and was also lucky to be alive.

Inside the cell, Yidar rested on his knees, his hands bound behind his back, his chin to his chest as he avoided looking at Uthari. The cuffs that restrained him were made from dragon steel —wherever had Uthari found them? It took a great deal of power to hold a zidarr, but Uthari had clearly planned long ago for the eventuality that it might be necessary. Malek made a mental note of that.

"Have you questioned him?" Malek asked, walking up.

"Not with force." Uthari spoke calmly, no hint of the frustration and anger he must feel in his voice.

Malek expected punishment for his failures, and doubtless a lecture about showing too much lenience to their archaeologists, but Uthari would give both in private, not in front of witnesses. That was not his way. He never embarrassed his zidarr.

"You will kill me." Yidar lifted his head, blood from cuts dried on his face and in his hair, and glared at them. "That is the punishment for a zidarr who betrays his master, is it not?" He sneered. "Why should I answer questions when you will kill me anyway?"

"Death for betrayal is in the Code," Malek said, assuming Uthari would not mind him speaking to Yidar—it was likely he'd called Malek here for the purpose of applying force. "You knew this when you turned on our liege. What prompted you to do it? Surely not money from Zaruk's spies. Was it a promise of power or a higher position if you switched loyalties to him?"

"I did not *switch loyalties*. I am *not* a traitor."

"Then how do you explain your actions?" It clicked for Malek then. The other ship. Yidar must have been the one to suborn the crew. But why? "Why did you order the *Flying Tiger* to help you attempt to steal the artifact?"

"Why did *you*—" Yidar looked at Uthari, "—order the *Star Flyer* to steal the artifact in the first place? For *power*. And to travel through a portal to a realm where dragons may still live and to obtain them as allies."

"I know why I seek the portal," Uthari said, not looking surprised by this outburst—he'd had more time to think about the betrayal and must have already realized what Yidar had done, "but I doubt our reasons are the same. What would you have done with this *power*?"

"Establish my *own* kingdom." Yidar jerked his chin up. "Be the ruler of my own city with my own human serfs to wait on me. Not to be second-rate to anyone else anymore." He glared not at Uthari but at Malek.

Malek hadn't realized he'd been such an oppressive first zidarr that Yidar had come to resent him. Was it only because he was young and ambitious? Or had Malek failed in some way? Later, when Gorsith returned from driving off the last of the attacking ships, Malek would discuss it with him.

"Ambition is understandable," Uthari said, "but to wish serfs and your own city... These are strange desires for a zidarr who was brought up from his earliest days to obey the Code, to long for nothing except to serve with honor, to admire those who live simply with few belongings."

"That is what you and all the other kings *wish* us to want, but only a fool lets himself be brainwashed by such drivel." Yidar stared at Malek again, though it appeared to be a pitying expression this time instead of a resentful one.

"To learn to desire little except to improve oneself is not an act of brainwashing; instead it grants a man power over himself and his baser instincts. What has throwing off these beliefs given you but the certainty that you require your own kingdom and servants to wipe your ass?" Malek shook his head, sharing his own expression of pity. "Allowing yourself to be moved by such desires only makes you easy to manipulate. Or, in this case, it sounds like you self-immolated without outside interference."

"Screw you, Malek, you sanctimonious ass."

Uthari lifted a finger and tilted his head toward the hallway. Malek followed him outside, the door shutting behind them so that Yidar wouldn't hear their conversation.

"It would be a shame to kill someone I've invested so many years of training into," Uthari said, "but is there any way to regain his loyalty or bring him back into the fold at this point?"

"Likely not. You would have to give him the opportunity to get what he wants."

"A kingdom? Maybe I should sic him after Zaruk and see what he could do. His reward could be Zaruk's city."

Malek snorted. "That would get him killed. Even with Stone Heart dead, Zaruk has more zidarr, and clearly, he has many allies."

"Yes, and he may soon have more allies after succeeding

today." Uthari grimaced. "Not that I intend to let him keep the portal, mind you. We *will* get it back."

Malek's chest ached, and he longed for a day of rest and recuperation, but he made himself say, "I am prepared to go after it."

Uthari rubbed his jaw thoughtfully. "I believe you and Gorsith had better stay here until we get the defenses back up and the fleet repaired. We dare not let others see our city or kingdom as weak during this time. But I am also considering how to retaliate. This cannot go without a response, or we shall also be considered weak. And then there is the need to reacquire the artifact—and our archaeologists. I am surprised they chose to flee from us and into the hands of another. Do they believe *Zaruk* will be more accommodating? He will not give them a suite. Or a zidarr to debate with." Uthari lifted his brows.

"Apparently, that wasn't as desirable an offering as one would expect."

"I told you arguing with women isn't the way to earn their trust."

"Should we cross paths again, I will attempt a different tactic with her." Malek remembered meeting Professor Jadora's gaze as she flew away on that wreck of a ship. He'd been looking for someone to shoot, even though it would have been a futile gesture born out of the frustration that he'd failed and been too weak to summon the magic necessary to drive the ship back to the castle. She'd had that same wary expression she'd had every time he'd been around her. Granted, he'd been pointing a weapon at her, but he suspected he had failed to win any sort of trust from her. Perhaps if they had not been pitted as enemies from the beginning...

Malek shook his head. For the first time, a request of Uthari's had been beyond his abilities to deliver.

"Good," Uthari said. "We *will* get her back and the artifact as well. I have not accomplished all I've accomplished in life by letting setbacks and failures stop me. We lost today only because unforeseen events conspired to complicate the city's defenses." He glanced toward the door to Yidar's cell, but he was probably thinking more of the attack by the artifact than his zidarr's betrayal.

Malek rubbed his chest. *He* was certainly thinking of that.

"I believe I will send Yidar after the artifact," Uthari mused.

An objection sprang to mind, born by a fear that Yidar would hurt Professor Freedar—and possibly kill her son, because of his potential with magic—but Malek halted the protest before it escaped. It wasn't his place to question his liege, especially when Uthari had been surprisingly patient with him over the day's failures.

He kept himself to asking a simple, "Oh?"

"Having him out of the city will keep him from scheming up any new ways to flummox me, and he may succeed where you did not." Uthari's eyebrow twitched at this first reference to Malek's failure. "I understand from the female servants that he's considered quite handsome. Perhaps he will earn the archaeologist's trust where you were unable to."

"They do not think I'm handsome?"

"Aloof is the term I hear used most often. But that is as it should be. A zidarr should not be so easily *available*."

Malek rubbed his chest again, though he was tempted to rub his head at this conversation. The Code forbade marriage and children, so except for rare dalliances, he'd always kept his distance from women. The thought of needing to win the regard of one—or at least the *trust* of one—for Uthari still boggled his mind, and he kept thinking his liege would say that was some kind of joke. He understood the professor's value and how useful she could be in dealing with the artifact —and the boy could be equally useful since he'd figured out how to draw upon its magic—but imagining Malek could bring them to his side by inspiring feelings of loyalty seemed ludicrous.

"I do not believe handsomeness was the problem," Malek said, attempting to consider the situation logically. "We kidnapped her. To win her trust in such a situation was... a difficult task."

"We will see if Yidar can accomplish it. If he can, perhaps I will assist him in gaining a kingdom. That ought to keep him loyal—or at least disinterested in conspiring against me."

"I agree on that point, though we will have to keep a close eye on him."

"Naturally. I will mage mark him, so I know where he is, can observe him at all times, and can punish him remotely if need be."

Malek nodded. For most of their kind, a mage mark was little more than a magical beacon, calling attention to the recipient, but Uthari was far more powerful than the typical mage, and he could do things that even Malek couldn't. Monitoring Yidar would be wise. For his younger colleague's sake, Malek hoped he didn't try to betray Uthari again.

"He will get only one second chance, assuming he accepts my proposal. I will go offer it to him now." Uthari placed his hand on the door but paused to look back before pushing it open. "While we are repairing the city and rebuilding its defenses, I want you to continue researching that artifact. When we recapture it, I want to know how to use it immediately, so it is not sitting in our court-yard, tempting enemies—and supposedly loyal allies."

"Yes, Your Majesty."

"Also, find a couple of our best ships that have little damage. Yidar should have a chance at catching up with the enemy ships and acquiring the artifact. It will be much easier to recapture *before* it is protected within Zarlesh's walls."

"Yes, Your Majesty."

After Uthari left, Malek considered whether the archaeologists and the artifact were truly on their way to Zaruk's sky city. Oh, he had no doubt that the mercenaries who'd helped steal it had been given orders to bring it back, but would the professor and her son have gone willingly with them if they believed they would end up under guard in another wizard's castle?

As requested, Malek *would* do research. He had made a copy of all the notes in the late husband's journal before returning it to Freedar, and he had other resources at his disposal. But his first priority would be to learn where that ship was heading. If it was not on its way to Zaruk's city, Malek would find out. And if Yidar failed, Malek would go himself and reclaim it and the archaeologists for Uthari. To serve his master was his duty, and he would not fail again.

As the *Dauntless* flew south toward the equator, a warm breeze whispered through the cracks in the hull, stirring the muggy air in the small cabin Jadora had been given.

She slept fitfully on the hard bunk, worried about pursuit, worried about Jak, and worried about the captain imprisoning them and taking the artifact back to his master. When she wasn't doing that, she wondered if they had any chance of finding the location where the portal could be opened before all those who wanted it for themselves caught up with them. Even if they succeeded, would they find help on the other side of the portal? Or would they go through a magical gateway to a world devoid of dragons or anyone else who could help them? Species went extinct on Torvil; what if the same had happened to the dragons on their home world? What if that was the reason they had never returned?

As she mulled, Jadora started to feel that she wasn't alone. She peered around the dark cabin, her mind conjuring visions of assassins springing out to kill her. She slid her fingers under the ratty pillow, wrapping them around vials. Though the ship's stores had been sparsely supplied, she'd found a few chemicals she could turn into weapons.

Seconds passed, and no assassins sprang for her throat, but she couldn't shake the feeling that she wasn't alone. Could mages turn invisible?

With her free hand, she reached for a lantern mounted to the wall beside the bed. It was powered by magic rather than flame, and the touch of a finger caused it to brighten enough to make out the sparse furnishings built into the little cabin. And to see a man in the shadowy corner beside the door.

She almost screamed. She *did* pull out the vials.

He gazed at her blandly, not reacting to the threat—or maybe not perceiving them as a threat. No, she realized numbly. It was Malek. He knew all about her vials by now.

"How did you *get* here?" Jadora lifted her hand to throw, her fingers shaking as her heart pounded so hard she felt it.

"I am zidarr," he said simply, as if that meant he could fly or transport himself a thousand miles with his magic. He tilted his head, the angle letting her see the fresh wounds on his face from his battles. The front of his shirt was shredded, the skin flayed away, showing blackened flesh where the portal's lightning bolt had struck. "I am not a threat to you."

"Oh, I'm pretty sure you are." She didn't mean physically, though he could certainly overpower her with magic or might. If she threw one of the vials, he would easily evade it. She slumped against the wall and lowered her meager weapons.

Wait, but *was* he physically here? When it came to Malek, she wouldn't deem anything impossible, but he'd been so injured that he couldn't possibly have left his city to give chase right away, and she had never heard anything to suggest that mages—even the most powerful wizards—could transport themselves across the world. Maybe he was communicating with her telepathically—making her believe he was in the cabin with her.

"You are not traveling to Zaruk's city." It was a statement, not a question.

"Are you sure?"

"I am. Where are you going?"

And *that* was why he was here—physically or in her mind. He meant to fly after them and get the artifact back—get *her* back. But first, he had to figure out where they were heading.

"Just taking a little trip. How are you?" Jadora asked inanely, trying to think of a way to evade any telepathic probing he was doing. *Could* he do that from afar? She'd heard mages had to be close to read minds. "I'm glad you, uh, survived your battle with that other zidarr."

"Are you?"

"Yes." If only because Stone Heart would have been commanding this ship, had he survived, and Jak never would have been able to bluff him. And because, if she had to deal with Uthari's people again, she would rather deal with Malek than Tonovan or someone even worse.

"Interesting."

"I strive to be so. But I'm trying to sleep now, so if you could return to whatever you're supposed to be doing back in Utharika, that would be excellent." She watched his face, hoping he would confirm that he wasn't truly here. She supposed she could verify that herself by walking over and poking him, but she preferred to keep space between them. Not that a little distance would matter if he chose to do something to her.

"Tell me where you're going." He didn't confirm anything.

"I can't."

"No?" He walked toward her, and fear shot through her body.

She opened her mouth to scream, but something compelled

her to stay silent, to tell nobody he was here. *He* compelled her to do that.

Malek stopped at the edge of her bed, close enough to touch her. Her back was already against the wall, so she couldn't scoot any farther away from him. She found herself looking at his scorched chest instead of up into his eyes. It was amazing that he'd survived that injury.

"Tell me," he repeated softly, "and I'll see to it that you aren't harmed."

"Implying that I *will* be harmed if I *don't* tell you?"

"Not by my hand."

"Is Uthari sending someone else after us?" She imagined Tonovan and grimaced.

Malek lifted a hand to the side of her head. It was a slow movement, as if reaching out to pet a wild animal, and she wrestled between the urge to shrink back and to see what he did. But there was no back—she would only clunk her head against the wall.

"Have you been reading *The Mind Way*?" He brushed his fingers along the side of her head.

And she felt it. It was real. *He* was real.

"I haven't had a lot of reading time," she croaked, "but I will. Trust me, I will."

"Good." He lowered his hand. "You'll need it."

Malek stepped back, as if he'd gotten what he wanted. *Had* he? She hadn't been thinking about the portal or their destination— she didn't even *know* their destination beyond the continent—but who knew what he could pluck from her thoughts?

He stepped back again and faded into the shadows. She squinted into the gloom, but the cabin grew darker and darker until she jerked up in bed with a start.

The lantern was off, as if it had been off all along. Had she *dreamed* that? Or had he somehow sent his thoughts to her and invaded her sleep? Did the zidarr have the power to do that? Across hundreds of miles?

Jadora rubbed her face with a shaking hand. If so, he might have gotten what he wanted. Their destination.

She slumped back against her pillow. In the morning, she would warn the others that Uthari's people were coming for them. Whether Malek's visit had been a dream of her own conjuring or not, she was certain she was right.

THE END

Made in the USA
Middletown, DE
06 December 2021

54497291R00314